# Short Novels, Shorter Essays

Frederic Weekes

iUniverse, Inc.
New York Bloomington

**Short Novels, Shorter Essays**



iUniverse books may be ordered through booksellers or by contacting:

iUniverse
1663 Liberty Drive
Bloomington, IN 47403
www.iuniverse.com
1-800-Authors (1-800-288-4677)



ISBN: 978-1-4401-0393-3 (pbk)
ISBN: 978-1-4401-0394-0 (ebk)

Printed in the United States of America

# Contents

# Bunny

# Bunny 1

Anyone standing behind them at an intersection, or better yet, off to one side, would notice the difference in their ages. She might be forty-five and he could be about twenty years older than she was.

At a busy intersection he would take her hand. One could see that they didn't interlock fingers. Rather, they clasped their hands as they would in a handshake. One might notice that she did not reach up with her free hand to place it around his arm and turn and smile and look up to say something. They did not stand close together.

When the light changed, they stepped off the curb while he looked in both directions repeatedly as though a truck might come out of nowhere. She looked straight ahead and left the navigation to him. Once on the other side, after a step or two, he would release her hand and they would walk to the next intersection.

He was dressed in a gray suit, a plain gray flannel without stripes. The collar of his shirt stood about an inch above the top of the jacket. The shirt must have been made by a specialty shop. His shoes were dark brown, highly polished, and had buckles on the sides, which came into view as the cuffs of his trousers moved about.

When he turned to say something to her, his profile could be studied. He had a large head, with a strong forehead, straight nose, good chin, but a mouth showing creases at the ends of the lips. The hair had been black once and now was half-gray. He had not changed his hairstyle in the past thirty years, during which time sideburns came and went, hair grew over the collar, and the tops of the ears were covered from time to time. All this business had been an affectation, he thought. He had his hair trimmed at the same shop near the office once a month. He would wash it in the morning, brush it before leaving home, and let it take care of itself the rest of the day. He might smooth it down with his hands occasionally. His posture was something out of General Pershing or General MacArthur.

She was a strong athletic woman. You might say that she was striding down the avenue, and you would use that term if you were following this couple as they walked south on Lexington. She was dressed for the fall. It was early October, 2002. Her skirt was one of those straight jobs made of tweed whose color could be approximated if you mixed a collection of leaves gathered on Columbus Day in Vermont. Her jacket was gray with green piping around the collar and the cuffs. When he looked at her dressed this way, he thought of his mother who would wear approximately this outfit finished off with a green felt hat that had plumes on the right side. The hats came from the Tyrol. There was a store in New York in his mother's middle years called Rogers Peet where one could buy such outfits.

This man, Zack, short for Zachary, never brought up the similarity of his mother to this woman, Jacqueline, who wished to be addressed by her entire name, at least in the course of business. Zack had learned early on about the perils of mentioning his mother to a woman in his life in the same paragraph. No amount of explaining could undo the harm. She wore a cream-colored blouse, which showed above the collar only when her head moved to toss her hair around. When she turned to say something to Zack, the hair would keep going as it does in those advertisements for shampoo on television. Its color was rich brown, and anyone walking behind her would have guessed correctly that it was thick and that she spent serious money on styling and upkeep.

When they were talking, the observer from behind would see these two handsome profiles gazing at one another, sometimes looking serious, other times smiling or laughing. His nicely formed nose must have been two inches farther in the air than hers. As she wore two-inch heels and his shoes kept the bottom of his feet an inch from the pavement, then he had to be three inches taller than she was. He knew himself to be six feet one, making her five feet ten.

He had become aware of her immediately she came to work in the same building. It was six years ago now, in 1996, that he noticed her at the small newsstand in the lobby. It was inevitable that they meet in the elevator, gradually, that is. First it was a nod, then a curt good morning, and finally, at the end of a day when they were leaving at the same time, he introduced himself. They were both married then and they exchanged a few words about the direction they would take to reach home.

"I have that dreadful commute to Oyster Bay," he said.

"You can read," she noted.

"Yes, but it's living in two universes. The one in Oyster Bay has fewer hours, lawns to mow, a dog to feed, friends to accommodate and a wife to placate. If that world were right next door to this world, these worlds would blend and I would feel so much happier about it."

"I just go up to Ninety-Sixth Street," she said.

"Does your husband have dinner on the table when you get home?"

"No, sometimes he has me in bed before dinner, then I cook."

Zack paused for a moment, and then asked, "What does he do for a living?"

"He's an artist."

"Unpredictable group," Zack said.

They talked in that vein for a few moments until they reached the subway entrance Jacqueline used.

"I hope you have something besides the law in that briefcase," she said as she started down the stairs.

He might meet her once a month in the lobby. She spoke in an exceedingly frank manner and he learned to treat her the same way. They had lunch once, only because they found themselves in the same establishment and decided to share a table. Her work had her recruiting executives. She joked that she might find some superlative position for him.

At the same lunch, Zack told her about his apartment. It was on the West Side in the low seventies and he kept it in the event the commute got to him mid-week, which it did quite often. On occasion his wife would come into town and they would attend a function, usually a dinner party.

Zack was expecting her to ask why he was telling her about the apartment but she was silent on the matter. She looked at her watch and said, "Back to the grind."

That lunch took place four years ago, in 1998. At the time of the lunch they had known one another in passing for two years. It was during her offer to find him a better job than the one he had that he got his first glimpse of her personality. She announced casually that no matter his situation she could improve upon it. At that moment he explained his position as managing partner, as though that would end the conversation. She asked, "How about a more prestigious law firm?" He explained that lawyers in a firm select their managing partner from among those who had made a career of it with them. They did not go outside.

She persisted, "Well, you can switch to top management at something other than the law, and I'll double your salary."

"Unlikely," he answered. "I'm sixty-one, couldn't be happier with the work, and my retirement funds are fairly tantalizing."

She let the matter drop but Zack concluded that she liked her work and was enthusiastic about it. He moved the conversation around to the weekend coming up and she talked about jogging in the park where she met her friends, those with and without dogs. She told Zack about going to the gallery where her husband sold his sculptures. She said they did that most weekends on a regular schedule to talk to would-be customers. It was clear to him that she was in love with this man and when she talked about the future her sentences were filled with hope. She started frequently by saying, "Next year, we plan..." Zack admired her enthusiasm for the days ahead. He was taken by her personality, at least by the portion she revealed, in part because it was different from his wife's, who worked diligently at remaining on a steady course right down the middle.

They would meet on the elevator now and again and walk to her subway entrance. He learned more about her, not the facts, such as schools attended, but he could identify the moments when she lit up. Her conversation could be about an executive for whom she had found just the right position. She would betray a liking for that person and she would anticipate a splendid outcome. She might discuss something that amused her, such as an event on the subway, an encounter at the market, or an item she had read in the tabloids. Knowing that she had no particular interest in current affairs, she stayed with the tabloids and would ask him to interpret important events.

Zack was sensitive to embellishments in personalities because many of his friends were victims of the disease. He could identify at a distance those who traded on genealogy, or old money, or schools graduated from, or yachts owned, or horses bet on, or children on top, or trips taken, or second and third homes, and all the rest of the rubbish. Zack thought he had heard it all and was sick to death of it. He had concluded that only two things mattered: the law of gravity and what you were able to accomplish on your own. The rest of it simply did not count. He detested mannerisms and special patterns of speech. He determined that Jacqueline had rid herself of all extraneous matter and was left with a spare, sparse, purged personality. Clean as a hound's tooth, he would say to himself. Perhaps she came that way. He never brought it up to her on the basis that he might ruin just what he liked best. From that lunch about four years ago, and from subsequent encounters, he concluded that she was warm, alive, enthusiastic, and optimistic, all wrapped in simplicity.

Two and a half years after that lunch – their situations had changed – she invited him to a reception she was attending, a reception for people in her profession. He arrived a bit late. When he entered the room he went up to her. She stopped, kissed him on the cheek, introduced him to the two people she was with, and said, "Would you get me a glass of white wine, and a plate with two cookies and some fruit?" She did not have to explain that she would be busy doing the room.

# Bunny 2

Zachary's father and mother, mostly his father, named their first born Zachary because there was a president named Zachary Taylor and they were Taylors. Parents and son never knew where Zachary Taylor fitted in the sequence of presidents. Washington was one and Lincoln sixteen, so Taylor had to be in there somewhere, closer to Lincoln than Washington. When Zachary read that Taylor made president because he was a general in the Mexican War, he realized that he had to be close to sixteen, perhaps twelve. When Zack took time to read about the president he was named for, in his fiftieth year or thereabouts, he was pleased to have the details at last, but it embarrassed him that he had shown so little curiosity during his adult years.

Zack's father had related to him that their branch of Taylors had come to Boston from England in 1635. This Taylor had lasted one year in Massachusetts and gone off with Roger Williams to Rhode Island in 1636. Zack's father, who had never darkened the door of a church, maintained that his own independence of things clerical was inherited from this ancestor who left the colony of Massachusetts because he couldn't abide religion as it was practiced there at that time. In Rhode Island, this ancestor was elected, or appointed, secretary of the colony, his father making the point that he could not have been illiterate if he held the position of secretary. So Zack Taylor knew he was an eleventh generation American, if he believed his father's calculations, and that he was descended from a literate person, and further that he was a New Yorker since 1644 when this ancestor, Francis Taylor, an Englishman, landed on Long Island, after sampling Massachusetts and Rhode Island. Zack assumed that Francis Taylor left Rhode Island because he couldn't abide Roger Williams' religion either. He knew little else about his roots and made no effort to poke around in libraries to find out. The subject did not interest him beyond the few facts that his father told him.

As he thought about the subject of family during his teen years, Zack wondered why his branch of Taylors hadn't amounted to much. After all, the Cabots, Lodges, Adams, and the rest of them had arrived from the old country at the same time as the Taylors, and they had prospered and produced successive generations of brilliant and accomplished individuals. Taylors, his branch at least, had melted away. Perhaps the first, Francis, in his capacity as secretary of the Rhode Island Colony, was the most productive of all. Zack wondered whether leaving Massachusetts was the source of the family's difficulties.

Zack never discussed this issue with his father, calculating that it would make him feel bad. Once in a while, Zack would suppose that he might be enormously successful, and therefore achieve some fame, and bring back luster to the family name.

Zack was born in 1937 in the Borough of Queens. His parents lived in an apartment building resembling so many others in the area. They appeared to take up an entire block. There seemed to be ample space for two parents, Zack, and his younger brother. Zack was eight when World War II ended. The Korean War started when he was thirteen, but by the time the Vietnam War came along he had entered the army and finished his two years of service. As the fighting grew serious, he thought he might be recalled but the military left him alone. He had been assigned to the armored forces and became an expert at using the new laser technology to aim the artillery piece mounted on a tank.

Zack's father made a career of working at one of the large department stores in New York. Zack was not certain, but he thought his father sold on the floor in the men's department as well as ordering inventory. His father left for work dressed to the nines, and Zack grew up thinking that all fathers looked that way when they left the house. It was Zack's father who dressed his mother. He knew the stores, the styles, and he knew particularly how he wanted his wife to appear.

It was the expectation in the family that both boys would attend college, even though it was obvious that there wasn't enough money. It was Zack's mother who offered a solution. At dinner, as the topic was being discussed, she said, "Why don't you go to a local college, get a part-time job, keep living here, save tons of money, and when you graduate you'll have a checking account and everything."

Zack understood the reasonableness of his mother's suggestion. He enrolled at City College and started on a curriculum of English literature and history. He found out promptly that his grasp of the English language was suspect. When his first paper came back from his American history professor, Zack saw, in red ink, the invitation, "Please see me."

On arrival at his teacher's office, Zack read the look on the professor's face to mean that he had dealt more than once with a student who demonstrated unfamiliarity with fundamentals. Zack closed the door to the office. The professor invited Zack to sit opposite him at his desk.

The professor asked, "Mr. Taylor, are you adverse to criticism?"

Zack replied, "Does that mean can I take criticism?"

"Yes, that's the question."

Zack lowered his head and thought for a moment. "Well, the answer to the question has to be yes."

"Mr. Taylor," the professor said in a weary tone, "Spelling's not your strong suit, and you write the way you speak. Are you aware of something called Standard English?"

"No sir, I'm not."

"Conversational English is what we hear around us during the day. It's not grammatical English, except on rare occasion. Standard English can be spoken in important speeches and you might hear it from a pulpit, or even in a courtroom, but Standard English can be found in good literature and well-written histories and biographies."

Zack understood that the professor, Alexander Shelton, was warming to the topic. "Do you read much, Mr. Taylor?" he asked.

"I read some, sir." Zack waited for an insinuation, sarcastic or otherwise, but was relieved that the professor did not press the point.

"Here's a list, seven biographies and three histories," Professor Shelton said, as he handed Zack a sheet of paper. "I've selected these not only because they are interesting, but also because the writing is excellent."

The professor was quiet for a moment. Zack said nothing.

"Let me tell you what to look for as you read these books. The first thing is brevity. Notice there isn't one word too many. Next, look for simplicity. You will be able to understand every sentence. Then, sequence. The author will have placed everything in the correct order. The author won't tell you something later on that you needed to know earlier." The professor had his hand in the air and he had made a fist. He hit the desk three times as he said, "Brevity, simplicity, sequence."

"Do you own a dictionary, Mr. Taylor?" the professor asked.

"No sir," Zack answered.

"Well, you need one. Don't buy the first one you see. Look at several, find one that gives the Latin, Greek, or French derivations of words. It's in parentheses right after the word. Take the word *adumbrate.* The *umbra* part is the Latin word for shade. The *ad* means *to.* So if something is placed in the shade it's less clear than it would be if it's out in the open. Then when you see the word umbrella, you know that it has something to do with shade. And there's a part of Italy south of Florence called *Umbria*. I've never been there but I'm forced to think there's plenty of shade, perhaps tall trees."

Zack thought it was time to acknowledge the professor so he said, "Yes sir."

"Where are you planning to find the books on that list?" the professor asked.

"I don't know yet."

"Do you have a library card?"

"No sir."

"Do you have a driver's license?"

"Yes sir."

"Find the nearest public library to your home, go there, get a library card, and show them the list. They're bound to have several of those books. Check out one of them and read it."

Zack hoped that the professor had traveled so far on his tangent that he would forget to comment on the paper. That was not to be the case.

"You covered the material well enough, Mr. Taylor. You discussed the important early navigators plying the North Atlantic: Frobisher, Cabot, Vespucci, Hudson, among others. You spelled their names correctly, I was glad to see that, and had the dates right. And the regions they sailed in, that was in good order. So that's about it, a dictionary and get a grasp of Standard English."

Zack stood up, said, "Thank you" and moved to the door. The professor had a final thought. "The study of the roots of words, their evolution, is called etymology. E T Y, etymology. Don't confuse the word with entomology, E N T O, the study of insects."

Zack couldn't bring himself to say "yes sir" or "thank you," one more time. He went out into the hall. He closed the door gently.

# Bunny 3

Life, as Zack viewed it, consisted of these segments: women, school, clothes, the part-time job, money, and relations at home. He did not place these in any order. They loomed in importance as events dictated.

Women, he decided, were better organized than men were. They tended to get to class on time, to have tackled homework, to do well in tests, to finish their papers on schedule, and to manage men. The women Zack became interested in managed him. That is, they kept him in his place. While he fancied himself good enough for the best of them, he was aware that many women he admired did not give him the time of day. He was puzzled, and wondered about his shortcomings.

Zack watched his classmates, slowly at first, more frequently in their junior and senior year, as they paired off with a woman of their choice and vanished. It was as though they came to college to find someone and with that done, the new couple would cast off in search of work, and surely babies, recreating a world that they had just left.

It was Zack's idea that one went to school to acquire skills, not a woman. Getting married before other matters were settled seemed to be putting one's life in reverse order. Selecting a woman to marry was something a man did after schooling was finished and a career launched, or at least defined.

The important women whom Zack associated with were of the same mind as he. They thought in terms of careers, marriage later on, perhaps a child or two, no more. As they described it, these women had the best in mind for themselves. They would go to graduate school, maybe become lawyers or medical people. Some wanted the master's in business in order to take the business world by storm. Why couldn't they end up managing a large department, a company even, and earn in the six figures, at least?

It was because of conversation with these women, sometimes one, usually two or three, that Zack asked himself what he might do after college. With nothing more than his imagination to guide him, he decided that people in medicine had to wash blood from their hands at the end of the day. The idea of touching blood seemed unattractive, making his other interest, the law, loom large. Once he had the idea implanted, he noticed the high percentage of elected officials, executives, and administrators who held law degrees. They need not practice the law on a daily basis, but having a degree seemed to provide choices. By the end of his junior year, he had settled on finding a law school on the East Coast, the closer to New York, the better.

He was twenty and a half and had not slept with a woman. That fact ate at him. He suspected his parents discussed it. He felt powerless as long as he lived at home. He told his parents he needed to study at all hours and that it was time to move out on his own. When they did not object, he knew they had been discussing it. His mother said, "Well, you have this good part-time job and the checking account; you ought to try it."

From the women he knew, Zack selected one who did not meet many of his criteria. Her name was Sylvia Landowski. He calculated that she might appreciate the attention. She did have long, tapering fingers and said she enjoyed playing the piano. They had met in a class on European History the year before and he recalled that the professor learned to rely on her. When no one knew the answer to the question he posed, she knew enough about the subject at hand to move the discussion along.

At the end of the summer, Zack pulled away. He announced, "Well, our last year. I suppose we're expected to redouble the effort." Sylvia understood the direction the conversation was taking and said, among other things, "I was a willing accomplice."

It came as a surprise to Zack how attached he could become to a pleasant, intelligent woman who was slightly overweight and had no features that would make him turn his head. He found her company light and easy. When he thought of her, he would say to himself, "Classy dame." He was surprised that he could abandon a woman who did not meet all his expectations in spite of her being a woman of substance. He learned about this trait in men, and was ashamed to find himself just like the rest of them, when he realized that he had plotted a strategy for a summer so that he might sleep with this woman, almost any woman, and in the end move on. The cost to the woman, if there had been a cost, had not been a concern.

Money had not been an insuperable problem. A grocery store in his neighborhood that Zack had been in and out of as long as he could remember gave him work during his freshman year. The owner liked to let on that he had a "college kid" working for him. He had hired kids from the neighborhood before. Zack lasted four years. He moved cardboard boxes of canned goods around the storeroom and kept shelves stocked. He learned about cleaning and displaying fruits and vegetables. The owner's daughter was the other actor in a two-person play in which Zack felt he was supposed to fall in love, marry the young heiress, and move into the apartment over the store where the parents were installed. The formula, Zack surmised, was that he and the owner's daughter would mail a check to her parents once a month to their retirement address in Florida.

Zack had known her from the beginning. He couldn't recall not knowing her. Although neighbors, they did not attend the same schools. She was named Elizabeth but was known as Lizzie. When she developed, or perhaps before, Zack had his fantasies about her. They left him around mid-life when memories of her faded. Lizzie was there in the back of his mind for years, a pretty girl, easy to talk to.

It was a simple matter to sense Lizzie's father's interest in bringing them together. He arranged their work schedule that way. Lizzie was attending the branch of the State University on Long Island. Zack equated Lizzie with the store. He did think about it some, life with her.

One Saturday afternoon, when she was operating the checkout counter, and Zack was replenishing candy in the appropriate racks, he asked her about her plans. She said, "Something in the media, papers or television. I like to write."

"So this grocery store's not in your future?" he asked.

She answered tartly, Zack thought, to the effect that the store might be in his future but not in hers. She was doing the same thing he was, becoming educated, moving up in her world.

When he graduated, money matters improved in that his expenses dropped nearly to zero. He chose that moment to enter the army for his two-year tour of duty. He went to basic training, and following that workout, he was assigned to tanks, driving them, and firing the cannon in the turret. In the two years he rose from private to corporal.

He had applied for admission to several law schools upon graduation, noting among the documents that admission was not possible until his enlistment was up. He would write them at six-month intervals to keep his file active. It was in the summer of 1962 that he took off the uniform. As he knew he would, he went directly to the admissions office at Columbia. He brought his degree from City College and his discharge papers. A young administrator, not much older than he was, pulled his file. They sat at a small conference table. The admission officer said, "This is unusual. Applicants don't ever show up in person."

"You've probably admitted the class for this fall and I'm relying on a cancellation," Zack said. He changed the topic to tuition, scholarships and financial aid. When they broke up, the admissions officer said, "I'll see what I can do."

Zack thanked him and walked down the hall to the office of the director of admissions. He made an appointment for three days ahead. This time he wore his uniform. The director and Zack compared the new tanks with the Shermans of World War II. The director was more interested in recounting his experiences as a member of an armored division in Europe than he was in discussing admissions. When the interview appeared to be drawing to a close, the director said, "Mr. Taylor, we'll make a place for you in this class under the assumption that there will be a cancellation or two." Zack learned several things from the experience. First, go in person. Next, don't be afraid to ask, because it lets them know you want it. And lastly, keep trying because you can't ever tell.

Zack felt from that moment on that nothing had made as much difference to him in his life as his being admitted to Columbia Law School. In any event, he would have continued to persevere if the director hadn't given him the nod. He was at a new level now. The idea of the store and Lizzie, as lovely as she was, and whatever that stood for, had been replaced by dreams of a life in a high-rise office, mingling with important people, and spending his days solving complex problems that helped these people achieve their goals.

# Bunny 4

Jacqueline Cronin finished the tenth grade and went to work. Personal computers were a thing of the future, not far in the future, and many women who entered the work force before computers had to sit at an electric typewriter and pound it out for four or five hours a day. Most of the young women on their first job did give it four hours, and then they spent some time making, serving and drinking coffee. In the time remaining, they filed documents and learned pieces of the jobs of their immediate supervisors. It was 1973. Jacqueline turned seventeen during her third month on her first job.

When she spoke of it, which was as infrequently as possible, she would say that she went through the tenth grade. That way of saying it came from her mother and father both of whom claimed to have made it through the eighth grade. Neither Jacqueline nor her parents ever used the expression, "high school dropout." They may not have heard the term until later.

Jacqueline's father was in heavy construction, working on tunnels, water mains, bridges and high-rise buildings in the city. He was not a day laborer any longer as he had advanced to be a regular member of a work crew for a construction company. Jacqueline's mother stayed home and raised the three kids, Jacqueline and her brother and sister. They were older than she was. With her brother and sister out of the house, Jacqueline felt it was time for her to enter the work force.

Her brother finished high school and started playing baseball in the minors. He lasted four years, married and had a child, perhaps in the reverse order, and shifted from baseball to driving a beer truck. He was still at it. Jacqueline's sister married her high school sweetheart. They moved to Brooklyn to be close to his work. It's a long subway ride from the Bronx to Brooklyn. Her sister almost fell out of sight.

Jacqueline's first job was at a manufacturing plant in Queens. She answered a classified ad for a clerk-typist. She had no idea about clerking but understood typing. She met her supervisor-to-be, a matronly lady, built low to the ground, who called her Dear and Dearie immediately. The interview went well enough. It consisted of Jacqueline's typing a page from an article in a magazine that the matronly woman had in her handbag and Jacqueline's filling out a standard application form. She did not know what "Social Security number" meant. During the first week at work she went to the local office of the Social Security Administration, stood in line, and had a number assigned to her.

The matronly lady took her to the owner's office. He asked Jacqueline to sit down. He looked at the application for a moment and asked, "First job?"

"Yes, sir," Jacqueline answered.

"Planning on living at home?" he asked.

"Yes, for a couple of years. I'll save up."

He asked her several other questions and as he did that he looked her over. Jacqueline had become accustomed to men looking at her that way since she started to fill out at thirteen. She guessed they were imagining what was under the clothes. At the end of the interview he asked, "May I telephone your mother?"

"Yes, you can call her," Jacqueline answered. Then she found the courage to say, "Why do you want to call her?"

He said, "I have kids around your age. I feel responsible for you in some way. Just want to talk to the family."

The matronly one, Beatrice Jenkins, whom everyone called Bea, hovered over the 110 employees. She had been after the boss for an assistant for about a year and overcame his objections when she announced that she could no longer take vacations or get sick.

Jacqueline was introduced to record keeping. The vacation time, sick leave and hours worked for each employee had to be reported to the accounting department every other week. She typed the reviews of all employees. New employees such as her were reviewed quarterly. After a year, this dropped to semi-annually. The senior employees were reviewed annually.

Over time Jacqueline grasped the characteristics that the people doing the reviews were looking for. She started taking sides, wondering whether the reviewer had been fair, she having formed her own opinions of many of the employees.

Beatrice's principal concern was over idle gossip. "Don't ever mention a word of what you've seen," she said more than once. Bea might add,

"We'd have to let you go if it got out that you were a sieve." Jacqueline learned quickly that her job was off limits and she scarcely talked about it with her parents. The unmarried men at the plant asked her out on occasion but she refused on the basis of being too young. In fact, she was avoiding discussing the evaluation process and how particular personnel files were shaping up. At seventeen, in any case, she wasn't in favor of going out right after work and then taking the subway back to the Bronx late at night.

She gave her mother part of the paycheck and stayed home into her twentieth year. She connected with a girl from her high school named Connie Ferraro and they moved into an apartment half a block from a subway entrance. She knocked off three stations in each direction on her commute. It was her roommate who introduced her to men, makeup and clothes.

The apartment building was put up around 1910. There were five floors and no elevator. The rooms were medium-sized and the ceilings were nine feet off the floor. Landlords over the years had made changes, or, as they thought, improvements. Apartments that had similar floor plans originally were now changed one from another. Closets had been added, kitchens enlarged and small front halls constructed at the expense of what had been generous-sized living rooms.

Jacqueline and Connie's apartment was on the third floor and faced south, over the street. There was some automobile traffic and all the parking places were taken at all times. Children, not many of them, played outdoors. Adults, perhaps a few more than the children, sat on the front steps or stood and chatted in small groups on warm days.

Connie and Jacqueline moved in over a Friday and Saturday. The entertainment for the move came in the form of classical music from the apartment beneath them. The occupant was rehearsing a repertoire or learning new pieces. Jacqueline had discovered classical music by accident. While searching the dial one evening in her bedroom, she came to music unaccompanied by the strident voice of an announcer. It seemed to her that, by a substantial measure, there was more music than talk. After a few years of listening to the radio at home in her bedroom, she was able to classify music by the century in which it had been composed. She knew that the pianist downstairs was playing either Debussy, or Ravel or another French person who had composed in the second half of the $19^{th}$ century or in the first part of the $20^{th}$ century.

"How late at night could this go on?" Jacqueline asked Connie, referring to the pianist one floor down.

"Don't you think the neighbors have negotiated this out?" Connie answered.

Connie checked the mailboxes and reported that of the thirty apartments, one was occupied by Abraham Ovitz, the classical pianist; two were occupied by single men; and two mailboxes were identified by last names only. The remaining twenty-five had couples in them.

"We're Cronin and Ferraro on the mailbox and we're two women. So some of those two-name apartments could have two men, one for you, one for me," Jacqueline said.

"You're right, of course," Connie admitted.

Jacqueline said, "It must be nice, dating a guy in your building. You have someone to bring you right to your door."

Connie was silent for a moment, and then she asked, "Have you ever been on a date?"

"No."

"So you've never been kissed?"

"I guess that's right."

"You're the only twenty-year-old woman in Manhattan who's never been kissed. We have to do something about that," Connie said.

"What could you do?" Jacqueline asked.

"I don't know offhand. They're plenty of guys over at the hospital. I don't have to go out with all of them. I'll find one the right size for you," Connie said.

# Bunny 5

"So, they don't ask you out, is that it?" Connie asked.

"Well, not yet. Pretty soon, I guess." Jacqueline answered.

"If you don't circulate around, you don't meet any new men, then who's gonna ask you out?"

"I don't know. Isn't something supposed to happen?" Jacqueline asked.

"It only happens when you make it happen." Jacqueline heard a tone of resignation in Connie's voice, as though many of her own efforts had failed.

"What have you done to scare up guys?" Jacqueline asked.

"Just about everything except go back to church."

"Would that be the end of the line?" Jacqueline asked.

"Yes, the guys there would have something wrong with them if they went to church in their twenties," Connie said.

"So what do you do?"

"Well, the young guys at the hospital, not the doctors, but the lab technicians, they ask me out. Maybe I'll snag a young doctor. And I have a big family and plenty of friends of relatives. So it adds up. And even the guys from high school. That wasn't so long ago."

"When do you think I could start?" Jacqueline asked.

"How about taking a course?" Connie said. She added, "Schools around here have night classes and you sign up and go once a week for fourteen weeks or maybe sixteen weeks."

"They won't take me," Jacqueline said. "I never finished high school."

"They don't care, they just want the money," Connie said. "You could study Spanish, or literature or take a class in painting. Guys take these classes to meet women."

"I suppose I could," Jacqueline said. "How do you start?"

"I'll call City College for you tomorrow and order a catalog," Connie answered.

The evening following the discussion on night classes, Connie volunteered her opinion on Jacqueline's appearance. "That ponytail has to go," she said. "It's for college girls who are rebelling against something, or they're saying that they're not about to put effort into looking their best, or that looks don't matter, so why bother?" Connie had a second thought. "Why don't we do something about it right now? Get a towel. I've got scissors and a comb."

Connie cut the hair to a length just above the shoulders and parted it on the left where it seemed natural. She brushed it out and handed Jacqueline a lipstick. "Go to the mirror and put on some of this. Probably the wrong color but put some on anyway." They worked on powders and blush and Jacqueline put on perfume, but none of that was necessary, they decided.

Jacqueline was at the mailbox first. She leafed through the catalog from City College as she walked up the stairs. She understood that by listing requirements for taking certain classes, the college expected students to progress through courses in the proper sequence and not sign up unprepared. Jacqueline concluded that she would let Connie go over the catalog before forming an opinion.

Connie had been thinking about the catalog, expecting it to arrive soon, because as she opened it she said, "Let's see if there's any music appreciation."

"What's that?" Jacqueline asked.

"You listen to that good music station all the time. In the class they play music, talk about what you're listening to, and tell you about the life of the composer."

"Sounds interesting. What are you thinking about taking?" Jacqueline asked Connie.

"I wasn't thinking about anything."

"Well, find something at the same time as mine and we can go together."

They settled on Thursday evenings at seven, music appreciation for Jacqueline and drawing for Connie. "I'll have to buy supplies," Connie said. "All you have to do is just sit there and listen to music."

"Do you think there will be guys we can meet?" Jacqueline asked.

"I suppose so. They might be a bit weird, but on the other hand they would know that the class would be mostly women, you know, happy hunting grounds."

On their first night of classes, as they were leaving the apartment, Jacqueline said, "Connie, you're overdressed, I mean, you're going to a drawing class."

"Well, you never know," she answered. Then she said, "Jacqueline, with legs like you have, you should never wear pants."

Jacqueline thought a moment and said, "This is just the first night. If there's anything out there, I can change."

During the half-time break, a man that Jacqueline had been watching, as he looked over the women in the class, came up to her and said, "There are coffee machines down the hall."

He wore a coat and tie and Jacqueline assumed that he had come directly from work, perhaps stopping for a bite to eat. She thought he was a nice looking man, certainly older than she was, perhaps twenty-eight. He introduced himself as Mark and said he worked at one of the museums in the "guard business," as he put it. Jacqueline imagined him in dark blue shirt and pants with a shoulder patch and a heavy black belt and black shoes. She asked, "What do you think about all day when you're guarding paintings?"

"I did that for two years," he announced. "It was pretty bad. You die of boredom by the end of the day, but they promoted me. I do administration now."

When they reached the coffee machines, Mark asked her why she had started taking the class. Jacqueline answered, "My roommate and I wanted to meet men so we got a catalog." She paused for a moment and returned the question. Mark answered, "Well, I listen to WQXR in the evenings, and this made sense." He had change in his hand and paid for two coffees.

"Your roommate's not in our class, is she?" Mark asked.

"No, she's in drawing class. Same evening, same time, so we can come and go together." They exchanged neighborhoods but not addresses. Then he said, "Well, I guess we can't do anything tonight because you go home with your roommate."

Jacqueline reached into her purse and pulled out a receipt for groceries from her local market. "Let me use your pen," she said. She wrote her name and telephone number and as she handed him the receipt, she said, "We don't have to go out only after class, you know."

Connie's father worked for Westchester County in the engineering department. Starting as a draftsman, he had risen to designing portions of projects that required civil engineering skills. He knew about roads and parkways, of course, and he had gained experience in dredging, some underwater work, foundations for bridges, and maintenance for the airport in White Plains. Connie's mother started as a teller in a bank and was now a loan administrator, principally for automobiles and home improvements. It was Connie's father who had urged her to apply at the hospital after graduation. "It's getting more technical every day. Just learn how to operate the machines and the instruments and you'll always have work." Her mother's advice was, "Keep your eyes out for a good Italian doctor who goes to church."

When Connie reminded her parents that they didn't go to church, her mother said, "Well, one who goes enough so you can have a church wedding and get the kids baptized."

Her father's family came from Naples and her mother's from Palermo, on the northern coast of Sicily. Connie's four grandparents were still alive. All had been born here. Connie had no reservations about her roots but she was disturbed by the appearance of the generation that came before her grandparents. The photographs had the women in black dresses nearly to the ground. All of them were short and overweight. The men were gnarled and looked like olive trees. Connie liked her brown hair and dark eyes, but she would have nothing to do with growing dumpy. She concentrated on diet and exercise, and on clothes and appearance. It had been demonstrated to her that men were endlessly fascinated by a woman's body, one that moved gracefully and energetically.

Connie admired Jacqueline's stature and the grace she exhibited, unconsciously, as she moved about. Prior to moving in together, she and Jacqueline had bumped into one another near Connie's house. They had talked about the work they did and left it that one would call the other and get together. When they separated, Connie watched Jacqueline for a moment as she walked down the street. She envied her that long easy stride.

# Bunny 6

Connie thought it was a good thing for both of them, being in an apartment, in a neighborhood, starting to be part of something more than their childhood homes. After graduation, Connie stayed with her parents for a year. She was the oldest of four children. Meeting Jacqueline by chance gave her the opportunity to head out. The family agreed the moment had come.

She was hired at the hospital without any experience, as a person just out of high school, who bowled them over with enthusiasm. Yes, she would work overtime if required. Yes, she would take any training offered to learn the operation of the electrocardiogram equipment, and any other equipment, for that matter. Yes, she would love to be an x-ray technician. Yes, she would always be on time, early even, if they wanted her to be. But it was real. She had a cheerleader's personality. The sun shone everyday.

In the first full year that Connie and Jacqueline lived together, 1977, Connie and Abraham Ovitz, downstairs, directly below them, noticed one another. She sensed that everything about him was compact, his mind, attitude, schedule, appearance and his treatment of her. And he was too short for Jacqueline.

Certainly he was passionate about his music, but it was his serenity around her that distinguished him from the rest of the young men. Connie assumed that he knew lady musicians and they would be competitive and driven, as he was. And she assumed further that he was a different person around her than he was with other women. He would discuss the "Jewish mind," as he termed it. "What is it about the Jewish mind that makes for so many great musicians, some great composers, untold numbers of physicists and physicians?" Once in a discussion of this nature, Connie had looked up from the paper and answered, "You work harder." She thought it was the answer he was looking for.

Abraham didn't have other women in his life. He had Connie and would see her on weekends. She had a standing invitation to come to his apartment Saturday afternoons when he was practicing. When she knocked, he knew it had to be she as no one else came by. He would let her in, and put his arms around her, and kiss her lightly. He might say, "You know where everything is."

The routine consisted of her making tea, then installing herself on the sofa and reading the *Times* and any magazines that were around. He practiced for two hours, and Connie usually showed up half way through. She would read most of that second hour but nap occasionally while he was playing.

He would join her on the sofa and they would talk and kiss. He went regularly to his parents' apartment Saturday evening. Sunday was their day together. They would be out of the building around noon, have lunch at any one of several small restaurants and return to spend the remainder of the afternoon talking and reading the paper. They spent the early evenings together in bed before Connie went upstairs.

He was her first man, so she could not compare. She speculated that if they met on a deserted island, it wouldn't take them long to calculate what to do. It seemed natural to her. He kidded her about her warm Mediterranean blood. "Well, that's home for Jewish people, too," she reminded him.

For Connie it had started the first time she laid eyes on him. The move in the apartment with Jacqueline was complete. Jacqueline and she had heard him practice regularly. Perhaps the third week after moving in, Connie trotted down the stairs as Abraham came out his front door. He didn't say anything until she made it to his floor, then he looked at her, smiled, and said, "Hello." She said, "You must be Abraham. I know your name from the mailbox."

"That's right," he said. Then he asked, "Does the playing bother you? I guess you're Ferarro and Cronin, also from the mailbox." Before Connie could say anything, he added, "I guess you're Ferarro. Cronin would be fair and Irish. You're brown as a berry."

"Does it bother you?" she asked.

"No, on the contrary." She was wearing white shorts and a white T-shirt and she followed his eyes as he talked to her.

"Where are you off to in that costume?" he asked.

"Just to jog a bit. Nothing serious."

"And where are you off to?" she asked.

"The hair cut. Why don't we walk that far together?"

The first thought that came to Connie was to ask Abraham to dinner. "I'm certain we can prepare a good meal for you and my roommate likes classical music. Listens to it a lot. She can ask you questions."

"Do you listen to classical music?" Abraham asked.

"Only when Jacqueline has the radio on."

They came to the barbershop and separated. She looked back and he was still standing there at the door. She had no idea if he was studying her body or just staying in contact until the last moments. She waved at him and turned and started off.

Connie had been thinking about intimacy from the moment she started understanding the process, and that had to be in junior high school. How is it going to be for me? That was the first question. What sort of man will he be? That was the second.

Nothing happened to her in high school. There was a new word around at the time, *relationship*. Connie understood it to indicate that men and women were supposed to mean something to one another before they experimented. But they weren't men and women yet, they were still boys and girls. Most of them meant nothing to one another beyond casual friendship.

Connie was waiting at an intersection for the light to change. It came to her that she and Abraham might be able to commit to one another. She could fall in love with him, easily for that matter. It seemed to her that he could fall in love with her even though they had been together for only two or three minutes. He might be the first man with whom she would feel secure, and the first man who was sufficiently mature to create a relationship with her, create and hold together something with emotional content.

Her interpretation of emotional content was that they would trust one another enough to do all the right things by the other. If he got her pregnant, he would marry her. That's what it came down to. The idea of becoming pregnant without marriage had its suicidal side effects. Yet the urge to do it, coupled with the methods of prevention that both sides could practice was a powerful combination that would overcome any reticence, moral or other. She would have to get the best deal she could; that is, have Abraham commit to her as much as he could, and then, when it appeared that love was planted in him, she would give herself over.

As she ran along the sidewalk, she knew he was thinking of taking her to bed. That much was obvious by the way he studied her, even in those few minutes. He couldn't know that he had hit Connie so hard, and he couldn't guess, as he was there getting his monthly haircut, that she was determining how far he would have to commit before she would make it available.

Without discussing it with her mother or with a friend, she knew that women had to strike the best deal possible. If a woman held out until marriage, she might find herself married to the man whose pride was at stake, whose pride demanded that he take her to bed, even if he had to marry her, with the result that the other considerations, the important ones, went out the window. If she went to bed too soon with the men she met, before anything developed, then the right one might never have the time to know her well enough to fall in love. So the idea, as Connie reasoned, was to find the one you liked, string him along, stay out of bed, then, when he committed, give it to him in a way that he knew that he could have it the rest of his life, and make that part so good that he wouldn't ever walk away from it.

She could sense over the months after they had met that he was in search of a woman. He took her hand as they walked back from their first lunch on a Sunday. He started saying things after they kissed, such as, "You're so right." He didn't say, "You're so right for me," as Connie hoped, but he was coming her way. Once he said, "You're a dream come true." Connie was quick to say, "Well, you can stop dreaming." When they were on the sofa together, kissing in the dark, he would always make flattering remarks. He explored with his hands but not so far that Connie had to restrain him.

One night – they may have known one another the better part of half a year – it became so intense that she wanted to stand up and take off all her clothes. She determined that rather than having it seem that he had conquered her, she would make a gift of it to him, which she did the following Sunday evening. She hoped that he understood by her action that she had committed to him, and that it was the moment for him to reciprocate. Her act had the desired effect, but it took longer than she expected.

He was on his back and she was against him, and not on him. She was caressing his face with her right hand and was plotting how to get it out of him what he felt for her. She didn't want to ask the direct question. She started with, "I like it about you that you're so all put together. You don't have to practice that much, but you practice. I could set my clock by it."

"How about, practice or perish?" he answered. She didn't say anything. He added, "I like it that you're here." She volunteered nothing, but ran her thumb over his eyebrows. He said, "I remember reading something about Louis Armstrong, that his third wife made him buy a house out on the Island. The article made the point that when he came off the road, he had a place to go and she was always there, waiting for him."

"That's a nice story," she said. She paused a minute. "You know, you could have any one of these Chinese cellists. They look very cute."

"We had some of them at the conservatory. They practice twelve hours a day and there's always a mother in the background. It's frightening."

"So you turned down the Chinese cellists. How about the Japanese violinists, or are they Korean?"

"Same thing. They want so badly to be on stage by fifteen."

"So you chose a slower pace?"

"Well, music isn't number one, as it is with that crowd."

Connie hoped that he would carry on and tell her that she was number one, but it did not occur to Abraham to say it, or he wasn't ready. He did say, "These Sunday afternoons are wonderful. I look forward to them. It's what you bring."

Connie let it go at that. He wasn't going the whole distance and, anyway, she was two months shy of being twenty-one.

"Do you want to stay over?" he asked.

"No, I'll go up and keep Jacqueline company for a while and get ready for work tomorrow."

"Do you think she knows what we do on Sunday afternoons?"

"Of course she knows, and I didn't have to tell her, either."

Connie and Jacqueline prepared warm milk into which they spooned honey. They avoided discussing the late afternoon events downstairs. They talked about Jacqueline's visit to her parents. She went there about once a month for Sunday lunch.

Connie lay awake, trying to identify the attraction between Abraham and herself. He was not able to describe it when they were in his bed earlier, at least not describe it in a simple phrase they both understood. If he was at a loss for words, then it seemed reasonable to Connie that she could be baffled as well. But she did recognize that she was more grown up with Abraham than with anyone else.

Being in bed with him transformed her from girl to woman. She was satisfying her man's urges and needs. That seemed to be an appropriate thing for her to do. In return, she felt he was protective of her.

Abraham suggested to Connie that she come to dinner with him and other musicians whom he had met at the conservatory. These were two couples, not married, who had formed a string quartet. They called themselves ABCD, for Ann, Bradford, Chandler and Deborah. Ann and Bradford played the violin and cello respectively, while Chandler played the viola and Deborah was the second violinist.

The members of the quartet were warm to Connie during introductions, but the conversation turned to music promptly. Connie listened to a barrage of terms that were foreign to her, such as *divertimento,* overture, *fortissimo*, *Eine kleine Nachtmusik*, treble clef, and Well-Tempered Clavier.

These terms meant nothing to her. Abraham tried to bring her into the conversation but his attempts failed.

The members of the quartet were obsessed, or so Connie thought, with the opportunities to record, the chances of finding concerts to play in, and the idea of going on tour, a wild dream, they admitted. If there was any other world for them, Connie was not made aware of it.

In the subway on their way uptown, Connie asked, "What was I supposed to do? Did you ask me along to humiliate me?"

"I'm terribly sorry," Abraham answered. "Their behavior was inexcusable. I thought the evening would give you a chance to see why they are too much of a good thing and having you in my life is so important. It backfired, that's obvious."

Connie held his hand and didn't say anything during the balance of the ride. As they walked toward their apartment building, Connie said, "You're wonderful, Abraham, but I fail to see what I bring to your life."

Abraham was quiet for a while, and then he said, "Give me a few more chances. Life's not easy for a specialist."

# Bunny 7

Jacqueline had heard some of the music the instructor played, although now it was being presented in chronological order and not at random as she heard it on her radio. Jacqueline's instructor made much of sticking to the proper sequence, but in truth she would insert minor composers in their proper place between the major ones she had introduced, forcing her students to readjust their written notes. Jacqueline pondered this method of teaching, worried over it, but could not come up with a better method of doing it.

The instructor, a certain Miss Everett, with the unlikely first name of Daisy, led off in the first session by announcing that not much happened before Bach. Miss Everett enjoyed dates, Jacqueline concluded, because she did not pass up the opportunity of placing them after a composer's name, particularly on the first occasions she mentioned one of them. So there it was, on the first session, "J.S. Bach, 1685-1750," written clearly in the middle of the blackboard. To the left she wrote, "Telemann, 1681-1767," and under Telemann, "Vivaldi, 1675-1741," and under Vivaldi, "Monteverdi, 1567-1643." To the right of Bach, she wrote, "Haydn, 1732-1809," "Mozart, 1756-1791," and "Beethoven, 1770-1827."

"My guess," Miss Everett announced, "is that you know the names to the right of Bach but have never heard of those to the left. Am I correct?"

There was a murmur of assent from the seventeen students. Miss Everett discussed each composer on the blackboard, and then started a tape of a Brandenburg Concerto, saying that this was number two of six. After playing the music for a few minutes, Miss Everett opened a large envelope and extracted a stack of papers. She called them "my handouts," and proceeded to pass them around. There were seven sheets for each student. On the first three were biographical sketches of the three pre-Bach composers, and the other four were a page each for Bach, Haydn, Mozart and Beethoven.

"Notice that all handouts are punched, so they go into your notebooks. I expect everyone to have a three-ring notebook and bring it to class," the teacher said in a determined manner. She let that sink in, and then added, "I will hold you responsible for all the material on these sheets. You may as well commit it to memory, and that includes the dates. We're here to learn." There was another murmur in the room, as though everyone had been belted in the stomach at the same time.

Mark, Mark Corona, the museum employee, provided her with her first date. He telephoned on the third week and invited Jacqueline to come to his museum the following Saturday afternoon. "From where you live, just take the Fifth Avenue bus downtown. I'll be at the front entrance at 3:30."

Jacqueline noticed that Mark bypassed the formality of buying a ticket. He took her coat and checked it at the cloakroom. Everybody knew him and addressed him by his first name. Jacqueline thought he wanted as many employees as possible to see her with him.

He led her around, explaining that they were in a former private home, a "mansion," as he called it. Jacqueline was impressed that he had facts about the paintings, and guessed that he had been made to learn something about each work of art to answer visitors' questions. It was her first guided tour of a museum.

At closing time he retrieved her coat and led her east, away from Fifth Avenue. They turned left at Madison and went into a small tearoom. She ordered hot chocolate and a piece of almond cake. He reflected a moment and ordered the same.

"Did you enjoy yourself?" he asked.

"Yes, beautiful things."

"What did you like the best?"

"The small paintings you talked about, the ones you liked."

"The Vermeers?"

"Yes, the Vermeers. So detailed," she said.

"There are plenty of other museums around here, as you know."

"Well, I didn't know," she said.

"We could make a schedule and knock them off one at a time," he said.

They did not make a schedule, but over three months they visited four museums. He had taken her to dinner once, and kissed her goodnight at the door of her apartment on the third floor at the end of every evening out.

After each class, that would be Thursday evenings, Connie pulled out the drawing she had worked on to give her opinion of the results and get Jacqueline's. Her teacher set up still lifes, something new each week. She used the standard compositions such as fruit in bowls, musical instruments, and flowers in vases placed on a table covered with cloth having some design. Jacqueline didn't have any sense that this was magnificent art, but she appreciated Connie's pride in discussing it. It was a revelation of sorts, that something you do yourself has more value to you than the same thing done by another person. The music appreciation class did not have that feature. Jacqueline couldn't see that she was producing something. She discussed the most recent handout with Connie and made a point of adding the composers on these handouts to the chart she had put on her bedroom wall. She learned quickly to leave space between entries as the instructor did not give up the habit of introducing yet other composers when it suited her. At the end of the course there were more than fifty names on the list.

Jacqueline would ask Connie on occasion how her relationship with Abraham was progressing. Her standard question was, "Is he getting closer to proposing?" Connie would assure Jacqueline that Abraham had no other love interest and that something would develop. One of her ways of expressing it was, "It's my safe place emotionally downstairs in his apartment. I know what it is to be loved and protected and wanted. I feel I contribute to his life."

"Has he told you he loves you yet?" Jacqueline would ask. She wondered how much of Connie's reaction was in the category of high hopes. Connie would answer that the declaration of love was on the way, and for the time being she was satisfied to have one man's undivided attention. And, picking up on Connie's concern that it was nearly impossible for her to enter Abraham's musical life, Jacqueline asked several times if Abraham had created a place for her. Connie would answer, using more or less these words, "I'm learning a bit, but that will never be at the heart of it. He wants a woman who makes him laugh, who keeps him out of a musical rut, yet encourages him to move the career ahead. And he wants this woman in his bed. That's obvious. He says so."

"You don't think the whole arrangement could be about that?" Jacqueline would suggest.

"I hope not. I don't think so. We're going to meet his parents. They should like me."

"You're not Jewish. Don't get your hopes up. His parents will want Jewish grandchildren," Jacqueline would add.

"It's a new world out there. If they felt their son was happy, they might let it pass." Jacqueline knew Connie well enough to expect a positive answer to any probing question she might ask.

At the end of the sixteen-week course, Mark Corona made his move. His offer was simple. He would rent a car and they would drive across New Jersey, into Bucks County, Pennsylvania, find an inn, and spend time "just looking around," as Mark put it.

Jacqueline's immediate thought was that he had put out this proposal many times and been successful at it often enough that he kept doing it with the next woman. He knew the roads, and probably stayed at the same inn. Maybe the management assigned him his favorite room, the one with a view of the hills or the river.

Jacqueline's reaction was to beg for time. She might make him ask her a couple of times. She said, "Thank you, Mark. Let me think it over."

Thinking it over meant discussing the matter with Connie. If she did take up Mark's offer, then she would achieve parity with Connie, but that was of minor importance.

After describing the offer, Jacqueline asked, "Well, what do you think?"

Connie did not hesitate. "Here's what it comes down to. Picture yourself naked in bed with Mark and he has his hands on your body. Does that sound appealing?"

"His hands, Mark's hands, no, not particularly."

"Do you know any men whose hands you might like on your body?" Connie asked.

"There are two guys at work that, well, yes, I'd like them."

"I think you've answered your own question. Mark isn't right for you. No use going all the way to Pennsylvania to do something you wouldn't do right here."

On their next night out, when the matter came up, Jacqueline said, in mater-of-fact tones, "I've decided against it, Mark, but thanks anyway." She wanted to add Connie's comment about his hands on her body but refrained. A smile came over his face, and then he asked, "What's the matter, are you afraid of something?"

"No. There's nothing to be afraid of. It would be my first time. Don't think there aren't some attractive parts about it. It's just that there isn't enough love there, me for you, or you for me." Jacqueline had no idea where those thoughts came from. She had not planned to say that.

The smile faded from Mark's face. He said, calmly and in a resigned way, "Well, nothing ventured, nothing gained."

Jacqueline didn't answer him. She was aware of the principle that one should venture forth in life, take risks, and that fear was the great enemy to be overcome. She had heard it said that those who risk nothing lose everything, as though the only way to expand your life was to try everything that came along. While that principle might have merit on most occasions, Jacqueline thought that the exceptions came when the price was too high. It wasn't what Connie had said, or anything that she could put her finger on that had occurred during her childhood, but she realized that the first time she would be intimate with a man, or the last time, or anytime in between, they would have to be crazy about one another. She felt more of a woman for having come to that realization than she might have by going to Bucks County. At least that was the conclusion that she carried around for a couple of years.

# Bunny 8

It appeared to Connie that quite some time elapsed between her first meal at Abraham's parents and the second. The reception at the second seemed warmer than the first, when Abraham's parents couldn't hide their curiosity. Connie listened as they asked their questions while taking in the glances as they studied her clothes, face, hair and body.

When Abraham's mother, Esther, remarked that Connie lived directly above her son, Connie detected a tone that said, "and I know you're sleeping with him." Connie had learned to ask her set of questions to place attention on the parents and relieve the pressure on her. Esther did her share of answering, but she did not let much time pass before she took up her recounting of Abraham's college degree and his time spent at the conservatory. Connie thought it was a version of "My son, the doctor." She looked at the piano in the living room where the conversation was taking place and wondered how many hours young Abraham had spent practicing.

Connie was trapped into listening about the first recital and subsequent minor landmarks. She was familiar with this material from listening to Abraham. He had not laid it out all at once in chronological order, but she had pieced it together over the months. The first recital at age nine appeared to be the most important date.

The second meal, five months after the first, carried a note of acceptance. Esther asked Connie to help her put on the meal, as she might ask a daughter-in-law, or as a daughter-in-law would volunteer to do. She even called her "Dear" once.

There were remarks whose significance Connie grasped at once. "I'll have to teach you to make this," was the most leading, with "Abraham likes this," a close second. It occurred to Connie that Abraham's parents were ahead of her. Abraham must be warming them up, getting their agreement, before popping the question. It happened on one of their Sunday afternoons.

They had returned from lunch at a small restaurant in the neighborhood. It was too cold for a walk. He was sitting on his couch, and she was facing him. She said, "You know, that barber of yours doesn't trim your eyebrows very well. You're starting to look like an old man."

"Have you ever trimmed eyebrows?" Abraham asked.

"No, I haven't. We could shave them off and start over."

"You'll find some scissors in the medicine cabinet," he said.

Connie came back with scissors and a towel, which she draped around his neck. Rather than sit next to Abraham, she straddled him, and after studying his eyebrows, started clipping.

Abraham ran his hands over Connie's body. He touched her lightly through her clothes, just exploring.

She said, "Abraham, if you want them to come out even, you better stop that." She said the words as lightly as he was touching her. She said them slowly and did not stop working on the eyebrows.

When she was finished, she leaned back to place the scissors on the coffee table. She rubbed his face with the towel. She then moved to sitting next to him, no longer straddling him. He rubbed a finger over her eyebrows and said, "Yours are perfect. How come?"

"It's just one more thing I have to look after. What would you think if they were bushy?"

"I would care for you anyway," he answered. Then he said, "I really love you a lot."

Connie heard the new level in his voice. He had more to say. He had told her that he loved her before but never added, "A lot."

"We ought to be together all the time, not just on weekends," he said.

"That could take many forms," she answered.

"I want to be with you permanently. I think we should be married." Connie's first thought was that Abraham's parents were looking at the clock, and Esther had just asked her husband whether his son had screwed up his courage. Then Connie said, "Abraham, I'm sure I want to do it. Give me a few days to let it sink in." That was Jacqueline's advice. "If he ever proposes, don't gush." Instead of gushing, she wrapped her arms around his neck and asked, "Do you have any empty closets?"

She was not able to concentrate on the events of the next thirty minutes. She was thinking of rings, gowns, reception halls, and the wedding trip. When they were resting, she asked, "Your temple or my church?" As the words came out, Connie realized that she wasn't giving much time to letting the news sink in.

Jacqueline's beau, Mark Corona, had departed the scene over his loss of the Bucks County challenge. They went out twice, and then the telephone calls stopped. There would be others, Jacqueline assumed. Men and women were constantly searching for one another, even when they were married and had no business doing that. It would just be a matter of time, she felt.

A day prior to the proposal, Jacqueline's neighbor, in the apartment across the hall, had knocked at the door. The women knew one another from chance meetings in the hall and on the street. The woman, Betty Wilson, whose husband did not reside with her permanently, asked, "Can you take my Hannah for a couple of hours? I have a bunch of errands to run."

Hannah was either six or seven and in the first grade. As far as Jacqueline was concerned, this was a normal, average little girl. She asked Betty Wilson, "Can she bring something to do? I don't mind having her, but I'm certain that I couldn't entertain her that long." The woman answered, "I'll load her up with books and crayons. And thanks a million." As an afterthought she said, "When you have your own, you'll learn to entertain them all day long."

Jacqueline left her door open. Hannah appeared with her equipment in a cloth bag. She said, "Hello, Jack." In the past she had said, "Jack," or "Jackie." The full name was beyond the child. Jacqueline installed Hannah at the small table in the kitchen. The radio was on. Hannah asked, "What's that funny music?" "It's one of my favorites," Jacqueline answered. "It's called the Firebird and it was written by a man named Stravinsky. It's ballet music." Jacqueline studied the child's face. Hannah was on the verge of shutting out the music and looking at one of her books when Jacqueline said, "I can show you pictures of the instruments they use to make the sounds you hear, and I can show you a picture of a man and a woman dancing in a ballet."

They spent part of the first hour leafing through a book illustrated with photographs of several orchestras, their conductors, famous soloists playing their instruments, operas being sung and ballets performed.

Hannah opened her coloring book and drew a violin in the horizontal position and a bass standing up. "I know this one's bigger than that one," she said.

Jacqueline fixed lunch. They napped and when they woke up Jacqueline read out loud the books Hannah had brought. Many were the same books that were read to her as a child. Betty Wilson returned mid-afternoon and announced, breathlessly, "It always takes longer than you think."

Hannah collected her books, placed them in the cloth bag and, as she was leaving, asked, "Can I come again and listen to the music?" She struck that awkward pose girls fall into sometimes, one arm over her head, the left leg straight, the right leg turned at the ankle so the outside of the shoe was on the floor with the inside raised slightly.

"Yes, just let me know," Jacqueline said. A few days went by before they found each other on the street, at the end of the day, returning to the apartment building. Hannah let go of her mother's hand and took Jacqueline's free one. She said nothing right away, but rubbed the back of Jacqueline's hand against her cheek. Then she asked, "Can I come this Saturday?"

Jacqueline understood several things at once. She had a new friend. This little friend was relying on her to open a new world. And finally, while this new friend might be a burden, she could turn out to be a blessing.

Word of mouth being what it is in an apartment building, the Saturday late morning music session attracted the children between the ages of six and fifteen. There were eight youngsters in this bracket. Most of them came. It required that she organize lesson plans, buy materials, and keep attendance records. She determined early on that children from neighboring buildings could join only if they were delivered and fetched by a parent.

The first Christmas, Jacqueline gave Hannah a toy piano spanning two octaves. Jacqueline figured out how to teach Hannah the tunes Hannah knew. The piano came with a folded-up sheet of instructions containing the rudiments of reading a score.

Several years went by before it occurred to Jacqueline to reward attendance. After fifty Saturdays, not necessarily in a row, she would take the faithful ones to a recital, or concert, or some musical event. Jacqueline recognized that the program was growing as big, if not bigger, than she was.

# Bunny 9

Connie and Abraham made the easy decisions in one sitting. A ring, of course, but the diamond would wait for an important concert. They would try to be married in the church she attended infrequently, with the reception in the adjoining hall. Perhaps a rabbi could attend if the two divines could work it out. Jacqueline would be the maid of honor. For Abraham, a violinist he had met at the conservatory would be the best man.

They did not differ from most prospective couples in hoping for a small wedding. The affair grew as they worked on the guest list. Foremost on Connie's mind was including a man or two whom Jacqueline would find attractive.

It was Abraham who said, "She might like my friend Sam McDonald from high school. He was very popular. Played football."

"Why didn't you mention him before?" Connie asked.

"I didn't know there was an active market to be Jacqueline's boyfriend," Abraham answered.

"She needs a choice," Connie said.

"I don't know if she'll like Sam. He's been in structural steel, now he's in ornamental iron, and he's contemplating a switch to being a sculptor, you know, welding scrap metal and all that."

"I thought sculpting was chipping at marble and them sanding it down."

"You're right, but this is new and they haven't figured out a word for it."

"Tell me about him," Connie said.

"We started as friends because we were neighbors and he would fend off the bullies at school. I was the smallest kid at the beginning. My mother didn't want me to get into fights because of the hands. Then we weren't neighbors any longer but still friends. He tried college, mechanical engineering. Lasted two years then went to work in the steel business. You see buildings when they're half finished, just a skeleton of steel beams."

"How old is he?"

"Must be about my age, say twenty-seven or twenty-eight."

"How come he's still single? Is there something wrong with him?"

"Nothing wrong with him. I think he's too popular. Tells me he can have any woman he wants."

"I don't think Jacqueline's a pushover," Connie said.

"It might blow him away if he met someone he couldn't have," Abraham said.

They were silent for a moment, and then Connie asked, "What does he look like?"

"Well, he looks a little like those buildings he used to work on. Did I tell you he switched from structural to ornamental?"

"I think you did, but I didn't understand it. Did it change his looks?"

"Yes. I'll tell you in a minute. Ornamental is all the other stuff in the building, the stairs, balconies, handrails, metal window casings, all that stuff. As for his looks, he let his hair grow. He needs a haircut."

"Is that why you think he's on his way to becoming an artist?" Connie asked.

"No, now that you ask. I don't know why he's let his hair grow. He just announced the business of sculpting to me a couple of months ago."

Connie summed up. "So, tall, thin, strong, with long hair. What color?"

"I would say auburn. Yea, light brown tresses. For my taste they look effeminate."

"Jacqueline could enjoy running her fingers through those curly locks," Connie suggested.

"We'll find out. Could work. My guess is that every woman he touched he's taken to bed."

"Won't work with Jacqueline. She didn't fall for that creep Mark Corona and his trips to Bucks County."

"You know her better than I do. I'm not placing any bets on it."

Connie and Abraham's parents met. It devolved on the four of them to put on the wedding, neither bride or groom having any money. Abraham's mother, Esther, said with a shrug, "A wedding is a wedding; we'll do what we can." By that she meant that the parents would control the guest list inasmuch as they had to pay for the affair.

Sam McDonald made the list easily. He was a top choice for both Connie and Abraham. Sam received a telephone call from Abraham about a week after the invitations were mailed. "Keep your eye on the maid of honor. She's your type."

"What would you think are her best points?" Sam asked.

"She's Irish and everybody likes her."

"How come she's still single?"

She's very picky and she's only twenty-two. It's at six o'clock so rent a tux," Abraham said.

The wedding party came to sixty people, evenly divided between the two families: relatives, close friends and a few important people. One of these was Connie's immediate supervisor at the hospital. Another was the person who handled Abraham's bookings. Rented tuxedos were in evidence. Most women bought gowns for the occasion. Jacqueline wore a white dress that went just below the knee with a matching jacket to cover her bare shoulders. Connie and Jacqueline dressed at Connie's parents. As they left for the ride to the church, Connie said, "You're ripe." When Jacqueline gave her a quizzical look, she added, "You're some armful."

Jacqueline and Sam first saw one another as Jacqueline walked up the aisle. Sam was standing in the third row. Each knew who the other was. Jacqueline thought of their eyeing one another as advance publicity. They were introduced in the reception hall. Jacqueline said, "I've heard nothing but wonderful things about you." Sam, with one of his infrequent insights, answered, "What you haven't heard may not be that good. I'll try to keep the level high." Jacqueline's immediate reaction was that it wouldn't work because the expectations were too high on both sides.

They were seated together at the dinner, each trying to explain what their work was about. It came time to dance and Jacqueline said she couldn't dance but he insisted.

"It's easy. I'll hold you close and go slowly." That's when she got a sense of his body, the strength of it and the sure, gentle way he held her. It wasn't difficult, as he had said. It was fun. She heard the beat and started moving to it. When they sat down, she said, "I enjoyed that." She left out the part that if he behaved toward her from now on in the same fashion he had in the hour or so that they had known one another, she would follow him for eternity.

At the end of the evening he said, "I want to see you. It's a long ride by subway, but I want to see you."

Connie explained to Jacqueline that men such as Sam had a full calendar. He would have to make a conscious effort to shed women. This conversation took place while Jacqueline was helping Connie move her clothes downstairs into Abraham's apartment. Connie said, "It's a new ballgame for you, kid, this living alone."

"Well, you're just downstairs, Connie," Jacqueline answered.

"No. I mean you're alone. Sam or any other guy who comes a long way to see you will want to stay over. You can't expect him to find his way home late at night."

It didn't turn out that way. Sam lived in an apartment in the town of Weehawken in New Jersey. When she asked where it was, he explained that the Burr-Hamilton duel had taken place on the palisade overlooking the river. When Jacqueline said that she had not heard of the men and their duel, Sam said, "I thought everybody knew the story." Jacqueline interpreted his remark as meaning she didn't know anything. The remark wouldn't go away. She knew a little about music and something about personnel matters at work, but that was about it. She concluded that she should start reading. She asked Connie about it one day. "Go to the library. They have all the books. If you want, I'll give you the book section from the *Sunday Times*. You can read the ads, find one you like and go to a bookstore and buy a copy. That would work." Jacqueline went to a bookstore not far from her apartment building. She found herself drawn to the music section, and noticed a biography of Mozart in paperback. It was a five by seven book with a purple cover. The print inside was small. She bought it and read it in a week. It was the first in a collection of such biographies.

Finishing the book gave her courage to bring Sam's remark up to him. It was six months ago that he had spoken about the duel. He contacted her about once each three weeks, not letting a month go by without seeing her. It was always on the weekend. He came late in the afternoon rather than early evening so that he could leave for home by ten o'clock. He took the subway and walked to the parking lot near the Port Authority to catch the van to Weehawken. It took nearly an hour and a half from her place to his.

He had just arrived and they were seated in her living room. She went right to the point. "You told me once that everybody knew about the duel."

"When did I say that?" Sam asked.

"I would say six months ago. I have taken it to mean that I don't know anything."

Sam said, "Now wait a minute. I should have said that everyone in Weehawken knows about the duel. That would have been more like it."

"Did you know about the duel before you moved to Weehawken?" she asked.

He didn't hesitate. "Of course not," he said.

Sensing that they were on even terms, she asked, "Tell me what you know."

"That's a huge question," he said. "I follow professional football. I know construction." They fell silent and then Sam said slowly, "Come to think of it we shouldn't worry about how much we know. We ought to concentrate on who we are. Take you and me. I keep coming back because you're a no-games woman. You don't play around with me – except now with this duel business. You're kind, polite, you pay attention to me. Makes me want to do that back to you."

They were still on the couch. She reached over and put her hand in his hair. She asked, "Do you wash it everyday?"

"Yea, and if you have to know I don't use bar soap anymore."

"Do the other guys at work kid you?" she asked

"No. They're wearing it over their collar. Some guys you can't see their ears. We even have one who wears an earring. I think it means the tough guys aren't that tough."

She turned around to face him. She put her arm around his neck and kissed him. It was the first time she had taken the lead in kissing. She kissed him so hard that her lips hurt a little.

When they broke, he said, "So it's going to be you and me, Jacqueline, is that it?" Connie's wedding had taken place ten months previously. It was almost 1980.

# Bunny 10

Zack felt fortunate being part of the student body at Columbia. He knew that his being there was the first step in the advancement of his branch of the Taylor family. The previous generations, starting in 1635, if he believed his father's date for the arrival in Boston of Francis Taylor, had been wallowing around in inferior circumstances of their own making. He, Zack, was on his way to add some burnish to the Taylor name. It would not be done in one generation. Perhaps he would succeed in his career, have three children, all of whom would attend good schools, and maybe two of them would in their turn amount to something. In two generations, the American dream would be achieved at last, and Taylors counted among the establishment. He allowed these thoughts to entertain him from time to time but wouldn't let them occupy him. He recognized a dream for what it was.

Zack's version of reality consisted of hard work, landing the correct position after graduation, and solving the social riddle. He did not know at the start of his second year, in 1963, that parts two and three would come together through the efforts of a friend and classmate. Part one, the hard work, paved the way for everything else. His reputation grew as an outstanding student. Friends, classmates and acquaintances did not hesitate bringing him into their circle on the basis that he was a safe bet. If he mastered the class work before him, one could assume that he would master the challenges that came along later.

The history of the law school interested him but he never brought it up for discussion. He thought it would be more natural for a friend to bring up the topic. Zack didn't know how classmates would react to someone who attached importance to events buried in the past. They might not care about history, being concerned principally with the day-to-day grind of law school. Zack located a pamphlet on the history of Columbia, starting with the formation of the school in 1754 under the name of King's College. The name would change during the Revolution. He assumed that the king at the time, George II, had authorized this institute of higher learning for his colony of New York. Zack was pleased to see that the school, when founded, was located downtown at the southern end of the island. In later years it moved to mid-town, and late in the 19th century it moved again to Morningside Heights. The location of the college had been dictated by the expansion of the city, staying ahead of the crowd as the farms were converted into streets, apartments and office space.

The law school was founded in 1858. Zack wondered about the law books in use at the time and when the practice of passing a bar exam came into being. He knew that in early times, a prospective lawyer would clerk in the office of another, and when ready, would present himself to a judge who would perform a cursory examination. If the apprentice met with the approval of the judge, he was allowed to pass in front of the bar, into that part of the courtroom where the cases were tried. Zack noted one anachronism, and wondered whether classmates did also, to the effect that the shield for Columbia contained three crowns. Certainly that was a holdover from the King's College days, but why three crowns?

Zack's thoroughness, driven by curiosity, was one of the reasons behind his reputation. In the class on contracts he heard Daniel Webster's name mentioned as the attorney who represented Dartmouth College before the Supreme Court. The year was 1819, when John Marshall was in the middle of his long and celebrated tenure as Chief Justice. It was not enough that Zack read the two paragraphs in his textbook and listened to his professor. He had to read the opinion of the court. The case was a simple matter. The overseers of Dartmouth College, appointed by one governor of New Hampshire, were dismissed when a new governor took office. This second governor thereupon appointed a new slate of overseers. The first slate sued for reinstatement, on the basis that they held their offices under contract. The Supreme Court found for the first slate, and these worthies were dully reinstated. The case was simple, but its ramifications broad. The sanctity of the contract had been established in the United States.

Not satisfied with this information, Zack went back to an American history course taught at City College by the man who had lectured him on owning a dictionary and paying attention to etymology. He remembered the professor's name: Alexander Shelton. It was about six years ago, but Zack could recall Professor Shelton intoning the names Clay, Calhoon, and Webster, and advertising them as the most important senators in the country prior to the Civil War. Knowing that Webster was a lawyer, Zack wondered whether Clay and Calhoon were also.

He read biographical sketches of these two and was elated to see that they, Clay and Calhoon, were attorneys. A thought came to him, that he might enter politics in mid-career and devote ten years to public office. The three men, between them, had occupied the important posts, except the presidency. The most remarkable piece of news Zack uncovered was that Henry Clay of Kentucky was elected speaker of the House of Representatives on his first day in that body, and never served a day that he was not speaker in his eleven years there. Zack concluded that Clay's training in the courtroom, his thinking logically and conclusively on his feet, must have been at the heart of his success. Zack reasoned that if he worked hard over the years, he could become what they called a silver-tongued orator. He wanted to be one of those, with the brains and the unassailable points of view that came with it.

Zack's friend and benefactor was one James Underhill. He had contracted polio as a child, a mild case that left no trace other than a limp when he tired, say if he walked a long distance. The condition had kept him out of the military. Zack was not yet a student of character so while he recognized some obvious traits of James, it did not occur to him to integrate this information into an understanding of James' personality.

James never asked questions of substance. In the matter of class work he would get the answers on his own from books. In other discussions, irrespective of topic, he would answer direct questions but never volunteer his point of view. Zack thought that if everybody on the planet acted that way, interaction would come to a halt, causing civilizations to die off. Zack counted on friendly give and take as a way of establishing one's points of view. He enjoyed arguing about current events that surrounded him, from the inequities of rent control, to the war in East Asia, to the coming presidential campaign. James would not engage in these discussions beyond a sentence or two. When Zack thought about James, adjectives such as subdued, introspective, contained, withdrawn, and distant came to mind. They sat together in class. Zack did not understand James' cultivation of him. He concluded that everyone needs social contact, needs friends, and that James had settled on him, perhaps at random. Zack had no idea that he had anything to offer, to James, or to any one else.

Toward the end of their second year, James invited Zack to stop by his apartment a few blocks south of the campus. He suggested they have dinner afterwards. On personal notes, Zack knew that James' home was Oyster Bay, on the North Shore of Long Island. He said he voted there. He had been to a New England boarding school that fed its student body to Yale, where James graduated. He had come directly to Columbia Law School. Zack guessed that James was two years younger than he was. He was a medium person who went unnoticed. James' hair was sandy and fine. It did not react to being combed. As with many people with light hair, he had fair skin and hardly any beard. Zack never saw him without coat and tie. On warm days he wore cotton suits. In the fall and winter, he switched to wool and mixed sport coats with suits. The shirts were mostly of the button down variety, some white, others colored, and still others striped. Zack concluded that James was a regular customer at a good store for men's clothes.

Zack arrived at the front door of the apartment, was let in, and announced. He took the elevator to the fourth floor and turned left as instructed. There was a small brass plaque at eye level on the door. It read, "James Underhill." Zack noticed it must be polished frequently and that the person doing the polishing had stained the dark wood around the plaque to a yellow hue. As he pushed the doorbell, he thought that it was inevitable that some of the polish would discolor the wood.

James answered the door promptly. He wore a blue blazer that carried the shield of Columbia sewed to the breast pocket, with its three crowns and white chevron on a blue field. It seemed odd to Zack that James would wear a piece of clothing that drew attention to him. Zack remarked on it by saying, "Very sporting, James." The answer was non-committal: "It's appropriate to wear something like this from time to time. Plenty of Columbia people in the family."

This piqued Zack's interest. He asked, "Do you know what the various pieces of the shield stand for?"

"In fact," James answered, "I went to the correct office and asked about it. The design is taken from the coat of arms of the first president, Samuel Johnson." Zack interrupted, "Dictionary Samuel Johnson?" "No, a different Johnson, but living about the same years. The crowns, of course, reflect the hand of George II."

It appeared to be a substantial apartment. Besides the entry, which led into a living room, there was a small pantry, a kitchen, and Zack guessed, two or three bedrooms. In the pantry, James poured two glasses of sherry. As he handed Zack his glass, James said, "Come, let me show you where I do law." They walked a few feet down a hall that led into a study, a small room with a desk, a table, and bookcases. The room was chaotic. Zack took it in quickly and asked, "James, how in the hell can you be such a fashion plate and yet produce a God-awful mess like this?" James answer was typical of him. He said, "Do you think it would be better if it were the other way around?"

Zack let go of the matter by saying, "Well, every man deserves one messy room." They sat in the living room and sipped the sherry. When they were finished, James announced, "I thought we might go downtown for dinner."

In the taxi, Zack went back to the brass plaque. He said, "You know, the person who polishes that plaque needs to get the proper colored paint and touch up the door."

"You're looking at thirty years of polishing," James said.

"How so?"

"The James Underhill on the plaque is my father. My grandfather bought the building in my father's junior year at Columbia. He went to law school after that. My father tells me he can't wait for me to get out of law school so the family can have its apartment back."

"Who's alive in your family?" Zack asked.

"They all are. Well, almost. My grandfather's eighty-four but my grandmother died a couple of years ago. My grandfather's tough as nails. I give him a wide berth."

The taxi pulled over to a curb in mid-town. Zack recognized the name of one of the important, established clubs. He assumed the family had been members for the three generations that he knew about now, perhaps longer if the club was that old.

# Bunny 11

Over dinner at the club downtown, it came out that James Underhill was the middle child. It was not something that James had alluded to previously. He talked about an older sister and a younger brother. If James was two years younger than he was, Zack reasoned, then the older sister might be his age. It was December, 1963. Zack was twenty-five. On graduation from Columbia Law School, in the spring of 1965, he would be twenty-seven. As they went over the menu and discussed the selections, Zack wondered about James' sister. Was she the reason for James' cultivation of him?

The names were traditional: Barbara, James and Douglas. James did say that Barbara was called Bunny. Zack interjected, "Does she object?" James replied, "You would think she might. At some point she has to rebel." Zack said, "Parents use the diminutive on their young ones not realizing the long-term effects."

In the hall leading into the dining room, Zack noted three or four painted portraits and many photographs. He asked James about the collection. "One president, several governors, a few senators, and I suppose a couple of members of the House of Representatives. We can study them on the way out." Then he added, "I'm certain they paid their bills here."

The room was lighted dimly. It took Zack a while to get accustomed to the low level. There was oak paneling far up and the windows were where the second floor might be. The chairs and tables were sturdier than necessary. Zack had not been in a room such as this but it resembled comparable ones he had seen in the movies. There were commons rooms adjoining the dining room. After their meal, they retreated to a small living room with a fire where they were served coffee and brandy. Zack could not tell whether it was in James' personality or whether he had been taught this behavior, but he was never-failing in his politeness to the waiters. They addressed him as "Mr. Underhill," although most of them knew him from the days he came as a boy.

By the fire, James came to the point. "You'll have to come out and meet the family, sister included."

"I'd like that," Zack said. He looked back at the fire and added, "Tell me something about your sister."

"She's out of college. Works at the UN in publications. She does a bit of writing but spends most of her time getting pamphlets printed that are sold in the bookstore and perhaps other places. Beyond that she doesn't say much."

"Is that a family trait?" Zack asked.

"The not saying much? It's not a family trait. It's a trait of hers. If you want to get her talking, get her interested, talk about sailing, tennis and maybe swimming. I'd say sailing is her principal interest."

Zack thought for a moment and said, "I'm awful at all those. I'm good at reading, studying, and carrying on conversations. I tend to come to a conversation with well-formed opinions."

"She likes to wing it. You two might get along fine."

They were silent, staring into the fire. In a while, James turned to Zack. "It shouldn't surprise you that I've been sent on a fishing expedition of sorts. Bunny asked me to find the right man for her at law school."

"She must know hundreds of men around Oyster Bay, from college and at work," Zack said.

"Yes, but she says they are all idiots, immature, insipid, game players, a complete waste of time."

"And you think I'm better than that?" Zack remarked.

They agreed on a Saturday a week and a half away. The weekend had Zack staying with the family, with lunch at home on Saturday and a dinner dance at a club in Locust Valley. Sunday was unplanned. James, Bunny and Zack would take the train back to town late in the afternoon.

Because Zack's father was in the clothing business, he made certain that his son had the outfits necessary for most occasions, and that included formal wear – not tails, but a tuxedo. In his thoroughness, Zack's father had selected a soft shirt with pleats on the front, a medium-sized bow tie, not one of those large butterfly affairs. There were gold studs and matching cuff links, and a simple black cummerbund. Zack's father had gone to the trouble of getting a dark wristwatch with a black face and band, as well as a thin black leather wallet to hold a driver's license and some cash. There was a dark blue overcoat of medium weight. As Zack packed these refinements into his suitcase, he realized how thoughtful his father had been.

For lunch he would wear the suit he wore on the train. He packed some casual clothes for Sunday. They were met at the station. It was not formal with a chauffeur in uniform. A man in his early sixties, whom the family called Windsor, turned out to be one-half a husband and wife team who lived on the property. Windsor's wife, Marjorie, appeared to manage the kitchen, but to Zack, as the weekend wore on, it seemed that Mrs. Underhill contributed in large measure to the operation of the house.

James introduced Zack to his mother and father in the front hall. His mother, Edith, sized up Zack and said, "Well, you're a fine looking young man." Zack expected her to add, "for my daughter." His father, another James, said, "So my son tells me you have your military service out of the way. Our Douglas has that to look forward to." It occurred to Zack that he had been the subject of considerable evaluation before the invitation was issued.

James and Zack went upstairs to a guest room where he unpacked his evening clothes. When they came down, Edith Underhill came into the hall and said, "We may as well start lunch. Bunny's never on time."

From his place at the table, Zack looked out on the bay. There were low hills on the right, and flat land on the left. The house stood a hundred feet from the water, Zack guessed. There was a stone wall, perhaps two feet high, at the water's edge. To the right there was a small wooden structure that must be a boathouse. Zack thought that there would be a motor boat, either inboard or outboard, and perhaps a small sailboat.

They had been served and were starting on the first course when they heard the noise of automobile tires on gravel. A door slammed and the car drove away. James' mother looked up and said, "Well, at last, she's here." Zack and James had been picked up at the station in Syosset and driven here. Zack had no idea how James' sister made it out from Manhattan.

Bunny went to her mother first, kissed her, and said, "Hello Mummy, I'm almost not late." Her father, James, and Zack had stood up. She kissed her father and said, just loud enough for Zack to hear, "Hello, Popsy darling." She kissed her brother and said, "So this is what you brought me."

"Best I could do," James answered. Bunny and Zack shook hands. She wore a two-piece dark red wool suit. The jacket was buttoned. Zack looked at the collar that came up around the neck, and noticed that the cuffs extended beyond the sleeves of the jacket. Everything that showed was frilly. Her hair was short, brown and wavy. There was not a trace of make-up and she wore no jewelry. Her lips were full and there was a natural pinkness to them. Zack thought she was delicious. At that moment it made no sense to him that men wouldn't be lined up around the block.

After Bunny had been served, she placed her elbows on the table, turned to Zack, and announced "Well, you know why you're here, don't you?"

Before Zack could answer, Bunny's mother cut in. "Bunny, won't you ever learn to control that tongue of yours?" In the moment that Edith's question took, Zack determined that he would let Bunny score all the body blows she wanted, and that he would come back with a rejoinder here and there, just enough to let her know that he hadn't been flattened. He thought he would let her win the points. That seemed to be a reasonable approach. Let her win the first rounds.

"Bunny, I'm here to dance with you tonight and very pleased about it, to answer your question."

"Let's face it Zack, you're here to look me over," Bunny said.

"It's a two way street, Bunny. I hope you avail yourself of the opportunity to look me over." Zack caught the smile on Edith's face. She must be feeling that he had fallen on the correct tone in dealing with her daughter.

The conversation was general for a while. Zack steered Bunny into discussing her job at the UN. After ten minutes of politeness, Bunny asked suddenly, "So you dance, is that right, Zack?'

Zack answered, "Well, I have three steps. I hope they'll do."

"And what are those three steps?" Bunny asked with a trace of sarcasm.

Zack hesitated a moment. Then he said, "I'm not about to tell you. I'll wait to see whether you can sort them out tonight."

James the father, who had been following the exchange, let out a small laugh that the table could hear. Zack thought he was handling the witness in a way that a senior attorney would approve.

They went in two cars to Locust Valley. At the club, young men took their cars and drove off with them to a parking place. The young woman accompanying James for the evening was named Amelia. When James introduced her to him, Zack could only think that she was a lovely rose, or some such flower. The manner was reserved, but she turned out to be friendly and open. Zack thought she might be curious about him, as one would be of any foreign object found in unfamiliar locations. She called James "Scottie." Zack concluded that with Jameses in all generations, "Scottie" was visited upon him for purposes of clarification. Excerpts of a conversation between Amelia and Zack, held during the dance that evening, are given below. Mr. and Mrs. Underhill were on the floor, as were James and his sister. Douglas was at the table, next to Amelia.

"Scottie told me that he dug you up at the law school. Do you understand what I mean by dug you up?"

"There's only one meaning," Zack answered.

"Well, that's not it. Scottie went to work with a pick and shovel on one of those playing fields at Columbia, and he dug up a large diamond, which he washed and placed on Bunny's lap."

"Do you suppose she'll polish it?" Zack asked.

"No. She won't want to change you. It's not her style. She wants to keep everything she has, money, position, all that, but add a new element. She couldn't bear to marry one of us."

"So she's not abandoning the life she knows in order to go out and explore the unknown?"

"You may as well accept that, Zack," Amelia said. Amelia smiled at Zack and changed the subject. "Tell me what your father's up to?"

"He works in a large department store downtown, in the men's clothing department."

"And your mother?"

"Runs the house and does a little volunteer work at a local school library."

"Your father dressed you nicely. You're beautiful."

"I'll relay that to him," Zack said.

They walked the few paces to the floor. Zack wondered whether this twenty-two or twenty-three year old woman was satisfying her curiosity or had been asked by others to set the record straight. They weren't like him. Was it worth it to try to join an unfamiliar tribe? He pondered the question the remainder of the weekend.

# Bunny 12

Zack Taylor had met Bunny, been introduced to the Underhill family, and benefited from their hospitality over a weekend. Now he had to make up his mind. Would he write it off as his first experience with the establishment, or would he start courting Bunny? She lived nearby and Zack guessed she was available. He calculated that if she were under siege from an acceptable beau, then James and family would not have gone to the effort of bringing them together. The family must have worked out the details.

Zack envisioned them in the small living room, fire lighted, and drinks served. Bunny, James, mother and father would be gathered of a Saturday afternoon. Douglas was off to college and in any event would have little to contribute.

Zack could hear Bunny as she started in. "James, you spend everyday in a sea of men. There must be one or two that would fit the bill."

At this point James would ask for details, starting with the physical parameters. He would move on to matters of the intellect. Did Bunny feel she needed a brilliant person, or would it suffice to have one who was interesting and well versed? After Bunny and James had batted the topic around for a while, Zack thought that Mrs. Underhill, or Mummy, or Edith, depending on who was addressing her, would bring the matter down to earth. She would ask Bunny why she insisted on marrying someone out of her class. To make her point, she would say, "Bunny, darling, you know perfectly well that David Sutherland is mad for you, and your father and I find him an acceptable husband. Plenty of young women your age would die for him."

"He's awfully nice," Bunny would answer, "but David's a bit of a twit. Not serious, too clever, too much money, and besides his hands are clammy."

"People grow out of that," her mother would answer. Zack guessed that Bunny would then state a belief she had hinted at, that their crowd had become ingrown and that after a while, sooner rather than later, there would come their descendants, an entire generation of idiots who would be swept into the dustbin. New blood was called for, as Bunny had told Zack when discussing the local residents on the dance floor.

Zack remembered that his father separated the customers that came into his clothing department into the while flannel set and the rest of the men. The white flannel set did not buy white flannels, these clothes no longer being available, but they were one generation down from the grandees who did buy them. White flannels were worn for tennis and yachting, and the cocktail hour, as that institution was being developed. For late afternoon imbibing, men would add a blue jacket with brass buttons in imitation of the naval uniform. When Zack's father spoke of the white flannel set, some disdain crept into his voice, as though these people had risen to the top but in the process yielded up their serious purposes.

Zack understood that his father had a keen sense that white flannelism was a temporary state, could not be sustained, and would be replaced by serious people with serious purposes. Emperors understood this when they were unable to persuade the youth of Rome to fight on the frontiers. Bunny understood this, Zack reasoned, when she hunted for the likes of him rather than settle for a sensible match.

On the train ride into the city from Syosset that Sunday afternoon recently, there had not been much conversation, and what there was of it occurred between James and Zack. Bunny seemed content to look out the window and be entertained by her thoughts. When they were in the station, and Zack and James were about to be off in the direction of the subway uptown, Bunny kissed her brother goodbye on the cheek and then gave Zack the same treatment. She did not add any of the standard phrases such as, "Wonderful to meet you," or, "I hope to see you again." She said, simply, "Goodbye," turned and went off carrying only a small overnight bag. Apparently Bunny had wardrobes in New York and Oyster Bay.

Zack liked her brusqueness. It was a purposeful part of her character. Zack wondered where the gene came from. He didn't classify her as rude, rather that she had a need now and again to belt people in the chops, surprising them, putting them on alert that she wouldn't let them get away with anything.

The Underhill house had an informal living room, perhaps it was a rumpus room, where they might have spent some time after lunch. Instead, James, Zack, Bunny, Amelia, and Bunny's younger brother Douglas drove to the yacht club where the family kept its thirty-foot single-masted sloop. As they came to the town of Oyster Bay from the Cove, they passed the high school on he left and a small Episcopal church on the right. It was built of stone in the English style. Zack wondered if any of the Underhills had attended the public school and whether he might marry Bunny in that church one day.

They passed through the town, and on the way to the yacht club he saw signs for Glen Cove and Center Island, places he had heard about but had never been to. When they were in the parking lot, Bunny pointed over the water to what Zack understood to be the Underhill house. It might be two miles away.

Bunny and Zack entered the clubhouse. It was simple in concept. There was an archway separating two parts of the dining area. A collection of pennants was nailed to the archway. They were small and triangular, the longest dimension being about six inches. Each had a single letter. Bunny pointed to the one with an "A" and said, "That's Arthur Underhill, my great-grandfather. He's one of the founders."

Zack wanted to ask why Arthur wasn't named James. He also wanted to understand the significance of these small pennants. Certainly one wouldn't fly them on sailboats. He refrained and let the matter drop. Bunny had made her point that her membership carried some territorial rights that he could not comprehend completely.

They walked from the clubhouse to the small dock. The others were waiting for them. They climbed into a skiff and rowed to the mooring to which the Underhill boat was tied up. Zack noticed that many of the mainsails on the other boats were rolled up over their booms, and covered with a blue canvas, while the Underhill boat and others appeared not to have mainsails. Bunny explained that the new technique was to roll the mainsail into the mast, it being kept hollow for that purpose. She showed him below where there were bunks for six, a kitchen of sorts, which she called a galley, and a small bathroom, called a head. Bunny couldn't explain the origin of these terms. Back on deck, she took him forward and told him how a spinnaker was used, sailing down wind on a long stretch. Bunny had said 'long reach' and Zack had asked her to interpret.

Zack was not defensive about being instructed, and Bunny was not heavy-handed. Her matter-of-factness appealed to him. It was his first time on a sailboat. He had borrowed sneakers from a stock at the house.

Bunny wore khaki pants and a blue jacket. She had on a white knit hat and a white scarf and white gloves, all wool. Zack wanted to put his arms around her. For the train ride to New York, she had only changed to a lighter coat. When she kissed him, Zack inhaled for the purpose of detecting an odor, soap, perfume, or even salt breeze. He detected nothing but she reeked anyway of that un-definable trait some men ascribe to certain women they know: sex appeal.

James was forthcoming with Bunny's address and telephone number. Zack decided to wait until Thursday to call so that they would make an arrangement for the week following. It was obvious that she was sensitive to his situation when she refused to accept an invitation that would involve an outlay of cash. Her offer was to show him around her neighborhood. He picked her up on the following Saturday afternoon. Her apartment was not as majestic as her brother's, but there was partial compensation in the view of the East River.

"You took me at my word and dressed for a walk," she said as she let him in. It was a crisp blue-sky afternoon. She wore gray wool pants and heavy shoes. On leaving, the white hat, scarf, and gloves came out of the closet. She wore a heavy wool sweater that might have been knit in Norway or Iceland, and over that a windbreaker that zipped up the front. Zack had that feeling again, that he wanted to put his arms around her, perhaps kiss her, but at least hold her close to him.

They walked in the direction of the river. She pointed out the bridges that led to Queens, all of which he had known about since childhood. There was some traffic up and down the river, which they watched for a few minutes. They walked some more, then she hooked her arm around his and said, "I'm chilly. Let's go back to that coffee place." Once seated she took off the outer layer and proceeded to ask him about his life, starting at the beginning, with date of birth. He took her through his schools and the years at City College. She wanted details on the grocery store where he worked, and particularly on the young woman, the daughter of the owners, whom he found easy to talk about, an old but accurate dream he carried around, the story of his first and only love.

When they returned to her apartment, Bunny announced that she would do something about supper. She offered Zack the place on the sofa that had the view of the river. There were magazines on the coffee table, as well as the morning paper. She said, "We're having wine, but ask me if you want something else, and the bathroom's down the hall, over there." An unadorned directness had replaced the bluntness of two weekends before.

During dinner she asked about his two years in the army, down to the details of laser control of the gun in the turret of a tank. In return she spelled out for him the contributions that she made in the production of pamphlets at the UN. For the moment she was in charge of the cover, front and back; the title page and table of contents; and a blurb about the author, or authors; and finally assembling an index, which required that she read and understand the material.

As they talked, Zack thought about the schedule. If he had been selected as the man who would marry her, that event would take place at the time of graduation, requiring a proposal six or seven months prior. If they were headed in that direction, he would have to bring the relationship along at the proper pace so that it didn't overheat in the early stages, requiring that he allow it to cool before re-heating it for the proposal. Zack told himself it made no sense to propose early, requiring that he maintain the relationship at a high pitch until the wedding day. He guessed that an intelligent woman such as Bunny would help him to set the correct pace, if indeed marriage was in the offing.

When he was at the door, saying goodnight, she leaned forward and kissed him on the cheek. He turned his face and kissed her on the lips. She stayed in place for that, but after the moment, stepped back, saying in effect that the exchange had been of the appropriate duration.

He said, "It was lovely of you and unexpected on my part that you fixed dinner."

She answered, "Perhaps you will cook me a dinner some time at your place."

They left it at that. Zack thought he should allow two or three weeks to pass before he telephoned again. He wanted to see her the next day, but he was in the grips of a schedule of his own making whose final episode would take place about a year in the future.

# Bunny 13

They were sitting on the sofa. The hall light was on and some light came through the window, the one facing the river. They had been out for dinner and each had had a cocktail and a glass of wine. Zack knew he felt mellow and turned down Bunny's offer of a drink. They were holding hands and Bunny said, "It's comfortable sitting here with you." He said, "Thanks, Babe, same here."

In a discussion about the term "girl," or "girls" collectively, that Zack used once in a while, Bunny had objected. She told him, "You can refer to us as women, if you wish, but not as girls."

"Saying women doesn't create the impression that most men are looking for," Zack had answered.

"Well, you can call me Babe if you want to. If you ever call me a broad or a dame, I'll kill you. So stick with Babe."

"It's a subtle difference," Zack had said.

"Babe means you have a body and brains, you have character and you are a bit of a character, you know, unpredictable. Men want to put their arms around babes," Bunny answered.

"You can call me Spike if you want," Zack had said. He liked "babe" and used it now and again when they were alone.

She said, "I meant to bring it up at dinner. Tell me if you've thought about what you want to do after graduation."

"I've thought about it, of course. My hopes are to find a law firm in the city. I'll have to think about the type of work they do and what I want to do."

"Grandfather could help," she said.

There they were, the words he knew would come from her sooner or later. He thought she was scheduling their lives, the work offer, the proposal followed by the engagement party, and then the wedding followed by the wedding trip. A feeling came over him to the effect that he had only to relax and let events rule. It was just a matter of reacting on cue.

"How does your grandfather arrange matters?" Zack asked. "I've never met him, you know."

"That can be taken care of," Bunny said. Then she added, "How does he arrange matters, you ask? Well, he calls the correct person and suggests an interview. I think that's all there is to it."

Bunny went on to explain that her grandfather knew the important personages. He had served for years in the New York Bar Association and had read examinations for the bar, handling certain types of questions. There was a law firm still carrying the name of Underhill but grandfather had retired and not been followed by his son. James, Zack's friend, Bunny's brother, made noises about joining the family firm, as he called it.

It went as predicted. Zack met the senior Underhill. When Zack couldn't identify a preference, Mr. Underhill suggested starting in taxes. He argued that many matters in the law such as real estate, corporate affairs and trusts had a tax component. He told Zack, among many things in an interview lasting an hour and a half, that after five years he could move on to a preference that would develop. He said, "You can even work in investment banking and mergers and acquisitions." The tone of voice Mr. Underhill used as he gave this last piece of advice indicated to Zack that these were the lowest callings. He never mentioned criminal law, either defending or prosecuting. Zack took it that these were matters to be dealt with by others and that the law as Mr. Underhill practiced it was a profession for gentlemen.

If Zack was to accept Mr. Underhill's kindness, he had to go along with the recommendation. The interview was set up. Zack met the managing partner and two other partners. They went to lunch. He received an offer in the mail ten days later.

It was Zack's first lesson in the power vested in privilege. He had made it on his own up to this point, but might not have succeeded quite so admirably at finding a position in a fine law firm. A day after receiving the offer, Zack went to his desk to write an acceptance. Midway he wondered whether there would be a price to pay.

Two months passed and the moment for the proposal came. Zack was ready to bring up the matter of marriage, but Bunny opened the negotiations before he thought it necessary. There were six months remaining until graduation. When Bunny made her move, Zack's immediate reaction was that he had underestimated the time needed for the steps between the proposal and the wedding. Bunny's schedule, he guessed, had taken into account that the interview for a job should not come too many months before graduation, that there had to be an interim between job offer and proposal, and finally that there would be enough time to arrange the wedding. It dawned on Zack that they could marry two or three months after he started work. That loosened the schedule.

They had been out on the Island for lunch with the family. They played croquet, at which Bunny was the undisputed master. This was followed by tea, and they were driven to the station for the train into the city.

Once in her apartment, she finished preparing a meal that they ate in the living room. Zack learned all he knew about wine from the Underhills. He now recognized that good red wine could not be sweet. He followed James' practice of sniffing the wine and he held his goblet the way Bunny did, the hand underneath, warming the wine a bit, which Zack realized released taste and odor. They had been talking about the war in Vietnam. When they finished the meal, and before Bunny made any move to take the plates into the kitchen, she turned to Zack and said, "I loved getting your letter. We should all write more often. What inspired you?"

"I wanted to tell you what I felt and what you've come to mean to me. I'd get lost along the way if I tried to say all that."

"No one has ever told me that I'm direct, straight forward, almost brusque, but never rude."

"Not even your mother?"

"No. She tells me to mind my tongue but doesn't go beyond that."

"I thought at the beginning that your lack of subtlety, let's say your complete candor, would sink us, but I've grown to rely on it. No question where you stand."

"I know that women are supposed to be soft and feminine and inviting to men. I associate it with erecting a spider web," Bunny said.

"Whatever the analogy, I find you highly desirable and have from the beginning."

They were silent for a moment then Zack said, "We've hugged and kissed at fair amount, but I want a great deal more."

Bunny placed her hand on his face and let it slide back to his ear then to his neck. She said, "Good."

Zack stood up and turned around and sat facing Bunny. He kissed her gently and played with her brown curls. Her arms were around his neck and he took that as an invitation. He caressed her breasts for the first time. She kissed him with more intensity and managed to say, "That's lovely."

Bunny said, "You know, we have some unfinished business."

"What would that be?" he asked.

"You realize we haven't been to bed together."

"I'm well aware of that. There's a reason, of course. It's that men can be suspected of wanting just that and then moving on."

"I guessed as much," Bunny said. "That's why I'm bringing it up. My guess is that you want more from me than just that, so I thought I'd get it out of the way."

"Bunny, your line of reasoning would never stand up in court."

"Well, this is just between you and me. There's no court." Bunny answered.

"You know, Babe, I haven't anything with me that will keep you from getting pregnant."

"I've taken care of that. I called the druggist across the street. He had them in a small paper bag for me. Very discreet. I opened the little box and put three of them under your pillow."

"Three?"

"Well, I didn't know, one two or three. I went for three. This will be my first time."

"You seem to be in charge here, Bunny. What do we do now?" Zack asked.

"We go into the bedroom, take off our clothes and get into bed. I don't think it's very complicated."

"No, Bunny, you're right, it's not complicated."

Zack stood up and helped Bunny out of the sofa. They walked the short distance to the bedroom. Once inside he leaned over and kissed her. She said, "Be gentle." She walked to the side of the bed with the alarm clock and pulled back the covers. He did the same. The only light in the room was reflected from the living room. She pulled the sweater over her head and started unbuttoning her blouse. She unzipped her skirt and removed a half-slip. Her arms went behind her to remove her bra. She stood looking at him with no embarrassment. She slid into bed and pulled up the covers.

Later on, when she was lying comfortably in his arms, Bunny said, "A big obstacle out of the way. And delightful. If you want to tell me what comes next, this would be an appropriate time."

Zack went back to the moment he was writing his note of acceptance to the law firm, the moment in mid-paragraph when he wondered if there would be a price to pay. His next few words were the down payment.

"There's a great deal I like about you, Bunny. We have a lot to talk about, what each of us expects and wants." The words sounded empty. Finally he said, "I love you, Bunny."

She said, "That's wonderful, dear. I'm building to it myself." He assumed she wanted him to try harder, be more attentive, improve in some ways so that she too could say that she loved him.

Zack didn't blurt out the question, "Will you marry me?" He and Bunny, over the next weeks, discussed living arrangements, money, children, work, and even elements of life style. When most of it was in place, he did let out the question. One of Bunny's early actions was to plan on meeting Zack's parents. In another move, she asked Zack whether it would be all right with him if she used her grandmother's engagement ring. It was one of her grandmother's last wishes, as Bunny put it. "I'll show it to you. It's very pretty. It has a diamond in the middle and an emerald on each side."

# Bunny 14

Sam McDonald timed his marriage to Jacqueline Cronin to coincide with his decision to leave the ornamental iron business and become an artist. He gave up his apartment in Weehawken, moved into Jacqueline's place on Ninety-Sixth Street, and rented space in a building downtown, a building that housed artists. They were mostly painters and sculptors, but not all. In the space adjoining his there was a fabric designer. It had not occurred to Sam that there needed to be a person who would create designs and have them printed on plain fabric. These fabrics became tablecloths, curtains, summer wear for children, and so on. Sam enjoyed his new world. He discovered that silk-screeners were artists, as were weavers and carvers of decoy ducks.

Artists in the building seemed to spend a fair amount of time drinking coffee and discussing their positions in, and contributions to, society. Sam determined quickly that the painters felt they were at the pinnacle – that their outpourings would grace the walls of the rich and later end up in the collections of important museums. Sam thought painters were too concerned with the school they belonged to, or failing that, identifying a school they might originate. One of their number, a certain Ian, said that he, and most of the rest, belonged to the Ashcan School inasmuch as most of their production would end up in an ash can. Another of the painters, a minimalist, who poured a single color of paint from a can onto a canvas and sold a few, called Ian "Sick."

Sam was trying to understand a particular phenomenon about the art world. He explained it as best he could to Jacqueline. The two of them could not conclude anything from Sam's story. It went like this.

Take a poor man living out in the countryside near a junkyard. The man might be one of those not so rare ones who felt a need for self-expression. By circumstances, indeed fortuitous, this poor man had on this property the ability to weld. That is, he had a tank of acetylene and another of oxygen. Hoses from the two tanks came to a torch where the two gasses mixed. When the amount of gas from each tank was adjusted properly and ignited, the resulting blue flame was hot enough to melt iron. Heating two pieces of iron that are adjacent to one another, then allowing them to cool, will form a weld and the two pieces are joined.

This man owned welding equipment for the good reason that his neighbors paid him to drive over and repair their farm machinery. He kept his own equipment running as well. One day this man decided to build an ornament to place in front of his house. He took out a piece of paper and sketched a horse, but this horse, rather than having four legs, had two wheels. He went to the junkyard and bought for two dollars enough metal and two front wheels from an old Ford tractor. He welded all this together and placed the horse in his front yard. It stood four feet tall and five feet in length.

One day, a man from the city drove by in his pickup truck and stopped to admire the horse. He got out of his truck and came to the front door. The occupant appeared. The man from the city offered to buy the horse. They arrived at a price of one hundred dollars. The horse went into the pickup truck and was driven to the city where it was installed in the new owner's front yard. The welder went to the store and bought a case of beer. That evening, as he sat on his porch sipping, he designed another horse, this time with legs. The episode changed his life.

When Sam told the story to Jacqueline, she said, "I'm so glad you saved plenty of money before leaving your job." They talked about how long he could last without selling any art. Then Jacqueline said, "You could make small horses."

Sam repeated the story to his new friend, Ian. Ian thought it over for a minute, then announced, "There's no market for horses in New York City. No front lawns." Then Sam threw in Jacqueline's comment. Ian said, "Makes sense. The market here is the living rooms of the rich. So that's your scale. Horses no longer than a foot."

Sam had already equipped his workspace with two tables, one of them covered with zinc, carrying his welding equipment. The other table was smaller and had a drawer in which Sam stored drafting equipment. He knew he wasn't a marble and chisel sculptor, and that he would have to make his way welding scrap metal. The horse had been on his mind since he heard the story a few years back. In his conversations with his wife and his new friend, the scale had been worked out. It was a matter of returning to New Jersey with a rented pickup truck and visiting junkyards for odds and ends of metal. There was no shortage.

Sam designed and welded together his first horse. It was exactly twelve inches in length and seven inches high. He carried it home to Jacqueline, not knowing the reception it might get. She, on seeing it, and having been forewarned of its arrival, placed it in the center of the dining room table in order to admire it. She said, "You can build another one, can't you?" The horse never moved.

Sam had always admired the stabiles of Alexander Calder. On the base, somewhere, Calder would weld his initials. Sam didn't recall whether the A went over the C, or the other way around. Sam didn't think his own initials lent themselves to this treatment so he shortened his name to McDo, and he etched it on one of the horse's legs with acid. The letters shone black against the grayness of the metal.

There were several galleries midtown that Sam had been considering. He made two more horses, an elephant, a zebra, a dog sitting on its haunches, a cat walking, and two birds, one still, the other in flight, attached to a small base by one thin wire. He fitted them into a crate, and went by cab to the gallery whose exhibits he liked the most. The owner wasn't there but the assistant was. She wore a black turtleneck sweater and black pants. A piece of Indian jewelry, hung on a chain, formed a pendant. The green of the stone was the only color she wore. Her glasses had black rims. Sam asked her name. She answered, "Penelope." He explained the contents of the crate and asked if he could show his animals to her. She said, "The owner isn't here, but yes, certainly." They pulled the animals out of the crate and removed the newspaper they were wrapped in. Penelope took one of the horses and placed it in the window. She arranged the rest on a glass shelf. She said, "Let's make a price list. Let's say five hundred for each horse and five hundred for the bird in flight, and the rest at four hundred each."

"Sounds fine. What's the split?" Sam asked.

"It's standard, sixty-forty, sixty for you." Then Penelope added, "The owner may not like any of this and you'll have to come back and take them away. I'm charmed, of course, as you can tell."

The horse in the window sold that afternoon at the end of the day to a collector who came in often and was interested particularly in the creations by new artists. He returned two days later to buy the bird in flight. A few of the other pieces went on Sunday. Penelope asked a collector, "Mr. Taylor, do you want me to call you if something arresting comes up?" He answered, "Yes, surely. No guarantees, but I'd like to see it." Sam was on his way. His animals started filling the rooms of the rich in their apartments scattered over the city.

Sam expanded his creations to include trees, flowers arranged in a vase, a four-door convertible, and ships, both steam and sail, each at fifteen hundred dollars. There seemed to be no end to his creativity. A gallery in San Francisco on Bush Street contacted him. He started selling on the West Coast. Collectors, knowing that not-yet-established artists might not be showing in a gallery in Los Angeles as well, would spend a weekend in San Francisco dedicated to making the rounds.

On hearing that Connie had a baby on the way, Jacqueline asked Sam to make a crib of the sort that rocks. It was eight inches long. It consisted of one piece bent in two places to form the bottom and the two sides. There were two other pieces that formed the ends. The bottoms were curved so that the assembly would rock. When Sam presented it to Connie, he said, "Maybe you can make a little mattress, or something." Connie turned it over to find the four letters, which Sam had placed on one of the ends, on the inside.

Connie was sporting a diamond on her left hand. It came about from appearances Abraham was making in concert halls. He had started to specialize in the concertos and sonatas of Beethoven. He was moving away from the romantics. Recording sessions had not arrived yet. They would have to wait until he was the soloist with a major orchestra.

The presentation of the crib turned into a dinner pulled together from the refrigerators of the two families. Sam brought down a bottle of wine, opened it, and poured a fair amount into four glasses. He toasted the baby who was seven months away. Sam drank his wine. The others sipped theirs. In Connie's kitchen, where she and Jacqueline were assembling a meal, Connie remarked in a light-hearted way how much they had accomplished in a few years. "It wasn't long ago that we moved here and didn't know anyone."

"I'm still sorting it out," Jacqueline said. They were silent for a moment, and then she added, "I like marriage. A lot of it is the same, but that's better than being kept guessing. I like the security of it. I've grown to like the daily routine. I thought it would bore me. And you know, somehow, the cold winter nights are the best. It's so simple."

"I think I'll work at the hospital until I have a month to go," Connie said. "In the Jewish tradition we're supposed to go back into Abraham's family and find a name. We've made a list. They're all from the Old Testament."

"It makes me want to have a baby too," Jacqueline said.

"Would you stop work and take care of your family?" Connie asked.

"I think that's the best way. I'll hurry up and we can push our baby carriages down the street together," Jacqueline said.

"Our husbands have to do well to let us stop working," Connie observed.

"So far so good, but it's risky in the arts," Jacqueline said.

At the dinner table, Abraham and Sam picked up the same theme. They might have overheard their wives. "This is a high-wire act, you know, this arts business," Abraham said. He added, "There's no reason pianos won't go out of style one fine day, to be replaced by a new instrument. Let's face it, harpsichords were the rage a while ago, and they were replaced by pianos."

"It's shaky," Sam said. "The money they spend on my stuff they used to spend on other artists. So those other artists are starving now. No reason some new concept won't come along and sweep away a lot of us. Down at the loft we talk about a new Picasso forcing me to go back to ornamental iron, or even back to structural steel."

Abraham asked, "What do the nest builders among us have to say?"

Connie said, "I'm having a baby. Abraham plays the piano. It'll work out." The three of them turned to Jacqueline. She turned to Sam and said, "Squirrels save nuts, but birds just live day to day. They don't worry. I'm not worried. Maybe it's time we had a baby." It was early in 1980.

# Bunny 15

When Jacqueline did become pregnant, which was soon after the night Sam presented Connie with the miniature crib, or perhaps that evening, she remarked to Connie that, yes, people can accomplish a great deal when they set their minds to it.

Jacqueline's baby came less than three months after Connie's. Jacqueline named the baby Constance and took time to say the whole name. Connie's baby, David, was given a metronome by his father in his first month. Connie put it away and told Abraham, "You'll drive him nuts."

Jacqueline had stopped taking the subway to Queens. She gave up her job in personnel after weighing the merits of work over staying at home. In the back of her mind she knew that if she continued to work and placed Constance in the care of a woman, she might shy away from having another child, but if she stayed home, the second would be inevitable.

Five years after the event of the crib, Sam's gift to Connie, both women had two children. They mingled everyday. Abraham practiced at home half the time. For the balance of his practice, he might go to the conservatory or to a recital hall where he was known.

Sam McDonald became fashionable. His work was analyzed in art magazines. He showed up, along with photographs of some of his outpourings, in Sunday supplements. Mostly it was hard work. Sam had doubled the space he rented and hired an assistant. He supplied galleries in about ten cities. He had hired the services of an accountant who did his books and paid the taxes.

The most productive gallery was the first, the one where Penelope held forth as the manager. The owner of the gallery preferred lounging in the Hamptons to work of any sort. Penelope would threaten to steal his artists and open up down the block but she said it with a smile. There must have been men in her life, Sam reasoned. He couldn't help being aware of some affection, not demonstrated, that they held one for the other. Sam would think about it from time to time and conclude that this feeling was based on admiration of the other's competence. Sam acknowledged that the warm feelings he felt for Jacqueline, the ones that made him reach out for her, and turn to her for counsel, were far stronger that the occasional lightning bolt he felt for Penelope.

It happened particularly in the company of others. They might be at a dinner for six or eight. Another artist or a collector would invite them and toward the end of the meal Sam might be explaining about his art, or swapping sensations with another artist, when Jacqueline would take his hand under the table, or touch him in some fashion, maybe with her leg. He didn't think she was being possessive, or that she was taking glory reflected off him. He thought he had it right that she was part of him. On evenings such as these, they never failed to fall asleep in one another's arms. They didn't have to say anything.

Jacqueline was seven years into her Saturday music classes. Twenty-one children had shown up once, but the average was fifteen. She faced the problem that schoolmarms do in one-room schoolhouses. Children who had been coming for several years were far advanced from the recently arrived. The old-timers needed different lessons.

The group of children was divided in two, the more advanced in her bedroom and the newly arrived in the kitchen. Jacqueline recruited from among the mothers to handle one or the other group. Music from tapes was played in both rooms and Jacqueline's curriculum continued to grow. She discussed the development of music over the past 500 years. The writing down of music eliminated the need for musicians to memorize scores and made it possible for composers to study the works of those who had come before. The invention of new instruments, such as adding valves to trumpets, expanded range and possibilities. Then, for unaccounted reasons, music went through its phases from the Baroque of Bach and Mozart, to the symphonies of Beethoven, Brahms, and Mahler to the romantics such as Chopin and Tchaikovsky. Then suddenly, for no apparent reason except that change is always in the air, Wagner and Stravinsky and other moderns hit hard, as though they wanted to clean up all that came before.

Jacqueline didn't know if these young minds grasped all she said, but she felt certain that a seed had been planted. She knew that the fruits of her labor would differ from child to child. Abraham fell under Jacqueline's sway. He enjoyed playing for the youngsters. He would ask fellow musicians living in the neighborhood to play their violin or cello.

The music world was not Sam's world. He preferred working in silence. There was a radio in his workspace but he had stopped tuning in the station that his wife recommended. Once in a while it was popular music but he found it distracting.

Sam went off to work Saturday mornings. It was understood that the education of these children was Jacqueline's affair and that it would play no part in his life. He showed no interest in her achievements and would not know that this or that child had decided to take up an instrument.

Jacqueline conceded that time given to her music was time taken away from Sam. She made it up to him by going regularly to the gallery located midtown on Sunday afternoons. She met collectors, a few of whom owned Sam's pieces, and she came to know Penelope. Penelope had a way of featuring Sam. Perhaps she treated all artists in this fashion. She listened to them, looked up at them, and tried to please them. It occurred to Jacqueline that the attention paid by Penelope to the various artists was related to how much each contributed to meeting expenses.

Over time Jacqueline met all the artists whose sculptures and paintings were on display and she concluded that Penelope held Sam in the highest regard. She wanted to say to Penelope, "Keep your hands off him, he's mine." She knew that any such confrontation on her part could be costly. The best way was to hold Sam to her with a long, loose cord that he could barely feel. Confronting Penelope would be tugging on the cord.

Jacqueline could sense two small clouds approaching her marriage. One was the time she gave to children not her own, and the other consisted of the women who were ready to exploit any weakness in her situation. She discussed these matters with Connie.

They were sitting around Connie's kitchen table, drinking coffee, as they did most mornings. Their children were playing on the floor. Jacqueline had had a girl first, and Connie a boy. On their second ones they had reversed gender. Jacqueline asked Connie, "Do you think I should give up the Saturday music business?" Connie knew her friend well enough to understand that this was not a question out of the blue.

"More and more it defines you. Families around the neighborhood look forward to it. They count on it," Connie answered.

"If I stopped, they'd fill in some way. I'm not life or death for anyone."

"No, they wouldn't fill in," Connie disagreed. "They'd let the children play out on the street on Saturday morning, that's all."

"Do you suppose I'm a victim of some minor success?" Jacqueline asked.

"Well, we all are, Abraham, Sam, and you on Saturday. You do something well and it tends to trap you. Take Abraham. His booking agent, the people who sell tickets, the ones who collect the tickets, the ushers, that whole business, they all depend on him. Same for Sam. The people at the galleries where he sells his stuff, they depend on him to send them more."

"Do you think I should tell Sam all that? Would he understand that a little success has come my way?"

"Of course he'd understand. It's a question of whether he's willing to make room for that in his makeup," Connie answered.

"Well, I'll give it a try. Can't hurt." Then Jacqueline added, "What about other women? I'm always worried about those other women. That Penelope, for example. I get the impression she's ready to pounce at any moment. Never mind that Sam's married and has two kids."

"Well, you know," Connie answered, "Some men are only good for ten to twenty years, then they're ready for a change. Not much you can do about it, even though you have a good marriage by your standards." Connie paused, then asked, "How's your sex life, by the way? An attractive man like Sam you don't want to short change."

"I'd say it's OK," Jacqueline answered. There was a tentative note in Jacqueline's voice that Connie caught. Connie said, "I don't know your brand, Sweetie, but give him plenty and keep it varied."

Jacqueline said, "Is that all there is to keeping a marriage together, plenty of sex?"

Connie answered immediately, "No, we both know there's lots more to it, but it's a good thing to keep in mind when you've got barracudas like this Penelope swimming around."

# Bunny 16

Sam McDonald had been aware of large-scale sculpture for twenty years. The uncontested leader in this art form had been Alexander Calder whose biography Sam had read. His father had been a sculptor and his grandfather as well. The three were named Alexander Calder, differentiated only by their middle names. Alexander was a graduate of Stevens Institute of Technology, in Hoboken, New Jersey, in mechanical engineering. Rather than pursue a career in engineering, he moved to France in the mid-nineteen twenties where he specialized in building things in miniature, most of it in eccentric fashion. He might make sconces from empty tin cans, or wind the outline of a fish from brass wire, and invent mobiles, the elegant small trees that could stand on a table or be suspended from the ceiling. And finally there were the stabiles, the twelve-foot high steel designs that could be found across the country, in plazas downtown, or outside a museum, perhaps other places.

Alexander Calder had passed on to another life, perhaps five years previously. Several sculptors would be moving in to fill the void. Sam discussed this eventuality with Penelope. His first question was the logical one – how to be selected as the artist who would win a particular commission. Penelope appeared to Sam as a person who understood the art business. She had given him advice before, particularly on how to sell his products in other cities after he landed his second gallery, the one in San Francisco. On the matter of large sculptures, she explained that the civic body proposing the sculpture would issue specifications and that artists would be invited to submit drawings, or even models on a reduced scale. Of course he would have to state price and delivery, delivery meaning the time required for construction, where the sculpture would be built, and how to move it and erect it on the site. Penelope ended by discussing the changes that would take place in his life.

"Your quarters downtown are fine for the small scale pieces you turn out now, but for stabiles you have to spend a fair amount of time in the country."

"Why go to the country when stabiles end in the city?" Sam asked.

Penelope was annoyed at his answer. "That's not the point. You need the space. These will be twelve to fifteen feet high, eight to ten feet across, and heavy. You'll need a barn out of town somewhere."

"I can't just go out and buy a barn," Sam said.

Penelope ran over Sam's objection. "There are barns no longer in use north of where I spend some time in Connecticut, on the road to Danbury. Beautiful land no longer farmed. You can construct your stabile right there, provided you win the competition, then dismantle it and send it off to its destination."

Sam was silent for a moment, and then he said, "Oh, Jesus."

Penelope asked, "What's the matter?"

"Can you see Jacqueline and the kids moving to Connecticut while I turn metal worker?"

"You don't have to relocate," Penelope said. "Spend some time there, commute a bit. You'll learn on the first commission. Do you know what you should do now?"

Sam's guessed from her question that Penelope had been anticipating this change of direction in him. "What would you suggest?" he answered.

"Take three cities, say Cleveland, Denver and Austin. Make believe they had opened a competition for a piece in front of city hall, and sketch out an idea for each. Cleveland is right on Lake Erie, Denver has all those Rockies to the west, and Austin, I've never been to Austin, do a long-horn cattle motif."

"Where do you get a twelve foot by twelve foot piece of paper?" Sam asked.

"First sketch on 8-1/2 by 11 inch paper, then a second drawing no larger than the long table in your workspace. The idea is to see whether you can come up with original ideas that symbolize some aspect about these cities."

When Sam said, "Oh, Jesus," in his conversation with Penelope, he had in mind Jacqueline's reaction to a move away from her beloved apartment near Central Park. Changes had come along. Connie and Abraham bought an apartment, more spacious, more elegant than the one they had lived in for eight years. At thirty-six, Abraham was entering international competitions, recording with one of the orchestras with whom he had been guest soloist, and was established to the extent that he could fill a recital hall. Connie didn't travel with Abraham, choosing to stay at home with the two children.

Jacqueline had become absorbed in her music. The collection of books grew. The material was more organized than at the beginning, about ten years ago, when they had married. There was a section on the composers, which consisted of short biographies, a description of the type of music they wrote, and a list of their famous compositions. Another section dealt with listening to music in which Jacqueline pointed out to her students sounds that the composers sought in their works, and how music had changed over the decades. Her third section was devoted to notation in which Jacqueline explained the symbols found on sheet music. To make this part clear, she had bought an upright. She could not play, but her little neighbor Hannah, now seventeen and all grown up, could and did for the class.

Sam speculated on the final disposition of this material. He wondered whether it was destined to be a book but didn't see how section two, the sound of music, could be presented in writing. His question was answered when Jacqueline announced that she had decided to submit a lesson plan to City College for a non-credit course similar to the one she had taken about twelve years previously from Daisy Everett. Jacqueline thought that Miss Everett had long since moved on, and if there was turnover among these non-tenured evening teachers, then she might find an open slot.

Sam's reaction surprised even him. He said, "You're abandoning me."

"How so?" Jacqueline asked.

"Well, you'll be gone one night a week and I'll be alone with the children."

Jacqueline was tempted to tell her husband that he might benefit from being with his children, but she let the moment pass. She said, "I need the stimulus of teaching this material. I really need to be with adults more. From the little bit you'll get, you'll see that time with the children can be good for all of you."

Sam talked about the contract married people entered into, that when the kids come the wife drops out of the labor force. Jacqueline countered with the notion that the contract was only for ten years. Sam rubbed his forehead, said, "Oh, Jesus," again. He mumbled, "What next?" Jacqueline fell back on silence and started taking the dishes off the dining room table.

This was not the first moment of discord between them, but both realized that they were on their way to some new arrangement. Jacqueline thought they would grow closer as she developed a professional side. Sam thought they would grow apart as his wife's concentration on their home life diminished.

There was one interview at which Jacqueline filled out a form. She posed as a high school graduate and was glad she did as the person interviewing her commented on her lack of a college degree. Jacqueline calculated that if she told the truth there would be no job offer, so the truth, one of the few times in her life, took a back seat.

She modeled her classes after those of Daisy Everett. She still had the three-ring binder crammed with the notes she had taken. During her first class, it occurred to her to look about the room and find among the students the young men like Mark Corona who had delivered her first kiss to her, and various women who were enrolled in hopes of making contact with suitable males. Both classifications were represented, Jacqueline thought, including a man older than she was. He looked at her in a suggestive way. Jacqueline was certain that he would develop into more than a student of music.

Not the evening of the first class, but after the second this man came forward and stood in line to ask a question. He gave his name as Neil Bellamy, which Jacqueline already knew from reading the names on the roster. The other students drifted out of the classroom. He kept a smile on his face and asked, "Tell me how this came about, your getting to the point that you can teach a class such as this?" Jacqueline recognized this as a contrived question that would get him face to face with her.

"I thought you were about to ask me Brahms' dates, or something else I knew," Jacqueline answered.

"You certainly know the answer to the question I asked," he said.

"Why do you want to know?" Jacqueline answered.

"You're an all-together woman," he said. "You're beautiful, intelligent, you have good delivery, and you have mastered the material. I think there's an interesting story there."

No man, not her husband, had been so direct and flattering. She wanted to believe what he said but she knew that he spelled disaster. Men such as this one move in on you, wreck everything, and move on, the smile still intact on their good-looking face.

She said, looking at the clock on the wall, "The class has been over five minutes. In ten minutes I'm walking out. You're not walking out with me."

That was their bargain. Although Neil Bellamy used all his powers of persuasion, he never broke the rule she laid down.

In the few minutes they had together over the weeks of the course, he extracted her life story. He suggested rendezvous during daytime, when her husband was downtown. He advanced lunch at his place. He invented the idea of meeting at a museum next to a particular painting, as though by accident. While Jacqueline never

gave in to his entreaties, she felt herself being transformed, not in a major way, just in her attitude.

She started dressing for class with greater care. More important, she now viewed herself in a new light, more intelligent than she had imagined and more elegant looking than she had given herself credit for. The greatest advance, though, was her abandonment of the complex over education. She had arrived at her station in life through diligence and thoroughness over the course of a decade. Neil Bellamy saw that in her. He said he was savvy in business and knew brains when he came across them. He endeared himself to her by not breaking their simple rule. At the end of the last class he handed her an envelope containing a slip of paper. On it he had written, "It's all true, everything I've said."

# Bunny 17

Sam submitted his first entry to the city of Santa Fe. This was his start in the field of large-scale sculpture, a sculpture intended for a place on the lawn in front of the state capitol. There were no specifications except for size. The concept offered by the artists need not symbolize New Mexico. Sam obtained a photograph of the capitol and noted that it was circular, built to resemble a large cake. He drew a model of the capitol, making it circular, and placed a topographical map alongside it that accentuated the mountains rising to the north of the city. He made a declivity that identified a tributary of the Rio Grande that runs through the city.

He showed the drawing to Penelope who said that she had been to Santa Fe and on her tour of the city had driven around the capitol. She found it odd looking. She thought the committee awarding the commission wouldn't want to be reminded of their building. She made no suggestions for an alternative design. They ended their discussion and were walking out to the front of the gallery when Penelope's hand landed in the middle of his back. She said, "I doubt that it will win, but submit it anyway. Miracles happen and you need the practice." Penelope proceeded to pat him on the back a few times. It was the first time they had touched.

Sam's second opportunity came when Biloxi, Mississippi, elected to place a sculpture in its principal park. Sam's research told him that the most notable citizen of the city had been Jefferson Davis, who retired there after a stint as president of the Confederate States. Sam drew a profile of Davis because he could not sculpt him full-face. He added in words around the base that Davis had been a senator, a graduate of West Point, and was a noted Episcopalian. When Penelope took a look at this set of drawings, she said she liked the concept on the basis that it might appeal to a contrarian's streak in the committee's make-up. They were sitting on a small sofa in the owner's office of her gallery. Their bodies were touching from shoulder to ankle. Sam guessed that Penelope knew what she was doing. She said, "I'm going to write out a few notes that you may want to include. I'll say that Jefferson Davis has been overlooked for political reasons and it's high time he was recognized." Penelope went to the owner's desk and returned with a pad of paper and a ballpoint pen. "I'm not a bad writer, you know. I produce all the sales material you see around here."

Sam received a letter from the committee in Biloxi informing him that he had lost. The winning design was not discussed but one member had added an unsigned note in his handwriting, saying, "Thanks a million. The South will rise again."

Time elapsed before Sam received correspondence from Seattle. He wrote the Chamber of Commerce for brochures of the city. He read the material that he received and canvassed the artists in his building. One of the painters was a refugee from the Northwest. The subjects of his paintings were totem poles, war canoes, pine trees, lakes and bays, and sea hawks. He made a meager living at what he did. He would brag that he paid his own studio rent and paid for his materials and only relied on his wife for the rest.

Sam found out the history of art in Seattle from this painter. The first museum had been located in Volunteer Park, located on the top of the hill behind the city. It had lost its place as number one museum when a new one was constructed downtown. Asian art remained at the original place, and the rest of the collection came down the hill. Sam's informant told him that the most newsworthy and controversial part of the new museum was the statue outside. It consisted of a human figure forty feet tall, the right hand holding a hammer, which stayed in motion while the museum was open. Sam's friend, named conveniently Ed Castle from Seattle, swore that the membership remained in turmoil over this statue, apparently a majority wishing to tear it down. Ed thought that if Sam were to produce a sculpture that lampooned the man with the hammer, he might strike a responsive chord in the evaluating committee. Sam referred to his maps of the city and found the park up the hill containing the original museum. He located the new museum downtown, and Pioneer Square, about a mile south of the new museum, at the heart of the earliest center of the city. His sculpture would be placed conspicuously in this square.

Sam thought that he could sculpt a couple of two-dimensional figures ten feet tall, a man and a woman, without the hammer, and have them symbolize the labor movement as it existed presently, members of both genders that did not use hammers any longer. He would encase these figures in a sphere made of many thin pieces of stainless steel arranged so that one-third of the sphere's surface was metal and two-thirds nothing.

When Sam showed his sketches to Penelope, she said, "Brilliant." Then she added that the committee might not appreciate his poking fun at the forty-foot hammer bearer in front of the museum. "It will be a matter of luck," she said.

They got up from the small sofa where they had been looking at his sketches. Penelope turned and put her arms around his neck and said, "I know you'll succeed soon. You try so hard." Even though Sam was clutching drawings in one hand and two pencils in the other, he managed to hold Penelope tight against him. She felt like Jacqueline in his arms, and on that note he relaxed his grip. Sam lost the competition. A sculpture not different from Ed Castle's suggestion won. It featured several salmon, a totem pole, a ferryboat going off across Elliott Bay to an island, with Mount Rainier in the background, and various other symbols of the region.

The fourth packet came from a medium-sized city, a suburb of Chicago. The sculpture would be placed outside city hall. The request for proposal gave him sixty days to respond. It stated that the sculpture should describe Chicago's importance in the westward expansion of the nation. Beyond that there were no instructions except that the dimensions of the sculpture should be such that it would fit into a cube sixteen feet on a side.

Sam was still holding the correspondence in his hands when it came to him that Chicago was known for railroads and stockyards and that he should construct a locomotive with horns. He dismissed the idea right away but it amused him that this would be his first impression.

He worked through the problem on paper and ended with a sphere consisting of two hoops placed at right angles to symbolize the earth. Inside he positioned one sheet of stainless steel in the vertical plane, which he cut to show the Great Lakes. From Chicago he welded ribbons of dark steel, symbolizing rails, which he extended to parts west, east, and south, and one ribbon north-west to Minneapolis. Much was left to the imagination, a feature Alexander Calder had initiated in his work. No need to be too obvious. Let viewers come up with their own interpretations.

On his usual visit to Penelope for suggestions and approval, they took their places on the small sofa in the owner's office. Sam wondered how Penelope might indicate her confidence in him. Could she be more demonstrative than the last time? He doubted it, unless she sat on his lap. They looked at his drawings. Instead of sitting close to him, Penelope stationed herself a foot away. She might be penalizing him for not having won any of the competitions, he guessed. When they parted company she reverted to patting him on the shoulder and adding some encouraging words.

Sam constructed a model in which the hoops were a foot in diameter. He stipulated that this would be enlarged to twelve feet in the final version. It was a bulky contraption to ship off to the small city north of Chicago, but Sam thought it was well worth the trouble. In his previous three attempts he had submitted models although accurate drawings would have met the requirements set forth in the bid package. In this proposal he said that in the event he was not the winner, his model should be returned to him at his expense. He had not so stipulated in his previous submissions and wondered at the final disposition of his models. In whose closets were they sitting? Penelope objected as it indicated to her that he wasn't certain of winning. Sam told her that the gallery he sold through in Chicago could fetch the model and exhibit it. No doubt some booster would want it badly enough to cover his expenses.

When he won the competition, he did allow Penelope to drag him up to Connecticut. She instructed him to get to Danbury on a Monday, when her gallery was closed, and gave him a telephone number to call on arrival. "I will have taken care of the preliminaries. We can drive around and look at some sites. We should be able to find a barn or something."

As instructed, Sam stood on the sidewalk in front of the bus station. He was dressed as he would for work and carried an overnight bag. Jacqueline wondered about the bag. She said, "You know, it's not that far." He answered, "It could take all day. I could find the right place late in the afternoon. I just might want to collapse."

Penelope pulled up in front of the station and waved at Sam who might have been twenty feet away. Her first words were "What do you think of country air?"

He said, "It smells imported." He had no idea what he meant by the remark and was surprised when Penelope did not ask for an explanation.

"I have two places to look at, so we can start with those," she said.

As they drove out of town, Sam stated his interest for staying within city limits. "If this place is anything like Weehawken, there'll be a run-down commercial district that has a couple of shops that have gone out of business, like a plumbing place. I just need one big room, running water, a bathroom and a telephone. That should do it. And if I'm in town, I can get supplies and maybe not need a car." That's how he stated his case.

The two places in the country were inappropriate. While they were buildings that provided shelter from the elements, they were low on amenities. Penelope had not inquired about 100-Ampere electrical service and running water.

The search in town brought results on the first try. Sam was forced to sign a lease for six months but was glad that he had found a suitable place in one day. He was prepared to retrace his steps to New York when Penelope said, "Let me drive you to a place where I spend some time. It's not too far."

Penelope had surprised him again. He asked her whether she had her own place. She explained that she had an arrangement with friends who were there only on weekends so that she could use it during the week. They were north of Danbury on a country road, perhaps four miles out of town, when she said, "That's it, under the trees, over there." The front of the house faced away from the road. Once in the house, Sam was led to the other side. The view was across a meadow to a small river. Penelope said that the hills to the west were in New York. She turned and looked north and remarked that those must be the Berkshires, but there was no conviction in her voice. Sam realized that such facts were not of interest to her. The hills could have been the Alps. She said, "It's cocktail time." Sam looked at his watch and indeed it was a few minutes after five o'clock. "What will you have?" she asked.

They elected to sit indoors because of a cool breeze. They settled into a sofa with the view behind them. Penelope steered the conversation to the details of construction, asking Sam how he would go about fabricating the pieces, assembling them, taking them apart for shipment, and finally re-assembling them in Illinois. When they were done with the details she asked him how he would spend the $25,000 commission. Sam said, "By my calculation, I'll break even, but it's the first one. No complaints."

He knew that he must be inventing the tension between Penelope and him because she had said nothing and done nothing that went beyond the matter at hand. When she brought the second drink in from the kitchen, there was mischief on her face. Sam knew that they would change the subject, having exhausted the topic of his work.

Penelope was silent for a moment. She turned to him and said, in ordinary conversational tones, "We are two normal people out in the country, alone in a quiet, comfortable house. Why don't you pick up your drink and come upstairs with me?"

Sam's thoughts went immediately to Jacqueline. He had discussed Danbury with her twice and on both occasions asked her to come with him as he looked for a place larger than his workspace downtown. He even suggested that the children would enjoy the country, which they had seen precious little of. In the first of these conversations it had come out that it was Penelope who was behind the idea of his having a place in the country to execute his large-scale sculptures.

Jacqueline turned down his invitation because taking the family to Connecticut would disrupt the children's schedules. She gave as an additional reason that at the time of those conversations he had not won a competition and had no immediate need for space. Why not wait to go hunting in Danbury when a need had arisen, she had asked. Sam had wanted to confront the issue. His wife was wedded to teaching music to neighboring children on Saturday and to her weekly session at City College in evening classes. He resented her inflexibility and what he considered her lack of adventurous spirit, not that a trip to Danbury required a great deal of that. He had felt for a while that he was losing his position in the family.

Penelope led him into one of the bedrooms and showed it to him. She discussed the two paintings on the wall and the destination of the little river across the meadow. She started unbuttoning her blouse as she spoke, in a most casual manner, Sam thought, and after the last button, took off the blouse and draped it carefully over the back of a chair. She explained that the silver on the dressing table had been her grandmother's. She slipped out of her jeans, folded them and placed them on the seat of the same chair. She went to the bed, pushed back the comforter, folded down the sheet on her side of the bed and looked up at him. He was standing in the middle of the room. She asked, "What's the matter, can't you unbutton buttons?"

Many questions came to him. Why would Penelope, whom he had never kissed, seduce him? Why did he throw his marriage vows out the window so easily? Was there some moral imperative that should prevent this turn of events? When he sat down on the side of the bed and leaned over to kiss her, he wondered who would ever know, and what difference did it make.

Sam thought they enjoyed it, but he wondered what purpose had been served. He knew that he was supposed to feel cheapened by the experience and elated at the same time, but in fact he felt nothing in particular. The moments reminded him of so many conquests in his days as a single man. He guessed that Penelope took most of her artists to bed. He became convinced that her actions had very little to do with affection for him, or for any of the others, when she married a psychiatrist six months later. This man had been divorced, but not before he had had two children. He was a regular customer of the gallery. Sam had met him. He had bought many small sculptures. Penelope would be able to look at the collection at her new address.

They were downstairs having supper when Sam volunteered that he would be better off staying the night. "I don't know how I'd explain coming in at 1 a.m.," he said.

"You're right," Penelope said. "Besides, we've broken in the sheets. I'll run you down to Stamford tomorrow morning and you can catch the train."

When he came into his apartment in late morning, the children were at school and Jacqueline was out on an errand. He left a note giving his whereabouts and telling his wife that he had found a place in Danbury proper. He went downtown and busied himself with cutting out metal prior to welding the pieces together into finished products. He thought he could drive the memory of the previous day out of his mind.

That evening Jacqueline welcomed him as usual. When she asked no questions, he concluded that she knew everything. She was beyond suspecting him. She must have guessed correctly at Penelope's involvement. Who else could it be? He knew it would be a long time before he could make peace with himself and reach out for his wife.

Sam finished the construction in six weeks. He took the sculpture apart, supervised the packing, and watched the boxes being loaded into a truck bound for Chicago. He spent two weeks on site re-assembling and painting the two hoops fire engine red.

Jacqueline had not come to Danbury to measure progress on the project. He refrained from inviting her because he dreaded hearing her say, "No thank you. That's Penelope's territory." Similarly, he reduced his outpouring of affection. He maintained a wide space between them in bed. He thought that if he touched her she would say that she hoped to be as good as Penelope.

After Sam returned from the Chicago area, Jacqueline let two weeks pass. She placed a small vase with two red roses on the bed table on his side. She came to bed and said, "I think that's long enough." It took him quite a while to get over the experience.

# Bunny 18

Bunny and Zack parked in front of the small church situated on the right side of the road as one drove from the Cove into Oyster Bay. They were using a family car, with Bunny at the wheel. Zack wondered how the rector would handle two Protestants who went to church rarely. Zack realized that the rector couldn't turn them down as he was captive of the Underhill family and many similar whose annual pledges paid the bills.

Zack noticed right away that the collar fit loosely, as though the rector had bought his clothes twenty years ago and had shrunk bit by bit. Bunny introduced Zack. She let go of his hand and said, "Dear, this is Reverend Buckingham." When Zack took the reverend's hand he could feel the frailness and wondered why the man had not retired. The rector looked Zack straight in the eye and said, "So you're the victim, is that it?" Bunny chuckled but didn't say anything. The reverend turned to her and remarked, "You must be the fifth or sixth girl I've baptized and now I'm marrying. Such a stable community."

He led them into his study and invited them to sit around a table for six. Reverend Buckingham went through the formalities. "How long have you known one another?" he asked. "Will you be living in New York?" "I understand you're about to graduate from Columbia Law School. Tell me about the job prospects." He moved to the marriage service, saying to Zack, "It takes such a short time. There's no comparable civilized activity that gets you into this amount of trouble in ten minutes."

To reaffirm the date, the rector reached behind him and took an appointment calendar off his desk. He turned to the month of June where he had already marked "Underhill-Taylor" on the last Saturday. The matter appeared to be closed when the rector asked, "When the children come, will you have them baptized here?" With that detail settled the rector stood up and said, "I suppose we'll motor over to Locust Valley for your reception." Reverend Buckingham had a reputation of imbibing a fair amount of champagne at wedding receptions as he moved around the room, on the lookout for candidates to make it to his church on Sundays.

Zack was relieved that Reverend Buckingham did not bring up the matter of their attendance at church. Zack guessed that most of the young people he was marrying had long since curtailed the practice, and that if he made an issue of it the results would be counter-productive, such as couples seeking out judges for the purpose.

They selected Bermuda where neither had been. Zack referred to the coming trip as their honeymoon, while to a man the Underhills used the term "wedding trip." Zack asked Bunny about this term new to him, although quite comprehensible. She explained the Underhills and the rest of them, whom she called her crowd, adopted the term first to be used, so that it was wedding trip over honeymoon, telephoning someone over calling them, and curtains over drapes. On hearing this explanation, Zack asked about the results if he did not adapt. Bunny replied, "It's not important, but you'd be setting yourself apart."

This brief conversation took place before the wedding. Zack wondered how many other adjustments were in store for him as he climbed a few rungs up the social ladder. The Underhills had accepted him. That was the deal they had struck with Bunny. He realized that he would encounter other adjustments when he was given sailing lessons, and when he had his first experiences with golf and tennis.

He was ever so thankful for his coming degree from Columbia Law School, although he realized that he could not invent graduating from a New England boarding school nor could he make believe there were four years at Harvard, Yale, or Princeton. He would have to compensate by being more successful than they were, the other men his age, thereby demonstrating that a graduate from City College could compete with the best of them. He thought about ventilating the entire issue with Bunny but decided against it on the basis that neither could change the past, and that Bunny, for her own good reasons, had rejected the advances of the young men she grew up with. He would conform and learn to say "curtains" and put the word "drapes" out of his mind.

The wedding trip held its set of surprises for Zack. While he and Bunny had been intimate on occasion after the proposal, that schedule was different from the infinite sex he ran into on Bermuda. It was inevitable at the end of the evening. It materialized before descending from their room for dinner. Sometimes it occurred after the morning swim, and twice it came as early as sunrise. After four days of this, Zack heard himself say to Bunny that he needed time off. She said, "That's fine, darling, there's always tomorrow." Zack thanked heaven that for budgetary reasons the trip would last only eight days. It came as a surprise to Zack that he could get his fill so soon.

On the matter of conversation, it came to both of them that they did not possess limitless material to discuss. They had turned to their books during the flight from New York. They carried these books and others to the beach and found that an important topic of conversation during meals was to comment on the material they had just read. Zack was thankful once again for the short time they had allocated. He wasn't certain he could have stretched the trip to two weeks.

Zack had been at work two months before the wedding. When he returned, he was greeted by the senior partner. He asked Zack, "Well, did you get it out of your system?" The question was accompanied by a knowing glance. Zack was tempted to ask him how long he had been married and whether his fires were banked, but he said nothing. Zack was reassigned to the partner with whom he had started. They were working on the tax treatment of a hotel as it went through renovations. The depreciation schedules had to be adjusted for the time and material invested into each space. These were the days prior to the arrival of software that could simplify these matters. Zack spent a fair amount of time with the accountants at the hotel, and more time than he wanted with the large desktop adding machine that made a great deal of noise.

Bunny was back at work at the UN, once again completing pamphlets. They devoted quite some time finding space for Zack's things. He had taken his furniture to a second hand store, the same place where he had purchased it, so that part of the problem disappeared. It was difficult finding a home for his clothes. Bunny had filled all the closets with her clothes for the four seasons. She was forced to vacate one closet and stash those items under the bed.

The serious discussion between them centered on when they might have their first child. On the subject, Bunny said, "Why don't we start trying in six months. It looks bad to get pregnant on your wedding trip. They never believe you when you say you're early."

During her pregnancy, the old lawyer, Underhill Senior, died. He had been the picture of health. On an afternoon in the fall, he had stepped outside to perform his baronial walk in which he surveyed his property, paying particular attention to the stone wall at the water's edge. He had returned to the porch of his house and taken his customary place in a garden chair when life ceased. He was eighty-seven. His wife had died some years previously. James Senior's departure created a vacancy on the property. He had occupied one of the two substantial houses. His son James and wife Edith were in the other. Wilson and his wife occupied the cottage. Conversations took place casually between Edith and Bunny, in what Zack took to be deliberately low-keyed negotiations. When the offer reached Zack's ears, after the preliminaries had been dispensed with, he realized at once that he would become a commuter, a regular client of the Long Island Railroad. It took him fifteen minutes to see that he would be getting the use of a house without buying it, that their child and subsequent children could grow up outside Manhattan, and that at some moment, perhaps twenty to thirty years away, Bunny and he would have to settle accounts with her brothers James and Douglas. It wouldn't do to grab real estate and cut out some members of the family. Zack thought the day of reckoning would come after Bunny's parents had died.

The issue of a name for the child arose. Zack's father had stuck his oar into the discussion, prefacing his remarks by saying that it was none of his business, then proceeding to ignore his own advice. His suggestion was that a male child should be named Francis as the first Taylor to make it to these shores was Francis and that the name had not been used since. Bunny agreed that the name James was out of the question and only remarked that Francis would be shortened to Fran, which was used more for women that it was for men. Zack knew she was keeping her powder dry for another moment. He knew her well enough by then.

On the second of their meetings, the male parents, Mr. Underhill and Mr. Taylor, found themselves sipping scotch and looking out over the water, across the bay. Mr. Taylor asked Mr. Underhill how long the family had been associated with the property they were on. Underhill said he was not certain but guessed that it was late 1600s or early 1700s, and those ancestors must have bought the land from the local Indians.

It was at this point that Taylor Senior discussed the arrival of the first Taylor in Boston in 1635 and his subsequent migration to New York. He also introduced the name of Francis as a possibility for a grandson. Mr. Underhill had changed the subject. When his father repeated the conversation to Zack, Zack said, "Don't anguish over it, Dad. I've learned about these people that when you top them they consider it unimportant and change the subject. When they top you, they let you know it."

Taylor Senior looked up at his son, indicating that he wanted an example. Zack said, "I've been made to understand that they're worth a hundred times more than I'll ever be. It's called controlling power, Dad."

On subsequent discussions about the vacant house in Oyster Bay and the name of the coming child, Bunny was direct, and Zack blessed her for that. She made her points but didn't browbeat him. A typical announcement went as follows: "The baby will grow up in clean air, next to the water. He or she can play on the lawn. My mother would love to have a grandchild on the property."

Zack asked about her idea of a schedule for the move. Bunny answered, "I'll give birth here in the city, and then we can move into the house." "And when might you quit your job?" Zack asked. "How about when I have a month to go?" came the answer.

They grew closer on arrangements. Finances were discussed, the eventual settlement with the brothers explored, and the hardship of commuting was acknowledged. Zack made one reservation, to the effect that his career would not be made to suffer, and by that he meant they would keep the apartment in the city and that it was understood that he would be obliged to work late on many evenings and not be expected to come home on the last train, only to turn around early the following morning.

When Zack agreed in substance to all the details, he uttered his first enthusiastic words, which were, "I'm looking forward to learning something about sailing." Bunny knew he was beginning to sell himself on the idea. At that moment she said, almost casually, that they could call the child Francis, or Frances if the baby turned out to be a girl.

At the christening, Reverend Buckingham cradled the boy in his arms and intoned, "I baptize thee Francis Douglas Taylor, in the name of the Father, the Son, and the Holy Ghost." The cold water on the baby's head seemed to have no effect. Zack thought little Francis was dozing through the ceremony. When the rector returned the baby to Bunny, he said, "I love the continuity."

# Bunny 19

The first time Zack became aware of Bunny's feelings their second child could walk. She might have been a year-and-a-half old. These sentiments were barely discernible but Zack reasoned that the emotion had been there for a while. He had simply failed to notice it.

A forty-six foot yawl whose owner lived in Connecticut would sail into Oyster Bay occasionally. The owner, Robert Sands, seemed to know everyone. They called him Bobby. He was born and had lived in Oyster Bay until he went to work in New York. He moved to Connecticut when the corporation he worked for moved its headquarters to Stamford. He never married but remained a popular figure with his old friends. He might come over from Stamford by motorboat and once in a while he would arrive in his yawl and take a party for a day sail on the Sound. There would already be a few people on board who had helped Bobby put up the sails.

Zack knew that Bobby had come to their wedding and reception but had no memory of him until he and Bunny were guests at a small dinner party a year later. Eventually the invitation came from Bobby for a day sail. Once they cleared the harbor and were moving east on the Sound, Bobby turned the wheel over to Bunny, suggesting to her that she keep the boat in the middle of the Sound with both shores in view. She sailed the boat most of the morning and made several tacks as they moved into the wind.

Bunny was always pleased to be around boats. A forty-six footer was in a different league than the yachts she had sailed before, certainly more of a challenge than the thirty-foot single-masted sloop that her father owned. During the morning, Zack would look at Bunny now and again. She didn't chat with the other people in the cockpit. Frequently she would look under the mainsail to determine that other boats were not bearing down on her. Zack was aware of her concentration and detachment, as though nature had determined that she should spend a fair amount of time at the wheel of large sailing vessels. There was no question that she did this well.

On the return trip, sailing down wind, Bobby set the spinnaker and took over from Bunny. Zack watched them as they went through the motions. Bobby held her shoulder for a long moment as he leaned over her and spoke. Zack couldn't hear the conversation. Moments later, Bunny went below and came back with a hat. It was the white hat worn by enlisted men in the Navy. Bunny folded down the brim and placed it on Bobby's head, adjusting it until it suited her.

Zack didn't know if he was witnessing familiarity. The effect on him was to make him rein in his emotions for a while, until Bunny made an advance toward him a week later. Bobby Sands and his sailboat, motorboat, near-par golf game, position in society and vast inherited wealth remained in Zack's mind. Any moment, he guessed, Bunny could be gone with their two children to the Connecticut side of the Sound, to sail the yawl and revert to the old life, a little of which she had given up to marry him.

On that subject, Zack would ponder just how much Bunny had given up. He acknowledged that she had a fixation for diamonds in the rough. At least that's how he imagined she classified him. In her accounting, it still seemed important that she had married out of her class. She would reinforce this by saying to Zack that his opinions were refreshing, original, not ideas he had heard somewhere and was just repeating. They were founded on what she called real life experiences rather than the notions of the privileged few. Zack didn't consider that his experiences were closer to real life, whatever that meant, than were the experiences of his new friends. He never debated the issue with Bunny. She had kept her membership in clubs, her life style, her money, and most importantly to Zack, her friends. She never attempted to recruit new friends who, she might consider, were from that other world that she thought Zack came from.

Over a few years, Zack integrated himself into this society new to him. He didn't feel different from the rest. He picked up their vocabulary and mannerisms, although not their tone of voice. He would listen to them speak and could hear that they didn't have a New York accent. He decided that he would meet them halfway by giving up his pronunciation but not adopting theirs. It took special effort to pronounce the letter <u>r</u> properly. When he mastered that he thought he had come far enough.

Their two children were the center of attention for the sets of grandparents. Zack's mother and father would come out frequently. Bunny was polite and welcoming to them. The senior Underhills didn't warm to the Taylors. Mr. Underhill explained to Bunny that they didn't have anything to talk about, and in addition to that, Taylor senior was a Democrat and therefore wouldn't understand the conclusions the Underhills had reached on politics. After all, as Bunny's father enjoyed saying, the Roosevelts lived just down the road, at Sagamore Hill, and his grandfather and Teddy were fast friends, and Teddy was a true Republican. Bunny never understood this line of reasoning but she did conclude that her father was not interested in sharing a drink with Zack's father and talking about this and that.

Bunny and Zack decided on a third child. They agreed that the first two were fine products. Bunny explained it to Zack by telling him it was the new blood he brought to the lineage. "You don't have that highly refined stuff we have around here. Your blood is the right mix," she had told him. Zack wondered how much of the recruiting of him had only to do with his genes. He didn't think it was important and refused to dwell on it.

Bobby was another matter. The Sands family was not exceptional when compared to other old, rich families on the North Shore. They fitted right in and had for a couple of centuries. As with so many families, they practiced law or worked in investments in New York City. Some members of the family owned a seat on the Stock Exchange. The Sands family held firmly to their class, money, memberships, positions in society, leadership in organizations that interested them, vacations to about the same place, a passable acquaintance with London and Paris, a place in Palm Beach, and life-long friends. Bobby fitted into this mold except that he hadn't married. His friends might press him on the matter to which he would answer, "Someday, maybe."

At a dance one evening it occurred to Zack that Bobby was in love with his wife. They didn't hold one another closely, that wasn't it, but they talked and laughed as they danced, seemingly unaware that there was anyone else on the floor. When Bobby escorted Bunny back to her table, Zack stood up. Bobby said, "Wonderful dancer. Thank you, Bunny, and thank you Zack." The way he said it made Zack think he was guarding and preserving Bunny so that he, Bobby, could take over one day at the appropriate moment.

As Bobby moved off, Zack noticed that he was wearing patent leather shoes with a bow on the front, not the lace-up variety most men wore. He asked his father about this and his father answered, "Yes, dancing pumps. A bit effete for my taste." Zack had seen a few men wearing these pumps at a Sunday lunch. He calculated that these men wished to signal that they hadn't put their dancing shoes away late Saturday night and couldn't be bothered to find their loafers by Sunday noon.

In the case of Bobby, Zack guessed that the pumps signaled to the world that he could do exactly what he pleased, moving dangerously close to eccentricity. He did exhibit all the confidence one might wish for.

Bunny's younger brother, Douglas, who was at the table watching his sister dance, did mention to Zack that Bunny and Bobby had dated the summer before she went off to college. "Eight years of difference in their ages," Douglas reported. He went on to say, "But they liked one another. He was out of college three or four years as she was starting. Obviously nothing came of it." To Zack it was obvious that it had never gone away.

The third child came, another girl. The nest was full, Bunny announced to her husband. Mrs. Wilson, who had lived on the property with her husband more than thirty years, and had cared for Bunny and her two brothers, now started to give more time to Bunny's children and less time to the senior Underhills. Over time, they slipped into using one another's first names. There was a time when Bunny had passed thirteen or fourteen that the Wilsons addressed her as Miss Bunny. It seemed stilted to the Wilsons but Mr. Underhill had suggested it.

An era of calm came over the people living on the property in the three houses. The senior Underhills were showing the first signs of creaking joints. Mr. Wilson did less gardening and ran more errands in the car. Bunny was satisfied raising her three children. Zack never moved from the law firm where he went after graduation. His practice grew and he spent at least one night a week in town in the apartment that he and Bunny shared when they were first married.

Zack and Bunny had two new friends, one a forty-six foot yawl, the other Bobby Sands. Ever so gradually it appeared to Zack that he, his wife and Bobby had become a threesome. It was nothing of his doing, Zack knew, but the other two enjoyed a familiarity, an ease together, that he and his wife could not match.

Zack was well aware that friends would always converse when thrown together. He recognized also that men and women who grew fond of one another would lean toward expressing that fondness in a physical manner. It was inevitable, a primal force. Bobby held an official position in their small family. He was the godfather of their third child. Zack reasoned that there wasn't much to be done about it. He could continue to be the best husband he knew how to be and hope that would suffice. If it did not, and Bobby's and Bunny's affection grew, he understood that their marriage would be over.

# Bunny 20

Bobby did not go beyond the boundaries of respectability. Zack never thought that he had propositioned his wife or stolen a kiss or held her too tightly during a dance. As part of the family, a godparent, Zack guessed that Bobby knew the terms of the contract: he would be familiar but wouldn't insinuate himself. The forty-six foot yawl showed up on occasion. Bunny still loved sailing. But the two of them must have reached a certain level of proximity and held it right there.

Bunny had kept that half-full figure that Zack liked so much. He wondered how she could be hard in some places and soft in others. She kept the business of bed very simple. She was always available, and more or less enthusiastic. Zack had no idea why the level went up and down. He knew it had little to do with him. She made it personal but not so personal that he felt that he was the important man in her life. He didn't think there was an important man in her life. He felt, lying in bed in the darkness, that he could be any man, the one she had selected to be the father of their children, the bread winner, but not particularly the partner.

As he looked back, he wondered whether he had ever been the partner. Being selected as the mate of one so well-positioned socially, he was flattered and had felt then more important than he felt now, although nearly twenty-five years had gone by. The evaluation that Bunny had made of Zack, early on, that he was a diamond in the rough and that he brought elemental views from the lower class into her life, had vanished. Those views tapered off after ten years of marriage and were now extinct. Zack wondered what Bunny thought of her decision, whether she regretted it, or whether it was a sophomoric sensation that she did not want to dislodge at the time and that her parents were not able to.

Their three children were succeeding in life. The oldest was out of college. The second child was enrolled. The third was finishing at boarding school. The club life had moved to the center: tennis and lunches for Bunny, some golf for Zack, who enjoyed the game, but viewed it as an affliction for those who made it a fetish of driving down their scores year to year, as though there was any long-term residue in a low handicap. Zack showed his disdain by using an old golf bag with old clubs and by changing the subject at the nineteenth hole when it got to be a bit much. In a way, he thought he had jumped over this old-money class he had joined by refusing to place his interests where theirs were, and continuing on a normal development of the intellect. Zack thought that most of them had stopped serious enterprises, except the task of making money, when they passed twenty-five.

Zack concluded that Bunny and he were reverting to type. She had dabbled in a class lower than her own, found that the process gave her some standing among friends (how bold and courageous, they said) and ended up with having brought forth three more-than-adequate children. Zack had to admit that the mingling of their genes produced results out of the ordinary. Her life away from the workplace did take its toll. The challenges of raising a family were different from those confronted between nine and five, and while Zack respected the resources that good parents had to find in themselves, he could see that the absence of the demands of work beyond the home had diminished Bunny. Her horizons were nearer than in the days she worked at the United Nations. She had become preoccupied with style and form, behavior and goings-on, and as Zack thought, had ceased to grow.

Zack, on the other hand, had been selected to be the managing partner. He now had to concern himself with personnel problems, growth of the firm, finding new clients to replace those who fell away, broadening the scope of the business, all the while continuing to accept his share of the tax work. He felt he had to consider ever more aspects of his firm in order to get through each day. He mentioned to Bunny that he made more money, but that he was working at two jobs.

She had not lost any of her appeal. Zack would think often of the day they met at lunch in the company of the family. It was about a quarter of a century ago, she walking into the dining room in her red wool suit, just a little out of breath, but unrepentant over being late, and in a few moments, provocative in her conversation. He still loved her and liked the feel of her in his arms but he sensed that they were drifting apart. He wondered if she was aware of it.

It was a new experience for Zack, perhaps for Bunny too, to live with someone who is not so much in your life as before, still an important part, but living in a situation in which the bonds are looser than a year ago. Zack stayed in town more often now, perhaps two nights a week. With the children gone, Bunny would spend these nights in her bedroom at the main house. It was not an unusual arrangement as the commute from New York City to Oyster Bay was time consuming, and for Zack, as for many who had commuted for years, it was becoming tedious. He wondered whether they might not move into town, and come out on weekends.

The threat from outside, Zack was surprised to see, came from a new breed of men. If a person were to come into their lives, it would not be Bobby, who had the decency to stay out until Bunny and Zack had ended their marriage on their own, if indeed they did. This new breed consisted of men wealthy beyond imagining. They worked in finance, at one of several firms, and had ridden the surge upward with skill and insight. They were in the middle of things everyday, could see what was happening, and on occasion made it happen. Many of these men were divorced. Their preoccupation with making money had left little time for the important aspects of life. Their wives, seeing the vast wasteland ahead, were willing to part company if the terms and conditions were orchestrated properly. The men could envision a stream of sweet young things for a few years before they were married again, perhaps to one of them. The wives would be placated by keeping the apartment in New York, and a hideaway on Nevis, or on another island in the Caribbean, and enough money to finance the operation.

This new breed of men had made so much money that they thought it was smart to use shorthand to describe wealth. As such, one hundred million dollars they called a unit. Zack detested the term, as though money, great gobs of it, had become the center of life and that there would be a pile of it somewhere, say in the backyard, and all who were connected to the pile would eat there, at the trough, until satisfied.

Zack still worked for most of his money. While a little of his total materialized because small pieces he might own had risen in value, it was not the case that the bulk of his modest wealth was due to some inexplicable device called market forces. Zack no longer counted pennies, he knew that, but at any moment he knew how much folding money was in his wallet. Zack didn't know how Bunny felt about this new avalanche of purchasing power, but he recognized that she was less unsettled by it than he was. She demonstrated this by befriending the crop of new rich. She told Zack they were amusing. When pressed, she explained that they tried so hard to conform in dress, manners and speech that she let herself be entertained by them at functions.

Among them was a Ted Andres, who originated in the mid-west, attended college in the east, and had been recruited by an investment banking firm. The sixteen-hour days, the travel, and the high-risk poker he played in investing his own money were part of the game. He parlayed all these efforts into a substantial fortune and by the time he was fifty, a year younger than Bunny, he had purchased a home in the Hamptons, a house in Oyster Bay and a medium-sized apartment in New York City. Zack thought that of those he had met, Ted was the easiest to take. To Bunny, Ted confessed that his purchases in real estate were not on the basis of need but rather that it extended his opportunities of meeting people that interested him. "As proof," he said, "I'm sitting next to you at this dinner party. I can't imagine anyone I'd rather be sitting next to." Bunny was flattered and said so. Ted Anders had not married and Bunny wondered if he had been so busy during his years at work that he remained innocent of women, not completely innocent, but inexperienced. Bunny sensed this urge in her to take him to bed and teach him the wonders of intimacy, assuming that he didn't know them already. Zack had been the other person for whom she had experienced that sensation, even though at the time it had been she who had no experience. That was a long time ago and Bunny was surprised that after all these years the sensation would reappear, and for a man she knew only slightly. She tried to dismiss the whole notion.

They would meet now and again and Zack noticed they sought each other's company to share a drink and some gossip. On one such occasion Bunny told Zack that Ted had this wild dream of either buying a yacht, or having one constructed for the Newport-to-Bermuda race.

Zack asked, "Ted's from the mid-west. Has he ever been in anything larger than a canoe?"

"I honestly don't know," Bunny answered. "Those are the big leagues, those long ocean races. I think it's 700 miles," Bunny added.

"How much will this set him back?" Zack asked.

"All the latest equipment, a perfectly functioning boat, all the supplies, and there have to be expenses associated with getting the boat back to Newport. How about ten million?"

Zack asked, "They refer to one hundred million as a unit. What's the term for ten million?"

Bunny answered, "I think it's referred to as walking-around money."

"The games the rich will play," Zack said.

Ted Anders would not keep his distance, as Bobby had. He spoke to her as though Zack did not exist. A new boat was being designed and would be constructed. Bunny was kept aware of progress. One day Ted said to her, "Perhaps you'll want to be part of the crew when we enter the race." Bunny hadn't said anything.

# Bunny 21

Jacqueline's class in music appreciation had gained in popularity over the three years she had taught it. Attendance was up to twenty-five students. There were sixteen the first time the class was offered. One student was repeating. When asked why, this woman, who always sat in the front row, explained that she only grasped twenty percent of what she heard, and that by taking the class again she would get more out of it.

After this explanation, Jacqueline remarked, "I take it you want me to cover the same material I did last time." The woman answered, "Word for word, if you can."

Jacqueline said, "Andrea, you don't know the sense of relief this gives a teacher. I thought you wanted all new material." The woman said, "That would defeat the purpose."

For Andrea's last name, Jacqueline had to turn to her roster. She couldn't understand why the name Simmons was difficult to recall. Andrea Simmons. It seemed simple enough. Andrea was medium in most respects. That made her shorter than Jacqueline and taller than Connie. She was pretty, had auburn hair, wore glasses, and came to class wearing a pantsuit of which she had an endless collection. Jacqueline envisioned a long closet from which Andrea would take today's pantsuit off the left end of the bar and in the evening put it back on its hanger and place it on the right end.

The one single man and the two married men in the previous class had buzzed around Andrea. She managed to shoo them away. That independence and Andrea's trait of speaking directly made Jacqueline wonder whether there were a black leather jacket and a motorcycle in Andrea's background, if not in fact then in her thoughts.

On the second evening of the repeated class, Andrea approached Jacqueline at the close and said that she wanted to chat for a moment, if not immediately, then over the telephone. Jacqueline's reaction was that the first words of a proposition might be in the offing. She wrote down her phone number on a slip of paper and handed it to Andrea.

The telephone call came the following morning. Andrea had started a placement business in which she dealt with secretaries, accountants and office personnel. There was plenty of work to do, Andrea said, and while the salary was slim, the commissions made up for it. Jacqueline was surprised at being asked. She had only told Andrea in an answer to a direct question that she once worked in a personnel department and was now at home caring for her two children. The office was mid-town. Would Jacqueline come in some time soon and discuss the opportunity?

It was an old office building. The three rooms occupied by Andrea and her assistant were in turmoil. Jacqueline noticed that each job to be filled was typed on a 5 X 8 card and tacked to the wall. The cards were placed by job type. Jacqueline asked how individuals were matched to jobs. Andrea answered that she advertised in the paper and selected from those who responded. Jacqueline didn't think the method was scientific. It struck her that there should be a more efficient way of managing affairs but no obvious solution came to her.

Andrea explained that her firm's income was based on receiving forty percent of the first ninety days' salary from the people they placed. Jacqueline's salary and commissions would come from that. Andrea, as though Jacqueline were already an employee, noted that the greater number of people she placed, the higher her take-home pay. Jacqueline had said, "If the formula holds still, I can make more money by placing people at a higher salary level." Andrea was not drawn in. She was quiet for a moment. Jacqueline guessed that she had made an obvious remark and that Andrea had been disappointed in it.

They left it there. Jacqueline would think it over. She thought about the matter for two days, calculating the pros and cons. Her broaching the topic with Sam might take a bad turn. He could object to the reduced time spent with the children and in some oblique fashion might bring to Jacqueline's attention that he was perfectly capable of supporting his family. Jacqueline's thought on that matter was that the income of artists could vary from high to low. She acknowledged also that it could go to zero in the event Sam broke away from the marriage. The conversation went as she had expected.

"I've been offered work at an employment agency, just the other day, from someone in class," Jacqueline announced one evening after dinner.

"How long ago?" Sam asked.

"Two days ago."

"So, you've been pondering for two days how to break it to me?"

"No. I've been doing all the things I normally do during the day and I let this new thought come into my mind now and then on its own."

"And what did you conclude?" Sam asked,

"That it would be a good idea. The children are growing up and I'll need a new challenge."

"The kids will miss you," Sam said.

"They're so independent already. Our evenings and weekends together should do it."

"Can you work, teach at night and do the Saturday thing, all of them at once?"

"No. I'll stop teaching at night and just keep the Saturday class. I get more out of that one with the neighborhood kids."

"Don't you have ten more weeks at City College?"

"Yes. I thought I could work half-time for the coming ten weeks."

"So, you plan to start right away?" Sam asked.

"Yes, if that's all right with you."

Sam snickered at her answer. "As though I had anything to do with it," he remarked.

They had been married thirteen years. Jacqueline understood that the relationship was weakening. There had been the dalliance with Penelope, but more importantly, Sam's attitude was changing from being an impulsively affectionate mate to one who seemed preoccupied with his work. Jacqueline thought that all artists had these questions about themselves. He was worried that his popularity as an artist might not stand up and wasn't sure that he would be able to sense new trends and accommodate to them. He would talk to Jacqueline about these matters, and while she tried to encourage him, a morose streak had seized him that she felt she couldn't do anything about. He would win a commission only to wonder whether it was the last one. She might say, "Do you realize that they are coming closer together?" "Will I come up with a winning idea the next time? That's what haunts me," he would answer.

Jacqueline's first suggestion for the office was the addition of a fax machine, a third telephone line, and the addition to the advertisements that résumés could be sent by Fax. Jacqueline lengthened the ad with the phrase, "Interviews arranged promptly."

Her second suggestion was to schedule a forty-five minute interview for each applicant. Jacqueline conducted them and working half time she could do four per day. Most applicants took a typing test. Jacqueline graded each person on appearance, previous experience, ability to speak English correctly, and a few other criteria. There were seven categories; grades could vary from one to ten. The highest score, therefore, was seventy. Andrea agreed that a score under fifty disqualified the applicant, as did any single score of five or under. Jacqueline went to the man who handled Sam's affairs and prepared their tax returns. They worked out a test for people in the accounting field. The test asked for an explanation of a Profit and Loss Statement, and a Balance Sheet. The applicant was asked to examine ten items on a list and identify them as assets or liabilities. And lastly, the applicant was asked to discuss federal, state and City of New York payroll taxes. In this last question, Jacqueline could check on their ability to organize material, to write a clear sentence, and produce it in a legible handwriting.

With the grading scheme in place, the percentage of people hired permanently went up markedly. Very few were let go after their ninety-day trial was complete.

Andrea remarked one day, "Well, ten weeks. You've interviewed about one hundred fifty people, or more. Most of them have been placed. You're coming to work full time next week. It won't surprise me that we'll have to expand to new quarters soon."

"I won't know what to do with all this money," Jacqueline said. In fact, she was buying clothes.

Jacqueline started by asking Andrea questions. Her purpose was to establish the difference between the operation they were running and an executive search firm. Andrea did know that executive search firms were hired by large corporations to find executives to fill certain slots at high levels. As examples, corporations might be looking for a chief financial officer, or a lawyer with particular knowledge, or an international marketing manager. Andrea said, "We get people by advertising in the paper. The high level jobs are never advertised. Recruiters go looking for them."

Jacqueline digested this analysis and wondered why they could not move up the ladder to finding more successful talent. Corporations around the city were calling them for the lower paying jobs. It was a matter of getting them to change their habits. She said as much to Andrea whose response was, "Well, we get our people by advertising in the paper. If one of our corporations asked us to find a chief financial officer or director of personnel, we couldn't advertise in the paper. I don't know how you do that."

Jacqueline's answer was, "I don't know either, but I'll find out."

Her plan was simplicity itself. She announced that she would go on one interview per week to the companies they were serving presently and ask the question of their contact, "How do you recruit people to fill upper level positions?" After a year, Jacqueline had visited nearly fifty companies and Andrea had seen half that many. They learned that they had to build a database of the names of executives who might be pried loose from an existing job to take on a job with more responsibility at a vastly higher salary. It was a time-consuming affair. During the year they were at it, they were asked to fill just two positions, a senior buyer for a department store and a transportation specialist for a freight forwarding company. Both women guessed that they had found a new path to success.

Jacqueline had remarked, "Pretty soon, Andrea, we'll have an office that has plants in it." Andrea's answer was, "Did you know that there are businesses devoted to selling plants to you and caring for them after you've bought them?"

# Bunny 22

As far as business was concerned, Andrea followed the path laid out before her. If she was to be in personnel placement, then she did what was required of her to place personnel. Jacqueline, on the other hand, looked at business as an opportunity to change existing methods in order to make the most out of the hours spent. This point of view was nothing she had been taught. It simply was obvious that if you went to work you ought to modify the approach until the return on the effort was maximized.

In their first year together, Andrea and Jacqueline had placed only two executives. In the process, Jacqueline had grasped the essentials of executive placement. She and Andrea had to collect names of high-salaried employees who would consider moving to a new position for a yet higher salary. They gathered names by securing telephone directories of companies in the area, and placing calls to executives during working hours in order to get their home telephone numbers. They found out that the mention of doubling a person's salary opened doors immediately, and tended to keep them open.

In the year following, Jacqueline's second with Andrea, the number of executives placed rose from two to fifteen. In the third year, there was a sufficient amount of business that they stopped placing secretaries and accountants and concentrated on executives at all levels. They moved from their cramped quarters to a more commodious space. Andrea contracted with a small firm to bring in two ficus plants and other vegetation. She signed up for a weekly visit from the people she referred to as the plant doctors. As they hired two more people, there would be one more move to the building where Zack's offices were, but that would be two-and-a-half years away.

Andrea, Jacqueline discovered, did not long for a motorcycle or dream of black leather jackets. When Jacqueline felt comfortable enough to bring it up, she asked Andrea about the men in her life, not knowing where the conversation might lead. Andrea, whom Jacqueline took to be attractive, said that men had come in and out of her life, but none had stuck. At last, Jacqueline asked Andrea why she had not married, to which Andrea answered, "No one's asked me."

With that out of the way, Jacqueline determined she would keep the topic open, or as she said to Andrea, "I'm staying on message." They understood that Jacqueline would be helpful in some fashion if the opportunity arose.

Sam's attention was wandering, Jacqueline thought. She could not detect that he had found a new interest, or been on another expedition similar to his layover with Penelope, but it became clear that he no longer focused on her. He had never understood that in order to place himself into the inner workings of her mind and personality, he had to care about her reactions and feelings for the world around her. He had not grasped this about a relationship when they married. The best Sam was doing now was to be caring and attentive on most occasions. Jacqueline thought these were traits of conduct that required no expenditure of effort. Sam didn't realize that he had slackened off. Jacqueline thought about it and concluded that Sam had become an average husband, someone who concerned himself more with day-to-day events in his life than he cared about any developments in hers. Jacqueline felt that Sam was now just her husband. He was no longer a pal, or a suitor; a partner in sex, yes, but not a lover, or an admirer, or a counselor, or a confidant. He was average and Jacqueline knew, or guessed, that under those circumstances they were both vulnerable. A new and different situation could come along to destabilize either one. It was just a matter of who would be hit first.

Jacqueline had heard the expression, "marriage of convenience." She thought it applied to old people who recognized the value of companionship; or that it described an American citizen marrying to bestow citizenship; or even a gay person who married to provide cover for his or her clandestine activities. But then Jacqueline wondered, could it apply to Sam and her? Weren't they waiting for something exciting to come along, something that went to the core, the way they had felt for one another at the beginning? She remembered the zing, the bang, of those early days.

Their marriage was convenient, Jacqueline knew. The second child had just become a teenager. Sam's parenting was based on his good memory. He recalled how those years had gone for him. He could guide his son and daughter through the obvious pitfalls connected to school and the opposite sex. Jacqueline didn't think he had brilliant insights, but he had maneuvered himself through those dangerous years to come out a whole person who had wanted her, and at the beginning, gave enough of himself that Jacqueline found him irresistible.

What happened to marriages, Jacqueline wondered? Connie had told her that many men were only good for ten or twenty years, and after that they found reasons to drift off. Sam must be one of these. He needed his life refilled as though he had spent everything in him to get through their time together.

Andrea's situation was simple to mend, or so Jacqueline thought. She remembered a man just entering middle age who had attended the last class she taught at City College. He was chunky and energetic and it became obvious to Jacqueline, and perhaps many others, that he was looking for women more than he was an education in classical music. He made the rounds during the break. In the few minutes that students were free to wander down the hall, Jacqueline noticed that he managed to speak to all the women during the fifteen weeks of the course. He even befriended married ones, perhaps on the basis that they had sisters, or friends, or even a disintegrating marriage.

Jacqueline found this man's name and telephone number in her final roster and suggested to Andrea that she call him.

"What's his name?" Andrea asked.

"Steve Oliver."

"What shall I say to him?"

"Tell him the obvious, what we do, how we came upon his name. Use my name, of course. Ask him what he does. Is he a candidate for recruitment? Ask him when we can interview him, some night after work or over a weekend. Ask him if his résumé is up to date. You know what to say."

"So you think he's romantic material for me, is that it?" Andrea asked.

"Yes. It's been a couple of years, but if he's available you might like him. At the very least we could make some money off him," Jacqueline said.

It didn't go exactly as planned. Steve Oliver accepted an invitation for a meeting, perhaps on the basis that he was being asked to have dinner with a woman, she picking up the tab. He was circumspect over the telephone when Andrea asked him about changing jobs, telling her that the matter could wait until they were face to face.

In the interview, at dinner, Steve explained that he was content working for his insurance company and would reject most any offer that came along. "Let's be reasonable," he said, "I'm only worth so much."

Andrea, ever professional, said, "Our business is founded on the premise that, given the right circumstances, most everyone is worth more than they suspect."

Steve changed the subject. Dinner had been paid for. He was holding Andrea's business card. He looked at it, then looked at Andrea and said, "Well, I have your telephone number now. Maybe we could see one another socially."

Jacqueline had described him as energetic. He was that, Andrea agreed, but it was energy directed at her, so Andrea thought of him not as energetic but aggressive. As she put it to Jacqueline, "He wants everything now."

Jacqueline remarked, "I think you were hoping for that."

Andrea asked, "Do you think it can last?"

Being aware of her situation with Sam, Jacqueline answered, "Get ten good years out of it. There may be fewer, or more, but build a plan for ten. It should be worth it."

# Bunny 23

Sam didn't know if this would be the end of his marriage or an interlude in which he fell out of love with his wife, only to come back to her.

Jacqueline's commitment appeared to him to be constant, although expressed with diminished enthusiasm. It was possible, Sam acknowledged, to have a marriage in name as well as a marriage lived at full force, and at all levels in between. Sam knew that he had been set adrift over the matter of Penelope. Even when he and Jacqueline came together physically the old ardor was absent. Sam looked back on the night when they resumed relations and wondered if Jacqueline hadn't been driven in part by her own appetite, the old longing.

Although the affair with Penelope in Connecticut, that one night, had been costly, it was not without its rewards. Sam had been given the opportunity of examining his marriage, its present condition and the hopes for it in the future.

It came to him that his life had descended into a routine. Their two children were growing up and asserting themselves with their tastes, friends, interests and aspirations. He and Jacqueline had less and less to say about their points of view and activities. Sam concluded that an important piece of his life with Jacqueline was melting away. The graduation from high school of the younger child would come, and then the apartment would be empty except for the two adults. In Sam's view, one of the principal reasons for their being together would vanish. A new arrangement would be required that took into consideration that the children were no longer a day-to-day preoccupation.

It had been brought home to Sam slowly over the years that he was one-dimensional. When he and Jacqueline were guests at a collector's apartment for dinner, he would discuss his metal sculptures, but when that topic was exhausted, fellow guests moved on to other subjects while Sam was shut out because of his lack of well-founded opinions. Jacqueline, through her teaching of music, knew more about the topic than anyone at the table. Her new career, which brought about associations with executives of all types, supplied her with insights into business. She limited her comments, leaving the impression that she knew a great deal more than was evident, which in fact she did not.

Sam thought it a bleak outlook that he would remain one-dimensional while his wife expanded her grasp of life around her. Sam knew that he had no interests beyond his art. He had given up sports and he cared little for reading and did not know where to begin to gain any competence with the generalists whom he met socially.

Sam knew that Jacqueline remained loyal to him. She would go to the gallery in mid-town and mingle with customers and artists, and chat with Penelope and a young woman named Martha, who shared the responsibilities with Penelope of interesting clients in purchasing the art. Jacqueline called Martha, "another thin one." By that she meant that the women she had met in the art world sported a thin body, were usually mid-height, and clothed in dark pants and top. When Jacqueline used this term, Sam understood that she was comparing them unfavorably to herself. She was proud of her full body and knew that Sam had enjoyed it over the years.

Jacqueline's work started to absorb time in the evenings. There were dinners with executives at client companies who would hire hers and Andrea's services and of course dinners with the people to be recruited as openings developed. Once in a while Jacqueline would keep an appointment with a potential placement at his home. It pleased Sam that the prospect's wife would be present. He was jealous of his wife but guessed that nothing had come of these encounters. It was just that she might find one of these men more attractive than he was. She wouldn't act on it, but the concept would be lodged in her mind and he would know that he had slipped a notch. He wanted it understood between them that if he were to hold her as number one in his mind, then Jacqueline would have to persuade him without doubt that he was number one in her mind. He had no idea how to arrive at such an arrangement. A direct conversation on the matter seemed out of his reach. Perhaps it would evolve.

The children were slipping away. Jacqueline may be slipping away, or at least not clinging to him. Her increased interest in her own work was at the expense of her interest in him. It could be that they might re-unite a few years ahead, but that seemed unlikely to Sam. What would he smash up if he broke away? The children would be affected, but not greatly.

Jacqueline might be relieved. She would be available as new opportunities appeared. Certainly one of those clients was single, attractive, successful and therefore rich. And what would it cost him? He would be the initiator, the one who told the children, the husband leaving his wife and bearing the guilt.

Sam knew the difference between his situation and Jacqueline's. He would have a new interest right away while his wife might have to wait until the right prospect came along. She might go through a year before finding a candidate.

Rosemary Chang had taken space about six months previously in the artists' loft where Sam worked. His first question to Rosemary was whether she was of Chinese or Japanese extraction. Rosemary had answered, "One syllable names are Chinese. Those with multiple syllables like Hashimoto are Japanese." The conversation ended abruptly. A few days later they met in the hall and he said, "Hello, Rose." That brought about an icy stare and the admonition that she liked the entire name, not just the first half. Sam didn't say anything. He drew in his breath, rolled his eyes, and moved on into his workspace. He wondered why women with long names insisted on using the whole thing.

Rosemary was the first of the painters to declare that all artists were equal and that painters had no reason to place themselves at the top of the hierarchy. This opinion of Rosemary's was repeated frequently enough that all the people in the building heard about it. The other artists thought it unusual that a painter advanced the idea.

There might be a new school forming among painters, led by Rosemary. The tenet held that the painters of the Renaissance were worth emulating. The followers of this trend tended to make their own colors and apply the paint in the same fashion as did the classic artists – many layers to achieve the depth they looked for. The resulting palette was more dull than a palette consisting of the modern chemically derived paints, but the artists made up for that feature by paying additional attention to the use of light in their compositions.

Rosemary was Chinese in her parentage and had been born and raised in the United States. Her personality, or character, or outlook, consisted of Chinese elements picked up at home combined with an American framework absorbed at schools and through friends. She was in thrall of her art and worked hard at producing full-length portraits. These tended to be at least four feet in height and sometimes more. Rosemary admitted to Sam that she chose this form of expression because no one else she knew was attempting it. Yet many women and a few men were willing, eager in fact, to stand for quite some time, wearing the same clothes and expression. Rosemary charged appropriately. In her subdued colors and type of art she thought she might become another John Singer Sargent or James McNeill Whistler. She contemplated adding bright colors on occasion but held to the old values.

A situation did not develop between Sam and Rosemary by a gradual process. Rather, she moved by increments as it suited her. She might poke her head in and ask, "Lunch?" One day she said to him, "You're the best man in this building." He had answered, "Yes, the best married man."

She waited a minute and said, "What does that have to do with it?" She was of medium height and wore shoes with one-inch heels. She would stand most of the time that a client was in her studio and these sessions would last two hours or more. She always wore trousers, sometimes jeans. While working she covered her clothes almost to the knee with a smock of which she had a collection. The get-up from the waist to the neck was about the same day after day, one of many loose fitting blouses, which came in several colors and were made of different materials. All blouses had one element in common, that they buttoned up the front and Rosemary buttoned them only high enough to ensure that the top of her bra was visible. These came in black and white and in the course of normal movement she granted ample opportunity for a man such as Sam to catch glimpses of much of the acreage that made up the front of her body. Without having made a study of the matter, Sam knew generally that women with Asian genes were small-breasted. Nonetheless, it was the temptation offered that captivated Sam. He knew they would be small, but he wanted to know how Rosemary would react to his standard offering and whether her breasts would be more or less sensitive to his touch and kiss than were Jacqueline's.

In the same fashion that San understood about the size of the breasts of many Asian women, he had also heard over the years that Eurasian women were meant to be beautiful. Rosemary was Asian and carried no European blood yet she had started looking European. Sam thought that the way she wore her hair and makeup had started to change her appearance. In addition, her way of speaking English as a native-born American tended to shield her origins, at least Sam thought so. She admitted to Sam that she had learned a modest amount of Chinese on her parents' request, but could not write a single character and had no interest in expending the time to learn a useful number of them. If she were to do anything oriental, she told him, it would be to learn the ways of early Chinese artists, the ones who painted the landscapes on scrolls. Sam didn't hold her to be a beauty, but he liked the almond shape of her eyes and the way her face lighted up at odd moments.

Rosemary's work required that the subject be present all the time that she worked on the painting, not for the background, but certainly for the face, body and clothes. Rosemary told Sam that she captured a face with ease, without having labored to learn the technique. There was discussion with the client on choice of clothes and background. Rosemary said to Sam that she knew that her portraits carried a good likeness. That came naturally. She was proud that she was able to give the painting an original touch that she could not identify with words. She saw it and hoped the client might too.

Because she felt the creative impulse when discussing Sam's art with him, or so she said, she would volunteer her opinions on solutions to problems, particularly on the commissions for the large objects that would decorate public buildings. Sam enjoyed working on those large objects more and more. He had always worried that his submissions would be rejected because his concepts would not be sufficiently imaginative. Rosemary supplied the missing piece. She would study the bid package he received from jurisdictions, be they cities, counties, or state capitals, and come up with three or four ideas. She might sketch a solution or put it into words. Sam started winning more of these competitions, perhaps because his reputation had spread, perhaps because his offerings were better than those of other artists.

Rosemary would be dismissive of herself. She would say, "I didn't do anything. Just a few concepts." This would be in response to his praise and thanks upon winning another competition.

Nine months passed since Rosemary had taken space in the artists' loft. He counted on her for her help with his art. She had most of the valuable traits that one hopes to find in a person. At least, Sam thought, they had a working relationship. He wouldn't insert himself into her portraiture beyond offhand comments, but he admitted to himself that she had taken a commanding position in his career, even if only by means of a sketch, a few lines, or a sentence. He could not afford to let that slip away.

Sam knew that something had changed when Rosemary came into his workspace and closed the door part way. It was enough to shield Sam from the corridor. She said good morning and came over to him, stopping only when she was inches away. She placed a hand on his shoulder and said, "I can't stand it any longer." She paused and put her hand in his hair at the back of his neck. "I can scrape up some lunch for us," she added.

As they walked along the avenue he fell a few feet behind her. The on-coming crowd had slowed him down. He thought of the many women in New York who walk their dogs. In the usual arrangement, the women make available food, shelter, and the services of a veterinarian. In exchange the dog supplies friendship and a little adoration.

# Bunny 24

Jacqueline's instincts told her to fight the separation, to insist to Sam that he would change his mind soon enough and recognize that they had become too important to one another. When he persisted by telling her that it wasn't working for him any longer his restricted personality couldn't be denied. That he would use that worn phrase, "It isn't working for me any longer," was an eye-opener. He wasn't shallow, really, that wasn't it, but she was disappointed that he could not come up with a better reason to leave her. She admitted there could be reasons, but when he could not organize them in a coherent fashion and present them to her so that she understood them, it might be acceptable to let him go.

Andrea's life had taken a turn for the better when Steve Oliver discovered her. He reacted to her fragrance the way no other man had. Andrea pondered why some women attract most men and others attract only a few, if that? Andrea and Jacqueline discussed Steve Oliver's pursuit of her. And they decided that he liked her lines and enjoyed her conversation and that might sum it up. Describing his approach one day, Andrea had used the word 'torrid.' The serious phase of their relationship had arrived, and there was a fair amount of each spending the night in the other's apartment. Andrea surprised Jacqueline at work in a dress. It was the first time that Jacqueline had seen Andrea without a pantsuit. Of course she brought it up. "Good old Torrid told me that he had never seen me in a dress and when I told him he'd seen me with nothing on he said it wasn't the same thing. Men are funny. So I'm buying a few." Jacqueline thought Andrea's legs were symmetrical and shaped nicely and that Steve Oliver had done the right thing.

Andrea and Jacqueline's business was in its final stage of expansion. They were discontinuing the placement of secretaries and administrative assistants completely so that they might concentrate on recruiting executives. The business was lucrative and the time had come to move to fancier offices. Each now employed an assistant. They searched for space in mid-town and signed a lease on 850 square feet. They looked at one another at the signing and, with nods and raising of the eyebrows, signaled to the other that there was no longer any room for error.

Jacqueline kept her marital status. Her business cards said, "Mrs. Jacqueline McDonald." She kept the rings in place on the left hand and would until the divorce became final and a little longer after that. She knew that most women in her situation shed their rings the moment the man departed. But Jacqueline was interested in preserving her marital status for business purposes even though it no longer had any meaning. The two rings balanced a larger turquoise ring she wore on the right hand, and by her reasoning if the two on the left hand vanished, then the one on the right, which Sam had given her, would vanish as well.

Perhaps on the third week in her new office building Jacqueline saw Zack at the newsstand. She had not thought about him for ten years or so but was certain he was a collector whom she had seen but not met at the gallery. She watched him at that time buy one of Sam's small animals, more than likely a horse. This time she turned away so that their gazes would not meet. If he worked in this building there was no doubt they would come across one another. There seemed to be little changed in him except for more gray in his hair. He looked well turned out. She thought he had the patrician look about him.

In another week they were in the elevator together. He looked at her, taking her in. After a few such encounters he smiled and nodded. Finally there were conversations on the sidewalk and the lunch together when they arrived by chance at the same place and shared a table. The foundation of his life, his marriage to Bunny, was crumbling and in short order he would find himself married in name only, living in the city, occupied principally with his work.

It had been a year or so that on Zack's initiative his firm started to make contacts with lawyers in Paris. He and his partners were not certain that they would have an office and employees outside the United States, but at first one, and then another of their clients asked for help in purchasing real estate in Europe. These clients would need the assistance of lawyers who could arrange the sale of properties and manage the transfers as required by local governments. They counted on Zack to handle the tax consequences.

Zack made a series of inquiries followed by telephone calls. He made one appointment per day for eight business days and booked a flight and a hotel room. He invited Bunny to come along, not at the firm's expense.

She turned down the offer on the basis that her calendar was full and she would need more time to plan if she were to go abroad for the better part of two weeks.

There were two such trips, one for investigation and the other for consolidation. On the second Zack selected two firms to whom he could channel work, his firm managing the organization of details in New York.

Bunny, when she brought up the crowded state of her calendar, it appeared to Zack, was admitting to a fascination with the completion of Ted Andres' new forty-four foot yawl. He had spent a year reading and studying, climbing through sailboats in this class, selecting a marine architect and a boat yard. The keel had been laid some months ago and the time for finishing touches was arriving. Bunny knew nothing about building sailing vessels, but she felt sure of herself when recommending furnishings for the main stateroom and the places where living, eating and cooking took place.

The Newport-Bermuda race had been abandoned. When Bunny told Ted that he would be required to hire a crew to sail his boat back to Long Island, Ted asked questions about loyalty. Bunny said that once the competitive half was over, the crewmembers would find reasons to fly back to New York to resume their careers. At this news Ted asked Bunny whether these sailors removed their suits for the race south. Bunny went over in some detail the opportunities for cruising north and south, particularly in the Chesapeake Bay, and Ted signed on. It had not come up for discussion but Ted would hint at Bunny's availability from time to time. "Are you any good with charts?" he had asked.

During one of the empty times when Zack was away, Ted telephoned to see if Bunny was free to take a swim. He showed up promptly. They wore bathing suits with shorts and shirts over them. Bunny led them to the boathouse where they lowered a rowboat into the water. This rowboat was an old friend of Bunny. She had not known it all her life, only since childhood. She had always known it was sixteen feet in length. She made certain that the oarlocks were in the boat but not in place. The oars were already in the boat. They rowed out into the harbor, Ted at the oars and Bunny in the stern. When they were a hundred feet off shore they turned to the right and headed east for a small beach where the Cove ends and the shoreline turns north past Sagamore Hill. They beached the rowboat, removed their shirts and shorts and marched prudently into the water.

Summer had just turned warm and they both found the water chilly, though not impossible. Ted dove in first, then Bunny. They exchanged the customary opinion that it wasn't so bad after the initial shock. Bunny guessed that Ted had been on a swim team, either in high school or college. She didn't ask but assumed as much from the graceful way he moved through the water.

They didn't last very long. This time Bunny rowed and Ted sat in the stern. After they put away the boat, as they were walking across the lawn, Ted suggested that they repair to his place. "I have food, drink, all the essentials," he said. "Give me a moment to change," Bunny answered. Bunny knew that there was only one conclusion to the afternoon, that they would end up in his bed.

In the back of her mind she carried the impression that as an unmarried man Ted had had little experience and that it would turn out to be part pleasure and part duty to teach him what she knew. She recalled having that sensation about Zack, not that she could teach him anything because she had no experience at the time, but that she could give herself to the project and they both could learn. But that was nearly thirty years ago.

When they reached Ted's house, he drove the car into the garage. They stepped out of the car and entered a room off the kitchen. Bunny noticed that Ted was barefoot. He put down his small canvas bag and asked, "Would you like a stiff drink?"

"Not too stiff," she replied.

He poured them and said, "I'm going up to get out of these wet things." She picked up her drink, took his empty hand and went upstairs with him. When he went off to shower and change she sat on the edge of his bed, sipped her drink, and stared at the view. When he came back he sat down next to her and kissed her several times around her face and neck. She turned and they exchanged a long kiss on the mouth.

"What should we make of this?" he asked.

` "You have been in pursuit of me from the first moment, Ted, and it might be up to you tell me what you make of it."

"I recall the first time I laid eyes on you, at the yacht club, outdoors one Sunday afternoon. You were wearing shorts. I had never spoken to you so all I had to go on was your appearances." He paused for a moment. "I don't know how it is for others, but your shape is just what I want. Some men go crazy over tall skinny women. I seem to like your proportions. I love your light brown curly hair."

"How about my front? She asked. "Your front has been committed to memory but I do find that I look forward to a refresher course now and again."

"Anything else?" Bunny asked.

"We could go on but let me add that the upper part of your back, your shoulders and neck, are edible. You have a light array of freckles on skin tanned just right. You can drive a man crazy with equipment like that. Then there is the smallest of ponytails that you and your hairdresser manage to keep shaped properly. I've always wanted to kiss you right there. But, let's move on to the important business."

"Everything you said was well received, Ted. This woman doesn't mind having her face and body understood and appreciated."

"I'm glad you didn't take me to task for being so candid, but on to important matters. I must start with your purged, scrubbed-clean personality. You speak directly so I conclude that you think directly. You're to the point."

"We've not had any important discussions," Bunny interrupted.

"If we were to, only the relevant material would be discussed. As an example, why are we in this bedroom? Why would you return with me to my house after a swim, knowing what I want?"

"I must want it too."

Ted paused for a moment. "I have been sensing that your marriage is starting to drift apart. Am I being a catalyst to all that?"

"No, not in this case. Couples start to drift apart and then a third party might come along to put it to the test. Sometimes there is no third party. They just drift apart."

"What's happening in your marriage, Bunny?"

"My husband and I have raised our children. I think we have been great parents. He has not been able to become part of the North Shore. He's remained a New Yorker, a Manhattanite, if there is such a word. His interests are the law firm and his new challenge, the expansion to Europe. I think he's discovering Europe. For myself I can't abandon Oyster Bay and the Sound and my way of life and my old friends. I guess that Zack and I know what's taking place."

"It sounds like continental drift, Bunny."

"Well, precisely, but it's moving quickly. When love evaporates it becomes difficult or impossible to pass affection back and forth between two people. At the simplest level, man and wife can't hold hands as they walk along. It gets to be embarrassing that there is no flow of love between the hands. It's so difficult. So you let go and that tells you all you need to know."

"Will you just sit down for a civilized discussion, the two of you?"

"Yes, I suppose so. And it won't come as a surprise for the one who does not initiate the discussion. My guess is that I'll go first and that Zack will feel relieved."

He told her he loved her and in what Bunny thought must have been an unguarded moment he let out his dream. "If the occasion should arise, it would be the best thing that ever happened to me that you and I were married." That was so straightforward, Bunny thought. She took his drink from him and placed both on the glass-covered night table. Quickly, without allowing an awkward pause, she pushed him back on the bed and put most of her body on his.

"You brought me over to your house for a reason," Bunny said.

"Yes, the room is so full of light. Shall I pull the curtains?"

"Yes, I'd like that. But I'll still be able to see you."

Bunny thought he might lunge at her. On the contrary, he was gentle and restrained. Bunny revised her opinion – he probably had lived with someone for a while and in the process had learned to please a woman, first by declaring his affections, and once that was established, by moving with care.

# Bunny 25

There were many important moments for Zack after he and Jacqueline started to move close together. These took place after the accidental lunch they had shared, when she had suggested playfully that she could find him a job at double his present salary. That was the occasion when Jacqueline came into focus for Zack. When he told her that he was the managing partner of his firm and would shy away from any offer, she left it open. He admired her persistence and her judgment. He realized that just about every moment that he shared with her became important. The beauty and the body were important parts but he knew that they would not carry the day if he had not realized that she was about the best-assembled human being that he had ever met. The blend of character, personality, values and brains was, in his estimation, as perfect as anyone could expect.

The breakup with Bunny was sudden. He returned from a trip to Paris to find her ready to ask for a separation. She did not mince words and talked soon about Ted Andres. She argued that if she stayed with Zack, her life would consist of a great deal of waiting, as was the case at the time. She would have to fall back on her own resources and her female friends for ways of filling her days. He would spend an increasing amount of time at work with intermittent trips to Europe. Zack reminded Bunny that she had always been welcome to accompany him. She responded quickly, "Yes, more waiting in a hotel room."

Bunny pointed out that Ted brought her male companionship on a daily basis, a full day at a time. With him she would cruise the Atlantic coast by sailboat, doing the thing she most wanted to do. Zack had learned that once Bunny had made up her mind there was little chance of changing it. He asked for a weekend in the house alone so that he could gather his things. When he went through the motions, it surprised him how little mattered. Besides the clothes, he gathered his golf and tennis equipment. He doubted he would ever use them. There were books from college and even two from high school. He wondered why he had kept math books but could not throw them away now. There were photographs of the children. Zack felt he could take some of them. There was a photograph of Bunny in a bathing suit sitting on a rowboat that had been turned upside down. He wondered whether it made sense to take it. He held the little horse he'd bought at an art gallery. It was one of his many gifts to Bunny. He left it.

He sat on his bed and examined the photograph of Bunny. It reminded him of the many times they swam in the Bay. So often they would be playful and intimate as they changed out of their bathing suits. He spent some time thinking about these occasions and how she had always participated and responded. There was no lack of enthusiasm and Zack knew that she had transferred her store of it to Ted. He put the photograph back on his dresser.

Her reasons for leaving him, Zack thought, were few and not presented with force. But he knew well enough that attitudes and conclusions such as Bunny's had grown over time even though he was not privy to them as they were forming. Once they came to him from her in a declaration they were old and entrenched. Bunny may not have been sleeping with Ted that long but Zack reasoned that she had been planning their life together for a while.

There were two cars on the property registered in both their names. He had no need for a car in the city. He arranged for a moving company to pick up the cardboard boxes and bring them to his apartment.

The final moment came for Zack back in New York. He sat in the living room of his apartment and thought about Bunny as she appeared in the photograph wearing her bathing suit. He knew he wanted what the photograph represented and knew at the same time that he could not have it back. It was obvious that he had to move ahead and build a new life. His life with Bunny had closed shut. That beautiful Jacqueline with the graceful stride came to his mind. He went over their encounters. She had been receptive but not in any aggressive way. She was open and friendly without any hint of moving beyond the normal barriers.

They were in the elevator together heading home their separate ways. He glanced down and noticed that her rings were gone. He said in a voice low enough that the others could not hear, "Would you walk out of the building with me?"

She turned her face toward him, smiled and nodded. Once on the sidewalk he said, "My situation has changed suddenly and I wonder if I might see you from time to time?" Jacqueline thought she could delay an answer. "And what form might that take?" she asked. "We could do the things that people usually do. There are two purposes. One is to do things that are pleasing and the second is to get to know one another."

"People get to know one another mostly by talking so we couldn't go to the movies," Jacqueline said. "Unless we talked through the show," Zack added.

Jacqueline let the matter rest. She looked down at her feet, looked at him and smiled, then said, "Let me think about it." They were at her subway entrance. Jacqueline opened her purse to pull out a token. She said, "We can talk about it some more."

Jacqueline moved ahead in a deliberate manner. If he wanted her, he would have to be patient. The end of her marriage was still recent. She pushed the first kiss into the future by shaking his hand and keeping a distance between them at the end of an evening. She held to this slow pace for half-a-year during which time they saw one another once a month. One evening she let the moment happen by turning into him at her doorway. She let the kiss continue long enough that he might guess this was her response for making him wait. By then both her arms were around his neck. She slid her face to bring her mouth to his ear and said, "I like you, all of you, and what we do together." She allowed her body to press against his. The next day, flowers arrived at her office.

Two new trips to Paris had intervened since that first kiss. They had participated in the standard things that people do such as dinners and plays. Neither rushed matters. She introduced music, making the selections and buying the tickets. He went along. Jacqueline didn't know whether he cared to learn about the topic or was agreeable by nature and wanted to be with her. It would develop, she thought.

Late one evening she invited him in for a drink after they had been to the theater. He held her in his arms and kissed her and then she said, "I think I know what you want, among other things. It might surprise you to know that I want the same thing, only we have preparations to take care of first."

He looked at her and said, "Heavens."

"It doesn't bother me that we both have short-term needs," she said, "but as a woman, I find it prudent to look out as far as I can see, to the end even."

"Makes sense." He wanted her to go on and said nothing more.

"We ought to think about an arrangement that we would both find suitable." She paused. "What would be our degree of commitment?"

Zack wasn't surprised at hearing the word. Most women, not all, wanted commitment, for the man to give up all other women so that a relationship could flourish without distraction. Zack had been giving the matter his attention over the months. He didn't like it that there was no woman in his life. He didn't like it that there was no one with whom to plan a life. And he didn't like it that he was starved for Jacqueline and found her still unavailable. He said, "Why don't you determine what there is to talk about. You can set the agenda."

"It's all up to me?" Jacqueline asked.

"Yes and no. You brought it up. I'm giving you first rights. Why don't I start by telling you that I love you? That's my first level of commitment."

"You caught me unaware, dear heart. I can't equal that tonight."

# Bunny 26

Zack suspected that he had shocked Jacqueline by telling her that he loved her. Perhaps he was too impulsive, but at that moment, having held her and kissed her, it just came over him. It occurred to him, without any planning, that he might start there.

Jacqueline had not repeated his words, which people do so often when some one tells them that they love them. On their next evening together she thanked him and told him that she was flattered that a man of his quality and accomplishment had fallen for her. Her words were, "I didn't expect it, but I welcomed it. How often does a graduate of Columbia Law School fall for a high school dropout?" Zack didn't ask for an explanation. He said, "You had me fooled."

Zack had not given his retirement a great deal of attention. There were ample funds. Bunny, their children, now grown, his home and his sports activities would occupy him. To these he would add charitable work and continue in the law, perhaps in another direction. He hadn't thought about it beyond that.

His home and sports departed with Bunny. He was once again, after many years, a resident of Manhattan. In his new situation he might increase his travel, find a hobby, and concentrate on replacing Bunny. His only complaint about his life with her was that it had ended. A competitor had offered a more attractive deal and she must have calculated that the time remaining to her could be spent to advantage with him.

He felt a compulsive desire for Jacqueline and he hoped that the attraction was for her and not caused by the lack of a woman in his life. It was not purely sexual, not particularly intellectual, but he valued her company in a way that he had not Bunny's. She fitted in better somehow.

It surprised him when she described herself as a high school dropout. He didn't quiz her on the matter knowing that she would elaborate at the appropriate moment.

He liked her eagerness to learn. He would bring an article from the paper to her attention and invariably she would read it, and then ask questions. She did not possess a reservoir of information, but she learned quickly and stored the material for recall, having the ability to connect facts, ideas and concepts in her own fashion. Zack decided that she had come by her originality naturally.

He didn't think Jacqueline was humorous. He wasn't aware that she made him laugh a great deal, but she was a cheerful person and laughed easily. Zack knew that the cause was not so much what he said, as that he made her happy. She enjoyed the time they spent together and events sufficed to bring a smile to her lips and bring on that soft, quiet laughter.

Her most captivating trait was the conversational intimacy she provided him. Zack guessed that these moments were reserved for special people in her world and she would be stimulated to speak that way by a need to confide. Zack guessed that these moments hadn't come up between her and her husband. They occurred in public places when she needed to relay a reaction that she was experiencing at the moment. It might be at a gallery over a piece of art, or during an intermission at a play, or over any topic at dinner. When in a restaurant he had learned that she preferred sitting side by side to sitting across from one another. She would be silent for a moment as she gathered her thoughts and Zack knew what to expect. She would turn to him and look him right in the eyes, giving him her undivided attention. He looked right back, savoring the moment. Usually her observations were self-effacing, such as, "I never guessed that anyone could be so considerate of me." She would be talking about some kindness that he had shown her. Or she might say, "The next time, don't wrap the package so tightly. It takes too long to unwrap." That was over her birthday present at dinner with her children. As best Zack could define it, she created a personal space while in public that only the two of them could occupy. When they were alone, she did not feel the need to do that. She was free to express herself in a more offhand manner. He felt that being attentive was winning the day for him. He thought, correctly, that her marriage had lacked that aspect and while Sam could have been satisfactory in many ways he may have lacked that sensitivity, that bit of introspection, that imaginative streak required to understand another person in a nearly complete way.

When Zack thought about Jacqueline's personality and character he included time for considering her face and her body. He had gone over the arguments many times in the past and could not resolve the issue of why men and women devoted any time to considering their partner's appearance. Why were looks important? What did those few fractions of an inch add to or subtract from the presentation? He knew the arguments on both sides, could not resolve them, and was at peace in the knowledge that Jacqueline was not beautiful, not pretty, but arresting. That's the adjective he settled on, arresting. By that he meant that if he were looking around and his eyes landed on her, he would stop looking around.

As for her body, he discovered what all people discover, that when an attraction develops between two people, the reaction cannot stop at the frontier, but must cross the border into the land of fondling, caressing and finally, intimacy. It bothered him that he could not think of Jacqueline without undressing her and imagining himself alongside her in bed. He chalked it up to a normal longing and could only settle on the thought that he did not have this feeling for any other woman. He went back to his start with Bunny and had to admit that his marriage did not come naturally from the selection process, that it was manufactured by the Underhills and Bunny, and therefore it contained a degree of artificiality. His feeling for Jacqueline, on the other hand, was pure and was his doing. He wanted her, her body and her soul, perhaps in reverse order. There was nothing to debate. It was the first time that he experienced two people blending into one.

Jacqueline had said that they needed to negotiate details when he brought up the matter of building a life together. She seemed to be in no hurry and let the matter drop. Zack decided that he could force the issue with a proposal. There were risks. She might turn him down and that could be the end of it. More than likely she would feel forced into discussion. Whatever accommodation they reached, it would be better than living in this unresolved state.

They were in her apartment drinking a glass of wine before walking to a restaurant in her neighborhood. They were sitting side by side and she was commenting on how much she enjoyed the new leaves as they appeared on the tree across the street. He leaned in her direction to have the same view as she did. In the tone of voice that he would use if he were to continue the conversation about the new growth, he asked, "Will you marry me, Jacqueline?"

She placed her glass on the coffee table, got up half way, turned around and sat down again facing him. She put her arms around his neck. The reddish-brown hair was in his face. In a moment she said, "You darling, you got there awfully fast."

"I think I must want it more than you do, so we're on different schedules. It's not fast for me." They didn't speak for a moment. He could feel the warmth of her body entering his. He had never held her in this fashion. She then took his head in both her hands and asked, "What do we do about the twenty-year difference in ages?"

Zack knew the subject would come up. He was relieved that she was being so direct. "Is that what it comes down to?" he asked.

"It leads to other matters. Age is the opening wedge."

"Other matters such as?"

"You've spoken of retirement and what you would like to do then. I can't see myself fitting into that life."

"How so?"

"I mean travel. On any long trip you would probably want your wife along. I'm not ready to give up my life as it stands presently."

"Funny. When you brought up age, I thought you meant that you didn't want to bury me."

"Not that. I could go first and you could outlive me by twenty years."

"Not likely."

"No, not likely," Jacqueline said. "So it's not that one or the other of us would have to arrange a funeral just as were starting out together." She reached back and picked up her glass. She took a sip, put it down and turned to him. She was not fully in his arms, more at an angle with one arm resting partly on his shoulder and partly on the cushion behind him.

"I like the work I do with Andrea. We're successful. I know you know exactly what I mean by that. We arrange to find good jobs for executives. They get to perform at a higher level than before. We get paid for that." She paused and said, "You know all that." She looked out the window behind him and said, "But the music part, you may not understand it. Sam didn't understand it. He never allowed himself to absorb the truth there."

"Let me have the truth," Zack said.

"Well, teaching the kids in the apartment has become part of me. I'm not interested in giving it up. I found out you are what you give. More than anything else, I give these kids my time. It's the most precious thing I have."

"Isn't that what we do at work, all of us, give our time?"

"It's different. We get paid for that. This, the music, is a gift to those children. I think they understand the transaction, those that keep coming back. I wouldn't want marriage to upset that."

"I could take care that marriage wouldn't interfere," Zack said.

"We ought to keep the reservation you made at the restaurant. Do you think we can find new topics to talk about at dinner?"

"I'm accepting the challenge," he said.

Jacqueline felt his body tense as he readied himself to get up. She tightened her grip around his neck, put on her most winning smile and said, "Listen, dream boat, I want something to come of all this, some way, somehow."

# Bunny 27

When they returned from the restaurant Jacqueline made a pot of coffee and broke up a bar of dark chocolate. Jacqueline said, "It's good for you, don't worry."

They went back to the sofa and took the positions they had before going to dinner.

"You proposed right here a couple of hours ago. It's the loveliest, most generous thing that a man can do for a woman, put his life on the line for her. Give me a little while to think it over."

"Usually there isn't much to think over."

"I know I want the blessings and security of a tight relationship. You must too. I mean, that's what the proposal meant to me."

"I offered marriage. I hope it would include the blessings and security of a tight relationship." He knew he was behaving like a lawyer and told himself to keep it simple.

"We'll have to be careful here," Jacqueline said. "I've never turned you away. In my own fashion I've encouraged you. Always been available. No games."

"That's true," Zack said. "How much time do you need to sort things out?"

"We could have lunch tomorrow," Jacqueline said.

"Could we get through this in public?" Zack asked.

"How about that quiet little place three or four blocks from the office? We've been there, as you know. I'm certain that proposals have been discussed in the back," Jacqueline said.

"I suppose we'll have to keep the emotions under wraps," Zack answered. He had eaten half the chocolate bar and finished his coffee.

"You know I love you," he said.

"Yes, that's clear," she said. "I have to find a way to pull this off. I'll never find another man of your quality. I'd be crazy to lose you." She paused a moment and then added, "Lunch tomorrow."

He telephoned her mid-morning and they determined to meet in the lobby at 12:30. He did not want to make her wait for him so he arrived a few minutes early. They discussed business matters during their short walk. The waiter who seated them in the back of the restaurant took their order for drinks. Usually both were dry until evening. This time both ordered a glass of white wine. They waited to be served, continuing the conversation they were having on the avenue. When they had each taken their first sip, Zack looked up at Jacqueline expectantly and asked, "And how far did you get?"

"Well, here's how far," Jacqueline answered. "When a man marries, he does not lose his freedom. It's always there. Perhaps diminished a bit, but he rarely takes the enormous plunge of giving up everything that he had for himself and putting it into a marriage. And I'm talking about the emotional part. I'm not worried about money and all that. Plenty of men put all their assets into the pot. But giving themselves over to another person so that they only have half the say, that's different.

"Women on the other hand, most of them anyway, give up their freedom when they marry. They do it willingly for the good of the marriage. Here's an example. If you wanted to see a game at Yankee Stadium, you'd ask me to go. But if I didn't want to go, you'd go anyway. On the other hand, if I wanted to go to an opera and you didn't, I might not go at all. I might think it would be disloyal to go without you. I'd let it drop."

Zack was grateful that the waiter came to take their orders. Neither had studied the menu. Zack ordered a hot sandwich and Jacqueline a salad. They ordered another glass of wine.

"So you like your freedom, is that it?"

"Yes, it's wonderful. I've grown accustomed to it. I'm a liberated woman now, like never before."

Zack put a smile on his face and cocked his head to one side. "I take it you're turning down my proposal, is that it?"

"Your proposal for marriage, as you envision it, I suppose so. But I'm interpreting the proposal differently than the way you offered it. I mean both of us are willing to give ourselves to the other. We just have to figure out a way to do that leaving aside marriage."

"We have a date to listen to some music, not tomorrow, but the night after. Friday. Is that still on?" Zack asked.

"Of course. I have the tickets and I'm looking forward to it. I've heard the Bach B-minor mass a few times but never seen it performed."

"I just asked because when someone turns down a proposal it's usually over. You shake hands, kiss, and that's it."

"Well, that's not it in this case," Jacqueline said.

The check arrived. Jacqueline reached for it and stood up. She said, "If we are about to work out something together, it's fifty-fifty from now on."

Anyone following them down Lexington Avenue would see the couple described in the first chapter, a good-looking couple striding back to their offices after lunch. These observers could not tell that the tall man was disappointed and doing his best to hide it. They could not tell that the attractive woman next to him was hiding her anguish. She had turned down a superior man because she could not give up her life and her sense of freedom. She pinned her hopes on being able to persuade him two days hence that he could have her but under a different formula than the standard one he had proposed.

They stood outside their office building before entering. Jacqueline held his hand. "The music is being performed on your side of town. I'll get a taxi and try to arrive at your front door at 7:30."

He leaned in her direction and kissed her on the cheek. "I'll be downstairs," he said.

# Bunny 28

The taxi carrying Jacqueline pulled up in front of Zack's building very close to 7:30. He was standing outside. Jacqueline said to the driver, "Yes, that's him on the right." He was dressed as she imagined he would be for the occasion. A dark blue suit, white shirt, and black shoes. As he climbed into the cab she noted that he was wearing a dark necktie with a small blue pattern on it. "Hello, beautiful," she said. They spoke about not seeing one another for two days, that both of them had wanted to call the other at work. She gave as her reason for not calling that she had nothing new to report. He said that she always had the sound of her voice to give, and that he didn't call because talking to her wouldn't help him put her out of his mind.

A block away from the music hall Jacqueline leaned forward and said to the driver, "Why don't you let us out here and we'll walk the rest of the way?" She paid him at the same time.

When they were on the sidewalk, Zack looked at her and asked, "Is that new?" It was a dark dress without a belt that fit her figure perfectly. The sleeves were quarter-length. The dress came to just below her knees. She was wearing a single strand of pearls and pearl earrings that she had bought for herself after Sam moved out of her life.

As they walked along, she took his hand and brought up his forearm and pressed it against the side of her breast. She knew he would be aware of it. He kept his arm there and made no mention of it. Instead he asked her where in the auditorium their seats were.

Zack thought about the signal Jacqueline might be sending him. Both were fully aware that she was holding his arm pressed against her breast. In the past few months he had kissed her hard and held her so that their bodies were in contact the full front. He had not gone beyond that to touch her body in a way that she might be forced to push him away. Zack acknowledged to himself that he could only tolerate a bit of rejection. Bunny had taken him to bed that first time and he hoped that some version of that might occur again. Zack couldn't guess that Jacqueline was ready for him and was waiting for his initiative. He thought it would be necessary to settle matters between them and arrange a future before they could be intimate. She, on the other hand, reasoned that if they allowed the romance between them to take charge, then a solution would present itself.

Waiting for Zack did not appear to be accomplishing anything. She had made up her mind that this was the evening to launch their life together. There was even a bottle of champagne in the refrigerator at her apartment. Jacqueline, without putting it into words, wanted to tell him that the time had come for them to become lovers. He had not brought up the matter of intimacy and Jacqueline surmised that he wanted to establish the terms of their relationship before starting out. But this evening she was determined to change their lives.

The B-minor mass lasted just under two hours without intermission. They left the hall a few minutes after ten and Zack suggested that they walk to his apartment building. "It's only six short blocks, or so," he said. Zack was unsure of how the evening might end. Jacqueline had bought the tickets and paid for the taxi and now he was leading them to his apartment. He asked, "Would you prefer to stop for a drink? We go right by a place."

"No thank you," she answered. "Let's go to your apartment. We can have a drink there."

They discussed the music and Zack asked her a question she had thought about but had no answer for. "Would it have made any difference if Bach had composed the piece in another key?"

She said, "You know, Bach composed the *Well-Tempered Clavier*, in which he wrote twenty-four pieces, twelve in the major keys and twelve in the minors. Let me say that Bach knew the difference. I'm certain that I don't."

"That's a deft answer, darling," he said. When they were in his apartment he fixed the drinks they usually had at the end of an evening. They were standing in the kitchen when he said, "I'm sorry to change the subject but can you guess how badly I want you? How can we arrange for you to stay over with me tonight?"

"The obvious way would be to ask. But I don't have a toothbrush, a nightgown and clothes for tomorrow morning. Why don't I ask you to come stay with me for the weekend. Do you have a pair of light blue pajamas with white buttons?"

"That's all I have, in fact."

"Do you have a small bag that will carry clothes for the weekend? Clothes for walking, clothes for a movie and toilet articles?"

"I have such a bag."

"Do you suppose you could pack such a bag?"

"Can you give me ten minutes?" he asked.

"In ten minutes we'll start our new life together. We'll have this weekend. We will be available to one another. We can live together. I want to give you everything I am, my companionship, my body, the sound of my voice as you said, my good days and my not so good days. I want to live with you to the end."

Zack didn't say anything. He was in thought as he absorbed the significance of Jacqueline's proposal. She said, "You're in a state of shock. If it works well and you still want to, we can get married in a couple of years. At least, we can talk about it."

They were still standing in the kitchen. He leaned over and kissed her lightly. He said, "This may be better than marriage."

The end

# Short Essays

# Birds

It's 5:10 A.M. I don't have to look at the alarm clock. It must be 5:10 AM. A so-called songbird whom I christen Morning Bird right away has arrived at the forsythia bush outside my bedroom window. The apartment is on the second floor and the top of the bush comes level with the bottom of the window. If forsythia does not grow that high then it's another bush with yellow flowers. Morning Bird alights on the same branch and warms up his vocal chords. In twenty seconds his chords are warm and he's singing his call, the real thing, which consists of three blasts of something followed by four blasts of something else. It's not a simple sound that one can write such as "tweet." This is a complex two-toned birdcall with varied harmonic content whose sound does not lend itself to our written language.

I get out of bed and go to the window and move one slat of the venetian blind to see him. I bend it just a tad. I don't want to disturb this damn bird. I just want to check on the brand of bird and his position. I suppose that if I yanked up the blind he would fly away. I have a perverse fascination in counting the number of mornings in a row that he succeeds in awakening me.

I have learned over the years that when an event is incomprehensible to me, either Russians or women are involved. The incomprehensible aspect in this case is why the same bird comes to the same bush at the same time. Can't be Russians. It must be women. Morning Bird is singing, if that's what it's called, to attract a female for purposes of mating and building a nest. If male birds resemble their human counterparts, this bird figures that his mate will do most of the planning and arranging of the new nest and plenty of the heavy lifting as well.

I go back to bed and listen to Morning Bird. He's in full throat now. If a mate came by they could get on with it and leave me alone. I wonder about birds' mating. I have taken my share of walks through the woods and never caught them in the act. They are so discreet with feathers covering all the important parts.

Morning Bird ends his song. I've not counted but while on the forsythia he repeats about forty times. He flies away. I am awake and decide to get up. The paper is at the door. The headlines say that the NATO Conference is in full swing. Morning Bird robbed me of my sleep. I want to call him birdbrain but then he can navigate from this forsythia to a certain tree in the rain forest of Costa Rica by looking occasionally in the dead of night at the constellations. I can barely make it from downtown LA to Pasadena without getting lost. It's six in the morning now and I hear Morning Bird and his pals holding a conference in the trees. I am reminded of the heads of state gathered in Washington discussing the future of NATO.

I read the morning paper but my thoughts go back to Morning Bird. He's doing now what I did at his age -- looking for a mate to build a nest and have children. It's good I didn't try singing. Morning Bird is no freeloader as may be those heads of state and their entourages who are talking about NATO and going to dinner parties at taxpayers' expense. He dives and swoops after insects in full flight but he may get some easy food by grabbing bugs crawling in trees. He comes the next few mornings and now I awaken in anticipation. His clock gets him to the bush at 5:10. My internal clock awakens me at 5:00. He does not let me down. I tell myself that I would gladly reach out and grab him around the neck, but how can I explain to him why I have put water and bread outside the kitchen window? He doesn't know it but we've become friends. He's my buddy and I look for him. One day he was on the windowsill, but when I came into the kitchen he flew away. He was light blue with white tips on his wings and his tail could spread out like a fan. I suppose he had been drinking the water and eating the bread that I had put out for him. One reads that bread is bad for birds; it does something sinister to their reproductive system. But our doctors change their minds from year to year. As an example, they used to say that eggs are bad for you, then it turns out you should have a couple of eggs every now and then. I put bread out for Morning Bird because I want him to have a few free lunches. I have had some.

One morning my buddy does not come. It may be that he's found Lamb Chop, or Sweetie Pie, and they are busy collecting twigs. In truth, I suspect that Lamb Chop selected him. All he has going for him is plumage, a pleasing personality, and a raucous voice. She has the organizational abilities.

As I read the paper in these post-Morning Bird days, I think about our view of birds in general. When we wish to indicate that someone is no-account, or flash-in-the pan, we say that person is fly-by-night. Of course if a bird is here in the afternoon and absent the following morning, then bird must have flown by night. How does that come to mean that the person we are referring to is not up to standard? And further, how can we say of something that does not please us that it is for the birds?

I go back fifty years and think about a style of humor we had then, mixing birds and humans to come up with rosy-breasted seersuckers, emerald-throated dowagers, midnight-bed thrashers, gimlet-eyed tit watchers, morning grouse, and ruffled spouse.

I suppose it was funny but the humor was at the cost of the winged ones. I go back sixty years to recall the cartoons of Munro Leaf in the Saturday Evening Post or the Ladies Home Journal, the two magazines in our house regularly. The cartoon always shows a bird on a limb looking down at a boy in the act of misbehaving. In this cartoon, the boy has come to the dining room table with unwashed hands and touches the food with dirty fingers. The bird in the cartoon always looks perplexed by the actions of the boy. We looked forward to the lesson in manners.

Songbirds are so fragile and ephemeral. They are beautiful but you know they don't know it. Their beauty in the grand scheme of things stimulates reproduction. They come into our lives for a few months then are away. Morning Bird and Lamb Chop have the nest built by now. They will be sitting on eggs soon. Their chicks will fly out of their nest on their own. Soon enough, Morning Bird will be thinking Costa Rica. Lamb Chop will slide out of his mind. I'll wait for him next spring when the forsythia blooms. But it may not be he. His destiny could limit him to one trip. It might be his son.

Two weeks have gone by. Whoa! It's Morning Bird. The call is unmistakable. I look at the alarm clock. It's 5:20. He's late. Then he's warmed up and he starts to sing. No more three strong blasts of something followed by four strong blasts of something else. Now it's two and three, or one and two, erratic, weak sounds. They tell me all I need to know. I've been there. Either he never found Lamb Chop or she jilted him. This must be a final attempt to land one of the girls who was left out. Perhaps he has a character flaw that all the girls detect, such as eating the bread I put out for him in place of bagging insects in mid-air, or he chews with his mouth open, or lands on one leg.

He could have been trying too hard earlier and the girls sensed it. I could be misunderstanding the new song. It could be saying "take it or leave it." Perhaps all young birds go through this phase. If I were he I would start the nest right away, working alone. That would improve his chances with the girls who detest domestic chores or those who arrive late, having lost their way from Costa Rica.

I'll put out some birdseed for him now.

# Tuxedo

Saying tuxedo to indicate evening wear is acceptable and founded on a historical event. The story goes that Pierre Lorillard, the son of a man bearing the same name, living in Tuxedo, New York, up-river from the city, having developed his land into an oasis for the rich now known as Tuxedo Park, grew tired of dressing for dinner. Toward the end of a century gone by, say about 1892, he sent a set of tails to a tailor in New York, instructing him to shorten the coat, producing in that act evening wear less formal than the full fish and soup that he, Lorillard, and many others, were required to wear to dinner. One doesn't hear "fish and soup" anymore, but in its day the expression meant evening wear.

Either Lorillard or some other worthy finished the job of decreasing formality by inventing the soft shirt and black tie in place of the boiled shirtfront and white tie. I bought my first tuxedo in 1953, and returned the one I had been wearing to my stepfather who had used his principally while singing in the glee club at Kenyon College, where he graduated in 1932. It has always stayed in my mind that I bought my tuxedo on the last year of Stalin's life. The association is not far-fetched. The Communists of Russia never wore evening clothes, and perhaps they do not to this day. They appear at state dinners in blue suits and dark neckties. It always seemed curious to me that the leaders of the Evil Empire would keep servants, limousines, and houses in the country, eat caviar, and drink vodka, but forsake the tuxedo. Men look their best in one.

Many will recall that President Truman, late in his second term, about 1950, introduced the black tie with design, a distinct break with tradition. The president said that he was tired of the plain black tie and wanted to liven it up. Seven years went by before I accommodated this change in fashion by buying a "Truman" tie, which continues to share space on my tie rack with the original version. As mentioned, Stalin had died to be superseded by Malenkov, who, in turn was pushed out of office by Bulganin and Khrushchev. B & K, as they were called, ruled in tandem until K demanded and obtained B's resignation, or perhaps, more likely, pushed him out. For the record, I did not wear the "Truman" tie, perhaps I should call it my "Bulganin" tie, for the first thirty years that I have owned it, sensing always that the black tie was the classier choice. Since the late 1980s, however, I wear the ties alternately and never fail to attract attention when sporting the "Truman" tie. I explain that I wear the tie in honor of that great president, and to the younger crowd I have to say that we in the old guard remember him for several courageous acts in foreign affairs, for cussing out the critic of his daughter's singing and for introducing the black tie with design. As I examine the tie, which I am doing now, I see that the design is abstract and Paisley, a mixture of Jackson Pollock and Laura Ashley, both at once. The label tells me that I bought it at Marty Sullivan's in Marion, Massachusetts, which fact I had forgotten.

Khrushchev's every-day trousers were the subjects of sartorial comments by most everyone. The legs at the bottom were so wide that they covered his shoes entirely. One day, when in my tuxedo, I looked down the legs and noticed that there were only shoe tips showing. I resembled Khrushchev! The tailor performed magic and made the pant legs look like other1960s American pants. I have Khrushchev to thank for suggesting this transformation which might never have taken place, allowing me to continue to wear my tuxedo with confidence.

Khrushchev, in his turn, was pushed out by Brezhnev. Details fail one, but K fell victim of his agricultural policy which produced too much of some commodities and not enough of others. As an expert on agriculture going back to the Stalin era, K could not take the heat and was forced to go. I had had the trousers cleaned and pressed as part of the alteration. I recall having the entire suit cleaned during the Brezhnev era, say in the late 1960s. When it returned from the cleaner, I slipped it into a strong, blue plastic bag with Brooks Brothers written on it, where it has hung ever since, except when in use. The bag arrived in my life with the purchase of a pin-striped gray suit, which had to be replaced eventually -- the suit, that is. The bag lives on after three trips to Europe, two by sea and one by air. Besides the cleaning, not much happened to the tuxedo during the Brezhnev era. In fact, with the exception that Brezhnev had a not-bad-looking daughter who misbehaved from time to time making him appear to be an ineffective father, not much happened in the USSR in the Brezhnev era. One cannot forget, though, that President Nixon gave Chairman Brezhnev a Chevrolet convertible, perhaps in his second term. That would be Nixon's second term. Most dictators get but one term. Brezhnev was in office from 1964 until 1982, or thereabouts, and President Nixon from 1969 to 1974, so they had plenty of time to exchange gifts. This was not a casual gift. Brezhnev was a car buff, perhaps having commandeered several limousines.

It's not fair to say that nothing at all happened during the Brezhnev era. In fact, I doubled my stock of cummerbunds. This is a word from the Hindi language meaning waistband. The dictionary says that it replaces the vest in formal attire. Pierre Lorillard could not have made this contribution as well as chopping off tails. Revolutions in any aspect of human behavior require time and contributions from many. I recall that a brother-in-law gave me this second cummerbund. It is made of a racy plaid, mostly red. I have worn it several times, but always to dances where no one would be offended. A cummerbund has pleats and one can wear it with the pleat-openings up or down. This relative and I fell into conversation about how to wear the pleats. He said that he always wore them up so that the cummerbund would catch the crumbs off the dinner table. Having nothing else to go by, I have followed this advice ever since. The relative in question is identified exactly by the label in the cummerbund: Robt. F. Ryan Ltd., Rochester N.Y.

Brezhnev died in office and was succeeded by Chernenko. I think I have that right. The talk at the time was that the Politburo could not settle on a leader and therefore punted, as we say, by selecting a man deathly ill. Chernenko did not disappoint the Politburo and died in office a year later. This event brought to my attention that not only are living things mortal, but inanimate objects are also. Or, said differently, how much more life was left in my tuxedo? Very soon it would be thirty years old. The trouser legs were acceptable but the waist would have to be let out soon. I remember clearly that it was during the one year of Chernenko that I realized there was no need to wear suspenders any more. Also that during the few years of Andropov, who came after Chernenko, I lived in hope that suspenders would be needed again because many years of the good life made them unnecessary. I found them in my closet and threw then away in the first years of Yeltsin. I remember nothing about Chernenko, the man, but I recall clearly that Andropov came out of the ranks of the KGB and the press led us to believe that there would be increased spying. Fortunately for our state secrets he died in 1985, to be replaced by Gorbachev.

In the early years of Gorbachev, I had to face the music and let out the waist. By that time it occurred to me that if I took this step, there was a chance that I could make it on one tuxedo. My stepfather made it on one, even though at the end his did look dated. He died in 1990 at the age of eighty. Another brother-in-law, not the one who gave me the cummerbund, has determined that he will make it on one even though he doesn't button the coat anymore, for obvious reasons. So I have made that vow, to get through this life with one tuxedo. At age eighty-three, I'm not asking a great deal.

For reasons unknown, fashions in tuxedos do not change rapidly, and when they do, one who wears a model from previous decades is not made to feel hopelessly out of touch. At parties, I tend to look around the room and guess the age of various outfits. I find out that I can't and that's reassuring. During Gorbachev, I was forced to buy a new pair of patent leather shoes. The old ones were cracked every place that leather bends, and as one who has believed that good-looking, well-polished shoes will compensate for some amount of un-dress on all occasions, I splurged and spent three times as much for this second pair of shoes as I did for the tuxedo. That would be in constant dollars, if that phrase means that there is no adjustment for inflation, a calculation that I am not able to carry off.

During Yeltsin, I bought a new dress shirt, an act made mandatory by an expanded neck. This shirt threw me a curve, and like most curves, it was of the unexpected type. There were four buttonholes on the front in the space where my original shirt had just three buttonholes. For years, since Khrushchev, when my bride gave me as a wedding present a set of gold cuff links and studs, the number of buttonholes on the shirt and the number of studs matched exactly. Dressing with one stud less than required by the new shirt, I am forced to keep the coat buttoned at all times and the cummerbund worn high on the waist. It never occurs to most men to check on the number of buttonholes as they buy a new shirt, and this sort of unfortunate accident keeps them out of stores in droves, me included. As I look back on the incident, I think that I would have returned the shirt except that I was one day out of New York on the QE2 when this new feature was discovered. As an aside, it should be related that a daughter took me to the pier on the West Side for the sailing. A friend of hers, asking for my destination, was told that I was on my way to Southampton to which the friend said, "I didn't know those ships stopped at the end of Long Island."

At the moment, we are with Putin. It is not clear whether he will seek a third term, pulling a Franklin Roosevelt on us. Putin is no longer a Communist nor is he any longer a member of the KGB, although such experiences could stamp one indelibly. As a leader bringing democracy to Russia, albeit at his own pace, I think he should reverse the habit of Kremlin's men showing up for evening affairs in dark suits and buy a tuxedo from Chirac's tailor. I don't know how dashing Sarkosy looks in his tuxedo. Putin is young and he might pass my current record of fifty-five years of dinner dances in one tuxedo, whose satin lapels are holding up nicely.

One of these summers very soon, I plan to walk south on the Appalachian Trail from New Hampshire, where I have two brothers who will start me off in the correct direction, to Georgia where the Trail ends. This activity will make the trousers less tight on me than they are now and guarantee that I will make it through on one tuxedo. I used to think that I owned this tuxedo, but lately I have come to realize that it's the other way around.

# Noise

I fell into one of those coffee places that are gaining in popularity across the country. After purchasing a 12-ounce cup I settled into a table and snapped open my paper. Soon enough, a blonde came over and took a table, leaving an empty one between us. She read. Minutes later, a brunette joined her and they commenced talking. In this last decade, while I have grown increasingly intolerant of noise, I have wondered why two people who have been alone and silent must start talking immediately they are thrust together. As is the custom nowadays, the women exchanged gossip at the conversational level. Whether they knew it or not, they were including me in events in which I had no interest. I shot them a double whammy, catching the eye of the brunette who may have misunderstood my signal, and moved to increase the separation between us. A phone rang. The blonde fished a portable out of her tote bag. She gave a subordinate hell over sending a stack of checks to the wrong bank, her voice rising as she administered discipline. I left before they did and went out the door, which I held to prevent its slamming. Very often, say ninety-nine out of one hundred times, I will hold the door, look behind me to determine if it needs to be held for someone following me, and then close it noiselessly.

On the way home from coffee, I parked in the basement of the bank that I use and came up through tunnels and stairs to the business area which is entered through a metal door. The hydraulic damper on this door, the device that adjusts the rapidity with which the door closes, has been broken for the two years that I have used this branch. If one goes through the door and releases it, the door closes with a noise that wakens the dead. When I open this door, I turn around, hold the knob, and close it gently, all the while asking softly, "I wonder if anyone has been around to fix the hydraulic damper?" I say it as though I am saying it to myself, but really I am saying it to the lady whose desk is by the door. Once upon a time she used to look up and smile. Now she pretends not to hear, ignores me, and gets on with her work. It's no accident that her hair is snow white.

I was coping with the annual increase in noise by making seasonal adjustments but, alas, the advent of portable telephones has been my undoing. This may be the moment to start a national association for the reduction of noise. Portable telephones got to me for the good reason that users raise their voices instead of lowering them when chatting. The fancy electronic circuitry and the satellites in space make it possible to hold conversations, or whatever, in very low tones. Apparently users are not aware of this feature. I have made a trip or two to Europe since the proliferation of portables, and find that users there are not more familiar than we are with how little audio signal is required for acceptable performance. It must be an international malaise.

Coming out of the theater last night I walked past a man with a portable glued to each ear. I had never seen this before. He may have been buying gold on the Hong Kong Exchange and selling it in Zurich. Little doubt he was reacting to a pent-up need to talk after listening for an hour and forty minutes to actors saying lines written by Euripides. That was yesterday. Today I risked my ears on a walk. Before lacing on boots, I thought about the noises of nature so that I could differentiate them from the noises that humans had invented during the last century. I was assuming that the year 1900 was the last quiet year.

I looked out the window across a lawn to a dogwood tree, then farther to some woods. There were birds eating on the lawn and other birds flying from tree to tree. They sang. Of all of nature's noises, birdcalls are held in the highest esteem even as they wake you at five. Others of nature's noises are waterfalls, winds through pine trees, ocean waves crashing, and grasshoppers in the summer. We are familiar with these noises and tend to revere them. We will drive miles to fall asleep at the ocean's edge and camp by a waterfall. So out the door it was to face the noises that we have created for our own torment in the past 100 years.

The internal combustion engine in all its forms is at the heart of our troubles. At the corner I ran into a triple whammy in the form of a gasoline engine driving an air compressor, connected by hose to a jackhammer. In the hands of a shook-up worker, the jackhammer was tearing up the pavement. Our neighborhood is being rewired for the 21st century when fiber optic threads will take the place of copper wire to bring us television, telephone, and the Internet from a single source, whatever that means. In the process all the streets in our neighborhood are being torn up.

Farther on I came to a backhoe converted into a jackhammer. A backhoe, you will recall, replaced the ditch digger, a man. While the worker with the jackhammer whom I was observing only minutes ago was tearing up the pavement retail, the backhoe operator was engaged wholesale. A steel spike that played the part of the jackhammer had replaced the scoop that we are accustomed to seeing on the backhoe. While the jackhammer was deafening, the noise from the converted backhoe was in the league with volcanoes and atomic bombs. Still farther on my walk, the neighborhood changes from apartments to single-family dwellings where three creatures of discomfort abound: lawn mowers, chain saws, and leaf blowers. I don't believe that I've seen recently the type of lawn mower that my brother and I used for many summers. We had an old-style push model to which we attached a strap and took turns, one pulling, the other pushing. Now owners of lawns have a hobby of cutting them with gasoline powered jobs and when there isn't enough time, the lawn service shows up and drives the mower off the back of the truck to cut the family lawn.

The use of chain saws should be restricted to forests where our economy requires the felling of trees. Male homeowners, however, prefer chain saws to arm saws to trim their bushes and use them during the only time off they have, Sunday afternoon, when the rest of the neighborhood is taking a nap.

Leaf blowers consist of a gasoline engine mounted on the back of a worker. The engine drives a fan that forces air out of a pipe. The purpose of a leaf blower is to avoid using a rake. In the old days we raked leaves into piles and either burned them or had them hauled away. Now we simply move the leaves around. A great deal of dust moves along with the leaves. I think the idea is to move the leaves off your property. Advanced cities, Palo Alto and Berkeley among them, have outlawed leaf blowers as too noisy, a rational position. One surmises that users, manufacturers, and sales agencies of leaf blowers were not able to make campaign contributions to members of these city councils quickly enough to prevent the passage of the legislation.

As I strolled through this neighborhood I did not meet a single device of the type that I'm complaining about, an aberration accounted for in the concept of statistical variation. I knew that I would pay the price for that bit of quiet on the way home and was not disappointed.

An under-muffled motorcycle went by me on the avenue. The trick in driving one is to see how fast the machine can be propelled from one red light to the next, in the process making as much noise as possible as you shift through the gears. The young cyclist must have felt the thrill of power as he harassed all within a one-mile radius. In effect he was telling all of us to go to hell. A few years back I asked a friend in France why the officials tolerated the noise from their motorcycles and scooters, which, as visitors know, has ruined the ambiance of the entire country. He said that the lobbies for users, manufacturers, and sales agencies have the upper hand and the elected officials have the lower hand. I have thought about suggesting to an elected person in our country that this might be the correct time to place noise limits on two-wheeled vehicles. I'm dissuaded from writing such a letter, as the answer is predictable, that the noise from motorcycles is not yet a problem. We know from past performances that our elected officials will wait until noise from that source becomes a crisis by which time they will be held motionless by the lobbies for users, manufacturers, and sales agencies.

No sooner had the motorcycle crisis passed than three helicopters flew overhead. They could have been on the White House to Camp David run. If I lived in another part of town, the helicopters would be on the White House to Andrews Air Force Base commute. Helicopters that produce as much noise as these have no business in the air. And that goes for helicopters used by television stations to report on traffic flows on the Beltway and across the bridges that span the Potomac. Let the TV stations send observers on foot and spare us the noise.

Yes, I would get jet noise as well on this short walk. Northwest Washington is on the flight path for Reagan National Airport. The original idea, back in 1940 when National Airport was opened, was to fly planes up and down the Potomac River so that people would not be disturbed on take off or landing. That technique worked well when we all flew in DC-3s but in the age of the jets, forget it. The unmistakable racket is overhead most of the time. There must be one per minute.

Senator John McCain – I think I have the correct senator – is advocating the addition of forty more flights daily in and out of Reagan. Or is it twenty landings and twenty take offs? That would make forty. We know the effects on our eardrums if he would be successful.

If I were a first cousin of the senator, I would call him on his private line. The conversation might go like this, after the usual preliminaries.

"Cousin John, you're running for president and attempting to add flights to the nation's already-crowded airspace. Doesn't running for president take all your spare time?"

"I would have more spare time if flights were added."

I pondered this brief evasion and said, "Cousin John, you're aware of the noise these additional flights will contribute?"

The senator answered, "I flew jets off carriers. Tell me about noise!"

I knew that I wasn't getting anywhere trying to put a half-nelson on this senator honed in the skills of dodging the questions of reporters and constituents. Nevertheless I went ahead. "Cousin John, I am starting a new organization called the Noise Reduction Alliance. I want you to be a charter member."

The senator cut in immediately. "I wasn't born yesterday. Noise Reduction Alliance and National Rifle Association have the same initials. What are you up to?"

"I'm recruiting important people, senators included, to join in the fight to end noise as we know it. I don't want it said about you that you are against the NRA."

"If you ever say that about me," the senator said in his serious tone, "it's no more Christmas parties at my house and other fringe benefits, cousin. Think it over." We fell silent.

After a moment, the senator came on. "See you at Christmas, I trust. I have to take this call from Phoenix."

As I approached the entrance to my apartment building a sports utility vehicle with ten speakers playing rap music drove by. It stopped at the light. I felt sad for the young driver's ears whose drums, an important part of his anatomy, were giving up their resiliency in a classic act of fly now, pay later. My rib cage started to vibrate in sync with the speakers and fenders of the car.

I fled inside the building and went up to my apartment. The fellow above me had his TV on too loud, but I was determined to attempt my daily nap. I trailed off thinking about people at the theater who clap too loudly, as though they owed performers more in adulation than their seat mates in courtesy. And thinking about women in museums who clack their leather-heeled shoes on the marble. And would Disney be interested in a theme park that featured the noises of the 19$^{th}$ century only? As I gave up consciousness, I wondered if the conveniences of the modern age, such as painless dentistry, could be achieved without cars and jets and leaf blowers. I ran out of thoughts but heard one last jet coming down the Potomac for a landing.

# Bad English

To our readership:

It has come to our attention that the incidence of errors in English and the consumption of martinis have increased recently. One need only hear fellow Americans to be convinced that errors have found their way into our language. As for martinis, we checked wholesale distributors of distilled spirits and found that sales of gin, vermouth, and olives increased 10% last year.

To determine whether these phenomena were related, we assigned Charles Piffle, reporter for metropolitan affairs, to lead the investigation. Here is his report, which we print in full.

Yours truly, in the name of good journalism,
M. T. Rushmore, Publisher
The Los Angeles Bugle

1 April 2008. Los Angeles. Luck ran with me in spearheading this assignment of determining whether the proliferation of errors in English usage and the increase in the consumption of martinis were related. I have a standing invitation from my neighbors to watch the news with them at cocktail hour. They have a preference for the program in which highly educated people parade by and are interviewed. A few evenings of watching could set the record straight. Are Americans committing more errors than previously as they speak? While finding the correlation between increased errors in English and rising consumption of martinis will have to wait until all the facts are in, we can make a start. I might mention that my neighbors are retired, have plenty of time on their hands,

and borrow my powered lawn mower. To commence gathering data, I wired myself with a midget recorder to avoid taking notes, which would spoil the ambiance. Not only did I want to catch errors, I needed their reactions as well. The following is a verbatim report of my first session.

I knocked at the door.

Mary – Well, if it isn't good old Charlie. Come in, Charlie. John, Charlie's here.

John – Hello, Charlie. Mary, where did you put the olives?

Mary – How do you expect me to remember a thing like that?

John – I'm putting more gin in the pitcher just for you, Charlie.

Charlie – I thought I would invite myself over to watch the news. It's six.

Mary – The box is on. I just have to crank up the volume.

John – Did you hear that? "There's two choices." Who the hell said that?

Mary – I think it's the secretary of something or other. One of the new ones.

John – We ought to recognize members of the cabinet.

Mary – I know, but they come and go. Give Charlie a martini. How many olives, Charlie?

Charlie – Two, thanks.

John – New channel, Mary. I'm not listening to anyone who's forgotten the plural. For God's sake, "There is two choices."

Charlie – Why do you say forgotten? Maybe he's never heard of the plural.

John – I can't contest that.

Mary – Good Lord, did you hear her say "Interim period"?

John – Who the hell is that? I can't see her under the hat. New channel, Mary.

Charlie – I get it. One mistake and you switch channels.

Mary – That's right. We have cable and more channels than we can use.

Charlie – If you switch channels that fast, how do you get the news?

John – Piece of cake. A sound bite here, a sound bite there. It all adds up. How's your martini?

Charlie – Fine. Did you hear him say "Deterate"? Can't even say deteriorate. Five syllables. Who the hell is that?

Mary – It's Prince something. He's Prince Charles' youngest brother. Got married the other day, perhaps ten years ago.

John – Switch, Baby.

Mary – It's a military man this time. See the ribbons? Refill, John.

John – There, he said it. "Nuculer." I knew he would. The more stars they have, the higher the likelihood of saying "Nuculer." Why can't they say "Nuclear, for Christ's sake?"

Mary – Don't bother me with silly questions. I'm counting the ribbons.

Charlie – Fewer wars, more ribbons.

John – Next case, dammit.

Mary – Did you hear him say "Not that big of a deal"?

Charlie – Should be "Not that big a deal." I guess you look for the smallest errors.

Mary – You've got it, Chuck Babe.

Charlie – How come you're letting this new one stay on? He started with "Big picture" and concluded with "Bottom line."

Mary – Right on, Chuckie. I'm eighty-sixing this dude now.

Charlie – By the way, how many "basicallys" do you allow before they're history?

Mary – Usually two. But if they have a bad case of it, John doesn't let me switch. He counts 'basicallys' to see if they set a new record. It stands at nineteen.

John – Who is this? Did you catch that "Period of time"? Makes me sick. Must send her a dictionary. Look up "Period" for God's sake.

Mary – I'm getting rid of her before you get her name. Tired of you buying dictionaries all the time.

John – Say "Tired of your buying dictionaries all the time. Use the possessive before a gerund."

Mary – You're right. Ti many martoonies. Let's look at a new one.

Charlie – Did you hear him say "Distrik"?

Mary – It blows me away when they are members of a transit district and say "Distrik."

John – Can't beat going to college. How's your drink, Charlie?

Charlie – Just a touch more. You set high standards for English in this house. I don't know if I could live here.

Mary – Good God, Charlie, you write for a living!

Charlie – Yes, but they fired all the re-write guys.

Mary – This one just said, "Time horizon." He's out of here, isn't he?

John – Of course. It's as bad as "caveat."

Charlie – Time horizon. I use that in my columns. What's wrong with it?

John – Anyone who confuses the passage of time with the curvature of the Earth doesn't belong in this living room.

Mary – Fix another pitcher, will you, dear?

Charlie – How come you just switched the channel?

Mary – The jerk said, "Between he and I." On the flagrant ones we don't even discuss it.

Charlie – What do you suppose this is?

John – A hearing. Yes, the House of Representatives. I recognize the chairman's name.

Charlie – I can't understand the one who's talking.

Mary – You've been drinking, Charlie.

John – Well, yes, Charlie's been drinking but the guy's difficult to understand.

Mary – You've been drinking, John.

John – Well, what's he saying, smart pants?

Mary – I don't know. I've been drinking.

Charlie – No. Come on. He's difficult to understand. No comprendo. He must be from the Deep South.

John – Let's listen intently.

Charlie – I am. The pitcher is full. My glass is empty. The guy needs a voice coach.

John – Maybe lobbyists could be voice coaches three days a week.

Mary – Wouldn't do any good. They're ex congressmen.

Charlie – I'm beginning to understand this guy.

John – Translate.

Charlie – He's asking a question about highways.

Mary – Let this guy drone on for a while. It's restful.

Charlie – Is he asking a question or making a speech?

John – He doesn't know either. Surf, Mary, surf.

Mary – I'm surfing.

John – Who's this guy?

Mary – I don't know. He's a spokesman. His eyebrows are touching.

John – Don't get personal.

Charlie – He couldn't find his razor this morning.

Mary – Charlie, don't stand on ceremony. Just pour yourself one when you need it.

John – He's a weather man. He just said Doppler radar.

Charlie – I just look out the window for my weather forecast.

Mary – He's said "Gonna" twice. Is he out of here?

John – Flip that baby, Mary.

Charlie – I have to go home for dinner.

Mary – Where's your wife?

Charlie – She's out mowing the lawn.

John – Impossible. Your lawn mower's in my garage.

Charlie – What's that noise I'm hearing?

John – Just the usual buzzing in your ears at this hour.

Mary – Go get your wife. We have plenty.

Charlie – She prefers onions to olives. Where was the door when you saw it last?

# Impacts Of An Obituary

The obituary of Alec Wilder appeared in *The New Yorker* late in 1996 or early in 1997, and, no doubt, elsewhere at about the same time. He had composed popular songs *("I'll Be Around," "It's So Peaceful in the Country," "While We're Young.")*, and written one book, *American Popular Song, The Great Innovators, 1900-1950,* Oxford University Press, 1972. I found the book in the public library of South Tacoma where I lived two moves ago. I read it through with great enjoyment. It tells about the careers of Jerome Kern, the Gershwins, Cole Porter, Irving Berlin, Harold Arlen ("*This Time the Dream's on Me," "Somewhere over the Rainbow")*, and the lyricist Johnny Mercer. The book must give particular pleasure to pianists as the author illustrates why great songs are great by providing portions of scores.

It was not enough that Wilder had composed popular music and written this one interesting and important book. The obituary revealed, as well, an unexpected aspect of his life. He had reduced the number of his possessions so that they fit into three suitcases. As one might imagine, Wilder had to dress about the same way everyday: sport coat, button-down shirt, bow tie, gray trousers, and loafers. The obituary went on to say that he lived six months of the year at the Algonquin and divided the remaining time between friends on the Cape and in Florida, with a bit left over for family in Rochester, New York.

The impressions left on me by the book have faded only slightly. The names of the six music men come spontaneously, and the impact of the three-suitcase saga grows daily. As age presses in on me from many sides, the need to settle my affairs increases. There is a will. The significant and valuable items have been distributed to children; that is to say, objects with either cash or sentimental value such as gold watches and medium-grade art that have been in the family now find themselves in the proper hands.

The money has been organized for easy distribution at death. But, alas, much more remains.

There is a saying concerning the accumulation of a lifetime that goes as follows: two moves equal one fire. The meaning must be that in a fire everything is lost, but that two moves are required to accomplish the same result. Old sayings notwithstanding, four moves in the past eight years have reduced my holdings only slightly, and my situation is not yet related to life with three suitcases, the life style that I hope for at the end. By the way, the three-suitcase plan has me spending my last days in Baja California, a bit south of Ensenada, in a one-room house. The house will be within strolling distance of the Pacific Ocean where I plan to swim daily. The services of a Mexican lady will be engaged. Her duties will be to provide coffee, tortillas, and other local foods. I hope to read the Bible, Shakespeare's collected works, and Proust's *Remembrances of Things Past* to while away the time.

Anyone can pass on art, gold watches, cuff links, and a silver service to children. It's the odds and ends that confound you. I realized recently, a few years after reading the obituary, that I needed a new point of view in the event that I didn't make it to three suitcases. The new point of view goes like this: picture that I haven't made it to Ensenada but that I died strolling in Glover Archibald Park in northwest Washington DC, or in some nature preserve in California. My children come to close the apartment. They find nothing of sentimental or monetary value. There are two cardboard boxes, one for each, containing a few undistributed mementos. These boxes can be shipped to their respective homes easily, or taken with them. They look in the Yellow Pages for a firm that buys the odds and ends of bachelor living, furniture as well as electronic apparatus. Presto, it's done.

That's the new model -- a compromise -- but still a last, great gift to the next generation. These children will not be asked by my ghost to spend months in an attic or a basement reading old letters.

Without knowing it, I started haphazardly on the new model a few years ago by determining that some of the objects that I possessed need not go to my children. It was a good start and should be accelerated. There is a little book on the early history of Grammercy Park. (Grammercy was spelled with a double *m* originally). In 1832, my great-great-grandfather, with four associates, purchased a farm at what is now 21st Street. They set off the small park in the center, in the style of a commons, and built their houses on the periphery. This ancestor was a big butter-and-egg man, as my father used to describe him. By that, my father meant a rich and influential person. He graduated long ago from Columbia. It was called Kings College then. He served twice as president of the New York Stock Exchange, although in his day that organization had a slightly different name. The small book shows that he dropped off the board of the Grammercy Park Association in 1858, so he may have died that year. I offered the book to the New York Historical Society, on Central Park West at 78th Street. They turned down the book for the good reason that they had two copies. My New York daughter appeared to be a good candidate and is now saddled with it.

A daguerreotype of my great-grandmother was on my bureau. She married my great-grandfather in 1842. He was the son of the president of the New York Stock Exchange. This Daguerre has been kicking around the family for 150 years. I sent it to Raynham Hall in Oyster Bay, a museum in the center of town that holds items such as these, gifts from local families in the same bind I find myself in. I did not know this ancestor but I knew her two daughters, my great aunts. They both died in the 1950s. The older, a spinster, spent the summers in Oyster Bay and the winters at 10 Washington Square with her bachelor brother after whom I was named. The younger lived year-round in Oyster Bay on sixteen acres of waterfront property. She kept a horse that she rode sidesaddle most days. She married briefly, unhappily. Her husband was an architect who had something to do with the Brooklyn Museum. I have a sketchbook of hers filled in between 1875 and 1882. One page is laid out like a modern comic, with nine drawings and observations in her handwriting. The page depicts a gentleman caller being snatched away by her mother who cannot understand that any young man might prefer the company of one of her daughters to herself, even in her fifties, after six children. Although the page is amusing, it does underscore the sadness that is part of an old family tale of a mother's narcissism standing in the way of her daughters' happiness. I have tried throwing away this sketchbook which also contains drawings of the Bay of Naples, columns in Egyptian temples, and profiles of a few European swains. Before each move I take the sketchbook out of its box and look through it, think about throwing it away, and dismiss the thought. The sketchbook will mean nothing to anyone else. Perhaps it should go to Raynham Hall as well.

There is an etching of my great-grandmother in profile, the same person whose Daguerre is mentioned above, and a watercolor that I found by accident. They go together. The frame holding the etching was damaged and had to be repaired. In so doing, the watercolor fell out. It may have spent 150 years behind the etching. I would classify it as belonging to the Hudson River School and probably be wrong. Each is in its own frame now but I haven't any takers. My young relatives seem to have their walls full already.

My grandfather married three times, losing his first wife in childbirth, losing his second wife and a son to an epidemic of diphtheria, and finally marrying my grandmother. I still have and use their 1911 edition, the 11th , of the *Encyclopaedia Britannica*. This is the edition with articles written by famous people. In spite of the extraordinary reputation of this edition, the articles in it that I have compared to the latest version, the 15th edition, are not written with the same level of detail. The leather bindings are falling off and the set should be thrown out, considering that the 1911 edition can still be purchased in new or next-to-new condition. I was brought up short the other day while looking up Nefertiti. No entry. Turns out she was found in a scrap heap by German archaeologists in 1912 and secreted out of Egypt to Berlin where she remains, too late for the 1911edition. If I throw away this set it will be over the already-stated objections of the New York daughter. If I try to give it to her now she will claim that there isn't enough room in her apartment.

There is a landscape painting that is another leftover of this marriage. It features two lovebirds, a man and a woman passing the time of day billing and cooing at the edge of some woods. The painting is far too large for modern walls and I store it in the back of the hall closet. As it is not of museum quality, no one will take it off my hands. Perhaps the solution is to cut it out of its frame and roll it up.

I have a leather box with six drawers of flies that are too beautiful to throw away. Grandfather enjoyed fishing and tied flies as a hobby. No one in the family fishes. On a trip a few years back, I fell into the fly fishing museum in West Yellowstone and hoped that I would be inspired to send the box to the curator. I couldn't bring myself to do it. Fly fishing in the Rocky Mountains for trout, no doubt, just seems too different from salmon fishing in New Brunswick. From the photographs, which I have as well, of course, it appears that gentlemen would camp out on the banks of the Restigouche River, catch and cook their dinners and, I suppose, drink bourbon, smoke cigars and tell stories. I have no idea how they made it up to Chaleur Bay in the northern reaches of New Brunswick. Perhaps I will give the box to an unsuspecting nephew.

Moving on to my father, there are texts from days at St. Paul's School. Latin and English could not have been his only subjects but these are the books that remain. As the saying goes, I can't give these away. There is a photo of him and his mother, taken when he was about twelve, of such high quality as to be a work of art. I can't part with it. There are letters addressed to me from various parts of the world. I like the one that describes a lunch he had at Fouquet's on the Champs Elysées. The tone of it is "see if you can top that." They say that letters are a biographer's dream come true but these are not historic. They live in the same paper bag they were in the year he died, 1973. I don't know what to do with them.

I have been discussing my grandfather's side of the family. If I move on to my grandmother's side there is her grandfather who graduated from West Point in 1823. He served continuously in the Army until 1869 when he retired to Washington. He lived and died in the Old Soldiers' Home here in 1888. As with the bulk of the regular army, he was in the Mexican campaign of 1846-47. I traced his assignments during his career while at the Archives on 8th and Pennsylvania in the District of Columbia and thought it accurate that he was the commanding officer of the Infantry Company that took Chapultapec Heights in Mexico City. The palace is there, where five cadets wrapped themselves in a Mexican flag and jumped to their deaths as Americans were approaching from the other side of the palace where there is a gentle slope. What an unhappy event to have tied to one's family! I have his photograph. It's not a Daguerre. He's wearing a colonel's uniform. He was promoted to colonel in 1855 and given command of the newly formed Tenth Infantry Regiment. Although a major general during the Civil War, he reverted to his peace-time rank and returned to command the Tenth Infantry at Fort Snelling, Minnesota, which post he held before that war. Perhaps I will send his photograph to the library or archives at West Point. There is no question that I am the last person on earth to think about this old warrior. His son, who would be another great-grandfather of mine, graduated from Yale in 1854 and joined the Army in 1856 as a surgeon. He served in various posts, including Santa Fe where my grandmother was born, and West Point where he is buried. He was the doctor for the post. At some time in his career he was the physician to General Sherman who took over command of the Army from Grant in 1869, when the latter was elected president, and held the post until 1883, when it went to Sheridan. The doctor and Sherman became good friends to the extent that, during both of their retirements, Sherman wrote letters of introduction for the doctor and his wife to our ambassadors in Europe. My sister and I take these letters out of their box from time to time, look them over, and put them back. No one could possibly be interested in them. We don't know what to do with them.

For reasons that are difficult to fathom, the doctor gave Sherman a book in Chinese on war tactics. It may never have been delivered, or the general returned it, claiming inability to read the language. The book lived in many trunks and attics until I determined to give it the University of Washington in Seattle. The Chinese scholar who took the book from me felt certain that the University's Asian Library had this text, so he accepted it on a provisional basis. A week later, he telephoned to say that this version was printed in 1540, or thereabouts, and antedated the copy in their possession by two centuries. This was a first edition of sorts. It was in excellent condition and written by a military man of high repute. As is the custom, I was to learn, their possession of the less desirable text was made known by the University of Washington so that other university libraries that did not have a copy could make arrangements, cash or swap, who knows, to add the newer edition to their collection. I have several photographs of the doctor, one strolling with a certain Mrs. Price Collier at an outdoor party at Piping Rock, I recall my father's telling me. I wish I knew why my father's voice carried an air of importance when he said Mrs. Price Collier. Perhaps he knew and admired her. I think she was born Laura Delano.

There are promotions signed by various presidents. My favorite is the promotion of the Army doctor to brigadier general signed by Theodore Roosevelt. It was the habit to promote to brigadier generals those who retired as colonels. They would henceforth be known as tombstone generals. I have visited his grave at West Point. There is not a soul who thinks anymore of this fine soldier and doctor of that century, or even knows about him, for that matter. I could be wrong about that. A second cousin in the Midwest has mentioned him to me. But it's as though his cardboard box is waiting for a good fire.

It goes on. Each cardboard box contains ever more challenges of placing objects in the correct hands. The mechanism at work is simple. Would-be recipients expect high quality, or rarity, or sentimental value, or monetary value. When none of these is present, you can't give it away. Not even relatives will take it off your hands. There are things that have meaning to me that none other can appreciate. With diligence, though, I can get through a box per month and be done in a couple of years.

I have known some of the people whose effects I am disposing of. Concerning those who lived too long ago for me to have known personally, I have been in their homes, or read about them, or heard tales from my father about them. The sum of the memories must define me in some way. When I go, these memories will go, too. I suppose that is as it should be. I will try to be less discriminating from now on and see more and more objects as useless.

When my daughters open their cardboard boxes with final mementos, each will find a small, stiff, red paper box. One contains a man five inches high made of cut-up paper and colored with crayon. The other holds a small-frame house complete with chimney, also made of paper. They were made as birthday presents for me years ago by these young children when we were on a trip, away from stores. They may not remember them. They may not understand the lasting impact of a child's sweetness. I can't throw them out.

# Pack Rats

The Collier brothers are remembered as two old bachelors, living in a brownstone in New York City, who were unable to throw away the daily paper. If this is a life-long habit, and the paper making it to the front door every morning is *The New York Times,* or many of our metropolitan dailies, then any house, no matter its size, will fill up over a half-century. In the case of the Collier brothers, their house filled, or nearly so, leaving tunnels as connectors between rooms. One day, when the brothers were in their eighties, a collapse occurred, trapping one of them. He gave up the ghost. The surviving brother was taken away by the authorities to live out his days in a safe place. All this happened in the late 1940s, or a bit later. The phrase "Collier brothers" has joined the lexicon and now symbolizes pack-rat-ism.

A certain couple living on the East Coast, whom this witness has known for years, has developed and now lives with an acute case of Collier's disease. The male and female that made up this couple were married about fifty years ago and produced the four children expected of them. They are spaced nicely and all are in their forties now. The first symptoms of the illness showed up in the lady of the house. These were the early signs that an observer with any wit could have picked up. As an example, she has to this day the entire collection of children's books that she bought as a child out of allowance money. Further, she became unable to throw away the magazine and travel sections of the *Sunday New York Times.* There must be something magnetic about that newspaper. The solution for her was to commence stacking these sections in empty corners of the basement. Over the years she was forced to compete with her children's junk, abandoned by them as they left home and went out into the brave new world. But that's another story.

One summer, when the children were small, the four of them and their parents spent a vacation in Europe. For transportation they picked up a VW station wagon over there. The trip went off without incident and the car was shipped home, duly arriving at dockside in Baltimore. This small green station wagon became the second family car and remained so until a new sedan replaced it. The same instinct that sent unread papers to the basement sent this station wagon to the back yard. After all, as the lady said, they might need the car some day.

It happened that the basement filled at the same time as the car landed in the back yard and the inevitable came about. The Magazine and Travel sections of the *Times* began to fill the station wagon.

In one of the unforeseen twists in her life, this lady's oldest son returned from the West Coast for a stay of a few months. Needing wheels, and spotting this old friend with newspapers up to the gunwales, the son emptied the car, got it running, and proceeded to buy tags for it. His mother said, "I wish you had asked me first about throwing out the papers; I had planned to read those someday." The car was totaled at an icy intersection that winter, ending that chapter in their lives. The son was unhurt.

Not for the reason that they were pack rats, the couple was divorced after four decades of marriage. Wife moved out, leaving husband alone on three floors. Either he had had the disease since birth and had not had the chance to show symptoms, or he had caught the disease from his wife and was at last given the chance to start his own collections. There are two. The first is wine by the case and the other is everything else. Old newspapers left the basement, to be tossed out and replaced by cases of white and red, mostly from Italy and France. Husband even had a portion of the basement walled off and a cooling system installed so that he could store these wines at the appropriate temperature. There must be a couple of hundred cases by now. The second collection came about on the discovery that one could buy a great deal of stuff over the telephone when equipped with a credit card and an attractive catalog. Wife had added an extension to the house for purposes of having an office. Now absent, the room was empty and what better place to store these new purchases? Presently, there is a rowing machine in the center of the room, surrounded by electronic products, unopened boxes of clothes and, not surprisingly, boxes with wine glasses of various sizes. On being asked why so many, he answered, "They make great presents."

Two significant events have come to this man's life in the last five years. A knee has gone out making it impossible for him to descend to the basement, thereby forcing him to abandon the wine to its own devices. Later on, a medical man told him to lay off the booze, making shambles of his life style. When last seen, this man had lost weight, the office on the first floor was jammed, and his children were beseeching him for a decision on the wine in the basement. Of course they should drink it, as it now has become a part of their inheritance.

We should pause for a moment. We say that pack rats cannot throw away anything. In fact, it is that they are not able to make decisions. Ridding the house of the daily paper on a regular schedule is a decisive act. We cannot expect pack rats to unload stuff when they are not able to make the simplest decisions, such as giving wine to loved ones before it goes sour.

We return now to the ex-wife. Her new house is a one-story affair, placing a crimp in her schemes for collecting. If only 1% of what comes into the house fails to leave on a regular basis, it doesn't take long to fill the corners. This lady has started a new life with another husband. We are not privy to the engagement, but it may have gone like this.

"Oh, Ann, I love you a great deal."

"Larry, dear, I'm mad for you."

"Do you think we should marry, Ann?"

"Are you a pack rat, Larry?"

"Of course, have you met anyone who isn't?"

The union between these two pack rats is working well. She is a vertical pack rat who stacks things in the corners, on chairs, on her desk, and on any flat surface. He is a horizontal pack rat who throws things on the floor, be it newspapers, scientific articles, books, clothes clean and dirty, and trivia, important or not. They are saved by her daughter and one of her daughters-in-law who make occasional sweeps of the place and throw away everything. Mother says meekly, "Please let me make the final decisions." The next generation pays no attention, as everything not nailed down goes into large plastic bags.

Of these two young women, these observations can be made. The daughter's house is monastic. The daughter-in-law's is nearly so and her refrigerator is empty as she does not allow leftover dinners to accumulate. Of course, they are reacting to the previous generation.

# A Movie Review

Several thousand residents of Los Angeles watched *The Razor's Edge* a few weeks ago. It was the feature film on our Public Television station one recent Saturday night. It's difficult to imagine a more pleasing presentation because the date of its filming, around 1950, guaranteed that there would be little if any violence and that the sex, what there was of it, would be normal rather than an exhibition of bad taste.

The story opens in 1919, immediately after World War I. Here we are at a country club dance on Chicago's North Shore. The clothes are exquisite, the music compelling, and you would give your last set of studs to be on the floor with one of those leggy, enthusiastic, airheads, all of whom can dance the Charleston thirty minutes at a time. They are not airheads, but the script suggests that they are.

The players are introduced. Clifton Webb, as usual, has all the money and malevolence. He plays the part of a sarcastic put-down artist. He plays the role well because he never is given another. He controls his widowed sister and her daughter, Gene Tierney, by allotting them just the correct amount of money to remain well fed, dressed to the nines, and dependent on him. The three of them are at the club waiting for their guests to assemble.

John Payne shows up. He looks fine in his dinner jacket but manages to appear weak because his role always requires that he lose the girl in the end. He must look forward to playing the rugged outdoorsman once in a while, if he could only persuade the casting directors. Then Somerset Maugham comes along in the person of Herbert Marshall. The story does not need Maugham, the author of this piece, but one guesses that he knew when he wrote the novel that it would be made into a movie and this was his chance to present himself to his readers as a sympathetic observer.

At last the hero shows up. Tyrone Power in evening wear is about as good looking as it gets, and forget that old phrase to the effect that "if you like that sort of good looks." Tyrone Power is handsome, and most guys would change places with him in an instant just to look out at the world from inside that face.

Well, Tyrone is mad for Gene Tierney, as who wouldn't be. He's just back from the trenches and must sort out a few things before organizing a life for himself, or marry Gene. To discuss this in private, Tyrone whisks Gene to a nearby gazebo where he plants some first-rate kisses on her. In the current version of the movie kiss, the male and female leads appear to pass chewing gum back and forth without using their fingers. In the style of fifty years ago, the camera moved to capture the back of one of the heads so that the audience was spared all the unattractive smacking and left with the pleasant and distinct impression that the two participants were enjoying themselves.

After the third kiss, Tyrone and Gene break. He moves to the other side of the gazebo and his story comes out. A few months ago, Tyrone's life was spared when a soldier gave his life to save him. No explanation is given for this sacrifice, but the act makes a strong impression on Tyrone, requiring him to examine his life. He wants to make certain that he does not throw it away as a bond salesman at some relative's brokerage. Such a job at a fine salary waits him.

Gene doesn't understand. She has the rich uncle and all the accouterments and needs only Tyrone to complete the masterpiece that their lives together would be.

We are off to Paris, the entire cast. Clifton Webb has a chauffeur-driven Rolls at his disposal to move the family about. Gene Tierney catches up with Tyrone who has been looking intently at life. She uses supplication, moving in on him. He backs away, claiming a need for space and time. Gene feels rejected, then thwarted. She doesn't say as much, but her clock is ticking. Tyrone announces that he must go to India to do more sorting out at the knee of a guru. At this point, Gene plays her last card, asking Tyrone how he plans to live on nothing.

He blows the story apart; or rather, Maugham blows his own novel apart by letting us hear that Tyrone isn't a poor rascal after all. He says that he has $3,000 per year. So much for searching one's soul, and working in a coal mine with average blokes, and gazing at the Himalayas from the portico of the guru's chalet. If Tyrone's $3,000 is in dividends, then the profits being distributed are earned by ordinary working stiffs engaged in boring, repetitive work in a dank factory. If his $3,000 is in interest, then taxpayers are coughing up money to pay back school bonds or to pay the interest on the federal debt.

So there goes Tyrone's inner search for truth. All he needed to know was that work is the answer. But then it would be a different novel.

As for the leads, they enjoyed one another on the set and their scenes together seemed to demonstrate a genuine affection that had nothing to do with the story. Gene Tierney, left pending by Tyrone, does marry John Payne and have two kids. Payne has a nervous breakdown. Power cures him with a bit of mesmerizing that he picked up in India. Several people die including Ann Baxter, whom I forgot to mention earlier. She plays the part of a weak woman who is tempted by liquor, drugs, and evil men. In the middle of the story, Tyrone Power proposes marriage, perhaps offered as a cure to her afflictions, but she drops out of the picture when her throat is slit and her body is found in a harbor. It's a good yarn. As for Gene Tierney, all she need do is sit quietly and read from the telephone directory, and most men would pay the price of admission.

Maybe some Saturday soon our TV station will show *Laura* and I can watch Tierney and Webb again, this time with Dana Andrews, in a movie that ranks up there with *Casablanca.* It doesn't take a great deal to entertain me – an old black and white movie with actors who remember their lines most of the time but are appropriately wooden when the action does not call for anything special. And a great looking gal and good actress the likes of Gene Tierney.

# The Thirties

With the exception of the Depression, which brought severe hardships to a quarter of the population, the thirties were not bad times. Perhaps I say this because the Depression hit our family only at the fringes. Had we borne the full brunt, I might avoid the topic.

I like to think that the population of the country was about right then, perhaps 130 million. There might have been 120 million of us the year of my birth, 1925. It is a fact that there were only four million people in California. Maybe people think that the population of their country is about right on the year they are born, irrespective of the year or the population.

The crush of population, the more than doubling in our lifetimes, has changed our habits and our points of view. We have had to accommodate this new crowding. The East is full. The West is filling in.

Our family spent a fair amount of time moving about. My father came out from New York in 1919 on his return from service in France in the Marine Corps. He came on his motorcycle, a four-cylinder Indian. There were no roads, so he followed the Santa Fe tracks from Chicago to Los Angeles, buying gas in livery stables, which were converting from tending horses to servicing cars. At night he either stayed out in the open or made it to a Harvey House. He asked my mother to come out three years later. He was not a romantic person so he may have sent her a telegram by Western Union. She came and they were married in Merced.

Father drove busses, or stages as they were called, for the Curry Company in Yosemite. You could go to Yosemite then, something we can no longer do without making a reservation. He drove from the valley floor up to Glacier Point and often made a run to Wawona to take visitors to see the big trees. This trip always involved driving through the tree with the cut in the middle so those passengers could have a photo taken of them to take home. He drove Pierce-Arrows mostly and occasionally Whites.

In the winter we lived on North Hill in Pasadena and Father did odd jobs such as chauffeuring. Mother, a determined woman, taught herself to drive going up and down North Hill. I think she must have been tough on a transmission. One of Father's failings was that he had to do everyone's thinking for them, hence couldn't teach anyone anything, nor could anyone take instructions from him. That's not absolutely true but it's close.

Getting back to population. We did travel the west by car in the thirties and my recollection is that it was empty. Roads were unpaved and they were called washboard roads. In 1937 we drove around, going first to Boulder Dam. The dam was finished but Lake Mead was just filling. We went down the elevator to see generators, all installed, but not yet making electricity for Los Angeles. No doubt they have been making electricity continuously since 1938, or whenever Lake Mead was full.

The road to Flagstaff, Arizona, was dirt, as was the road up to the rim of the Grand Canyon. It's difficult for a twelve-year-old boy to get excited about geological beauty but easy to be impressed that one could ride a mule down to the river and back in one day.

To get across the Colorado River, we drove to New Mexico, through quiet, small towns such as Gallup, and drove north, and then turned left to go to Zion National Park and Bryce Canyon before coming to St. George, Utah. I remember St. George as an oasis, a place with milk shakes nearly a quart high for fifteen cents. St. George was different from the other towns we went through. It had a main drag, neon lights, and drive-in restaurants. St. George seemed misplaced after going through Gallup. Then north to Salt Lake City. We weren't about to leave out Salt Lake and a swim. It's true that you can't drown.

The trip continued. There was no missing Yellowstone Park and Cody, Wyoming. After watching Old Faithful erupt and walking over the shaky, steamy ground we went east to the town of Cody. We stopped at the small museum, but I came out soon to chat with an old man sitting outside named Bronco Charlie Miller. He said he had known Buffalo Bill Cody and that made sense as Cody had put together the town named for him, and anyway didn't die until 1917. In fact, he had dammed the North Fork of the Shoshone River, which rises in the Park, and had a power station put in to electrify the town. Bronco Charlie told me that he had spent most of his early days driving stagecoaches. I went back to Cody fifty-six years later and the old museum had become the Chamber of Commerce and a new museum stood across the street, a museum at least as large as the Norton Simon is. It has a fine collection of Remmingtons and

Farneys. I entered the Chamber of Commerce to tell them they used to be the museum. They had not known this but were not impressed to find it out. We drove around Lake Tahoe on the way home. There was next to nothing there. It should have become a national park but the important people were distracted. The Depression kept money in short supply, with the result that the Federal Government did not buy the land in the Tahoe Basin.

Over the years we drove again through the west. It was a place of wide open spaces, bare-bones motels, simple restaurants, gas for less than twenty cents, long, straight roads, and plenty of open range. It cost money that ranchers did not have to fence property, so the range stayed open for miles. Cattle used the roads as much as cars did. We should have preserved the west in the condition it was sixty or seventy years ago. It was a country of great beauty and few people. It was not on purpose that the people who lived there imposed an ugly layer over the original, simple, beautiful one, the one they had found fifty years previously when they arrived in the mid-to-late 1800s. They did it in the name of making a better life for themselves and to accommodate the new settlers who followed them by the millions.

# Reading "The New York Times"

A source of great pleasure is visiting a friend on Sunday afternoons. We read *The New York Times,* her subscription, and drink the strongest coffee in the west, her concoction. On a particular Sunday recently, I turned to the Arts Section first because a portrait in cartoon style of Jean Philippe Rameau caught my eye. I find out that he was a French composer who lived in the times of Bach, Handel, and Vivaldi. These four, among others, were composers of the Baroque period, which ended about 1750, the year that Johann Sebastian Bach died. One must have a far more educated ear than I do to detect the elements of the Baroque when it is played. All of that came to an end when a new wave of composers came on the field, of whom Mozart (1756-1791) was the most celebrated.

It turns out that there was an Italian architect with approximately the name of Baroque. To achieve its present spelling, some art historian gave the name a French twist, no doubt. The architect, in the course of his career, added more and more frills and ornamental features to his designs. As we know, and it happens in all fields, when the artistic outpourings become too frilly, a new wave of creators comes along and takes the particular art form back to its basics, blowing away all the extraneous nonsense.

Rameau was a contemporary of Bach, Handel, and Vivaldi, but less well known than they. And that is one of the points of the article. This year we celebrate the 250th anniversary of Bach's death, and therefore his compositions are being re-examined in depth and presented live and in recordings in new versions in the western world. It is anticipated, then, that in the year 2014, the 250th anniversary of Rameau's death, the music establishment will do the same as it is doing now for Bach, and who knows the treasures that might be uncovered. Perhaps Rameau will become as famous as his three contemporaries.

As I read on about Handel, I recalled a story and determined that it was good enough to interrupt my friend for the telling of it, even though she was buried in the first section. Anyone who has attended a performance of Handel's Messiah has stood up during the singing of the Hallelujah Chorus, which comes near the end. This much we know about the piece and the custom of standing during the Hallelujah Chorus: that it was composed in 1741 and performed first in Dublin in 1742. For its first performance at court, presumably in London, George II was in attendance. As the Hallelujah Chorus began, the king stood and, naturally, all in attendance stood as well. We know that at the end of that particular chorus he sat down. The following is speculation. George II and the others had been seated for more than an hour listening to verses from Isaiah and the New Testament set to music. At the first note of the Hallelujah Chorus, George said to himself, "Hallelujah, this baby's over, and I can go to bed." He was ready to clear the hall at the sound of the last note. At the end, however, when the orchestra and chorus moved on to the next verse, George had to decide. Would he make a break for it, or sit down and stay to the end? He did the latter. But the tradition had been born and to this day we stand for the Hallelujah chorus. My friend smiled dutifully at the correct places in the story.

As I read on about Vivaldi, I wanted to tell her that I couldn't distinguish his Four Seasons from Respighi's Pines of Rome. Perhaps a little plagiarism took place there. I saw she was reading intently and remained silent. I came to a mere mention of Haydn in the article. He lived from 1732 to 1809 and therefore spanned Baroque and the era after. I wanted to tell my friend that Haydn left off frills and embellishments because he was too prolific to work them in. How can one compose over 100 symphonies and have time for frills? I also wanted to tell her that Haydn's friends claimed that he was killed by the noise from Napoleon's guns. This worthy was on one of his campaigns in the summer of 1809, when he, his army, and the frail Haydn, converged on Vienna. Napoleon was intent on bringing another autocrat to heel, this time the Emperor of the Austrians. The cannonades were too much for Haydn, forcing him to pass away one warm afternoon during the battle of Wagram.

Friend and I finished reading at the same time. Her nose had been buried in the genome project. Live by storytelling; die by storytelling, I thought to myself. So, as she explained it to me, I learned that there are 23 chromosomes and about 80,000 genes in our DNA. My mind wandered when I contemplated the word chromosome. The chromo part must have something to do with color. Surely chromo is the Greek word for color. She went on. It was interesting but I couldn't get into it. The entire topic is for the next generation.

# An Eye Operation--the Left Eye

So many friends my age broadcast the wonders of the operation. "Have those old lenses out," they said, "and you'll see like any twenty-year-old." I made an appointment with the ophthalmologist recommended by a brother-in-law. He's in the medical profession. I thought that I would tell the doctor how it is and see what he had to say.

Here's my problem. When I drive east out of Los Angeles in the morning, heading for San Bernardino on Interstate 10, I cannot read the white letters on the large green road signs that are suspended over the freeway. The sun is out in front of me and the light from the sun breaks up as it goes through the cataracts in the lenses, sending mixed signals to the retinas. The freeway signs appear to be large green panels without lettering. If I get in the wrong lane, in no time I'm on my way north to Sacramento, or south to San Diego or, just as time-consuming, thrust out on the streets of East LA. And these signs, of course, are vital, because they let you know the lanes to stay in for San Bernardino. Here's the explanation for the existence of the problem. In old age, cataracts, or foggy spots, can form in the lenses. When the sun is at your back in the afternoon, in the trip described above, the rays that say "San Bernardino" make it to the retina and can be understood. When the sun is out in front, a profusion of light rays is added to the rays that say "San Bernardino" and the resulting overload makes it impossible to separate the signal (San Bernardino) from the noise (extraneous rays from the sun). There are other problems associated with cataracts, such as not being able to recognize one's friends across the room, and not being able to appreciate good-looking dames anywhere except up close. The temptation to remove these difficulties is irresistible. Here's the solution. Ask a surgeon who operates on the human eye to remove the original, foggy lenses and replace them with new, clear, plastic ones. Piece of cake.

In anticipation of the first visit, I went through my recitation. Doctor would be interested in the freeway sign story. As well, I could tell him that when I made a fist and didn't close it completely, leaving a tunnel to look through, I could knock out stray light and read neighborhood road signs from my stationary car. These are not the signs over freeways, but the small signs on residential streets. They are green and white mostly, but the letters are minuscule, selected for the various towns in our country by young persons with perfect vision. Their time will come. Before seeing a doctor, one must spend time in the waiting room. A word or two about that time consuming activity.

A great, unsolved problem concerns the proper handling of patients in waiting rooms. Rather than have patients wait forty minutes with old magazines in the company of other fidgeting victims, some doctors have patients sit half the time in the waiting room and the remainder in an examining room. In keeping with this new crowd-control practice, Nurse ushered me into an examining room and made me read the eye chart. She handed me a paddle resembling a large lorgnette that had one hole and one non-hole so that depending on which hand held the paddle, I could see the eye chart through one or the other eye, not both. In addition, there is a perforated disc that can be rotated in place so that the eye whose vision is being tested looks through a sieve. Looking through several small holes improves vision (you can read farther down on the chart). I found out that by selecting one hole out of a dozen, I could read one line farther down on the eye chart, indicating, perhaps, that all paths from the eye chart to the retina are not equal. Nurse completed her examination by saying, "Good." I have learned to say, "Please turn on the lights so I can read my magazine." She said, "Doctor will be right in." I have always wanted to say, "If you believe that, you have no sense of time," but have refrained in the name of cowardice.

Doctor arrived and turned off the lights. We met in semi-darkness. Before I could get into my stories about freeway signs and nearly closed fists, he made me place my chin in a rest, part of a complicated instrument. Of course I couldn't say a word. It occurred to me that he had heard all the stories and was only interested in making his diagnosis. He looked into both eyes, not at once, and said, "They're not ready to be operated on." He went on to say that when lenses with cataracts are ready for surgery, the lenses want to pop out. These cataracts need to be ripe, mature. He used these words.

Doctor wrote out a prescription for glasses and told me to make an appointment six months away. This was springtime a year ago. I had the glasses made and tested them on the freeway on the way to San Bernardino, in the morning and the evening. They did not help. I reasoned that if the lenses inside the eye were fogged over, no amount of clever work by lenses outside the eye could help. I was out $160. Being as cynical as the next, I suspected that the act of prescribing glasses on the part of Doctor was in keeping with that worldwide, highly-prevalent, not-limited-to-physicians practice of saving one's behind. The glasses and associated clip-on anti-sun shield stayed in the glove compartment of my car. I used the combination when I forgot my dark glasses.

Six months went by. Doctor looked into both eyes. "You're ready," he announced. "Which eye should we do first?" I asked. He said without pausing, "The left." I suspect he alternated. He gave no reason for his choice.

Doctor assured me that of all operations this was the simplest and least invasive. One slit across the top of the eye, some activity to break up the old lens, a yank to pull it out, followed by a maneuver to insert the new lens, and the process completed with six stitches to sew up the slit. Some surgeons perform this operation in their offices. Not Doctor. He used the local hospital and operated with the services of an anesthesiologist. I went under to the music of Respighi's "Pines of Rome." Respighi has become quite the rage. I know this tune because both daughters danced endlessly to it while learning one of Isadora Duncan's numbers. I regained consciousness forty-five minutes later, the operation complete. Two weeks after, I played bridge without glasses for the first time in twenty years. Not long before the operation I had "reneged," perhaps the only time in my life, playing a club when a spade was called for. One of the adversaries went through my stack of tricks to locate the error and found it. Two trick penalty. He is young. His time will come as well.

A few weeks later, I went to the opera to see "Tristan und Isolde." As is the practice in many opera houses now, superscripts were used to project the important aspects of the plot. Much of the trivia of the story is lost, but the operagoer knows when the duke is in trouble. I couldn't read the superscripts and had to rely on the skimpy notes in the program, which are fine as far as they go but cannot overcome the problem of identifying the exact moment in the third act when the duke gets in trouble. Is the duke singing a love duet with his enamorata or is he warning his daughter that the man in her life won't do? I do not recall whether there is a duke in "Tristan und Isolde," but it's a good bet there is.

At my regular checkup I related the following to Doctor. "Sir, I went to the opera the other night and couldn't read the superscripts. And, as well, I can't see the numbers of the hymns on the placard, which is about thirty feet from where I sit in church." Doctor said, "I've never been to an opera." I was stunned, not by his not having seen an opera, but by the non sequitur. I went on. "It was Wagner. You might like opera. If you don't care for Wagner, you could start with Verdi or Puccini." He eyed me, not cautiously, nor insolently, nor surreptitiously. I realized he was thinking of what to say next. At last he declared, "I like Wagner." I realized I had patronized him. The damage was done. At my age I have not yet learned to avoid patronizing anyone on any subject, particularly inadvertently. I could not let go, digging a deeper hole for myself. I said, "You can buy one ticket to an opera with four acts. You and your wife take turns. One watches the opera while the other reads a novel in the lobby." Doctor said nothing. I guessed he had heard all the attempts at conversation, all the weak humor, and was getting on with business, already thinking about the next patient in the other examining room. He wrote out a new prescription. He said, "You will be able to read the superscripts at the opera." He left out any mention of the hymns. Mindful that I was out $160 for the first pair of glasses, he added, "Make sure you use the old frame and just buy new lenses."

We parted company and the prescription went into my wallet. I thought about filling it but realized that as the months went by and the right eye was operated on in its turn there could be a series of prescriptions for new lenses. On the third or fourth day, I pulled the prescription from the wallet and placed it on my bureau, an act, for me, of unprecedented defiance against medical authority.

Several weeks went by and I was back for a scheduled check-up. Doctor went immediately to the point. "How are those new lenses?" he asked.

I came right out with it that I was too cheap to buy lenses that would only see service for two months. Doctor said nothing. How punishing those silent moments can be. I had no idea what he was thinking as he put drops in my eyes. Perhaps it occurred to him that in his career he had never encountered this level of insubordination.

The drops in, he came back to the topic. "Your left eye is stable now and set for reading without glasses, but the focal length must be changed for driving. Why don't you use the prescription that I gave you and just change the left lens? That should be a permanent solution for driving. When your right eye stabilizes after we operate on it, we can change the right lens."

This solution was so rational. It provided me with a perfect left eye for driving at half the cost. I had to acknowledge this new suggestion. It came to my mind to say, "Very well," but I knew it had a condescending tone to it. From a couple of tours in the Navy I knew that a ship's captain said "Very well" to the starboard lookout when the lookout said he had spotted a Japanese cruiser on the horizon. It wouldn't do. I searched my repertoire and came up with "By God, I'll do it." It was an inadequate response, but all I could come up with on short notice. This phrase implied camaraderie between us that did not exist. It was as though I was saying to Doctor, "You have a great idea, you've expressed it well, sold me, in fact. I'm going along with it." Doctor let it go at that but he may have felt patronized again.

Leaving the lens crisis behind us, I turned to science. "Doctor," I asked, "how is it that the pupil is always round without regard to the size of the opening?" He answered, "There's a circular muscle in the eye which adjusts the size of the opening to let in the light required. Most animals have circular pupils but some have oval (I knew he was talking about cats) but none has square pupils." He gave a little chuckle and I knew he liked what he had said. Then he added, "The eye, someone upstairs designed it."

There it was. He was acknowledging my not being able to read the numbers of the hymns from thirty feet away. He was willing to discuss the superscripts in the opera house but never mentioned the hymn board. Now, in this circumspect fashion, he was connecting the Almighty to the eye. The sly fox. He could have told me to carry my binoculars to church, but no, he waited a month or so and made reference by innuendo.

I repaired to the optometrist who had made the glasses and handed him the prescription, with instructions to manufacture the left lens only. He went to a file cabinet and pulled out the records on his original work. He studied all the documents in his hands and said, "It will be too confusing to leave the original lens for the right eye in place while we insert the perfect lens for the left. I'll call Doctor to find out if I can remove the right lens when I put in the new, left one. You will end up with glasses that have just one lens." I was rocked on my heels at this development. Few things strike terror in me more than experts disagreeing. I said "OK" and went out to my car, weaving slightly.

Speaking of experts, I left out a portion of this story because I thought it insignificant at the time but I see now that it has to be included. Doctor, with years of experience and batteries of equipment, knew down to a wavelength the troubles with my eyes, and when and how to fix them. Yet, before setting the date for the operation he dispatched me to another doctor who specializes in the health of retinas. I thought then and do presently that this was a case of overspecialization. Retinas can suffer from macular degeneration, or failure to grasp the image and transmit it to the brain. Doctor wanted the opinion of another doctor that it was not macular degeneration but cataracts that my eyes suffered from. The level of behind-covering that I was causing among these doctors gave me insight into the financial difficulties experienced by Medicare Part B, the portion of Medicare that reimburses physicians.

In a few days, Optometrist called and I swung by for my new one-lens glasses. Optometrist had called Doctor and they had agreed to remove the right lens. I tried them on. Wow! Out the shop window and across the street I saw detail that I had forgotten existed. Yes, I was out $40, but what a difference a lens makes.

I drove the car carefully onto the avenue and realized that something was wrong. My brain was trying to make sense of the combined signal from the eyes, one being operated on and the other not yet. The signals wouldn't mix. The glasses went back into the glove compartment. I was seeing very well without them but watched traffic like a hawk. A few months would pass before I mastered the one-lens glasses.

The operation on the right eye was scheduled and I had to see Doctor on the day prior for another routine check-up. I hoped to come up with a way of telling him that the newly formulated glasses were the cat's pajamas without telling him that I never wore them. It would take some doing.

Lady Luck ran with me on the day of this final examination. Doctor did not bring up the matter of the new lens. Of course he knew that I had placed the order for it as Optometrist had telephoned him about the advisability of removing the right lens. So why plough old ground, he must have said to himself?

Doctor was satisfied that the eye he had operated on was in perfect shape and that the other eye would be perfect after he had operated on that one. He said as much. I realized that surgeons couldn't be modest. What would be my reaction if Doctor said, "I gave it my best shot. Looks like everything will be OK. Listen, be grateful, you can still see. Not all my patients can say that." I would have been too shocked to have a reaction.

As the examination drew to a close, Doctor spoke about adding drops of pure water to the eyes three times a day to keep them irrigated. After receiving that instruction, I changed the subject drastically to racial ophthalmology and asked, "Why do so many Asians wear glasses?" He took the question in stride and answered, "The gene for near-sightedness is very powerful. If either the husband or the wife has the gene, and the other one does not, the odds are very good that all the children will be near-sighted." I asked the obvious question, whether there had been many near-sighted people in Asia over the centuries. I should have realized that before the advent of a census, before eyeglasses, doctors, and statistics, no one could have had an answer to my question. I had learned that Doctor could bob and weave around a question with the best of them. He said, "Asians take care of one another, and those with poor eyesight were not eaten by tigers." I knew by then that Doctor could speak in code. Here he meant that the Law of Natural Selection did not apply to Chinese with poor eyesight. I caught this reference to Darwin and had visions of all near-sighted Chinese living in two or three contiguous provinces, surrounded by a wall that they are good at building, protected from tigers on the outside by the wall and 20-20 Chinese sprinkled here and there. We paused to allow our separate images to settle in, and then Doctor asked me, "If you or I had gone to the Galapagos, do you think that we would have grasped it?" I could see that Doctor was one of those rare individuals who could skip past large blocks of useless conversation, knowing in advance the contributions of each party, to get at the conclusion that interested him. I said, "No, we probably could not have ," then added, "but Darwin for all his brilliance sat around for twenty-five years before committing his findings to paper, and then only because he was pressed forward by the competition, an all-too-human trait." I realized that this was a long sentence for me to say aloud as I mixed several irrelevant notions. Doctor nodded, and then said that more and more Americans were turning up near-sighted, but that modern surgical techniques were coming to the rescue. I wanted to ask him if the cause was a surge in Anglo-Asian marriages but I realized that time was up.

Once in the car, I stopped to conclude my thoughts on the matter. First, he ignored my problem with reading the hymn board, and then he acknowledged a suspicion that the Almighty had been in on the design of the eye. His latest maneuver was to bring Darwin into focus. Clever man. He stands in many places at once. I had always thought that Asians were near-sighted because they spent their days looking into microscopes, but not so, apparently. The second operation is scheduled for tomorrow morning. I'm glad Doctor's on my side.

# The Right Eye

Before recounting the events at the hospital leading up to the operation on the right eye, it makes sense to write the vignette that follows to illustrate that our lives move along in strange and fascinating ways. We are aware of this phenomenon but need reminding occasionally.

My sister's house has a dish on a tower that is aimed at the satellite that re-broadcasts France's TV Channel 5. The daylong coverage includes a weekly half-hour with the darling of French intellectuals, Bernard Pivot. This gentleman gathers authors around him and they tear into topics. On his Friday program recently, M. Pivot discussed the prediction by Nostradamus that the French King, Henry II (1519 – 1559), would die in single combat. The event did take place, the jousting match, and Henry II died from a wound to the eye. A member of the panel added that with one eye out, the king soon enough lost sight in his other eye.

I had only a vague notion about Nostradamus and therefore sought him out in the encyclopedia. He was French, carried the name of Michel de Notredame, and lived from 1503 to 1566. His career began with medicine and ended in astrology, perhaps a natural progression. His predictions were made in four lines of verse called quatrains, the quatrains being packaged in sets of 100, or centuries. Nostradamus produced ten centuries, the seventh incomplete. Plans for the eleventh and twelfth centuries were interrupted by his death.

At the library, "The Further Prophesies of Nostradamus," by Erika Cheetham, (Putnam Publishing Group), gave these details. Quatrain 35 of Century 1 says this of the king, not specifically Henry II. "The young lion will overcome the older one, in a field of combat in single host: He will pierce his eyes in their golden cage; two wounds in one, then he dies a cruel death." The King's wife, Catherine de Medici, alarmed, summoned

Nostradamus to Paris where he arrived 15 August 1556. He was received by the queen the day following. They discussed the prediction. There appears to be no record of their conversation. Nostradamus had a brief interview with the king as well.

In 1559, as part of celebrations surrounding two weddings, the king engaged in single combat with the Conte de Montgomery. On the third of their charges against one another, Montgomery's lance broke and a piece entered the king's visor and blinded him in one eye. Neither the text nor the encyclopedia discusses the failure of the second eye.

I brought up the matter with Doctor, leaving out all the extraneous matter, going directly to the point, which was, does sight leave the second eye in some sympathetic manner if the first eye is damaged? Doctor said, yes, that it could. He said that the body's immune system, fighting to heal the wound in one eye, could blind the other. I thought that this was a design failure on the part of the heavenly personage responsible for mankind, but could not pursue the topic as the conversation concluded when he had to tend to the next patient. Doctor had the last word, saying that the sympathetic dimming of the second eye used to happen on rare occasions after failed operations for cataracts but these events no longer occurred because of the excellent microscopes now in use. He looked at me to make certain that I was reassured. He concluded by telling me that there are drugs available now that pick up the slack should the excellent microscopes fail at their job. I knew I was in over my head.

This has been a long detour on the way to the operating room but it makes the point that the pieces of one's life have a tendency to intertwine. I could have gone to my grave without knowing the little I know now about Nostradamus and Henry II had it not been for cataracts.

* * *

The person responsible for scheduling told me to be at the hospital at 6:45. I asked her whether anyone else would be there at that hour. She assured me that the hospital came to life at five. The operating rooms are on the fifth floor and it is in surrounding spaces that one sheds clothes and dons a surgical gown, answers the same questions for the third time, and waits to be wheeled in for the operation.

While in the waiting mode, I noticed a familiar face. "I remember you, you were my anesthesiologist when we did the left eye." "So I was," she said. There followed a few perfunctory questions about how the first operation was progressing, and a comment to her colleague, an anesthesiologist, a male, who would be knocking me out for the right eye. I could sense her alertness, watch her smile, be made aware of her confidence, and recognize the beauty in her. She had the other beauty as well but it was concealed from the casual observer by the green pants and shirt that medicos wear around operating rooms. For an instant I wished that she had drawn me for the morning, but had she, I would not have seen her in this slightly different role, much of her interesting personality made evident, compressed into a minute or two.

Doctor said no fluids after midnight and perhaps because of that, intravenous feeding of water and glucose was started before being wheeled to the operating room. The bag containing the water hung about two feet above my body. The plastic hose that connected the bag to my hand where the needle entered the body had a plumbing fixture halfway, which was used to insert the knockout drops.

On arrival at the operating room, Anesthesiologist affixed electrocardiogram sensors to my chest. I suppose that vital signs are monitored during the operation. I remarked that there was no music. Nurse said, "I can fix that." Instead of Respighi, the room filled with a mixture of elevator and dental office music. Doctor said, "If it's heavy metal, I have it turned off." Nurse and Anesthesiologist tied my wrists to the side of the operating table. He said, "I don't want you to assist Doctor in this operation." A good line, I thought, and wondered how many times he had used it.

When I came to, Doctor patted me on the shoulder and said everything went perfectly. As it was he who deserved congratulations, I should have been patting him on the shoulder but my wrists were still attached to the sides of the bed.

In the recovery room I was able to promote a cup of coffee. I answered more questions from yet another nurse. She was as attractive as the lady anesthesiologist and I wondered whether the hospital recruited on the basis of looks. All that aside, I was struck by the high level of competence and supposed that an expectation for excellence had become the norm for all departments of the hospital.

* * *

The day after the operation, Doctor removed the bandage from the right eye, pronounced that the eye was recovering nicely, and that I had a constitution that promoted rapid healing. He had me stare at the eye chart, blanking one eye then the next. The line containing the smallest letters that can be recognized determines whether sight for that eye is 20-20, or 20-30, etc. This prompted me to ask Doctor for a definition of this measurement. He said that the simple explanation of 20-30 is that if he had 20-20 vision and I had 20-30, he could see as clearly at thirty feet as I could see at twenty feet. I did not think that his definition was simple at all because it involved two persons. I should have let it go at that. He went on. The technical definition is that a person with 20-20 vision can detect five minutes of arc at twenty feet. Let's break this down. There are 360 degrees in a circle and 60 minutes in each degree. If one is situated at the center of a circle twenty feet in radius, then one degree of arc at twenty feet is the circumference of the circle divided by 360 degrees. This would be $2\pi$ times 20ft. divided by 360, or 0.35ft. This distance, 0.35 ft., approximately one-third of a foot, turns out to be 4.2 inches. But as each degree has sixty minutes of arc, 4.2 inches must be divided by sixty then multiplied by five to give us 0.35 inch. So a good set of orbs can detect a gap of 0.35 inch, or a third of an inch, at twenty feet. I didn't care to ask him about the gap that a set of 20-30 eyes could detect at twenty feet.

While I was at it, I asked him why German generals wore monocles in the First World War. Or did they wear them only in the films? He said that a monocle is a simple way to correct one eye for reading without the bother of something as massive as glasses. I thought of German generals reading maps on the western front. Doctor added that it was not uncommon presently to correct one eye for close work and the other for distant objects by prescribing different contact lenses. I thought of how scrambled the brains would become and thought of the glasses in my glove compartment that were sitting idle.

* * *

Between weekly visits, I became intrigued about measurements of the eye's ability to see. Particularly, I didn't know the difference between 20-30 and 30-20. And I didn't understand Doctor's first definition well enough to tell another person about it.

A certain Dr. Snellen, it turns out, had made measurements about one hundred years previously and determined that the Gaussian distribution curve, or the bell curve as it is called often, applied to the ability to see. He assigned 20-20 as the norm, the top of the curve that characterized the vision of most young people. To the left of the center of the curve he placed people with vision that he described as 30-20, 40-20, 50-20, etc. In this set of numbers, the first number indicates the distance that the individual is away from the object that is being observed and the second number indicates the distance away from the object that the average person must be to see as clearly as the individual under discussion. So a person with 30-20 vision can see an object as clearly from thirty feet as the average person can from twenty feet. The lucky people with 40-20 vision must be the ones who can see the hands on a clock tower two miles away. The Gaussian curve of distribution tails off on both sides as you leave the center. There are fewer people with 30-20 vision than there are with 20-20, fewer with 40-20 than with 30-20, and so on. People with 100-20 are rare birds indeed. Perhaps they are visionaries. Dr. Snellen was Hermann Snellen (1834-1908), a Dutch ophthalmologist.

How about the unlucky ones? They have vision described as 20-30, 20-40, 20-50, etc. The first number, twenty, is the number of feet that the person is away from the object, and the second number is the distance away from the object that the average person must be to see it as clearly as the person being described. So a person with 20-40 vision can see an object twenty feet away as clearly as the average person can see the same object standing forty feet away. These people tend to wear glasses most of the time.

After giving me these details, Doctor said, "You will certainly end up knowing something about the eye." I guessed that he suspected me of obtaining this bizarre information with some devious purpose in mind.

* * *

During a follow-up examination Doctor warned me against swimming. Concerning pools he said that chlorine doesn't kill everything and that there are objects floating around, presumably small living things that I wouldn't want to know about. He was imagining that one of these animals would work itself through the half-healed slit he had made to change the lens, and once inside my eyeball, would just raise hell. He scared me off pools. What about the ocean? He said that the ocean was not as clean as it once was. He knew I wanted to dive into the surf. He could have scared me off as he had done with pools, but he said that I could go in backward up to my chest. He didn't want waves breaking in my face. A few days later I found myself with a companion at the shore, well south of Los Angeles, and determined that some salt water jumps into your eyes no matter the precautions taken. Doctor's warning had not been strong enough.

The next-to-last examination was routine, so much so that Doctor was free to chat about the weather. "Has it started to rain?" he asked. I assured him that it had and he told me his wife would be pleased at it was she who tended the garden. "I never do any gardening," he said. Then he added, "I don't mind carrying the mulch around for her, but I just don't garden."

I didn't know where he was going with this departure but I suspected he would accomplish closure, if not right then, perhaps during the final examination. I knew him well enough by this time to know that he would not introduce gardening without having a purpose that made some point in the matter of eye care. I had been made to wait before.

* * *

Three weeks had passed. I was in the examining room and Doctor had finished measuring the pressure in my right eye. He said, "Twelve." I asked, "Is that good?" He answered, "Perfect." All his examinations of my eyes had ended on that note. I wondered what he would say if a measurement did not suit him.

There was a moment of silence, and then Doctor said, "Gardening is the opposite of operating on your eyes. In gardening you go from course to fine. Look at the tools they use, the rough treatment of the ground, the casual way my wife plants seeds. And yet the outcome is so fine. Is there a more beautiful sight than a well-tended garden in bloom?" I managed to slip in, "Of course not," before he went on. "When I operate on your eyes I go from fine to coarse. Phenomenally accurate instruments, latest techniques, yet I can't predict the final shape of your eye and therefore cannot select the focal length of the plastic lens that will do a perfect job for you. It's an approximation."

"The left eye is settling nicely, as you can tell," I said.

"Past performance is no indication of future results," Doctor replied. He smiled and I knew he was satisfied.

I asked him, "Did you carry the bags of mulch around the garden for your wife?"

"Oh, yes," he said. "It's my contribution."

* * *

One night not long ago, I was driving in my neighborhood and objects looked a bit bleary. I pulled over and reached for the glasses in the glove compartment. The frame had only the left lens. I slipped them on and presto, all came clear. Doctor had forgotten to tell me that the glasses might be perfect for driving at night. Perhaps I had distracted him with my questions.

# Short Fiction Pieces

# Saving The Planet

Brian Osborn was pushing his old-style lawn mower in straight lines across the small lawn. He tended to do this on alternate Saturday mornings. His neighbor of twenty years, Nat Edmonds, held to the same schedule. Without discussing it, they both knew that they could care for their gardens and solve the world's problems simultaneously by working together on the same Saturdays. If pressed for an opinion, both would admit that talking was more important than gardening.

Their gardening was ritualistic. Brian always arrived on the scene first, and for the fact that Nat was always second there could only be one reason, that he looked out the window at his neighbor's lawn, or listened intently for the correct sound before making an appearance himself. Brian had never brought up the matter of his arriving first, sensing that Nat's participation in gardening was only for camaraderie, and that gardening was simply a vehicle to that end. Nat's opening line was also ritualistic; that is, he always said the same thing. "Hi Brian, how in the world are you?" This particular Saturday Brian answered, "Not bad, except for yesterday afternoon." Nat was forced to say, "Well, what happened yesterday afternoon?"

"I was at the library doing research, back in the corner of one of the reading rooms, and a stream of employees kept coming out of the door and letting it slam. Drove me nuts."

"Why didn't you move, or is that too logical?" Nat asked.

"The books on the topic I was researching are located in that corner, so it made sense to stay there," Brian said.

"Don't you think you might have researched another topic?" Nat asked.

"Nat, I have to research psychiatry at some point, and neither the door nor the books are about to move, so I thought I may as well get it over with," Brian answered.

"It's only Freud and Jung, so you might have bought the books and done your research at home," Nat said.

"That gets expensive if you plan to do research on several topics," Brian answered.

"You retired too soon. If you were still working, you wouldn't have time to do research," Nat said.

"As I've told you, friend, my company wanted me out of there at sixty-five. Any way you slice it, the trouble is with the door and the people who pass through it. No employee at the library holds the door to keep it from slamming, and the door closes wood to wood, or wood to metal. No rubber bumpers. The noise wakes the dead," Brian said.

Brian knew that once Nat was satisfied he would generalize the subject by fitting it into some large category. The fact that Nat paused told Brian that the moment had arrived. Nat was in the process of determining the category into which he would place all this business of doors slamming.

"Do you suppose we are talking about noise or architects?" Nat asked.

"Some of both," Brian answered.

"If we limit it to noise, then our topic heads off in one direction. If we discuss architects, then it's in another," Nat said.

Brian and Nat were seated on the top step of the stairs leading from Brian's lawn to the sidewalk. Brian's lawnmower was where he left it, in the middle of the lawn. Nat's was where he had left it, in his driveway.

"Let's do architecture," Brian said.

"OK, let's," Nat said, and he started in. "As I analyze it, the slamming door is the responsibility of the architect. The fellow ought to know how to design a door that closes slowly at the end, finally coming to rest against a rubber bumper. Not very demanding technically, really. I mean, given a week or so, I could design something."

"I know you could, Nat. Your screen door doesn't slam. I don't know what you did, but it's quiet," Brian said.

"I'll show you sometime," Nat said. "But you remember *The Bridges of Madison County*? I read the book and couldn't resist seeing the movie, Meryl Streep and Dirty Harry. You remember the whole story revolves around the screen door? The hero comes to town with his cameras and meets this woman whose family is at the state fair. He doesn't slam the door to the back porch and ends up in bed with her."

"There must be more to the story than that," Brian said.

"Yes, but without the screen door there wouldn't be any story, believe me," Nat said.

"Architects ought to be made to sit next to their doors for a month after one of their buildings opens. That should show 'em," Brian said. Then he added, "But you were about to open the topic to something bigger. I could sense it when you gave me a choice, noise or architects. Do you remember what that was?"

"Remember? Of course I remember," Nat said. "It's about the design of men's rest rooms. That's definitely the responsibility of the architect. Plenty of them are designed so that when you open the door from the hall, you can see the guys standing there relieving themselves. It shouldn't take any brains to move things around so you don't have that view from the hall."

"I know what you mean," Brian said. "Makes a guy nervous. All the architect has to do is interchange the wash basins with the urinals. Piece of cake."

Nat asked, "How come they do that? Architects ought to know better. Certainly they use the facilities in public buildings. How do you account for it?"

Brian fell silent. Finally he said, "Beats me." Then he felt that it was his turn to enlarge the topic beyond noise and architects. "Nat, my friend, we've just begun. The prime faults of architects have been isolated – slamming doors and embarrassing layouts for men's rooms. Why don't we enlarge the scope? I'm thinking about something big. How about a manifesto, an analysis of all the changes we could make to save the planet?"

"Just you and me, we're to save the planet?" Nat asked.

"Sounds ambitious, but we have to start. Nothing happens in this world unless one person, or in our case, two people start something."

Brian and Nat remained on the stairs a while longer, discussing this ambitious plan of issuing a manifesto on saving the planet. Before their wives called them for lunch, they broke off and finished their lawns. They raked up their cuttings and put them into a green garbage can they shared. Brian asked, "Shall we do our hedges tomorrow? We could talk some more."

* * *

Twenty-four hours later they were back to gardening. Nat led off. He said, "I've come up with some topics. We only touched the surface yesterday. My list is not endless, but we have enough for a few chapters. I also thought about the entire topic of manners."

Brian chimed in, "That's good. Do you want to tackle the field of signs; you know, road signs, signs in subways, all the illegible small type on modern packaging?"

"Sounds great. Do you want to venture into politics? After all, this is a manifesto," Nat said.

"That could be beyond our ability," Brian admitted. "We don't have any expertise there."

"But remember what you said, you have to start," Nat reminded him.

"Well, OK, let's get the other stuff out of the way first, then we'll look at politics if we can get up the energy," Brian said.

They sat on the top stair again. Both had placed their shears on the ground and leaned their rakes against a magnolia tree on Brian's lawn. Nat pulled a piece of paper from his pocket and announced that he had worked up an organization for the topic of noise. Brian said, "Let's see." Nat handed him the paper and Brian read out loud.

"Conversation, announcements, music." Then Brian said, "That's to the point." He followed by reading the entries under each of the three headings. Under conversation, Brian found 'general rule,' 'cell phones,' and 'shouting on the street late at night.' Under announcements he read, 'railroad stations, airports and planes,' and under music he read 'restaurants and cars.' "I like it," Brian said. "You've put a lot into it. Where would you put slamming doors? Under architects?"

"No," Nat said. "Because we covered it yesterday I didn't think to add it to the list, but it's so important that it has to go on the top line with conversation, announcements, and music. My mistake. And by the way, we're not through with doors. When we discuss manners, we'll talk about holding the door for the person behind you."

"This might turn into a matrix," Brian said. "Tell me your general rule on conversation," he added.

"It's obvious, really, as most universally accepted rules and conventions are, particularly in the scientific fields. This one isn't scientific but it might become so. The rule is this: the level of sound need only be loud enough to reach the people taking part in the conversation. That's Nat's rule of conversation."

"That's brilliant, and therefore obvious. You may be introducing whispering as an art form," Brian suggested.

"Well, it makes sense. You don't raise your voice in the middle of the night when you're talking to your wife in bed."

"How about when you're arguing?" Brian asked.

"Well, that's the exception, of course. But in general, keep it down. People in airplanes, restaurants, or at the office should remain aware of surroundings. It's called consideration."

"I think we'll find that consideration will play an important role before we're through," Brian said.

"Yes, when we get to manners, it should dominate," Nat agreed.

"How about conversation on cell phones? What's your thought there?" Brian asked.

"A great deal has been said already on the topic. Our minister started his sermon on it a couple of weeks ago. Had to do with communicating with God. I had the point of it at the time but it escapes me now," Nat said.

"That is a bit of a reach, communicating with God, as though there were an 800 number. But people raise their voices for no good reason, and that's a violation of Nat's rule right there. I mean, who cares what you have to say on your cell phone?"

It was Nat's turn. He paused for a minute, then in a reflective tone he said, "I think we'll find that the rule on conversation fits into our manifesto. Rules, axioms, and principles go down better than a mere collection of words when you're writing something as important as a manifesto."

"Agreed," Brian said. "I think it's time we move on to announcements on our list. What's that all about?"

"Well again," Nat said in a voice filled with pontification, "Let's look for the underlying principle. In general, loudspeaker systems don't work. They make noise, but they don't convey any information. The signal to noise ratio, if you want to get technical, is zero."

"Right on," Brian said.

Nat carried on. "In railroad stations and airports, the announcements echo around the large spaces and there's no content. That's the technical problem. The psychological problem comes when you're asleep on a red-eye flight, or any flight for that matter, and the pilot comes on to tell you that you're over Grand Junction, Colorado. Well, I'm sorry. First, I don't care. Second, I can't see Grand Junction from 37,000 feet in the middle of the night, or in broad daylight, for that matter. And third, the pilot overdrives the mike – he holds it right up to his mouth instead of eight inches away, so that when he says the consonants it's a bass drum right in your ear."

"Nat, you're getting a lot off your chest," Brian interjected.

"I almost forgot the fourth – some of the pilots are low on grammar. They say 'there's two points of interest out the left side' instead of 'there are two points of interest.' They've abandoned the plural."

Brian thought for a minute. He said, "That's good. We could add grammar as a category by itself. It's being assaulted pretty seriously on all sides."

"Our manifesto could grow into a book," Nat said.

"Well, Karl Marx's manifesto was book length if you add the introduction," Brian reflected.

Nat was silent, perhaps thinking about Communism. Then he said, "Marx and Engels, they both had beards. Let's not go there. We can keep our manifesto short. Just end it on announcements by saying we need new technology. Just admit that the loudspeakers don't work. Look at the name, loudspeakers. Should be softspeakers."

"Very well thought through," Brian said.

* * *

They clipped their hedges for a while. Brian's wife Madge came out with two glasses of lemonade. "Looks very good, gents. You haven't been clipping all along, have you?" she asked.

"No, dear," Brian answered. "We're saving the planet. Writing a manifesto on the changes required to our civilization to save it from itself."

"That's so charitable of you both. Thoughtful and touching, really. Put it down on paper, and I'll be glad to type it up."

They said, "Thanks, Madge," in unison.

# Space Ship

Caleb Shepard's car radio had been left on. It came to life as he turned the key in the ignition. When he put the car in reverse, he heard the announcer say, "The sun is a space ship." The news followed, and Caleb failed to note the station, the program, or the announcer's name. The sentence that he had heard didn't seem important to him at first. Not until he arrived at work would it start to play in his mind, not going away.

On his drive home he concentrated on the idea. Had he been listening to the end of a bit of science fiction, or a comment by a professor of astronomy, or the conclusion by a serious scientist on the purpose of the solar system? Nine or ten hours had passed since the announcer had said the words. Caleb wondered whether other listeners had been swept up by them. He guessed that most listeners just let the words glide by. Caleb had never thought that the sun was a space ship. It had never occurred to him. His concept of a space ship had been established by the ones he saw in films. They were large metal affairs, sheets of steel or titanium riveted together, rocket engines that emitted a low-frequency rumble, with men and women in futuristic suits at the controls, engaged in mortal combat against alien galaxies. These space ships were the stuff of movies, not to be taken seriously. The stories surrounding them tried one's patience. How could anyone believe in such foolishness?

The sun as a space ship, now that was reasonable. Had every intelligent person on the planet realized this to be the case? Was he the last to know? He might ask a few friends. They could answer, "Where have you been?" Alternatively, they could be dismissive, saying, "What have you been smoking?" Perhaps the truth of the matter would come to him and he wouldn't have to bring it up to anybody. He would just wait and see. Perhaps from one source he would figure out that everybody knew the sun was a space ship. From yet another source he might learn that someone was joking around on the radio. In truth, the sun is no more a space ship than Mars or some old asteroid. But Caleb liked the notion.

The sun as a space ship had a feature that all the make-believe space ships lacked. The sun carried its own energy. By Jove, the sun was energy. Most space ships of fiction contained a nuclear reactor for propulsion. They seemed hokey to Caleb. On the other hand here was a source of energy with an estimated life span of fifty billion years that emitted light, heat, and gravitational pull, and was at the center of an orderly system, one of whose planets had life. It started to make sense to Caleb. The space ships in the movies didn't even have bathrooms, while the sun owned the earth on which everything imaginable existed.

Caleb saw that a new vision of the universe was coming his way. He would go easy, and let it fit into place in his mind. He wouldn't work on it. He would let it come to him. Perhaps he was the one chosen to make the Revelation.

When the flat earth people went away for good, and those who held the earth to be center of the universe gave up the struggle, mankind was left with a workable model. Neither a group nor an individual had come along in the last five hundred years to suggest a new arrangement. Caleb knew all that. Peace of sorts had reigned among scientists and intellectuals for five centuries. The sun was a medium-sized star off to one side of the Milky Way, consuming the time allotted to it as it drifted through space. But this settled notion might change, Caleb suspected. If the sun was a space ship, then it had a destination, and objects with destinations have missions. It could be, it dawned on Caleb, that the view developed five hundred years ago, while satisfactory, was incomplete.

As Caleb pulled off the highway into his neighborhood he wondered whether it would be appropriate to discuss this concept with his wife of 28 years, Ann M. Shepard. The M stood for Modulowski. During a severe argument about ten years ago, Caleb had organized a paragraph that questioned his wife's intellect on the basis of her ethnic background. She had shot back that while his forefathers had gone fishing for whales, and hers had grown sugar beets on Polish farms, neither occupation required any brains, and that he and the entire Mayflower crowd could go to hell. With that out of the way he had apologized, they had had a drink, and he vowed to himself to understand condescension for what it was and be rid of it. Ann, for her part, knowing that she had established parity with her husband, unloaded the few vestiges of dumb-blondism that remained in her personality. Caleb concluded that on the basis of how well they had been getting along these past ten years he would risk discussing his new idea with his wife. At the very least she would humor him. At most, she would sign on.

Caleb turned into the driveway and turned off the ignition. Rather than get out of the car, he determined to view his new domain. He placed his mind one hundred million miles above the sun and studied the expanse of the solar system. There was little Mercury, perilously close to the sun, then Venus, followed by the earth and Mars, then a gap to the giant Jupiter, and on out to the others. Pluto was faint.

Caleb's father had been a high school science teacher and it was not uncommon that he turned dinner table conversation toward activities in the classroom. One of his favorite topics was infinity and he would go after the Big Bang theorists once in a while. Caleb's brother and sister knew the arguments and participated on cue. They had no choice. Their father would say, "You go to the end of the universe and arrive at the wall. But there's a door. Caleb, you open the door and what do you see?" Caleb would answer, "More universe, Dad."

"So the universe is limitless, isn't it?" the father would press on. "Yes, it is," the children would say in chorus. Caleb's father would follow the same line of reasoning for time and matter, and then deliver his crushing blow against the Big Bang, saying that if matter is infinite, it would never have been gathered into a thimble so that it might explode.

Caleb felt at ease with the solar system. He reached over for his briefcase, pulled the keys out of the ignition, and stepped out of the car. As he came in through the front door, his wife called from upstairs. "Were you solving a banking crisis in the driveway?"

It hadn't occurred to Caleb that his sitting in the car for two minutes was unusual behavior that his wife would ask about. Now that she had, he realized the convenient opening he had been handed.

"Other deep thoughts," he answered.

"Pour yourself one; I'll be right down," she said.

Caleb knew that Ann, as was her custom, had come home from work, gone to the refrigerator, opened the bottle of white wine, poured a glass and taken it upstairs to nurse on while she changed out of her suit into something casual. Ann, a nurse, had worked in the wards, in the operating rooms, and now found herself in administration. Her entire career had been at the hospital. In fact, they had torn down the original hospital about fifteen years ago and had built a new one around her. His career had been at the bank. They met in high school and married when they were both starting out. Ann had never asked him why he had married her. Had she, he might have lied. He had been lonely after serving his two years in the Army, desperately lonely, and the thought of limitless sex appealed to him. He admitted that he was desperate for sex at that time. On those two pillars, loneliness and sex, they had built a strong marriage that weathered children, a mortgage, and the normal imbecilities that accompany any union of 28 years. At least Caleb thought so.

Ann came down the stairs and turned into the living room. Her glass was still half full. Her hair was pulled back in a bun and her face washed clean of all makeup. She had put on tan shorts and a blue shirt left tucked out. She wore no shoes and this much body usually destabilized Caleb. She kissed him and said, "Well, what were you thinking about in the car?"

Caleb poured out his new point of view on space. Ann did not interrupt him. When he came to the end of his recitation, she said, "The mission and the destination, those are the new pieces, aren't they?"

"Yes, and the idea that our local God and the sun are linked inextricably. Those old Egyptians and their sun god, they were on to something," Caleb answered.

"In your thoughts," Ann asked, boring in, "did you come up with a destination and a mission?"

"I realized that important conclusions take years, if not centuries, to be formulated and take their rightful place. Look at old Copernicus, he cleaned it up after less able scientists and philosophers had obscured matters for four thousand years."

"He was Polish," Ann interjected.

"Yes. I'm aware of that. Nikolai Copernik, or something. He didn't grow sugar beets."

Ann smiled. It had become a small joke between them used on occasions. They drank white wine from their tall stemmed glasses.

Ann resumed. "You can't use that as an excuse, the fact that you just thought of it. Your idea means nothing if you can't flesh it out with at least one destination and perhaps several choices for a mission."

"The signals are very faint, my dear," Caleb said. "Mankind is young. The Copernicus theory is the undisputed model now, but in that position, it will give way to a new model soon enough. That's the way it works. Look at what happened to Newton. Einstein downgraded him into a local, slow-motion physicist. I mean, you step off the earth, and everything's relative."

"For a banker, you know a lot of stuff," Ann said.

"My father, the high school science teacher," Caleb answered. Then he went on. "You know, we're moving out of our galaxy. We're leaving the Milky Way, on our way to visit other constellations."

"What would be the purpose of that?" Ann asked.

"So that humans could gather ever more knowledge, and perhaps, just perhaps, plant the seed on unpopulated planets around distant stars," Caleb said.

He paused and filled their glasses. Ann said, "That's brilliant. No direction except for drifting; and as for purposes: populating distant planets, uncovering the final truths, finding the reasons behind all this."

"That should work," Caleb said.

"You have no proof?" Ann asked.

"None at all, but if I announced this revelation, this prophesy, the great scientists would jump on it and supply the details."

"Bankers aren't prophets," Ann said. "And prophets certainly are not white," she added. She went on, "Gandhi was brown as a berry. You'd look awful in a sheet."

"Still, I have to get out the word," Caleb said.

"How about posthumously?" Ann asked.

"You mean append it to my will?"

"Our wills," Ann said. "It will be known as the Modulowski-Shepard Accord. If you don't have some Polish in there it'll never fly."

"That could save us some embarrassment during our lives if we're wrong," Caleb said, falling into agreement.

Ann looked at Caleb and said, "I haven't started dinner."

Over the years, during a rough patch, or any moment when her husband's mind had gone into overdrive, off on some tangent, Ann had always been able to return him to a stable place by drowning him with good sex. She thought they had a fine marriage.

# Fourth Of July

Abner Cochrane had two children, one from each marriage. He could not understand why his children still gave him the time of day. Perhaps it stemmed from the genuine affection he felt for them, which he could demonstrate by small acts of kindness once in a while, such as cleaning a garage.

Both his wives threw him out, the first for womanizing, and the second for boozing it up on the way to being found out that he was a womanizer. Abner loved women and in his early years, say fifteen to forty, graded them on their susceptibility to his charms or entreaties. He was interested in them to the extent that they could be talked into sleeping with him. While Abner used to chat about women at work, before he retired, and talked casually about women with his friends, on the whole he remained discreet.

There was a part of his love of women that he never discussed, not with anyone. It was his deepest secret. The topic had to do with his views on race. The Cochranes were from Kentucky, and Abner, as an adult, had moved to the West Coast and never left. He had been collecting impressions of Asian women from the time he hit California, and his impressions of black women went back to the age of twelve or so, when he discovered women, as a young lad living in Kentucky. As he grew up, he used the term "colored" when discussing African-American citizens. Later on, people stopped saying "colored" and went to African-American. Abner noticed that this term, in turn, was replaced by "black" and his orderly world was thrown into confusion.

While he had slept with more white women than he could count, he had never had sex with either an Asian or an African-American woman. He felt that crossing the racial divide called for a commitment that he was not willing to make. He would be glad to marry any woman he fell in love with, but he could not see how he would be accepted into either Asian-American or African-American society.

Of the two, Abner preferred black women. He felt that Asian women were closed corporations. They had invented the tea ceremony. They knelt down and kept their eyes averted. How in the world would he approach one of these ladies? What could he say? Black women, on the other hand, were open and cheerful, laughing and in motion, apparently easy to get along with. Abner's secret, and he would never let this out, coming from a border state like Kentucky, was that he loved dark skin. He had always wanted to touch, feel and kiss women with that smooth, brown skin. He knew that it was one of the few smart aspects of his long entanglement with women that he had never allowed himself that pleasure. He guessed other men had their secrets.

The daughter from the first marriage invited Abner to accompany her to a Fourth of July party given by her neighbors across the street. She would include him in affairs of this type and he reciprocated by helping around her house and by taking her to dinner once in a while. They kept the proper distance from one another, or so Abner thought.

Abner knew from his daughter that the family across the street was black, and that the husband was from Nigeria, and his wife an African-American. His daughter had told him all that. He knew as well that it was a second marriage for both and that he could expect two sets of children, their spouses and offspring. Although there had been costly repercussions to Abner over his women and booze, there was the positive result that he was socially at ease. He had been in all the situations, failed in some, succeeded in other, and now in his mid-seventies he felt entirely relaxed in any and all surroundings. Many situations were the same, after all. This party would be a piece of cake.

Abner wondered how mixed the crowd would be, not the number of blacks and whites, but the mixture of black and white genes in one person. Certainly the host, a Nigerian, would be 100% African and Abner expected this man to be black. The others, African-Americans, would be a mixture and their facial characteristics and color would reflect the particular combinations that had made them. Although Abner didn't expect any Asians at the party, he did take a moment to review his opinion of Asian-Americans, which was that the Asian genes were far stronger than their Anglo-Saxon counterparts so that he couldn't tell an Asian from an Asian-American. He also thought that Asians, or Asian-Americans, were the smartest people in the world, worked and studied harder than anyone else, stuck together as a group after landing in the United States, and all drove Japanese cars. He recognized that these views could brand him a racist so he never spoke of them. These were his private notions and as long as he didn't act on them he was in good shape. He did admit to himself that this attitude might have affected his behavior at some moments, but he couldn't remember an incident.

Around three o'clock in the afternoon of the Fourth, Abner and his daughter, still Mary Cockrane, walked across the street and to the front door. After being introduced to the host and hostess, they walked through the house to the patio, shaded with trees and furnished with tables, chairs and benches so that groups could form.

Abner sat on a bench with his back against the table. He twisted his body to engage in conversation an African-American lady his age. She was the mother of one of the female guests who was married to the host's nephew. Abner thought he had it right. After sipping wine, eating potato chips and talking to the lady, he turned his body around to address the person who had sat down next to him. He caught her profile first, and then she turned to face him. She was the most beautiful combination of black and white he had ever seen, or would ever see. He assigned her a name right away, Milk Chocolate. Her name turned out to be Shandra and Abner thought, as she must have been born in the mid-sixties, that she had been given an Anglo name with an African twist. The thought came to him that Leopoldville on the West Coast of Africa had been renamed Kinshasa. Perhaps Kinshasa sounded like Shandra. This young woman had a collection of perfect Anglo-Saxon features mixed with slightly full lips and a wide mouth in which Abner could see a set of perfect white teeth when she smiled. Her hair was long and a bit wavy. She hadn't stood up yet, so Abner had no notion about the rest of her. They talked easily. She gave him a who's who around the patio. Abner noted that most of the people were better educated than he was. No doubt they had devoted less time than he had to chasing the opposite sex, and had used the time saved to good advantage.

The host announced that he would say Grace before the meal. Everybody stood. Abner didn't recall being instructed to hold hands but suddenly he was in one of three circles doing just that. He had hold of Milk Chocolate's left hand and could feel the rings. He would have given her teacups of diamonds under different circumstances. The host gave the invocation. He went to the core of his personality and thanked God for the blessings that they were about to receive and didn't leave out the blessings they already had. His words seemed to be unrehearsed.

Abner was now standing next to Shandra. She looked as though she ran the 400 meters in college. They talked some more. She belonged with a fine looking man across the patio and two of the children playing in the garden were theirs. Abner wanted to lean forward and take a bite of Milk Chocolate. She was extraordinary. He hoped that by some miracle her parents would become the Adam and Eve of a new race of people. Anglo-Saxons and West Africans mixed together were destined to become a new race of beautiful, happy, accomplished people, with perfect teeth.

They stood in line for the evening meal. Abner, as was his habit, checked out all the women, trying to calculate which ones would have been worth the chase a few years ago. At seventy-five, his sex life consisted of looking back and reminiscing far more than it had to do with planning action. He was happy that he had plenty of memories to reflect on. A stray thought came to him on the naturalness of men being wild about sex in the years when they were able to partake. Men with power, at least some of them, gave in to their impulses. They couldn't get enough of it. Juan Peron concentrated on teen-aged girls. Napoleon binged on all the women between Paris and Warsaw. There was one he was particularly fond of in Warsaw. Abner speculated that Napoleon cut short the winter of 1812 in Moscow when he found that the local aristocracy had vacated the city with their daughters as Napoleon approached. He was back in Warsaw months before the spring. She was waiting for him. And Abner had heard that one of our presidents got a headache if he didn't have sex twice before tea time.

Abner had a paper plate in his hand and was waiting for short and long ribs. He kept speculating along the same line and wondered what was in it for the women, the ones who went to bed with the great men. Certainly it wasn't love. They must have known they were being used. Was it enough that they were servicing great men, so that in their old ages these women could reflect on having slept with this one or that one? Maybe to them, just maybe, exciting, dangerous sex was enough. In his case, Abner had never asked one of his conquests why she was doing it. There might be another opportunity tomorrow, and no use drowning all that hard work in truth serum.

Abner was a dedicated circulationist; that is, he did the room, as the politicians say, and met all the guests. This wasn't a charitable activity on his part. After all, he had met plenty of women by moving around to meet them, this one in a fur coat in the ballroom, that one in shorts at the end of the pier. He wasn't next to Milk Chocolate anymore. He would look across the patio from time to time and admire her beauty. At the moment she was sitting next to her husband in a circle of young people. They were laughing and telling stories but Abner couldn't hear what they were saying.

Someone in the garden started to sing the *Star Spangled Banner.* Everyone stood. This was nothing like singing the anthem at the ball game. This was personal. Abner looked at the faces. They were filled with joy and ardor. These were black Americans singing this song, they whose ancestors had suffered such indignities, distress, and physical abuse for so many years. It occurred to Abner that through this suffering black Americans had forced white Americans to organize a country in which people with differing races and religions could live side by side. Black Americans did not make whites organize this society to make whites feel good. They did it for self-preservation. Whites did not go along with this reorganization willingly. They went along because their own legal and constitutional arrangements prevented them from doing anything else. It was nearing the end, Abner guessed, and blacks were freer and more equal than they had ever been and were gaining a little every year. Whites began to be proud of taking part in the changes, in the process toward full equality. Abner knew that he hadn't done much more than let go.

Abner looked at the young faces. These twenty-something kids knew the words. It was their country. They seemed proud to be living here, where their hopes were bound up. Christ, this was some Fourth of July for him.

# The Fifth Gospel

"Oh, that's wonderful news!" Lisa exclaimed to her husband Stephen as he put down the telephone after talking to his agent.

"Yes. I only half expected it, you know. Collections of short stories aren't as popular as they once were," her husband said. "I'm one of the lucky ones, I suppose, with an aggressive agent in New York pounding on doors regularly. I have to conclude, though, that there is some merit in those stories."

"I don't understand it, frankly," she said. "Our attention span as a nation is plummeting and, with television, you would think that we don't read, yet there are thousand-page novels produced every day."

"Remember, there's plenty of time on airplanes. Reading has become the opiate of travelers."

"Good, I like that," she said. "So what will you be working on next?"

"I have two stories. Perhaps I can connect them. They hit me more or less at once so I suspect I was meant to connect them. Do you recall the other evening coming back from dinner? Meg turned to the lady on the passenger side, I don't remember her name..."

"Evelyn Trowbridge," his wife interjected.

"Evelyn Trowbridge, my that's a nice name. I'm sure I can use her in my story."

"Be certain to change the name, dear," his wife said.

"Thanks, and Meg told her that she had the best house in Bermuda. I think I have it right that Evelyn has invited Meg and others to spend a week there in the spring."

"What's the story, Stephen?" his wife asked.

"I don't know yet. But the remark about the best house has lodged in my brain. The angle for me is that this woman is known for her house, not for anything that she stands for or anything she has done."

"Well, you don't know that," his wife Lisa remarked. "She could very well support the symphony and a museum or two, and throw in a hospital."

Stephen thought for a moment. "You're right, of course. But no need to identify her in the story. I can even change the island. It juxtaposes in some fashion with the other story."

"Tell," Lisa said.

"You'll think this the height of something, but we need another Gospel. We must get back to basics."

Lisa said, "If you can link Evelyn Trowbridge and her perfect house in Bermuda to the need for another Gospel, you will have ascended to new heights as a writer."

"It's just an idea that struck me. I find the need for a new Gospel quite compelling," Stephen said.

"Are we straying like lost sheep?" Lisa asked.

"Yes, we are. Too many complications. Life was meant to be simple. Follow the Golden Rule. Don't be a lousy bastard all your life -- or any part of your life, for that matter," Stephen said.

"I think we enjoy the rituals," Lisa said.

"Can you see that painting by Giotto, the angel kneeling on the left, facing Mary on the right: *The Annunciation*?" Stephen asked.

"Yes," she said. "He has on a beautiful red robe trailing out behind him and she's dressed in the fashion of 13th century Florence. I think she's holding a lily. It was simpatico of the Divines to announce to Mary that she would give birth without benefit of sex."

"Exactly," he said. "The people who came after Jesus insisted on the virgin birth. They wanted a Jesus without baggage. They couldn't allow that he was tainted with sin carried down from generation to generation, from the beginning."

"Not so fast. You know that the virgin birth is in two Gospels, Matthew and Luke?" Lisa said.

"Well, there goes that story," Stephen remarked.

"Not really. Skip over the virgin birth. Go after some other concept that you don't care for, such as transubstantiation," Lisa suggested.

"You must tell me," Stephen said.

"It's the belief that when we take communion, the bread and wine become the body and blood of Christ even though they remain bread and wine."

"Well, I can attack that. Thank you. You're sure the virgin birth is in two of the Gospels? I would have thought that the concept would be invented later on."

"If you're about to write a fifth gospel, you could take a moment and read the first four, I should think," Lisa said.

"Well, fair enough," Stephen said.

Lisa went on. "Your objection to the practice of religion over the last two millennia is that people have had the audacity to construct theories based on the life of Christ, and that these detract from the original message. And now you would like to add to the stack of writings by putting together another gospel. More audacity."

"Yes, but mine will be different, somehow. It will not be fanciful theory, just a reminder to study the first four Gospels."

"Do you just flat-out write it, say your piece?" Lisa asked.

"A little invention is needed. One morning, the staff of a museum arrives to find a marble vase on the floor of the director's office. There is no known entry that anyone could have used while escaping detection. In the vase, there are sheets of parchment containing a story written in Latin. The lettering is modern. The marble is not recognizable as coming from any particular quarry. The parchment is new. The ink is analyzed easily enough in a laboratory, but it is not a formulation ever used before."

"So?" Lisa asked.

"So, the director telephones the head of the classics department at the local university who is a Jesuit priest. He comes right over and translates the contents."

"Is there a title?"

"Yes, it's called the Fifth Gospel, and it's signed by the Holy Ghost."

"Then?" she asks.

"The director makes one hundred copies of the text in Latin and one hundred of the translation, calls a press conference for purposes of exhibiting the vase and the document. The director tells the press that he has nothing further to say, which the press doesn't believe, and that the story is contained completely in the Fifth Gospel. The vase and the Latin document go into the museum's vault."

"Are you up to writing a new gospel, dear?" Lisa asks.

"It's a bit of a challenge. You're right, as usual," Stephen said.

"Will you let me read the story as you go along?" Lisa asked.

"I guess so," Stephen said, "but I'll finish the gospel before I let you see it."

* * *

*THE FIFTH GOSPEL,*
*translated from the Latin*

*"It has not been revealed to you the arrangement between yourselves and me. I supposed you could calculate the association on your own; but for reasons sometimes distressing, other times comical, you have not risen to the challenge. There has always been a remarkable unwillingness by millions to act on the fact of the Deity.*

*"The vastness of the universe cannot be comprehended by you, and with difficulty by me. There are collections of stars that go beyond those you can see. Infinity exists. I have been told that on good authority. There are powers that go beyond my power. My power is local. There is one God, and the powers vested in that personage are almighty. I derive my powers from that personage whom I have not seen, only sensed. Most of you believe that the senses are sight, touch, smell, and hearing. You leave out spiritual conveyances, which guide me and could guide you, save that you are unable to abandon earthly habits in order to take up the life of the mind.*

*"The very advanced among you ask questions about the origins of time, space, and matter. One cannot imagine a universe prior to the arrival of these three, therefore one cannot believe that these three were not always here. That is one of the dual aspects of the universe. I have accepted the concept of infinity in time, space, and matter. Time is infinite in duration. Space is infinite in dimension. Matter is infinite in mass.*

*"It is difficult to accept that infinity exists, as well, in spirituality. Humans consider themselves as the sole possessors of spirituality on Earth, and that the only other level is God, but spirituality exists in all living things, providing many levels on Earth. I, in my position, have greater powers than humans do. There are infinite layers beyond mine. The universe is infinite in all respects.*

*"Those who ask unanswerable questions also wonder about the purpose of life and mankind. I have never been told the purpose, but it has been related to me that the elements, carbon, oxygen, nitrogen, and hydrogen, and so on, were formed so that some of them could unite to create life. Others remained in the pure state or combined to form inanimate objects, such as water and rock. Having completed that arrangement, powers above me arranged for the construction of cells and for the division of one cell into two. The evidence around you that you call life comes from the God-given ability of one cell to reproduce itself by dividing in two. All life flows from that phenomenon. Accept my word; the cell and its ability to divide are from God.*

*"My powers are limited to creating individuals who may, or may not, follow a path that I hoped they would. That is, I am not able to guide an individual throughout that person's life. I am limited to starting a few persons toward a*

*goal. I am pleased that I do not have more power. I suspect that I would abuse it.*

*"I created Jesus at a time when brute force dominated affairs on Earth. I could have placed Jesus in any part of the Roman empire, or in Rome itself, but it seemed to me that he should be part of a faith and grow up to test believers and attempt to change some of their practices of worship. So many faiths start nobly, only to require alteration or to suffer collapse from within. I gave Jesus kindness and reason and thought that, through his use of these traits, he could accomplish great things. I could not have anticipated that some of those around him would abandon him, or that agents of the Empire would destroy him. Although these events were significant, it is his life that deserves re-examination.*

*"We can start with the fable of the virgin birth. My intention, it should be obvious, was to create a man who emanated from the most humble beginnings, but who could change the world. I had hoped that humanity would understand that every one of you is endowed with extraordinary talents and that the challenges of a life are to locate these talents and put them to use. I was taken by surprise by the fable of the virgin birth. I played no part in it. Matthew and Luke place this story in their Gospels. They had no proof.*

*"As mentioned, I gave Jesus kindness and reason and the ability to heal the sick. It was my purpose to focus attention on his kindness to people by giving him the power to cure. People have misconstrued this as the working of miracles. In the matter of reason, he was the most brilliant person, demonstrating that he had a clear view of how a society should re-align itself in the direction of rational behavior. Not one human bested him concerning the relationships between people and God, and not one faulted him in telling about the practice of religion, and not one knew better than he how each person should treat all others. The progress made in the past 2,000 years on these issues has been discouragingly slow.*

*"The story of Christ's life as contained in the four Gospels is accurate enough. These four Gospels can be treated as gospel, as you say. There are errors and omissions, but the principal points are there. Study the four Gospels and learn the Sermon on the Mount. In other matters, you may retain the sacraments of baptism and communion. These are reminders of the beginning and end of Christ's ministry.*

*"I have created many other individuals in all the corners of the Earth. Some have followed my desires. Most have failed. Two whom you will remember are Gandhi and King. Gandhi was to teach that nonviolence has a place in your violent world. He was successful. King was to combine the practice of non-violence with the concept that individuals cannot be responsible for the circumstances of their birth. King, in his short life, whose end I could not control,*

*was as successful as Gandhi was. It should not be lost on anyone that good and noble works gather momentum.*

*"To those of you who practice the Christian faith, or are tempted by it, read the Gospels, understand their lessons, and allow them to guide your conduct. The writings that are based on the Gospels, but prepared by others, may have merit; but the individual's responsibility is to study the original works and construct a life based on the lessons therein. The greatest among these are that we must love our neighbors as we love ourselves, and that we must let our light so shine before others that they may see our good works. Of course, we are admonished to love God, but the remoteness of that personage renders the task difficult. I have difficulty myself from time to time.*

*In the name of the Holy Ghost."*

* * *

Members of the press continued to show up, but in smaller numbers each day. Theories were advanced, only to be routed. Experts were allowed to examine the sheets of parchment and the marble vase. A source for neither could be identified. The director of the museum had the good sense to require that the experts come to his premises. The originals did not go on tour.

The telephone on Winston Elliot's desk rang. As the director of the museum, he let his secretary answer. She said, "It's Mrs. Trowbridge. Shall I put her through?"

"Yes, thank you," he said, guessing that the matter at hand was the vase. Elliot heard the cultured voice with imperative overtones.

"Good morning, Winston. How are you? A bit fed up with it by now, I suppose?"

"It's dying down a bit. I'm getting back to my work. You realize that I have been an agent of God?"

"Who do you guess was the prankster?" Mrs. Trowbridge asked.

"Evelyn, no one has unseated the Holy Ghost. He's the prankster, or culprit, or whatever."

"Winston, I have a proposal to make to you, in person. Any free time today?"

"After lunch, say two o'clock," Elliot said.

"Fine," she said and hung up.

* * *

"We've talked about my collection, Winston."

"Yes, we certainly have."

"I have offers from three museums in New York, and from the museums in Cleveland, Cincinnati, Chicago, and a brush with the museum in Los Angeles, and a serious encounter with the people in Seattle. They are talking about building a new wing just for me."

"Yours is the last great private collection in the country. Little wonder you have them standing in line."

"What would we do for me here in this museum?" Evelyn asked.

"As chair of our board, you know as well as I do that we would do back flips to have your collection end up here. I don't think there's any mystery about that. Your name in marble. Three rooms devoted to the collection. Thirty pieces up all the time. The rest in the basement, but rotated regularly. People coming from Europe to see the new items on exhibit. It would be a boon to us. An enormous shot in the arm even though we already have the best collection in the United States."

"Yes, I know," Evelyn said.

"Did Turner explain the difference between giving the collection now and bequeathing it?" Winston Elliot asked.

"Yes, he explained it. I asked him to get it down to two pages, double-spaced, leaving out all the legal nonsense. It's a test of Turner's grasp of the matter. Let's see if he can be brief."

"I hope that your association with this museum over the decades will make a difference. We have been your museum, after all," Elliot noted.

"Yes, it does make a difference. The vase. That's my proposal. I get the vase and the museum gets the collection now."

"Is that the offer, Evelyn?" Elliot asked.

"Yes. Make it the first item on the agenda at the next board meeting. And I have a request. Let's go to the vault and take a look at the vase. You know I haven't seen it face to face."

"You speak as though it has a life of its own," Elliot said.

They repaired to the basement, past guards, and into the area where the most precious objects were kept. The vase stood in the center of a table, illuminated by a single bank of fluorescent lamps. They stood before it and in a moment Mrs. Trowbridge said, "It's exquisite. The perfect shape, with the handles in the correct proportion. I suppose they are of the same material as the vase itself."

"Yes," Elliot answered. "The marble is continuous. The vase is made from one block of marble. No one can identify a quarry where this particular pale yellow marble comes from."

"It's not some plastic, is it?" Mrs. Trowbridge asked.

"No. The laboratory assured us that it was crystallized limestone throughout."

"Has any museum in the world reported a missing vase?"

"No," Elliot said.

"It's magnificent. I love the square base under the curves. The color is perfect."

* * *

The twenty or so members of the board of directors acquired money in different ways. They were all rich. Evelyn had inherited and married great amounts of money. As some said, she represented serious money. Several had inherited and were second or third generation aristocrats. They worked, but their principal occupations were maintenance of wealth and the creation of new wealth through thoughtful investments.

Several more had made their money and bought their way onto the board by means of generous contributions. They had established a foothold in the art world by collecting the works of modern artists and entertaining lavishly. The old money did look down their noses at the new money, but the members of the board did not divide over that issue. The board had three factions, one led by Evelyn. These were called the Dinosaurs, and the term was used freely, face to face, without offense. The objective of the Dinosaurs, always, was to maintain the buildings and grounds and to ensure the safety of the collection. After all, they said, they had the best collection in the country; the basement was full to overflowing, so why not continue to do superbly whatever we do?

The second faction, led by Winston Elliot, was known as the Rotators. Elliot, as director, attended all meetings of the board, but had no vote; however, he was the spokesman for the Rotators. Their point of view was that the public would be served well if the pieces on exhibit were changed frequently, either by trading places with pieces in the basement, or by being consigned to the basement while works of art were brought in from other museums as traveling exhibits. Their best moment came when they were able to consign the Hobbemas and Ruysdaels, the landscapes of those Dutch masters, to the basement and cut in half the number of Rembrandts that were hanging, and in the process make available a fair amount of wall space for other pictures. They never let up in their quest for change; but Evelyn, as a way of indicating that the Rotators might be going too far, once said, "The Leonardo goes to the basement over my dead body."

The third group consisted of the Avants, short for avant-garde, of course. None of them pronounced the "t" in "avant," making certain to use the French inflection. The Avants were interested in twentieth century art -- the more modern, the more daring, the better. Their best moment came when they secured a traveling exhibit of Picassos, painted by him between the ages of 11 and 18. One of the Dinosaurs remarked, "Well, he was conservative as a youth. None of that two eyes on the same side of the head."

The first item on the agenda was to consider the swap of Evelyn Trowbridge's collection for the vase, the exchange to take place immediately, or as soon as Evelyn could empty her houses. Elliot read the item aloud, then there followed a few remarks by Turner, the museum's lawyer, who attended regularly but had no vote. At the close of his remarks, he said, "Evelyn," turning the discussion over to her.

She said, "I need an incentive to strip my houses of the collection. I know it belongs here. I don't think I'm asking for much. Turner explained that we have clear title to the vase. Perhaps each of you would like to express your opinion."

Silence. Prolonged silence.

One of the Rotators reached for a bottle of sparkling mineral water and unscrewed the top. It was as though the members had let out their collective breaths. Others reached for bottles of water or soft drinks. An Avant poured himself coffee at a side table. When seated, he said, "This is an enormous responsibility."

A Dinosaur spoke up, "Do we have all the data about the vase?"

Evelyn answered, "If you think the Holy Ghost planted that vase, I have a bridge to sell you."

The Rotator who had opened the first bottle of water said, "Exhibited properly, it would pull in millions of people. We could have an expensive poster and a book ready."

Others joined in and it became obvious that the factions were not holding together. Evelyn's Dinosaurs had deserted her. One Avant said, "This is modern art. We'll see more from this sculptor."

One Rotator said, "Evelyn, it may not be in our power to bargain for this symbol."

With that, an Avant introduced a motion to table the exchange of Evelyn's collection for the vase, which carried unanimously with the exception of Evelyn. Her vote was, "Abstain. I guess you know what that means." Her remark was accompanied by more silence. Winston saw her collection going to New York.

* * *

Lisa had received the invitation from Evelyn for a weekend in Bermuda. She had been stewing around during the afternoon, waiting for her husband Stephen to come home so that she could spring the news. When he came in the door she announced, "Well, Stephen, it's social climbing at its best. Pack for Bermuda."

"Good Lord, Evelyn's desperate."

"She took it personally. Too bad, really, ditching friends she's had for years. So we end up with an invitation to Bermuda in place of her old pals."

"When it got into the press," Stephen said, "Evelyn was shown to be someone who couldn't hold her board together. Some might resign over that. Looks like she just unloaded most of her friends."

Lisa asked, "Do you have a clear conscience over drinking her booze, eating her food, and taking up space in her house?"

Stephen thought for a minute. "I just write fiction. I don't have a dog in that fight."

* * *

Evelyn, Lisa, and Stephen were on the same flight. "I'm so glad you're along," Evelyn said before they boarded. "The place is too big to feel happy in alone. The rest are coming tomorrow, and let me tell you not a one of them is from the museum's board."

They were not seated together on the plane, but had a chance to talk in the taxi. Stephen said, "I'm sorry your swap for the vase didn't go through."

"It made me look toothless. That hurt," Evelyn answered.

Lisa said, "There was just enough of the supernatural to make any decision difficult."

Evelyn said, "They were wimps. I wasn't asking a great deal for the best private collection in the world."

"You had a good deal of support in the Letters to the Editor. Lots of letter writers want to see your collection. Why not consider this the first part of the negotiation? The motion was tabled, not defeated."

"Those are kind words," Evelyn said.

They entered the house and Evelyn showed them downstairs. They came to the last room, the library off the living room. Evelyn opened the door. A vase was on the writing table in the center of the room. Evelyn said, "It's smaller than the other one." They walked into the room and stood around the table, studying the vase. It was not the same as the other, blue in place of pale yellow, smaller, but of the same design.

Evelyn looked into the vase, and then reached into it to pull out a small piece of parchment. She looked at it and handed it to Stephen. He looked at Lisa and read the English, "Oh, ye of little faith."

# The Brothers

# The Brothers 1

He stepped on the escalator to go up to the street. It was the end of the trip he had made quite a few times from Minneapolis to National Airport, then by Metro to Capitol Hill. It was only a one-block walk to the south side of Independence Avenue where the House Office Buildings were lined up. He went up the stairs of the building that held his brother's office, and stayed on the first floor, walking down the familiar corridor, past the doors of various members. There were signs giving their names and their state flags were on display. When he arrived at the door marked Warren Montgomery of Minnesota, he turned in, to be greeted by the receptionist whom he had known for nine years, all the time his brother had been a member. She always addressed him as Reverend, no matter what he wore. This particular day he was dressed in his clerical garb. He had an appointment tomorrow at the Cathedral and knew that the Presiding Bishop appreciated it when his troops showed up in uniform.

When he became ordained, Ralph Montgomery would correct people who called him *Reverend,* saying that *reverend* was an adjective, so that while it was fine to address him as Reverend Montgomery, it didn't work to call him simply *Reverend.* After a few months of using that objection, he tired of it. That had been thirteen years ago.

The receptionist, Ellen Rodriguez, said, "I'll tell your brother you're here. He's alone. Go right in."

"Hello, Warren," the minister said.

"Hello back to you, Ralph," the congressman answered. "Good to see you, as always. Nice flight?"

"Just a commute, really. As you know, it's about four hours from take-off to this office, when everything's working correctly. National's been redone since my last trip. It's a pleasure to go through there."

"You'll have to start calling it *Reagan.* We all do here," Warren said.

"Old habits die hard," Ralph said.

"So what brings you on this trip, Reverend Montgomery?" Warren asked.

"The old issue again. The church has been struggling with same-sex marriages for a while, as you know, and the Bishop calls in some of us from time to time to measure progress."

"I recall that the last time we talked on the matter, you told me that it had gotten down to the choice of each congregation, or perhaps each diocesan bishop," Warren said.

"Yes, that's where it stands now. The next General Convention will be held in Denver and I expect the Church will take the plunge."

"A lot of good it will do you," the congressman said. "As long as the states don't recognize same-sex marriages, you can conduct marriage services all day long, but they won't have any standing in the law."

"That's true," Ralph said. "And we have to come up with a new term for it. The term *marriage* drives them crazy. I mean most people don't care, but for those that do, it drives them nuts."

"They must be the ones that have lousy marriages," Warren said. "Insecure on the whole matter," he added.

"How about *Legal Union*, does that do anything for you?" Ralph asked.

Warren thought for a moment and came back, "Nothing. Does nothing for me. Can you imagine entering into Legal Union bliss?"

"Not exactly. Listen, we have bishops galore. We can put several on the case. We'll come up with something," Ralph said.

They changed the topic to focus on the legislation that was occupying most of Warren's time. "Have you ever heard of the Alternative Minimum Tax?" Warren asked.

"I hope not," Ralph answered.

Warren explained, "It's designed to trap taxpayers who find too many deductions, legal deductions, that is, and it forces them to pay more tax than they would if they used the 1040 and itemized on Schedule A. As an example, it snags plenty of couples with eight children because as a family they can claim ten personal exemptions."

"Serves them right," Ralph said.

"Well, eight children, that's plenty. You may have a point. But the tax code has always been pro large families. The nation has come to expect it." Warren added, "We had hearings on the subject about three years ago. Didn't get anywhere. We rarely act unless there's a crisis."

Ralph reflected a little. "Of course that's how you make certain that crises arise on a continual basis, by waiting for a crisis before acting. I imagine that in business, the successful executives do enough planning to ward off crises. If you allow a crisis to creep up on you, then you've failed."

They chatted some more on various topics and agreed that Ralph would have a late lunch at Union Station and end up at Warren's apartment. They took their leave of one another. Ralph walked from the House Office Building, along the back of the Capitol, past the Supreme Court to Union Station for lunch before he caught the Metro. He rode the Red Line to Dupont Circle. A bus took him up Massachusetts Avenue, past the embassies, to Wisconsin Avenue. He walked the short distance to Warren's apartment. The offices of the Bishop at the Cathedral were nearby. This would be the Presiding Bishop. In Ralph's mind the Presiding Bishop was connected directly to the Archbishop of Canterbury who, in turn, had a pipeline to God.

They met the following morning. In attendance were two bishops, one from a diocese in the northwest and the other from the south. There were three deans of cathedrals and three parish priests of whom Ralph was one. The discussion revolved around progress on the issue at hand and the resentment made obvious by some members of congregations. One of the parish priests reported that his church had two young lesbian ministers on the staff who had formed a union and adopted two children. "Obviously, they would welcome some religious and legal acknowledgments of their status," this priest had said.

"How did your parishioners take it?" the Presiding Bishop asked.

"Those who care about such things left us long ago and settled in conservative churches. The ones who remained don't care. In our church we recognized about ten years ago that a small percentage of men and women are homosexual, so what's the fuss about?"

"We have a long way to go in this country," the Presiding Bishop said in his closing remarks. "Keep up the good work." He added, "In a decade or so, the first state will permit same-sex marriages, and it will be because churches changed public opinion. It's just a matter of time. We want to lead on this one."

Ralph Montgomery left the meeting, satisfied that his church was contributing to the level of acceptance and understanding. He had been swayed a few years back by a member of his vestry who had said casually, "Hell, Ralph, the big shortage in our country is commitment." Ralph knew that this simple statement trumped all the tortured arguments.

He made his way to the intersection of Massachusetts and Wisconsin Avenues and walked down Wisconsin toward Georgetown. He turned into one of the apartment buildings, walked past the concierge's desk where he was welcomed. The person said, "Good afternoon, Reverend. On your way up to your brother's?"

In the elevator, Ralph took out of his pocket a key ring on which he kept a key to his brother's apartment. He let himself in. The door slipped from his hand and made a substantial noise as it slammed shut. He went to the kitchen for a drink of water. The phone rang. A female voice came on and said, "My, you're home early this afternoon."

"Perhaps you thought you would be talking to Warren. This is his brother," Ralph said.

"Oh, I'm sorry," the voice said.

"Would you like to leave a message?" Ralph asked.

With that the other party hung up.

# The Brothers 2

Muriel Egstrom was off the farm in Minnesota. She was thirty-eight years old and in her estimation had led a varied and full life that had brought her from the nearly forgotten position of fourth and last child in the family to being legislative assistant for a congressman. At first it was clerical work in the office of a member of the House from her state. Presently she worked in a demanding position for a member from Illinois.

Muriel's family resembled many other farm families across Minnesota. Muriel's mother and father were both of Swedish extraction, both strong Lutherans. In the general lowering of standards that was taking effect in all aspects of American life (at least, that's how the parents saw it) one could sense moral decay, unattractive clothes, distasteful music, late hours, excessive drinking, some rudeness and a measurable decline in attendance at church. When Mother and Father discussed these phenomena, in bed before they went to sleep, they included the possibility that their three sons, and Muriel perhaps, were engaging in sex in the back seat of cars and elsewhere. When Father would say, "Well, we can't be too hard on them," Mother knew he was referring to their carrying on in the same fashion in their day. Mother would say, "Well, I hope they don't get into trouble, and I hope Muriel doesn't lose her reputation."

Mother was clinging to that last vestige of respectability, associating abstention with high moral character. She was unwilling to accept that most of the country had moved beyond that position, considering only sexually transmitted diseases and unwanted pregnancies as threats. In an attempt at explaining all this nocturnal activity, Mother had remarked to Father once that children living on farms were surrounded by animals reproducing, and that these examples of behavior had not undermined their morals but rather made the process appear normal and therefore something to engage in. She was unable to make the leap from that thought to the idea that her daughter was caught up in a planetary change in habits called the sexual revolution.

Muriel hit the State University when the anti-establishment movement had seen its best days, to be replaced by the feminist movement and such pressing questions as what to do about apartheid. While the feminist movement meant to some women on campus that they should engage in the struggle for equality with men, to Muriel the movement signified that the old expectation about falling in love with your man beforehand was a waste of time. Her classmates were forced to admit that Muriel was having a very good time at the university.

She selected political science. Her favorite subject was European history and her particular interests within this topic were diplomacy and military affairs. She was elected to the Phi Beta Kappa society. One of her friends, who was wretched over Muriel's success, asked her how she did so well academically when she spent a fair amount of time on her back. Muriel answered, "I spend an equal amount of time in the library." It was incontrovertible that she was a gifted student.

Her first job after graduation was at a large manufacturing plant where she was given the task of scheduling. She became one of several low-level administrators who would track large, important orders in their progress through the plant to ensure that they were shipped on time. Muriel was surprised to find that she could be diplomatic to people who weren't performing up to par. When she had mouthed off as a kid, her father would say, "You can catch more flies with honey than you can with vinegar."

The company would send her in advance to the location of major exhibitions in which they participated. The crates arriving on trucks had to be located and delivered to the proper place in the auditorium. The contents were assembled into booths and displays. The manufactured products that were the heart of the exhibit had to be set up and made to work.

There were men in Muriel's life, from inside the plant and out. She knew that not being physically attractive made it unlikely that men would notice her and keep her on their minds. But the idea of waiting for men to call her wasn't her style. She would call a prospect and ask if he was free that Sunday afternoon. If he came back with a yes, then she would say, "I'll be in the park at three o'clock feeding the ducks. Why don't you show up?" With another man she might say, "I'll be in the parking lot at such-and-such bar after work at five thirty. I drive a blue Buick. Let's go in and have a drink and we'll take it from there, and it's my idea so I'm paying." On the second or third date she might feed this person in her apartment and allow him to take her to bed. These men stayed hooked as long as she wanted them.

The man who finally landed Muriel was one Monty Oldenburg. He was of German extraction rather than Swedish. He had black hair, shaved twice a day when he went out at night, and moved around like a prizefighter. They would come into contact once in a while when she was expediting an order. She wondered why he hadn't called her. She called him one afternoon.

"Oldenburg," he said.

"This is Muriel. What are you doing after work one of these evenings?"

"I thought the men called the women," Oldenburg said.

"Well, why haven't you called me?"

"I'll call you when I get damned good and ready," he answered. "See you around," he added.

This was the first time Muriel had been stiffed. Four months went by before Monty called. He caught her at home one evening. She had to decide on the spot whether to stall him and make him call again, but he might let four more months pass by. She accepted and broke another date.

Muriel understood that Oldenburg believed in the traditional approach. He had to call the shots. She could dump him, or learn to wait by the phone. She liked his answer when she pressed him on the four-month delay. "I've been shedding women," he said. She liked it that he had to cut back before he took her on.

She discovered that waiting by the phone wasn't excessive punishment. Monty had regular habits. He always telephoned Monday nights and planned the remainder of the week. He filled her weekend. He usually telephoned again on Thursday nights.

On the night of their fourth date, at the door to her apartment, Monty got around to kissing her. "What's he been waiting for?" she wondered. She was leaning against him and asked, "You're in no hurry, are you?" He said, "It moves fast enough without hurrying it along." She thought about asking him in but sensed that he had adopted a reserve uncharacteristic of other men she dated.

Muriel admired his seriousness and the good work he did on the job. He wasn't a funny person. While he grasped her humor and laughed appropriately, it was not in his nature to initiate pleasantries. Muriel thought he had made so much headway in life by being aloof that it had not occurred to him that he might develop other parts of his personality.

Muriel and Monty married after a seven-month courtship. He was thirty and she was twenty-seven. It would last a year.

# The Brothers 3

The principal wave of German immigration into the United States occurred between 1840 and 1860. Many of these new citizens settled in the indus trial cities of the North. Minneapolis and Saint Paul received their share. These newly arrived found employment in the industries that were forming at the time.

Monty's great-great-grandparents, married in the old country, settled in Saint Paul in 1857. Monty had a photograph of the couple framed and mounted on his living room wall. The photo may have dated from 1875 or so. Their four children, two girls and two boys, one of them Monty's great-grandfather, were standing behind the couple.

Monty knew their names, which he had written on the back of the frame. He held in his head the names of most family members from the beginning. His relatives counted on Monty to keep the record straight. Indeed, he had constructed a genealogy, which he had written up on two large pieces of paper. These could be aligned with one another to show the entire clan of Oldenburgs. Monty was a fifth generation American, but the sixth generation of his family had started arriving.

There had not been any success stories in the family. The men had learned trades. Most of the women married and raised families. There were several college graduates, Monty not among them, but there was no Uncle Max to tell stories about, how he had built the big house on the hill.

Monty, the oldest of three children, prided himself on his trim, strong body. He was too slight to play football at his high school and not fast enough to make the track team, but in the summer he played softball and swam, and he skated in the winter. Concerning his face, he liked what he saw in the mirror. He parted his black hair in the center. There was a slight wave. He had a heavy beard and full eyebrows that he kept trimmed. His ears, eyes, mouth and nose appeared to be mounted appropriately about his face. It gave him comfort that he resembled his father closely. People said his father was handsome. Monty enjoyed knowing at every turn what he would look like twenty-six years in the future. Other matters of interest to Monty beyond body and face were clothes, and the effect that body, face and clothes had on women.

While in high school, Monty had little choice in clothes but he preferred dark trousers and lighter jackets worn over a white shirt. He liked the contrast. Concerning his impact on women, he knew they gossiped about him and a few flirted with him, but he knew that until graduation he would be immobilized. While he could borrow the family car, an old clunker, and his mother and father would give him money, Monty knew he would need additional resources to make an impact. It appeared to him to be dignified to wait until after graduation.

When the senior prom came, three of Monty's friends joined him in renting a limousine. Monty asked a classmate to be his date and asked her early. He thought no one else would ask her and the chance of being turned down would be next to nil. He didn't want it to get around that he'd been turned down. He knew girls did that in hopes of being asked by someone higher up the ladder. Isabel was big up front. She wore her hair piled up and put on a strapless gown. Monty knew that his classmates would realize that he had what it takes to pick out a girl who might not be popular, yet who turned out to be attractive.

The pressure of going to work after graduation came from his sisters. In a three-bedroom house with three children, same-sex children would be paired off. His sisters shared one room during the entirety of their childhood. In Monty's senior year, their longing for his room couldn't be suppressed any longer. His sisters started asking for a promise from him. They wanted to know how long it would be after graduation until he had a job and moved to his own place.

The only company he had ever worked for was hiring the year he graduated. He landed a job as the lowest assistant in the test department. He had to learn about electronic instrumentation so that he could conduct tests and interpret results. Monty made good progress over the years. He came to work at age nineteen. Muriel and he discovered one another and married in his thirtieth year. He was forty now and second in charge of all quality control for his firm.

His first apartment was small but new. If he was about to invite women to the place, it had to be clean and neat. It was a two-story building with all the front doors facing toward the parking lot. The front doors on the ground floor opened directly where he parked his car, the way motels work. It would be to his advantage to minimize the time his women could be viewed by neighbors. He reasoned that his women would appreciate the lack of exposure.

His parents equipped the kitchen. His sisters bought an iron and ironing board. They offered to teach him how to press his shirts. For the rest of it, the little furniture he needed, he went into debt. Those payments, along with his car payment, ate up most of his salary after rent and food.

The first woman that came to mind was Isabel Jensen. He thought they had danced well and had a good time at the prom. She still lived at home and, like himself, had elected to go to work rather than continue in school. As she related it to Monty, she "typed like a whiz" and found work in a lawyer's office. On their third date, a Sunday afternoon walk followed by a meal he had prepared, Monty brought up the pressing matter. He said, "I'm up on birth control and I have condoms, and it would be wonderful if we tried it. It will be my first time."

"We're both nineteen. It doesn't make sense to wait any longer," Isabel had answered. Monty doubted that it would be the first time for Isabel because a couple of his classmates had kidded him and wished him luck after the night of the prom. It surprised Monty that he could simply state his case and succeed. The signal was that he might not need to express love for women in order to take them to bed. As his resources grew, he expanded his circle of women. Perhaps half succumbed on being asked. The remainder turned him down. None of these expressed anger or disapproval over his behavior.

As long as sex became available on a regular basis, mostly for the asking, Monty steered clear of romantic attachments, until he met Muriel. She was the most interesting person, male or female, he had met. There was no subject that came up in their conversations that she was completely unaware of. She was the first woman he had dated who had graduated from college. After a few encounters, Monty realized that Muriel's mind contained a table of organization, which arranged facts in categories and orders of importance. She would not jump from topic to topic. She tended to exhaust one topic before moving to the next. When she changed to the next one, that topic had some relevance to the previous one. Some men came halfway to Muriel's standard. None of the women he went out with came near. That he had found this mind in a woman made him ask whether this was an exclusively female trait.

It was not enough that Muriel was informed. It dawned on Monty that she reasoned. It seemed normal for her to assemble facts and draw conclusions. None of his friends had that habit. After waiting four months to call her back and being offhand by saying that he needed time to shed women, he realized that he might have lost her. He had telephoned one evening because there was no other person to call. He was flipping through his address book and found her listed under M as "Muriel at work." He had to ask someone in his office for her last name before locating her in the phone book.

Before Muriel, it would be dates followed by the proposition and a few nights in bed. Nothing had ever happened. Monty could not get interested in any of them. He was thinking about marriage, and his family had asked, but he couldn't get interested. With Muriel, all changed.

It came to him that Muriel might limit conversations to topics she knew a great deal about so that he would always come off second best. He could put this idea to the test by finding a topic she knew little or nothing about and reading up on it. Would she be interested in a field of his? He found his field through her. On a weekend when they had been dating for three months, Muriel asked him if he had ever visited old Fort Snelling. He told her he knew the original fort was built on a bluff overlooking the river, but beyond that he thought of the place as an army camp that had been the assembly center for draftees during the second war, and maybe the first.

Some history was available at the fort, which had been reconstructed as a memorial to the old army. Monty read that the government had built forts on the West Bank of the Mississippi to encourage migration into the Louisiana Purchase. These had been erected in the 1820s. He learned that the army had expanded and contracted depending on the country's needs, expanding greatly in 1846 to prosecute the war against Mexico. It had contracted after the conclusion of that war, but expanded again in 1855 by the creation of the Tenth Infantry Regiment, to be stationed at Fort Snelling. The regiment's purpose was to exercise control over the tribes of the Sioux, who from time to time rose up against white settlers. The formation of the Tenth Infantry and its arrival in Minnesota Territory occurred two years before the arrival of the Oldenburgs from Germany. The first commandant of the regiment was a West Pointer from the class of 1823 named Edmund Brooke Alexander. So it said in a pamphlet. Monty wondered if his great-great-grandparents had seen this colonel on the occasion of a Fourth of July parade, or some other function.

From Fort Snelling, Monty went on to read about other forts built at the time of the expansion, such as Fort Leavenworth in Kansas and Fort Smith in Arkansas, before these territories became states. He read of the army's role in moving the Cherokee Nation out of the South toward empty land west of the river. They would settle mostly in Oklahoma Territory.

While his reason for developing this interest was to test Muriel, he found that with or without Muriel he had discovered a subject that interested him. He took books out of the library and learned about army history and became familiar with the names of the authors. There was ample material. Muriel did not take the topic as her own, but she became his disciple, a willing one at that. Monty contemplated marriage.

One night, at her apartment, Monty asked Muriel if she could describe her ideal sex life. She proceeded to give him frequency and preferences in some detail. At the end, Monty said, "I can deliver that." He proposed shortly afterwards. She accepted.

Monty had made his conquest without emotional commitment. He told Muriel as part of the proposal that he loved her. He told her again on their wedding night. Beyond those occasions, he limited himself to being polite and considerate. He didn't sense that he became a different person after he declared his love. He knew that it was the accepted thing to say. He assumed that love did not imply a commitment beyond living together in harmony.

# The Brothers 4

For no particular reason, perhaps because she sought new experiences, Muriel became interested in a primary campaign. One of her co-workers had attended a committee meeting of volunteers who would attempt to capture an open seat in the House of Representatives for a young lawyer. His name was David Morris. Muriel had no idea about the work involved in a campaign but she was curious. At her friend's invitation she attended the next meeting. She decided on precinct work because, as she looked over the list of voters in her precinct, she recognized several names. It would be an interesting experience, she thought, to knock on their doors, hand them literature on her candidate, and ask for their vote.

In that process, it surprised Muriel that so few of the voters she met face-to-face had questions on pressing matters. Here was an opportunity to discuss any one of ten issues on which she had been tutored, and only a handful of voters asked about any of them.

How could democracy function, Muriel wondered, if the electorate was so ill-informed? During the campaign, she sent answers to the few constituents that inquired about problems that affected them and their district. When her candidate won, and the spoils were divvied up, Muriel was offered a job in the office in Washington answering mail from home. It would be the least senior position in the office among a staff of eight. There was the matter of what to do about her husband and their marriage.

Except for the question of having children, they had settled quickly into an orderly life together. Having a family was the only point of friction between them. It had not occurred to either during the courtship that one or the other might not be keen on that. It came to Muriel that the idea of raising boys who might inherit some of Monty's personality didn't excite her. A couple of girls, well, that would be all right. When the job offer came, Muriel was surprised that moving to Washington held far more appeal than staying home and remaining on the old job. Monty withdrew from the discussion on the topic of their life apart. Muriel said they would write, telephone, and see one another on weekends as schedules permitted. Scheduling, it turned out, was more a matter of money than it was of finding time.

Once in Washington, Muriel was surprised at the rapidity with which the young chose up sides. The housing arrangements came in all imaginable combinations. Soon enough, the sleeping arrangements were settled. Muriel selected an apartment for one, expandable to two for the rare occasions when Monty flew into town.

On his first visit to see his wife, Monty said, "So this is what they call a double bed in Washington." He was thinking of their expansive apartment back home, two bedrooms, two baths, and the rest to scale. Muriel said, "I need the space only when you're here."

She expected a remonstrance out of Monty but it never came. Her explanations for his silence on the matter were as follows: first, that Monty didn't miss her because he had found another woman promptly; or, Monty cared for her and was being patient while she worked through this phase of her life; and finally, Monty was dazed. He didn't know what had hit him. He would fight back soon.

Muriel didn't find out how he felt because they never discussed matters at that level. They were on the telephone one evening, six months into her new career, when Monty interrupted her mid-paragraph. He said, "Listen, this isn't going anywhere. See you around." He hung up without waiting for a response. He had had the last word.

It surprised Muriel that she could let her marriage slip through her fingers so easily, and that it didn't seem to make any difference to her. She knew that it wasn't a matter of career over marriage. Answering mail hadn't turned out to be that exciting. She concluded that she didn't want children, at least not with Monty. With Monty she had the rings, the name change and some status, but no fire. Perhaps it could be different with another man, and then again, there might not be any man who could wake up the romantic side in her. It dawned on her that Monty had remained true to form to the end, aloof from the fray.

One of her co-workers carried the name of Susan McAllister. They had adjoining desks in the limited office space allotted to member's staffs. The morning following the final conversation, Muriel told Susan, "I think it's over." Susan remarked, "We've been betting that way."

Muriel wore the rings until the papers arrived from a law firm in Minneapolis. The attorney's letter was cordial. He related that her husband wanted an amicable settlement in which each party walked away from the contract. There was next to no property of value to divide.

The rings off, Muriel readjusted her sights. Her plans included rising in importance to become a legislative assistant. The congressman she worked for, David Morris, as a freshman, did not have important committee assignments. He was a member of the Committee for the District of Columbia and had a seat on the Agriculture Committee. Not much came his way. Muriel thought she might hook up with a senior member. During her short time on the Hill, she had decided that the House Foreign Affairs Committee worked on programs that interested her.

That was the work portion. For the social side, she concluded that a reversion to past practices would not work. She was approaching thirty, and rather than being up front and obvious with men, she would do what most women did, let the men come to her. She might add a fragment of her former self if the situation called for it.

In her reading of history, she had been attracted to the biographies of the great mistresses such as Madame du Barry and Madame Pompadour, whose appeal, it turned out, was not restricted to folding back the sheets. These women created situations in which the king in question could enjoy intimacy in relaxed circumstances with ministers, advisers, persons of importance in the arts, and finally, the mistress herself.

It was obvious to Muriel that effort along these lines would be wasted on staffers her age. If she was setting out to be a serious, interesting person who added to the lives of those in some circle she hoped to enter, then she had to shoot high. The target would be a member, perhaps ten years older than she, perhaps a senator, perhaps a person of importance in the administration. If she met an attractive man who was married, and he showed interest in her, then he would go into the dustbin immediately. She didn't want any part of providing for the married men, only to listen to their tales of woe and promises about divorcing their wives. The man would have to be single, divorced, or widowed. She didn't have to marry. It was enough that she had a circle of friends made up of influential people and that among these, one would be her lover.

Muriel looked forward to the work required. The best apartment she could afford, somewhere off the Hill, up one of the avenues, Connecticut, Massachusetts, or Wisconsin, or perhaps 16th Street. Good furniture, starting with used pieces. Fine china, silver, and crystal, and lastly clothes. She knew that few men noticed these things individually, but they did sense the values held by the women they met. She wished to be thought of as intelligent, well read, dignified, attentive, quiet and cultured. She had met a few women with these traits, all older than she was. They were the wives of important men. If she never touched one of their married men, they might let her in at the outer edges first, then closer into their confidence. It should be worth the work.

# The Brothers 5

When Warren arrived home, he found his brother where he expected him, watching the evening news. He was sipping his favorite drink, a mixture of orange juice and tonic water.

"Well, no late night votes, I see," Ralph said.

"No. We were in committee after lunch," Warren answered. "Then it was constituent business the rest of the afternoon. When someone misses a social security check, we jump in."

Ralph returned to watching the news. As an afterthought he said, "Some woman called. Heard the door slam. Must live within earshot."

"She's right above me. Did she complain about the noise you made?"

"She hung up before that," Ralph said. Then he added, talking slowly as one does when watching the news and attempting to express a thought, "The only sound I heard was the sound of clothes coming off."

Warren shot back, "What a hell of a thing to say." He paused a minute, then speaking more to himself than to his brother, he added, "We have to go out. No food here as usual. How soon can you get your shoes laced?"

"I can get them laced by 6:55 when this program ends," Ralph answered. He was still speaking slowly, paying more attention to the news than to his brother.

"We'll walk. Just down to the bottom of the hill. Across the street from the supermarket." Warren drifted off to his bedroom where he changed out of his suit. When he came back he poured himself a glass of wine in the kitchen, and then went in to sit next to Ralph. He said, "Look, Ralph, no tie."

They were quiet during the balance of the program. Ralph changed quickly out of his clerical clothes. They walked down the hill past the Russian Embassy, then a gas station, followed by a liquor store. They commented about some kids playing ball in a small park across the street. They went past more commercial buildings. Ralph said, "You realize we'll have to regain all this altitude on a full stomach." Warren answered, "About all the exercise I get."

When they were seated in the restaurant, Warren asked, "How did it go with the bishops?"

"Well, they like *union*, and they like *covenant.* So it's not *legal union* as I suggested this morning. Just *union.*"

"I thought *covenant* had to do with a deal that God cut with the people of Israel."

"That's right," Ralph said. "This is covenant in the general sense, an agreement, same-sex people coming into agreement. We may come up with other choices."

The waiter came by to take their order for drinks. When he left, Ralph asked his brother, "OK, who is she?"

"As I said, she lives upstairs."

"Are you sleeping with her?" Ralph asked.

Warren studied his napkin for a while and played with his knife and fork.

Ralph persisted, "Just a simple yes or no, then we can get into the disclaimers."

Warren brought his head up and managed to look for a moment into his brother's eyes. "Yes," he said.

"I thought you and Alice had the perfect marriage," Ralph said.

"Well, there are no perfect marriages," Warren answered. "And this is a little different," Warren added. "There's no emotional content."

"It's always a little different," Ralph said. "And no emotional content, what does that mean? Is this just recreational sex? Did she carve a notch on the bedpost for nailing another member of the House?"

"Hey, don't play hardball," Warren said. "It became available. I didn't go after it. It came to me. And guys cheat on their wives. Wives cheat on their husbands, but less often. This is very nice. She's been married. It's a fine way to end an evening."

"Boy, are you in trouble with the big scorekeeper in the sky."

"Now what does that mean?" Warren asked.

"On the day of the Second Coming, you'll pay," Ralph said.

"Can I write a check?" Warren asked.

"Stop it, Warren. By the way, the standard penalty for philandering is no sex for a century."

They ordered dinner and another round of drinks. Warren said, "OK, I came clean. Now it's your turn. What's going on in Minneapolis, brother?"

"I'd hoped we'd get there. Feels good to tell someone. I'm lusting in my heart."

"Where have we heard that?" Warren asked. He didn't wait for an answer. "Who is she?" he asked.

"Sings in the choir."

"Ministers can't seem to stay out of choir stalls. What's her name?"

"Colleen Murphy"

"She's in the wrong church."

"A transfer," Ralph explained.

"Are you planning a little *divertimento?*" Warren asked with sarcasm.

"Not yet. It may be on our minds. I don't know."

"What has she got that Marla doesn't have? Does it come down to a big pair and nice hips? I thought we got past that after high school."

"Dream on," Ralph said.

"Well, what's bothering you?" Warren asked. "Is it the seven year itch?"

"I suppose so. Married thirteen years. First five OK. A bit rarefied since then."

"Marla cut you off?"

"Not cut off exactly, just hard to come by."

"It's a lousy trick. Get some pill to slip in her coffee."

"Yea. Do you think the product exists?"

They walked the mile or so up the hill to Warren's apartment. Warren went into the kitchen. He emptied a tray of ice cubes into a glass bowl and took a bottle of club soda out of the refrigerator. He came back for glasses and an unopened bottle of Scotch. They sat in the den and proceeded to get good and drunk, but not incoherent.

Warren: "I think you ought to lay waste to that Colleen Murphy and stoop to my level. You deserve it."

Ralph: "I deserve Colleen, Colleen deserves me, and it's Marla who really deserves it."

Warren: "You know, lusting in your heart is the same thing as doing it. That's what it says in The Book."

Ralph: "I could quote you chapter and verse."

Warren: "You're in the same amount of trouble with the big Kahuna in the sky whether you do it or not."

Ralph: "You already said that. Don't call him/her the Kahuna in the sky. Use neutral. The Big Spirit."

**Later in the evening.**

Ralph: "I think I'm a little drunk. Starting not to feel anything."

Warren: "Think about Colleen Murphy. You'll feel something."

**Still later in the evening.**

Ralph: "When I'm in bed, you can sneak upstairs and tear one off for me."

Warren: "I didn't tell you. She's very busy socially. Probably not at home."

Ralph: "OK, try later."

**At the end of the evening.**

Ralph: "Going to bed. Can't see."

Warren: "Setting the alarm for eight. Gotta legislate."

Ralph: "Get me up at eight. Gotta navigate. God, am I drunk."

# The Brothers 6

Muriel worked five years for David Morris, the congressman who brought her to Washington. At the end, she spent more time on agricultural matters than any other activity. The congressman had gained in seniority and working on legislation started to take some of his time. When he discussed with Muriel the idea of giving up correspondence with constituents so that she might replace the assistant who was heading back to Minnesota, she had said, "I know farms. Grew up on one." It was understood that she had the best mind in the office.

Muriel's subsequent departure from David Morris' office and her leaving agriculture behind in favor of foreign affairs came quite by accident. While going through the line in the cafeteria, the book on her tray slipped to the floor. The person immediately behind her, a middle-aged man in shirt sleeves, picked it up and handed it to her. "Interesting title," he said.

"Yes, I read on treaties," Muriel answered. "Sort of a hobby," she added.

"Macabre hobby," the man offered.

"What's the Treaty of Rapallo?" Muriel asked.

"Dunno," the man answered.

"Treaty between the new Soviet regime and Germany in 1922. Just on commercial relations. Men by the names of Chicherin and Walther Rathenau respectively. They were the foreign ministers. And what's the Treaty of Brest-Litovsk?"

"Dunno," the man said again.

"It ended the war between Russia and Germany in 1918," she said.

"You'd better stop. I can discuss the Treaty of Versailles and maybe the Congress of Vienna, but after that it's a blank slate. And my name's Roger Paige."

They sat opposite one another. Roger Paige turned out to be the second in command of the staff for the House Foreign Affairs Committee. They discussed the work that the staff undertook. Muriel, barging straight ahead, asked about any vacancies. It turned out that there was none, but then Roger Paige said he was certain that a congressman from Illinois was in the market for an assistant, and this congressman had a seat on Foreign Affairs.

The interview with the congressman from Illinois had two awkward moments, the first when he asked about travel abroad. Muriel answered, "None, I'm afraid. Don't have a passport, for that matter."

"A birth certificate, two photographs, and eighty-five dollars will cure that," he said. He then asked about language skills. She told him that she had been studying Spanish for a year. He frowned, as though studying for a year didn't count. He handed her a pamphlet on immigration patterns from South and Central America to the United States. He said, "Read it aloud."

She read the first page in a fair Spanish and followed with a rough translation into English. He said, "Keep going to school." She got the job. Her first assignment was to track the work of the Immigration and Naturalization Service as it applied to the large number of Latinos who were settling into the congressman's district. The legal immigrants in his district pestered the congressman's office for progress in smoothing the way for illegal immigrants.

The congressman from Illinois was divorced and had acquired a reputation for making what were termed power lunges at single women. Muriel knew that *power lunge* was not a part of the lexicon. She found out that it became associated with this man because he was known to be dangerous when alone in an elevator with a member of the opposite sex. He was handsome and intelligent and in his early forties, so he met Muriel's requirements. She was apprehensive of entanglements with somebody in her office for all the good reasons that those relationships were often cause for disaster.

Quite by accident Muriel and the power lunger lived on the same block. They had not been aware of one another until Muriel started to work for him. When she discovered her proximity to his place she decided the time had come to move, and it was in this fashion that she ended up in the same apartment building as Warren Montgomery. She was on the third floor, and he immediately below on the second.

Most individuals using the same elevator manage to meet after a while. Muriel and Warren met the day of her arrival. The doorman had helped her wheel two suitcases onto the elevator when Warren appeared. He stepped in and asked, "New here?"

"First day," she answered. She studied his face and asked, "Ways and Means?"

He showed surprise. "I travel through Washington in total anonymity then someone recognizes me in my elevator." They had traded introductions by the time they arrived at the third floor. He had not pushed the button for the second. When the doors opened he said, "Let me give you a hand with those."

When they were in the hall, Muriel said, "I know you because I worked for David Morris for five years."

"Yes, David. His district's not far from mine. Know him well." He paused, and then asked, "For whom do you work now?"

"Jack Enriquez, Foreign Affairs."

"Illinois?" Warren asked.

"That's the one," Muriel answered.

"Jack couldn't be his given name?" Warren wondered.

"No. It's Juan. Goes by Jack."

He went in with her and said, "You have plenty of work to do." The furniture had been arranged but he guessed there were thirty unopened cardboard boxes. He said, "If you haven't used it in a year, throw it out."

They would meet now and then, either coming in or out of the building, or on the sidewalk, or at the bus stop. One day about a year after she moved in, they were both on the bus returning from work. She asked, "Why don't you come up for a drink?"

He hesitated for a moment. Muriel was certain she knew what he was thinking about. "Let me get out of these clothes and check the mail. How about thirty minutes?"

Muriel found out that over half the time he flew in from Minneapolis on Tuesday mornings and flew home on Thursday evenings. His wife had elected to stay home after they had agreed that their children would fare better completing their schooling where they had started, rather than being uprooted. "You'll only be gone two nights a week," Warren's wife had said.

"Legislation doesn't come off an assembly line on some schedule," Warren said to his wife, suspecting that she was well aware of the phenomenon. "So, of course, I can't keep to the two-nights-per-week pledge all the time."

He found out from Muriel about Monty and their brief marriage. He registered on the similarity of names, that her former husband's first name was Monty, and that his family name was Montgomery.

"His first name, it's the thing I liked best about him. Perfect fit. The rugged good looks." Muriel trailed off into silence.

Warren went off on a new tack. "You've done wonders in this place. Same floor plan as mine, but how much more inviting."

"I tried to make the living room, dining room and this den a bit austere and the bedrooms quite feminine." Muriel remained silent. She thought he was imagining himself in her bedroom, by invitation.

After a moment, he said, "Well, I'm off. Thanks a million for the drink and a half. I suppose you know what I'm reading tonight."

"Penetrating material on the new tax bill," she guessed.

"And you?" he asked.

"How drug shipments make their way out of Colombia and arrive in Florida."

They walked to her door. He leaned over and gave her the lightest kiss on the cheek. She reviewed her pledge about married men.

# The Brothers 7

Marla Mitchell and Ralph Montgomery met at the seminary. She worked as an administrator for the director and Ralph was moving through the three years of study that precede ordination.

Marla had paid little attention to her family's roots. She knew that a Mitchell had migrated from England to Canada, perhaps around 1850, and some descendent had come to Minneapolis in the 1880s. This person would be her great-grandfather, she knew. Concerning the women these Mitchell men married, Marla knew only their names. Her mother was Cecilia Mallory. As Cecilia was an only child, Marla had no aunts or uncles on the Mallory side. The same situation existed on her father's side. Marla herself was an only child. She knew early on that there could not be first cousins and that her closest relatives would be second cousins. There were three such people approximately her age who lived in Duluth. Marla might see these three, two brothers and a sister, once in five years.

Ralph, on discussing this situation with Marla, before they were married, had remarked that it must be like living on a planet revolving around a sun, with no other celestial objects in view. On hearing this, Marla had stopped conversation to reflect. "No moon, no other planets, no stars. Terrifyingly lonely, wouldn't it be?" It struck Ralph that she was describing her life to date.

Ralph evaluated women on the basis of their acceptability as wife of a minister. Marla examined men as potential husband, father, provider and partner, how adaptable they were in mastering the details of family life.

Sex was important to Ralph. He thought about it often and thought himself fortunate to have engaged in this activity with three women. He knew that his male friends were far more aggressive, and therefore more successful than he was. He did believe that one's sex drive was to be attended to. It pained him that there was an argument that the drive ought to be under the control of a code. Ethics notwithstanding, if he found a woman with the same point of view as his, who agreed that it was a pleasurable activity to be engaged in, then morality be damned. He regretted that the occasions came rarely and that when they came, they were not followed by repeated performances with the same partner. But it bothered him that he knew on some level that it shouldn't be simply fun.

Ralph's first encounter occurred at the age of nineteen on a camping trip. There were a dozen young people in six canoes fishing on a lake north of the city. On the second of these nights the rains came. Most had brought tarpaulins that they suspended from low branches. Ralph and the woman with whom he had paired off made a shelter from an overturned canoe. Within minutes, in this close proximity, they were kissing and fondling. Warren, two years older than Ralph, had given him a dozen condoms. He said, "Take these with you. You might get lucky."

His second occasion took place in college, not long after the incident under the canoe. A woman in one of his classes, with whom he had struck up a friendship, invited Ralph to her apartment near campus for the lunch break. Both had classes in the afternoon. The young woman explained that her roommate was at home across the state. She kissed Ralph and announced, "I don't think you've ever done it." The afternoon classes they missed were confirmation to Ralph that some women had a sex drive as strong as his.

His third opportunity came on a walk back to his house from the local shopping district. He passed the elegant home of a family whose daughter he had known since third grade. She came out the front door at the appropriate moment. They chatted. She asked him to stop over for a swim on Saturday. Ralph speculated on the type bathing suit she might wear. In the pool, Ralph was overcome by aggressive impulses. He kissed this young woman and placed his hands on her. They spent most of the afternoon in the pool house conducting an exhaustive study of the human form.

Marla, after becoming acquainted with Ralph's family, concluded that her goals in life could be met by marrying him. Ralph, who moved slowly in her direction, felt that he had to balance his desire for a woman on a permanent basis with the demands on his time until graduation. In the second of three years at the seminary, he devoted himself to his studies. In his third year, he concentrated on Marla and even joined her often for lunch in the cafeteria. It became obvious to classmates that they would take the step after his graduation.

An evening in March in his final year, Ralph brought Marla home and was sitting on the two-seat sofa in her apartment. She was on his lap. He kissed her and allowed his free hand to clasp one of her breasts.

Her clothes were about the same, day after day. There was variety in color but Ralph realized that each costume was meant to accentuate her front and rear. He thought both were near perfect. All tops were tight fitting, be they sweaters or blouses. Her dresses were cut square across the front so that the start of the curves and the beginning of the cleavage were on display. The skirts and dresses were short enough to show all the leg from the knee down, and frequently more. The pants she wore were always tight across the rear. Ralph wondered at the quality of thread that prevented the two pieces of material from bursting at the seam.

After a long kiss, Marla broke away and whispered in Ralph's ear, "It will have to wait, sweetheart." He removed his hand from her breast and placed it on her hip. In the instant that the movement took, he calculated that if he proposed early in March they could marry in late June.

It was bliss at the start. Marla gave Ralph what he wanted in the amounts that interested him. She reasoned that in a year she could drain him of most of his enthusiasm. At the end of that time, she suggested to Ralph that she might go off birth control and allow chance to rule. They decided on two children. Ralph understood that he had six months after Marla became pregnant. That would mark the end of boundless sex for him. He knew that the new child would displace him in her affections. Marla talked that way. "I didn't realize that I wanted a child so badly," she would say.

The son came first. He was named Don after his maternal grandfather. Marla continued working at the seminary until two weeks before the birth and went back three months later. But her heart wasn't in it. The family money was in place, providing sufficient income. Ralph was installed as the assistant at a parish downtown. There appeared to be no reason to carry on. They selected and bought the house they were destined to live in for several years, Marla more years than Ralph.

A daughter, Kate, arrived two years after. She was named after the actress in *Philadelphia Story*. Ralph thought it was the best movie ever made. That was their family. The affection that had been so plentiful now required negotiation. Ralph fell back to campaigning for it. He would start by bringing home flowers. He would be flattering in conversation. If Marla wanted to deflate him, she could say, "Well, aren't we romantic tonight," or, "Up to your old tricks." If she was ready for him, she would say, "It's a good idea, handsome." He made the grade half the time.

Being the assistant at the principal church downtown had many of the same features as working for his father. He inherited administration and finance. He had been responsible for those tasks in his few years working in the family business. He worried about the annual budget, fund raising, adjusting wages, maintenance, and all the rest of it. The rector hogged the giving of sermons and had a political agenda that he dispensed in large segments from the pulpit. Ralph wished that he were given more opportunities to preach even though he did not agree with Marla that any man or woman of the cloth had the right to advance a political point of view through sermons. He thought rectors should exhort their flock to adopt and live by Christian virtues and then go forth into the world and do good works.

It was not lost on Ralph that the rector had a large following. Many parishioners had left over his positions, but more had arrived to tilt the balance in the rector's favor. Ralph concluded that politics sell well from the pulpit, but when it came his turn to be rector at another parish after six years as assistant, he could not take the example along with him and put it to use. He realized that he was an Episcopalian who believed in blocking and tackling. The important aspects to him were the plant, the grounds, music, Sunday school, outreach to charitable organizations, the liturgy, and finally, his ability to deliver a good sermon. He had problems with maintaining high standards in sermons. Ralph blamed his lack of experience and worked to improve. He allowed his assistant to deliver a sermon about a third of the time in an effort to give that young woman far more opportunity than he had been given.

Some of the coldness that descended over Ralph and Marla's relationship could have originated with this decision. Marla might ask him, "Aren't you giving her too much exposure at your expense?" Ralph would go through his experiences as an assistant and recount to Marla that training this young priest was one of his important duties. "How can the church survive if we fail to breathe life into these young people?" Marla's answer, said differently on several occasions, was approximately, "She's young and capable. Let her take care of herself."

The second element of discord was the matter of Ralph's unwillingness to preach politics from the pulpit. Marla had enjoyed the sallies of the rector at their previous post. Ralph understood that Marla did not read the newspaper carefully and had assembled few, if any, facts on current affairs. But it was clear to him that Marla valued the opinions of that rector, perhaps because she was in no position to organize her own. Ralph held the view that the rector was opinionated and ill-informed and, therefore, in no position to discourse on international affairs. How could a priest in Middle America pretend to know anything about international diplomacy and the intricacies of modern warfare?

From Marla, Ralph would hear, in a mildly exasperated tone that the congregation might be tiring of being preached to on Christian values. They were ready for excitement. In fact the membership had grown slightly, and no parishioner had transferred to another church.

Ralph made no distinction between the slow pace of his sex life and the reduced flow of affection from Marla. They were the same. He acknowledged that having two children to care for could take Marla's attention away from him, but he could not fathom why, with the lights out and in bed, his wife could not devote twenty minutes to him twice a week. It made no sense. From a practical point of view, to keep him balanced, she should make herself available to him, even if her heart wasn't in it. At least, that's how he felt.

On the other matters, featuring his assistant and separating his church from politics, Ralph concluded that Marla was attempting to affect her will through him. She was telling him what she would do in his place. "Why don't you see it my way?" she was asking. Ralph guessed that Marla was punishing him for his failure to comprehend her wishes and act upon them.

He would sit in his office at church, gaze out the window, and wonder what might happen if he said to Marla, "Why don't you go up now, bathe, douse yourself in eau de cologne and come to bed? We'll make love until smoke comes out of my ears." But he couldn't say those words, or any resembling them, with the result that the small smoldering fire of resentment grew in him year after year.

# The Brothers 8

During the years that Muriel lived on Wisconsin Avenue, in the apartment above Warren Montgomery's, she had accomplished some of her goals. The furnishings were first rate. Her clothes, likewise. Her inclination was to own fewer but these would be of the best material, cut in a classical style, made to last a long time. Her body hadn't changed. Her face held its lines because she ate and drank sparingly. The hairdressers, make-up experts, and fingernail people did the best they could. There was no particular feature that impressed those who met her socially, but the package stayed in their minds. They knew that attractive woman from Minnesota, the one with the slight mid-western accent. That's what they would say.

The social ambitions were met, most of them, at any rate. She had continued the study of Spanish and made it a point of associating herself with Spanish-speaking people at the embassies. The fact that she worked for Jack Enriquez gave her all the reasons and excuses required for contacting any diplomatic mission from South and Central America, visiting their offices, and meeting the mid-level diplomats. She did not try her hand at diplomacy. Her forays were for the official purposes of gathering information. Her unofficial purpose was to enlarge her circle of friends. The parties at the embassies were much alike, but Muriel used them to increase her language skills and meet single men.

Her married men followed a pattern. They flirted and propositioned. If there was any loyalty among them, it was to be loyal to the practice of bedding as many women as possible the moment their wives left town. The mastery of Spanish was reaching acceptability, her circle of friends had grown, and the women liked her because she kept their men at arm's length. To date there was no man for her. She did not need a man to marry. She wanted only those close ties that take care of loneliness.

The men in her life who counted, in chronological order, were her former husband, Monty Oldenburg; David Morris, who brought her to Washington; Jack Enriquez, for whom she worked; and Warren Montgomery, who lived in the apartment below hers.

Monty and Muriel had never closed the door completely. She never looked him up on her occasional visits home, but he arranged to be in Washington about twice a year, perhaps less frequently. His stated reasons were to see the sites in the nation's capital, to visit Civil War battlefields, and to try the beaches at the ocean, but not museums. He would telephone in advance, say a month ahead, and settle on a date convenient for Muriel. When he arrived, always on Friday evening, he went straight to her apartment.

They never discussed the underlying reasons for his coming. Muriel was pleased to be taken out of town, to places she would not get to on her own. Her embassy crowd would be occupied with entirely different activities. When he came, Muriel donned the rings and played at marriage. Monty noticed, of course, and on the first of these post-marital visits he took her hand and said, "That's nice. Thank you."

While he used the guest bedroom to change, they always slept together. It never came up for discussion. He wasn't rough, but then he wasn't gentle either. He was strong. In one aspect his behavior hadn't changed. He was as thoughtful and considerate as he had always been during the marriage. On occasion, he'd say 'I love you' as though he'd let it slip out. He never followed up with hopes and plans. She assumed he had not found someone to replace her and perhaps was not trying that hard. He would leave Monday mornings. Once they met Warren in the lobby and Muriel introduced Monty as her former husband.

David Morris had won all re-election bids. He continued on an upward path that would lead to a position of power in the House. His wife had moved to Washington at the onset along with the children who were no longer young. By now they were easterners. David's secret, as far as Muriel understood it, was to concentrate on getting the job done irrespective of how popular his votes might be. He seemed not to measure the cost to him before he embarked on a new challenge or adopted a position.

Jack Enriquez was incorrigible. He flirted, insinuated, propositioned, alluded to, and suggested, but in her case never lunged. Perhaps he didn't deserve being called the power lunger. As Muriel grew more competent in handling Latin American affairs for his office, he tended to defer to her on steps to take. He had her making outlines for the short speeches that he gave at home and she always prepared the questions he might ask of witnesses in front of the Foreign Affairs Committee. Muriel could have opened a relationship with Enriquez, but she refrained on the basis that he had never understood who she was. She recognized that he was incapable along those lines. People, women and men, came into his life to take on tasks, to socialize, to go through the motions of the day and plan for the next. She understood that he could not bring a woman into his life so that the two of them could build something of value. She was certain that it was this crater in his personality that had brought down his marriage.

Warren Montgomery, on the other hand, had all that Jack Enriquez was missing. Although it was agreed between them that they would not discuss mutual attraction, they both sensed the ease and comfort that existed between them. And he was very tender with her in bed, perhaps the opposite of Monty. It seemed to go to a different place in her brain. Muriel guessed that their having outlawed love made possible a friendship without expectations. They acted naturally, without guile, both placing the entirety of their personality in view without reserve. More than once, at the end of an evening, when she was still in his arms, she would say, "It's perfect, Warren." She knew it was her way of saying, "I love you." He might kiss her again or answer, "I know."

Muriel recognized that if she and Warren were ever to permit love to enter, requiring him to sever ties with his wife, then their relationship would pick up expectations, with each partner having a role to play. She knew that the current arrangement was preferable to any that she might imagine, but she also knew with certainty that matters would continue to evolve. She and Warren would heat up, or they would cool down. It was not in nature's plan that they would continue to live in this ideal climate.

Halfway through the four years that she had lived in the apartment over Warren's, Muriel felt that curiosity was getting the better of her. She asked herself obvious questions, such as, who might ever know, what would it be like with him, and finally, why not? She knew as well as any woman that disaster could be around the corner. But she recognized that many women served for years as the mistresses of men who lived some distance from their wives, or across town, for that matter. The men enjoyed their families. They had no notion of leaving them. They saw no harm in a liaison, a bit more than casual that they didn't permit to go anywhere, but that would keep them calm in the early parts of the evening.

On a particular winter night, Warren came home by taxi, as was his custom when he worked late. On entering his apartment, he dropped his briefcase by the door, took off his raincoat, left it on the sofa and walked into the kitchen. He telephoned Muriel, who picked up on the second ring. He said, "I need energy, female companionship, social intercourse on the highest plane, and a drink."

Muriel said, "I have those four covered."

"Ten minutes," he said.

Muriel let him in. He was surprised, and must have shown it, to find her dressed in a housecoat. It was the first time when he had come up that she wasn't dressed for the street. "It's not that far from bedtime," she volunteered.

When he was on the sofa, and had taken one sip from his drink, she came over, knelt next to him, facing him, and kissed him. She didn't say anything. He edged forward on the sofa, moved his legs to be under him, stood up and carried her into her bedroom.

That had been the start of it, the first times followed by conversations on how to contain the damage, how to be discrete, and the need to enjoy the present. They strung together all the popular lies about adultery with the intent of putting the best face on the activity.

Muriel found it unavoidable that she would keep Tuesday and Wednesday evenings free. Warren was starting to stay an extra day to catch up on the work he might have done in the mid-week evenings.

It was on an afternoon following an evening of particularly sensuous loving that Muriel heard the door slam downstairs. It was one of the few times she had telephoned him, and the first time when not returning one of his calls.

# The Brothers 9

Colleen Murphy had not switched allegiance from the Roman Catholic to the Anglican faith. She was born in Northern Ireland, in Belfast, to an Anglican family who migrated to the United States when her parents grew weary of the violence that beset the six counties. Ralph Montgomery had assumed she had started life as a Catholic. They had never discussed the matter. In fact, they hadn't discussed very much at the beginning.

In the twenty years from the age of ten to thirty, Colleen did not attend services. Her parents had dropped out. At thirty, Colleen started at the church closest to her apartment. There were several reasons. She wanted to sing, and a choir with a choir director seemed the appropriate place to start; she wanted to meet people her age, men and women; and she did not object to resuming her spiritual journey. These were her reasons as she thought of them in their order of importance.

Colleen played piano and therefore could read music. She sang in the range of a mezzo-soprano, and the choir director appreciated right away that if she wished to be trained he might have found a soloist. In the course of things, the choir director reported his new find to Ralph. He had said, "You can't miss her. All that red hair."

On the Sunday following, at about ten to eleven, the participants in the service formed outside the main entrance. There was a verger, who would lead the procession. There were three boys, one carrying the cross and the other two holding lighted candles. The choir would file in behind them. Ralph found her immediately. The choir robe did not hide her figure completely. The red hair and the slightly sad expression made him think of the way the Pre-Raphaelites painted their women. He was studying her while thinking about the painters of that group when she turned around. They smiled. They acknowledged one another this way for about a month. Then, on a Sunday evening, Colleen appeared at a get-together of newcomers. Ralph talked about the history and mission of the parish. On succeeding Sunday evenings, other members of the staff led the discussion, but Ralph was always present to introduce the speaker and lend a hand.

Colleen and Ralph found reasons to talk at the end of each session, if only for a moment. He might ask, "How are you enjoying the choir?" She could say, "I enjoyed your sermon today, particularly the part on ..." Ralph looked through the records. Among choir members he found her address and phone number. She lived in an apartment building not far from the church. He drove by it every evening on the way home.

Approximately two months after Warren had advised his brother to lay waste to Colleen Murphy as they were sitting in Warren's den, both under the influence, Ralph took that step. On an evening that his wife had driven out of town to visit her parents and taken the children with her, Ralph stopped at Colleen's apartment building. He walked up to the entrance and pushed the button on the intercom. He heard the voice with the slight brogue ask, "Yes, who is it?"

He answered, "It's Ralph Montgomery. May I come up?"

She answered, "I'll buzz you in."

When he got off the elevator on the fourth floor, he looked to the right and saw her standing in her doorway at the end of the corridor. He wanted to run but he held a steady pace, all the time taking in that long face, the pale skin with the few freckles, and the wavy, red hair.

She let him in and closed the door behind him. They said nothing beyond hello. He put his arms around her waist, not knowing whether she would reject him. Her arms came up around his shoulders. They kissed at the door. They kissed and explored a few minutes on the sofa and stayed in bed together for the next two hours.

On moments that Ralph had free and his wife was out, he made his way directly to Colleen's. At the beginning he thought there might not be anything beyond physical attraction. He realized soon enough that in Colleen he had found the first warm, affectionate, responsive and understanding woman of his life. The contrast between an early evening with her and any time spent with his wife was beyond what he could have imagined. He did not know that women such as she existed.

Colleen had identified Marla at services on Sundays, and as one woman will of another, had sized her up. When there might have been laughter, Colleen found severity. Colleen was not surprised that Ralph had appeared in her life.

In Colleen's view, when ministers dropped their priestly garb, as Ralph did frequently at the foot of her bed, they reverted to being flesh and bone, all mystery set aside. Colleen liked the good looks and his short hair always tousled. The first time she saw him she wanted to reach out and rearrange his hair with her hands. She thought he had that look about him, that combination of warmth and boyishness, which made women want to involve themselves in a personal and physical manner.

The other two men in her life – they had come and gone – were regular, average men. She recognized mixed motives in them. They wanted her body, and for some time they made efforts to enter her life on a permanent basis, but both of them wandered off. Ralph wanted her body and it seemed to her that would be the end of it, and then he too would wander off. When he had satisfied the urges, however, he started talking. Colleen found out about his youth, education, decisions in life, even a bit about his marriage. He got around to remarking on what was going on between them six weeks after the affair got under way.

"You've given yourself so freely to me. Do you realize you never raised a barrier?" Ralph said.

"When you rang the intercom the first time, I knew right away what you wanted. I suppose you needed it. I had it to give."

"What would happen if most women had your attitude?"

"Misunderstood men in this country would have mistresses. Frustrations would be worked out, perhaps marriages saved."

"You have this volcano inside," Ralph said. "I didn't believe anything like that existed on this planet."

"It's not a volcano, it's a furnace I've had banked for several years. It's been waiting for you, I guess."

She held him more tightly and rolled over on him and kissed him around the neck. Her red hair fell over his face. He made no effort to move it away.

Six months after the start of it he found out that Colleen had just become pregnant. He called his brother right away. On hearing the news, Warren said, "Well, one career's over. Do you want to join me in politics?"

"Be serious," Ralph had responded. "I'll have to resign my position, divorce my wife, perhaps she'll divorce me, and I'll have to struggle to keep a relationship going with my two children."

"That's all true," Warren said. "It's OK to resign from your parish, but don't stop being a minister. It's all you know how to do. You'll need a job and a pretty good one. You'll be a father again in a few months."

# The Brothers 10

On the day that Ralph let the door slip from his grasp, Alice was two days from her 40th birthday. It happened on a Wednesday and Warren would be home that Friday to celebrate. Wednesday was a day like any other, except that their two children, aged twelve and fourteen, came home and announced that their school had been singled out by an association for excellence in academic matters. Neither of her sons could relate this achievement to the world at large, but the older, Ned, did say, "I guess all that homework added up."

Alice had selected the school from several others on the basis that graduates were accepted at decent colleges, and that senior classes contained no more than sixty boys. Her education had been about the same as her sons', at a girl's school on the North Shore of Chicago. She went east to college and managed to purge herself of the slight mid-western accent that people from Chicago can acquire. She wanted to sound like her New York counterparts. It was not lost on her that the rich young women from Boston to Washington did not sport regional accents. They all spoke a cleaned-up English that was meant to pass anywhere as the correct version of the language.

Alice's father was a neurosurgeon, now in the closing days of what had been an outstanding career. Alice's mother came from an old family, or as old as a family can be in Chicago, say five generations. The source of wealth had been railroads, but the current investments were in real estate. The family, sensing the coming decrease in the worth of rolling stock and track, and appreciating the nearly perpetual rise in the value of land, shifted from railroading to owning office buildings and the portions of downtown on which they stood. During the first half of the twentieth century, the family had managed to buy up small parts of the hearts of the four largest cities in the United States. Alice received income from a trust set up by her grandfather. The proceeds from another trust came her way on her mother's death.

Warren's family had entered manufacturing around 1900 and various members still controlled enterprises, either as members of a board of directors, or as fully employed executives. Warren felt ill-suited for a life in industry and when he won his first election as a city council member in the bedroom community where he and Alice lived, his father settled three million on him, handing out the advice that as long as Warren wished to be a public servant, he need not be one in poverty. Warren's father had chosen the sum of three million so that Warren and Alice would have approximately the same net worth. He had said at the time, "It might be unhealthy for a wife to be richer. She could lord it over you." To avoid envy between brothers, and because the father was fair, he gifted Ralph in the same amount at the same time. It was in the personality of the brothers that nothing of their wealth could be gleaned from their behavior. That went for Ralph's wife, Marla. It was not quite true of Alice.

The neurosurgeon and his wife had built a five-bedroom house that had two living rooms, a dining room, a den, hallways, an entryway, kitchen, pantry, and two screened porches and ample baths. There was a full basement where the family kept their luggage and such used-on-occasion necessities as Christmas decorations. There were bicycles and skis in the proper number to equip Alice and her two siblings as they grew up. There were also boxes of clothes from Alice's grandmother, and these Alice and her younger sister would try on over winter weekends. Alice's grandmother had died in the house. She considered her clothes and jewelry her most precious possessions, which she distributed freely to her two granddaughters. To her grandson she gave the toilet kits of her husband, who predeceased her, and she threw in two sets of cuff links and shirt studs. There was also a gold pocket watch.

The clothes had not belonged exclusively to Alice's grandmother. Some of them were from previous generations. They spanned the years 1890 to 1940. Alice liked best those from the 1920s because she felt that the low waist and short skirts of that era suited her best. When decked out in one of these costumes, she resembled the ladies in the editions of *Vogue* from past years. She worked on a collection of hats to finish the presentation.

Alice did not know whether her body had formed her personality. She knew only that she didn't want any other body than the one she had. There were long arms and legs and a long torso. She stood two inches shorter than Warren. Her hips were slim and her breasts small. She was pleased about this latter feature because she felt that women who were large up front had difficulty swinging a golf club. Golf was her game. She had learned to hit a drive with all her force by letting the left arm lead the club head through the swing, and by letting the club head follow the ball until it was well on its way. It was pretty much straight down the fairway time after time. She had never devoted herself to mastering the rest of the game, the approach shots and putting. They had not seemed important to her.

Leading her life was important but there was no passion anywhere. Her two sons received attention and affection. Concerning Warren there were difficulties. She admitted that, but found it simpler to attend to the two boys than to understand and satisfy the needs of the mature man in her life. Her interests hadn't changed over the years. As with so many of her friends, it came down to music, art and literature. She participated in the organizations that brought the arts to her city, but she knew that her involvement was superficial.

They had met at the airport in Chicago. She was waiting to board a flight to New York. He had changed planes after arriving from Minneapolis and found himself in the same waiting area. He sat down besides her, thinking nothing of it as the area was filling. He asked her whether she wanted part of his paper. She answered, "We probably read the same material." He took her in, as was his habit. He imagined how she had looked as a child, and then wondered what she would be like in middle age. He guessed that one day the long neck would wear a choker containing four strands of pearls. He could visualize a tiara in her hair. He thought she resembled one of those princesses the Danes sent to England to marry into their nobility.

They were both in the rear of the plane and after takeoff he came down the aisle and asked if he could sit next to her. They arranged to meet in New York on that weekend. He never let her out of his consciousness. The courtship had involved a fair amount of time flying between cities. He had known right away but it took Alice a while to decide.

He was surprised that he found her plainness and simplicity so attractive. This was not a sophisticated, clever woman. Her approach in conversation was direct. He grew fond of that long face, the eyes set slightly higher than expected, and the hair piled up with scarcely a part. She did not understand his attentiveness as so few men had gone out of their way to single her out.

For her birthday she asked that Warren change into a dinner jacket. She wore one of the dresses from her grandmother's collection complete with hair ornament. It was neither a hat nor a tiara, but a band around her hair holding a single feather standing straight up. She hired a cook and a person to serve the meal, which opened with champagne. The boys were at table, dressed in their blue suits.

The evening passed off uneventfully. She opened his present, a simple diamond bracelet. She got out of her chair and walked around the table and kissed him. He snapped the bracelet in place. She said, "It's lovely, Warren," and kissed him again.

He awoke at about two in the morning. Alice turned over and asked, "Who is Muriel?"

He paused a moment. "There's a Muriel in my apartment building. Why do you ask?"

"You took me for her. You put your arms around me and called me by her name. Twice, in fact." There was silence, and then Alice asked, "Are you sleeping with her?"

Warren didn't hesitate. "It has happened."

Alice sat up in bed. She said, "I need a drink." She picked up the bathrobe at the end of their bed, slipped into it and left the bedroom. Warren got up, found his bathrobe and slippers, and followed his wife.

Warren could see by the color that she had fixed a strong drink. He prepared one for himself and followed her into the living room.

"I didn't think I had to live in Washington to supervise my husband," she said.

"Apparently it's not supervision that I need."

"Tell me what happened."

"She lives directly upstairs."

"And?"

"It started with a drink after work, perhaps three years ago. The serious business, maybe a year ago."

"Do you want a divorce?" Alice asked.

"Not in this lifetime," he said. "And you?" he asked.

"No, of course not. It is not I who has wandered. Why should I be expected to pay a penalty because you behaved so poorly?"

They were silent. Both took swallows from their drink. "I don't want to give you the pitch about lonely man away from home," Warren said.

"Well, thank heavens."

"But there's more to the story. It's important that you understand."

"Do tell," she said in a sarcastic tone.

Warren stood up and walked across the room. He turned off the lights and returned to the sofa. He used one hand to hold her face, thumb on one cheek and fingers on the other. He placed his other hand on the back of her head and proceeded to kiss her for a long time. When they were finished, bedclothes were strewn around and they lay naked on the sofa. Alice asked, "Well, where did that come from?"

"From some deep recess. It's related to how I feel about you."

"A bit animalistic," Alice ventured.

"No, very humanistic," he answered. He went on. "Here's what I found out with Muriel. You may as well hear this. Muriel and I have never made plans or taken vows or suggested some different life for one another. But I did learn from her that the physical part could be an expression of love. She doesn't make love. She expresses love. You, on the other hand, this isn't going to be very nice, treat the whole business as a duty, a minor unpleasantness that a dutiful wife goes through to keep her husband at peace. You dish it out once every two or three weeks as though it's prescribed medicine. I suspect you look at the calendar."

Warren wasn't finished. "I'll make you a proposition. I'll give up Muriel, gladly, if I can have from you what she gives me. It's not Muriel. It's the unfettered affection. Knowing what I know now, if I can't have that from you, we may be finished. Can you look inside yourself?"

She put her arms around him. They slid slowly from the sofa to the floor, she landing on top of him. He said, "Look inside yourself. See what's in there. Figure out what you can give."

Alice lay on top of her husband. She was quiet, breathing deeply, not in an agitated way. Had this been the customary event she would have retrieved her nightgown and slipped it on. As it was, she lay naked on him even though the nightgown was on the sofa next to her.

"What am I supposed to do now? How do I look inside?" Alice asked.

"I like your exterior just fine. It's what's inside that I'm after. Once in a while I see in there and it's wonderful."

"You talk in riddles."

"No. When I start the sexual activity, organize it, and satisfy myself, then it's me taking from you. That's all right from time to time, but when it's time after time, it's embarrassing. More often than not I have my way with you, roll off and go to sleep. It's demeaning. I guess you put up with it as part of the job. It's not been that way in Washington."

"Cruel of you to bring that up."

"I'm sorry. No cruelty intended. I'm trying to isolate some instinct in you. I know it's there. Once in a long while, maybe once a year, you participate. It's only on those occasions that I feel any love from you. I don't know what brings it on and why so rarely."

"Am I getting heavy on you?"

"No. It's wonderful. Are you getting chilly?"

"No. I'm trying to answer your question. I know the moments you mean. I don't know why they come when they do, and why so infrequently. Is that really the problem we have?"

"That and the fact that it's impossible for a man to ask for it. It's like begging. What would you think if I asked you to be more demonstrative?"

"My sense is that it would be the wrong question. If you asked me to be more demonstrative I might think you want me to develop new techniques."

"That's the quandary for men, perhaps for women as well. The idea is for love in both directions and when the moment for the physical expression comes that's fusion, or something."

Alice answered, "Looking back, I associate physical activity with the way you want me to be in our bed. Once in a while physical activity awakens that part of me. Or something outdoors, or dancing with you."

Warren said, "That could stimulate you, something we do together that has physical activity. But beyond that, the next layer consists of generosity, affection for the other person, some appreciation of the other person. I think that's what love is."

"When it's there for two people, is it there all the time?" Alice asked.

"When each person is the most important person to the other, then it's there all the time."

"Maybe this Muriel is some sort of catalyst. Through her you got to ask your question."

Warren didn't say anything. Alice was quiet pondering the next remark. She asked, "Would you admit that it can't be the way you want every time, that there will be times when it just doesn't work?"

"I will admit to that, if you agree with me that waiting a year between times has nothing to do with two people in love."

She put her long fingers through his hair and started kissing his forehead. She moved to his eyelids, then his cheeks, and finally settled on his mouth.

# The Brothers 11

The following morning at the breakfast table, before the children had roused themselves, Alice volunteered, "Interesting evening. I thought we got a lot accomplished."

"Do you want to come to Washington Tuesday morning?" Warren asked.

"No. I'll let you deal with your Muriel. I don't want to meet her, even by accident."

"Do you trust me?"

"I have to. You're trusting me to find what's been missing between us."

Warren telephoned Muriel Tuesday evening on returning from the Hill. He asked if he could come up. He recounted the events at home over the weekend. "I used your name at two o'clock in the morning. Hardly a brilliant thing to do."

"Were you in the middle of it and the wrong name slipped out?"

"No. I was asleep and the wrong name slipped out, and I didn't deny anything."

"Is she calling lawyers?"

Warren answered, "We never got that far. I told her what I thought you and I had between us. Then I made the point that's precisely what she and I don't have. I went on to say that if we, my wife and I, were not able to find it, the missing ingredient, our life together would be over."

Muriel said, "Because we never discuss these matters, I haven't any idea of what we have, as you put it. I mean, I'd like to hear your view of what we have."

"It's the freedom to be intimate on all levels. With my wife those moments happen so rarely. When you can be intimate physically it turns out that it is because intimacy comes easily at all levels. In the case of my wife and me, there's so much left unsaid, so little expressed. Life together has this superficial air."

"It's that simple, dear. The physical part doesn't clear the way for the rest of it. It's the reverse. You work on understanding and appreciation at all levels, then the physical part is a cinch. I'm just repeating your thought in different words." Muriel added, "What did you say to your wife at that point?"

"I told her I couldn't beg for it, that she had to find it in herself to let me in her life, to give herself to me, more than just occasionally."

"It's interesting that over the years of your marriage you weren't able to blurt it out, but you could say it when forced to," Muriel said.

"Just saying it once in a while over the years might have worked. Men hate that. They want their women to understand and to volunteer the best in them. If you ask for something, then receive it, you wonder whether you've extorted it."

"How did it unfold?"

"We were in the living room. I turned out the lights. Clothes came off. It wasn't rape, but I was forceful. You know, I love the woman."

"That must have been acceptable because she didn't throw you out. Then what happened?"

"After more conversation, she returned the favor, on the floor." Warren paused and added, "It's all there. Just has to be shaken loose."

Muriel let the conversation die. Then, assuming a light air, she said, "This is traumatic business. Freshen your drink, go in the den and turn on the news. I'm about to prepare dinner for us. Microwave dinners and salad. How about that?"

"If it's not too complicated," Warren said. They had just stood up and Muriel slapped him lightly on the fanny.

They ate dinner in silence and when the news program was over, Warren said, "You recall the pat on the *derrière* you gave me a while ago?"

"It wasn't distinguished from others I've given you, was it?"

"Well, that's affection. Some mixture of understanding, appreciation of the other, pleasure in the other's company. I feel at ease around you. I want to reach out and touch you most times when no one's looking and all the time when it's dark. It's so nice. It's obvious we would be good together."

"We promised we'd never talk about it," Muriel said.

"We assumed that our lives weren't changing. But nothing stays the same very long."

"I guess you're suggesting changes. Which changes do you have in mind?" Muriel asked.

"I have to move. I'll find one or two rooms on the Hill somewhere. I don't trust myself in the same building with you."

"Did she make you take an additional oath?"

"On the contrary. She left it up to me. So moving, that's change number one. Change two is that I shouldn't run for re-election. I think my life is with my family."

"I can't imagine your giving up politics," Muriel said.

"I can always run for governor. Shorter commute."

It was about eight in the evening. Warren stood up and moved one step toward the door. Muriel put her arms around his waist and pressed her face against his chest. "One for the road?" she asked.

"It would be superlative, except for the guilt. When they let you loose on your own, the honor code comes into play. Those damned codes are stronger than steel."

"I'm going to miss you," Muriel said.

# The Brothers 12

Ralph had been contemplating how he would tell Marla. Would it be a weekend afternoon when the children were out? Would it be late at night, up stairs, under the cover of darkness? Knowing Marla, the lights would come on and she would start yelling at him, with the desired effect of waking the children. "Your father's leaving us. He's starting a new family."

He could delay. Colleen might lose the child. She might decide to leave town. He didn't think she'd abort. When she told him about the pregnancy, she said that having a child answered her fondest hope, but added right away that she could disengage herself from his life at a moment's notice. Ralph understood that to mean she would settle with her parents in Milwaukee. He could hear himself rejecting the idea, saying that it was his baby as much as hers and that his abandoning her at a moment like this was out of the question. He did wonder whether she had stopped taking the pill on purpose and if that was the case, then it was her baby, not his, and perhaps she should leave town and allow time to heal wounds.

He would start with Colleen, and sound her out before confessing to Marla. Colleen might have decided to leave town. He had to know her point of view before heading into the maelstrom that Marla would create.

They were face to face in Colleen's apartment. "I have to tell her, Colleen," Ralph said.

"If you hold to the theory that all the news will come out in the end," Colleen remarked.

"Well, it will. That's our experience nowadays. Your life goes up on a bulletin board, particularly if you have any public exposure."

"I suppose there's no advantage in waiting," Colleen said. "What do you guess your wife's reaction will be?"

"She'll want the house, the kids, and half the money. She'll want a divorce. I sense she has a vengeful streak. She may want to destroy me."

"Can you support her and your children and find a little left over for this birth?"

"There's a fair amount of money. Father, God bless him, set up Warren and me fourteen years ago when Warren won his first election. So money's not an issue except that I'll have a lot less of it."

"You can afford this birth?"

"Yes. We'll have to find a place for us to live, large enough for three. I'll have to resign from my parish. You'll be finished in the choir, by the way."

"I'm not showing yet, by the way," Colleen reminded him. They both laughed. "So you're going straight home, have dinner with your family, then when the children are in bed you'll broach the subject. Sounds like the worst day of your life."

"There's no question of that. You know, in weak moments I thought of providing enough money to send you off to Milwaukee or Chicago and set you up on your own and hope that you would have the baby and start a new life."

"I thought of that myself, just from the financial standpoint," Colleen said. "I wondered about it but concluded it was impossible, just too expensive. But now that you've indicated there's money, we can both look at it in a new light. You don't have to wreck everything. I can disappear and you can go on about your life."

"You recall the first evening I pushed the button on your intercom?"

"Of course."

"I was so desperate for the warmth and comfort that a woman can bring a man that I put everything on the line – my career, reputation, family, future -- everything. And I don't regret it one instant. I knew in some instinctive way that the treasures one woman has locked away, treasures that she can give to the correct man, one man, are worth more than all the rest of it."

"You may be overdoing it, darling," Colleen said.

"No. It's true, and if the gift lasts one day only, I wouldn't be surprised that the one day is more valuable than the rest of your life."

"Ralph, now you are overstating it. I gave you what you needed at the moment you needed it, but you may be able to get that from Marla now."

"I don't understand you. I assume that I will get nothing but grief from Marla."

"Your bargaining position is very strong. You are and you have everything she wants. You may be able to strike a bargain. If all you're asking for is what I give you, well, that's not much. She should be able to turn that on with a snap of her fingers. Most women can."

They were sitting on a sofa in Colleen's small apartment. Ralph placed his arm around her shoulders, kissed her lightly, and said, "She'll throw me out. I might come back here tonight."

"Yes, of course. If you don't come back tonight I'll assume she's forgiven you and you've worked out something. But call me as soon as you're free to."

The drive to his house from Colleen's took thirty minutes in early evening traffic. Ralph was rarely punctual. Marla understood about last-minute telephone calls from parishioners and that he might visit a patient in the hospital on the way. This was an ordinary evening at home. The family ate dinner together. The children went upstairs to their rooms to tend to homework. Both rooms had twin beds in the event a friend stayed over, and there was space left for a desk, a small bookcase and a chest of drawers.

The situation was so much on his mind that he knew he could not wait until late in the evening. He was in the living room, holding the paper. Marla came in carrying a magazine that had come in the mail. They took their customary places.

Ralph said, "We have some things to talk about."

"What would they be, dear?" Marla asked.

"There's no way of saying it except to barge in. I've been seeing something of a woman and she's pregnant."

"And it's your child?"

"No question."

"And what do you plan to do about it?"

"There isn't too much I can do. In six months or so the child will be born. I'm surprised you appear to be composed."

"I don't know. Women these days learn to expect most anything. Wouldn't you guess that thousands of men are telling their wives tonight, across the country, that they've cheated and that a baby's on the way?'

"I suppose so. Hadn't thought of it that way."

"Well, what do you plan to do? It's not as though you're thinking about it for the first time this instant. And by the way, do I know her?"

"The redheaded girl in the choir, Colleen."

"The big cow from Ireland?" Marla asked.

"She's not a big cow, for heaven's sake."

"Well, her breasts are bigger than mine. Couldn't you have had the decency to find someone across town, someone I didn't know?"

"In extreme circumstances you work with what's at hand," Ralph said. He was surprised that Marla hadn't thrown a fit, although that might come later.

"What am I going to do, you ask. I went to her because of some need. Well, not some need, a definite need."

Marla cut him off. "We all know the need. Men can't seem to grow up. For heaven's sake, Ralph, you're in early middle age. Can't you keep your zipper up?"

"Marla, we're so far apart on the issue that it would take five years of psychotherapy for both of us to reach an understanding."

Ralph outlined his choices. He could use money to dispatch Colleen to her parents or any place she wished to go. He guessed at the amount of money it would take. His other choice was to take up life with Colleen. He didn't say "abandon" in conversation with Marla. He said that he could "give up his family and career." In his heart he knew that he would be abandoning them.

Marla asked him how long it would take to make up his mind. He said that he couldn't stand the indecision, living in no man's land, as he put it. Marla asked him if he wanted tea. She prepared it. They stayed in the living room, reading. Ralph thought it was as though nothing had happened.

Before the usual time for bed, Marla got out of her chair and said, "See you upstairs." He read for a few more minutes. When he heard the bath running, he went up and changed in his bathroom. He lay there, perplexed. The bedroom was dark except for light from the street. In a few moments Marla came out of her bathroom. She went to the door leading to the hall and locked it. She wore only the top of her pajama. She stood at the edge of the bed, removed the top and asked, "It's still all there, isn't it?" He had folded down the sheet and blanket. She slipped into bed with him and he felt a little overwhelmed by the scent of the eau de cologne.

When it was over, she said, "If that's what you want, you can get all you need right here." This was the same woman who had said to him, on the occasion of his moving close to her and placing his arm around her, "Well, let's get it over with." That was eight years ago. Colleen was right. Most any woman can turn it on with a snap of her fingers.

* * *

Warren and Alice tried isolating the reasons for the unraveling of this marriage. They admitted that they had trouble dissecting their own, let alone understanding what went on in Ralph and Marla's case. Warren had sensed trouble when his brother admitted to his lusting over a certain redhead in the choir. He knew disaster had struck when Ralph telephoned him to announce that Colleen was pregnant.

On a weekend when Warren was home from Washington, he and his wife fell to searching for reasons. "I wonder how flexible they were." Alice asked. Before Warren could answer, she said, "We've accepted lots of change, you and I, your moving to Washington, the whole business of politics that I was not prepared for."

"Their lives changed when they became parents. And of course, there's simply the matter of growing older," Warren said.

"Perhaps Marla changed when she decided to have no more children. It's the beginning of a new life for women when that happens," Alice said.

"It might have been better for them if they had moved out of town, done some missionary work, traveled. Ralph's been the assistant at his first parish and now the rector at his second, perhaps not for long. Pretty much the same stuff day after day."

"Stale, you mean?" Alice asked.

"Yes. You need new challenges, difficult ones that force you to come up with another set of goals and to meet them the person has to evolve, grow, and develop additional resources, powers you can't even imagine you have."

"Do you think we've grown?"

"I've grown around the waist," Warren answered.

"I'm changing the subject," Alice said. "A mistake so many people make is to delay gratification. They put off pleasure. I say live for the moment. That's what I say. We only have so many moments, why not make the most of them?"

"It's normal to postpone," Warren said. "We become preoccupied with the serious side." He paused, and then added, "You don't." She smiled at him. He went on, "You need to have a powerful personality to live for the moment. Means taking out the trash in your life on a regular basis. I doubt Ralph and Marla could do that. Far too serious."

"You don't think they had much fun?" Alice asked.

"No, I don't think so. If you're serious at work, in the dining room, in the living room, you take all that serious business upstairs with you."

"Through it all, we've remained pretty good friends," Alice said. "That counts for something."

"Counts for a lot," Warren said.

"I never noticed that bond between them," Alice said.

"I sensed they came together with a crash now and then but that they had no idea of going through life holding hands."

"Do you think they were committed for the long pull?" Alice asked.

"Evidently not," Warren answered. "Commitment's the state of mind that brings you back after a terrible falling out, when you think it's impossible to go on. Haul out some more trash."

"You like that analogy," Alice said.

"Well, trash is the stuff that accumulates in people's lives. We have to confront one another, get it said, get it on the table, and work through it. We all get to that point, with spouse, with friends. It takes confrontation to get rid of the trash. Then you can build something."

"Do you think we avoid the issues once in a while?" Alice asked.

"Yes, I'm sure we do," Warren answered.

"Do you promise not to do that anymore?"

"Yes, sealed with a kiss," Warren said.

"Something Ralph and Marla and you and I are guilty of," Alice said, "is that we don't look out at the world together. I suspect it's important. I do a few things in the city. You do your politics in Washington. We don't do anything of significance together. Ralph is a priest. Marla does the altar guild, but beyond that they operated alone, or so it seemed to me."

"What do you suppose they could do together?" Warren asked.

"I don't know. Even if they read the same book and just discussed it," Alice answered.

"We're sure picking them apart," Warren said.

"I guess most couples have the same ills," Alice said.

"Just a matter of degree?" Warren asked.

"Yes, I suppose so," Alice answered.

"You know, darling, there's a need for forgiveness in marriages," Warren said.

# The Brothers 13

"Would you think it over?" That was Muriel's closing question addressed to Monty over the telephone. She had explained to him that ten years in Washington might be enough. There could be positions of greater authority and responsibility than those she had held, but they would be in the executive branch and the odds of making the transition from the legislative to the executive branch were slim.

Muriel aimed to return to the university and devote three years to course work toward the doctorate, followed by two years given to research and writing a thesis. The question she had asked Monty was, "May I start out living with you?" When he had demurred, she asked him to think it over.

Monty's answer had covered the issue of permanence. He said, "You're always welcome here but so that I don't go out of my mind, I'd have to know if you intend to stay until you found a place of your own, or if you're coming back for keeps."

Muriel's answer was equivocal. She said, "I can't tell yet, Monty. I counted up in my diary. You came to Washington twice while we were married and fourteen times after the divorce. I enjoyed the visits but they were different from marriage. I would call the visits part tourism and the remainder sex."

Monty interrupted her, "You're wondering which part was the more important to me, I suppose."

"For me," Muriel answered, "I learned some history and I always like what you do in bed."

"And for me," Monty said, "both were necessities. I gave up other women about eight years ago."

Muriel changed the subject. "Your visits were different from marriage in that difficult situations never were resolved. Never enough time. When I was ready to right some wrong, you were in the blue van headed for the airport. I want to see if we can get through the rough spots, resolve issues, and come out stronger. That's marriage. That's what I want you to think over."

It was a simple decision for Monty. He would read less and talk more. The lonely evenings and empty weekends would be a thing of the past. They would convert the second bedroom to a study for Muriel. If he made her feel welcome and created a comfortable home for her, she might stay. And her body, pleasant in all dimensions, whose every square inch he knew from exploration, would be his. He loved her. A part of that came from Muriel's response to him. He was keenly aware of the pleasure and satisfaction he brought her. He wondered about the men in Washington. Was there one, or were there a few, that she responded to? He assumed there must be at least one. It would be unnatural if there had been none. He thought his decision to give up other women eight years ago had been unnatural. Monty wanted to believe that she would come back one day. Perhaps two or three times he had said to her, "You're the only one I want." She had kissed him and answered, "Thank you, that's dear."

* * *

When Warren came into his office, the receptionist handed him three telephone slips. Mrs. Rodriguez said, "A Mrs. Oldenburg called ten minutes ago. She asked that you call her back at your earliest convenience."

"Can do," Warren said.

The familiar, soft voice came on. "I miss you living below me, Warren," Muriel said.

"Two rooms on the Hill aren't the same for me, either," he said.

"Are you still contemplating the run for governor?"

"Yes. Put out my first feeler. The money people. The power brokers."

"How did it go?"

"I would say positive. But, as you know, when an office becomes vacant the hats come flying into the ring from all directions. I guess my candidacy is in a pending file for the moment."

"The reason for my call is to let you know that I'm planning to go home and start work on the doctorate. I'm hoping to live with my former husband. It's provisional, really. Maybe we can pull it off."

"Are there any statistics on how many couples make it who remarry after a divorce?" Warren asked.

"I'm certain there are and I guess they're dismal. The reason they're dismal is that people don't fix up what went wrong before the divorce. They're not around one another to work on it."

"You're a rational woman, Muriel. Why would you fight against the odds?"

"I never gave Monty and me a chance at marriage. You know, children and all that. Too immature. I don't know why I came to Washington, maybe for a change, something different to do. Obviously Monty meant very little to me then. He's quite a guy. He's made of hard stuff. He's waited for me, I guess. He wanted children and I denied him that. What remains between us consists of a few visits and some old memories."

The conversation went on at length. Muriel dove in. "When I get home, I want to meet Alice."

"Why in the world would you want to do that?" Warren asked.

"To ask for forgiveness," Muriel answered.

Warren described Alice's reaction to the news of the infidelity. He wanted to make certain that Muriel understood that while she, Alice, was no friend of infidelity, she acknowledged that in this instance the news had awakened a response that placed their marriage back on track. Warren said that in effect his wife had forgiven both parties and that any direct contact might produce unexpected results. "Why not leave well enough alone?" he asked.

Muriel answered that the act would bring about closure. Warren responded by saying that the value of closure was overestimated, and that Muriel could try leaving matters open, that is, let this matter die a slow, natural death.

At this point, Muriel said, "I thought it would clear the air in the event I volunteered some time in your campaign."

"Another bad idea, Muriel," Warren said. "The press -- and it takes only one reporter -- will sniff out the fact that you and I lived at the same address for three or four years and the questions will start. They won't be able to extort confessions from us but we'll find ourselves issuing denials every other day. I don't have to tell you what that does to a campaign."

"How many people know?" Muriel asked.

"Alice, you and I, and Ralph," Warren answered.

"How did Ralph find out?"

"He answered the telephone that afternoon he let the door slam and you called."

"Of course," Muriel said.

They discussed the subjects in history that she would study, and the tentative topic for the thesis. To this last question Muriel said that she would find a treaty whose consequences had not been explored to the satisfaction of her thesis committee.

Warren asked Muriel when she might leave. She answered, "When I receive an all-clear from Monty. When he issues one, I'll start the extraction process, giving notice, packing, all that."

As the conversation wound down, Warren asked Muriel whether she had been accepted at the university for her program. "Yes, I did that first," she said. "Played the Phi Beta Kappa card, and then told them how I had contributed mightily to the foreign affairs initiatives of the Congress these last five years."

"Maybe you can petition the university for the degree and forget all the rest," Warren said.

# The Brothers 14

Colleen stayed awake until after midnight. When Ralph failed to show up, or to telephone, she concluded that Marla and he had found a solution. She thought their most obvious plan would be to ask her to settle in Milwaukee with her parents. He would pay for the move and give her as much as fifty thousand dollars for all expenses. It would be up to her to decide whether to put the child up for adoption. Their second choice might be to have her stay in Minneapolis, give birth, and put the child up for adoption right away, the problem disappearing as she, Colleen, disappeared from the lives of Marla and Ralph. Colleen tried to imagine other solutions but was overtaken by sleep. Her last thought was about the baby within her. She felt her stomach by rubbing both hands against it. It felt the way it always did.

Ralph reached her in the morning at work. He asked her how she was. He told her that there was a scheduled meeting of the vestry the following evening. "I plan to resign," he said.

"No, you mustn't do that," she pleaded.

They arranged to meet for lunch at a restaurant near her place of work.

"You have a pained expression, Reverend Montgomery," Colleen said. "How did it go last night?"

"Well, I was shocked by the calmness Marla exhibited, and shocked again by her performance. I guess you could call it a performance. Don't I wish that the real Marla resembled the fake Marla I saw last night?"

"She turned up the heat for you, was that it?"

"It's interesting that she knew all along the missing element in the relationship. I didn't spell out anything."

"Don't you suppose you can make a go of it?"

"I assume not. That's why I'm resigning."

"Will I be named?"

"Not on your life. Keep working and singing in the choir and drop out at your convenience."

"When we're seen together, people will make the connection."

"I plan to live on the family place at the lake for a while. The children can visit me from time to time. You can come up on weekends. It's really quite remote, but lovely."

Warren and Ralph's parents had purchased a large house on the shore of a northern lake. It happened to be the same lake where Ralph and his partner slept under the overturned canoe two decades ago. The place was large enough to house Warren and Ralph's parents, and Warren and Ralph's spouses and children. They had spent a fair amount of time together on the premises. Ralph's notion was that he would occupy the guest cottage, which could be heated against the coming winter.

"You don't have to hide on my account," Colleen said. "I get out of town and you and your family carry on as though nothing happened. This approach that you're talking about, in which you give up everything, doesn't make sense."

"I don't deserve the congregation's trust any longer. That's the reason. The idea of your paying for my transgression doesn't sit well with me."

"Listen to me, darling Reverend, it's our transgression, not yours, and we are having a baby. You've had two and now you're having a third. One of my purposes for being on this earth is to have a child. I see difficult times ahead for everybody, but I see a great deal of joy."

They talked back and forth. Colleen wanted to know how Ralph would spend his time at the lake. He claimed he would walk in the woods, read a great deal, and think about his character and how events had overwhelmed him. He said that his great failing had been to avoid confrontation with Marla on the issue. Why couldn't he explain to her that, as a man, he needed her affection? It had turned out that finding affection elsewhere was simpler than stating his case to his wife. "Another quandary," he added, "was that if I had explained my desires to Marla and she provided what I wanted, it would haunt me that I had forced it out of her. I know it's not in her heart, anyway."

"It's become clear," he went on, "that I want the real thing as a gift, just the way you give it to me."

"There's no answer to that one," Colleen said. "Some women give it easily to the man they love, no questions asked. Other women can't find it in themselves to give it. It's a cold, hard piece of their personality. I believe in my heart that if it's important to you, that important, you have to go find it and pay the consequences. You've done that. No amount of walking in the woods can make it clearer to you, clearer than what I've just said."

Ralph was silent for a moment. He brought up the topic of money. He would make certain that expenses were met. They discussed schedules. After tendering his resignation he would talk to his children, pack a few clothes, and be off.

"Will you come by?" Colleen asked.

"Yes, of course. And because you're without a car, I'll drive down to get you when you want to spend a weekend with me."

"That'll make me miss choir. And by the way, you're paying an extraordinary price, just about the ultimate price, so you must place great value on what I have to give you. That being the case, you'd be crazy not to avail yourself of it in great quantity."

He smiled at her. "You have many beguiling traits about you," he said. They had finished their lunch and left the restaurant.

* * *

The conversation with his two children was as painful an episode as he had endured. He was unable to find words of explanation beyond, "These things happen between husbands and wives."

"Mother's at the Wilson's house. We're supposed to call her when you leave," his daughter said. She was eleven. Ralph packed some clothes and picked out several books. He told them he was on his way to the lake and that they could telephone any time. He said he looked forward to their visits on weekends.

When he was ready to leave, he suggested to the children that he place the call to the Wilsons. When he went out the door and walked to his car, he began crying. He drove half a block and stopped the car to regain his composure. In thirty minutes he was at Colleen's. His first comment was to admit that he had failed to bring up their situation to the children. "I could not calculate how to tell a nine year old and an eleven year old that there's another woman beside their mother, and that there will be a baby soon enough. We'll have to face that someday."

"We'll work our way through these problems over time. By the way, you're not in any condition to drive to the lake. You need a drink. I'll fix dinner, and we'll go right to bed."

# The Brothers 15

"Your brother called," Alice announced. "He asked that you call him some evening when it's convenient."

"How did he sound?" Warren asked.

"I couldn't tell, really. He did say that he had seen Colleen and his children, but not together. His children don't know about the baby yet."

"I'll call him tomorrow evening. I know his habits. Around seven o'clock after the news he'll be starting to wash his dinner dishes," Warren said.

"Should either you or I, or both of us, drive up to see him?" Alice asked.

"Excellent idea. I'll sound him out."

It was Thursday evening. Warren had caught the mid-afternoon flight from Washington. Alice would track his flight and pick him up. She had started meeting his plane after launching what Alice referred to as "Our new life together." She looked forward to that first kiss in the car. It excited her. She knew precisely where it would lead.

Warren had discussed his candidacy with two members of his party. They wanted to know about the campaign he might structure. They held him in high repute, but now he was planning a statewide campaign and it would focus on issues inside Minnesota. Previously, as a candidate for the House of Representatives, he campaigned on national issues and how his views, and votes, would affect his constituents.

His brother's situation forced him to rethink his position. No one knew yet, but some acquaintance, or reporter, or member of the congregation would connect Ralph's resignation with Colleen's pregnancy and her dropping out of the choir. The obvious question to ask Colleen was, "Who is the father?" If she did not provide an answer, plenty of people would speculate.

Warren wondered whether he should confront the electorate with the truth in the hopes that most would forgive. Should he wait until matters developed and let Ralph deal with it? Should he abandon the idea of a run for governor on the basis that he was guaranteed to lose? Should he avoid the whole business of pregnancy because it was none of his concern? Colleen could lose the baby any day. She might still move away. Perhaps if he waited a little longer, time would come to his rescue with one of those miracles.

The talk at dinner was politics, discussing the events of the previous few days in Washington. The boys participated and enjoyed an insider's view, the only view they had heard. After dinner, Warren carried on along the same lines, and Alice said, "Don't be too serious with me tonight, dear. You know I have my limits on the issues."

At seven Friday evening, Warren called his brother who came on right away. Warren asked, "Just starting the dishes?"

Ralph laughed and said, "What else?"

Warren asked him how he was filling his time. Ralph answered that he was reading a good deal and walking the trails around the lake. Warren said, "Are you solving any problems?" Ralph's answer upset Warren mildly. "The trails around here don't lead to those places."

The chatted some more, then Warren asked if he and Alice could come up and spend Saturday night. Ralph said he planned to pick up Colleen Saturday morning and bring her up for the weekend. "We may as well bring the boys along," Warren said. "They'll have to know sometime."

Warren and Alice debated which of them would explain the events to their sons. It was agreed that Alice would start. She was surprised at their questions and reactions. "What's better about Colleen than Aunt Marla?" "If we went to church regularly we could have done something." "What happens to Don and Kate? Do they stay with Aunt Marla? Uncle Ralph and Aunt Marla seem so nice together." The boys showed no interest in discussing the sexual arrangements. It was not until the older son had met Colleen and taken in the slight bulge that he asked his mother, "Did Uncle Ralph do that?"

The women prepared dinner, although Colleen, who had been at the lake since noon, had settled on a menu and bought supplies at the general store where the dirt road meets the main road into town.

After the boys excused themselves from the table, they went to the bedroom they would use to watch a video the younger one had brought. It was Warren's turn to address the three adults. He started in with, "I think it's a mistake to let things drift along." He made his point that the family had some public following and that it would be to everyone's advantage if the news got out, managed by them, and time were allowed to temper the impact.

"It's not going to help your political career," Ralph said.

"I'm not running again. Coming home. Might do something in state."

"Governor?" Ralph asked.

"Possibly," Warren answered.

"Obviously I don't care for the public part," Colleen said. "Do you suppose the pain is of shorter duration when you give out the news than when it leaks out?"

"If I give it out, the pictures of you, Ralph and myself, and perhaps Marla, will make the front page. There will be a follow-up story on the second day. That should be it. On the other hand, if a reporter is assigned to the story it might be converted into a scandal, lasting who knows how long? If we go public, I should be the spokesman for the family. If I'm not the spokesman, the reporters will come to me for a series of statements on the effects on my political future and all that. They probably will, anyway."

"I'm desperately sorry about all this," Colleen said. "Just the smallest accident and people are brought down. You know it was never my intention or Ralph's."

"Colleen," Alice said, "you could have left town. I'm so glad you didn't. Ralph needs and wants you. That's obvious. I think you may need and want him, perhaps not to the same extent. And you're having this baby, a niece or nephew of Warren and a first cousin for our boys. Let's celebrate all this good news and stop walking around with long faces."

"I'll drink to that," Ralph said. That was his second sentence since the conversation had taken a serious turn.

"And you're pregnant, Colleen, so you can't drink to it," Alice said.

On their way home Sunday, Warren pulled in to the general store. He said he was going in to buy soft drinks for everyone for the trip. They each gave their selection. In the store, Warren addressed the owner. "Charley, how's my brother doing?" Charley reflected for a moment. "I think I know what you're asking, Warren. He's drinking half a bottle a day. One of my good customers. But listen, get him out of here before the real winter sets in. I don't have to finish that thought for you."

* * *

Moses Staats, most people agreed, had a funny name. He had been active in Minnesota politics since returning from the war. He entered the university, majored in economics and, on graduation, entered the world of commercial real estate. His affair with politics centered on finding candidates for his party in the primaries. He had been part of a group that selected mayors, members of congress, attorneys general, and plenty of men and women who served in Minnesota's two houses. Now in his seventies, Moses had become the person one turned to for political advice. He had a locked jaw. He never repeated and never talked out of turn. He had a rare virtue, that of being incorruptible. He might do a favor, but it would not be in exchange for something of value to him. He might alter one of his positions, but it would only be on the merits. It occurred to Warren that a conversation with Moses would be time well spent.

They met for lunch at a downtown club where Moses had been a member for forty years. Warren and Staats had had lunch in this room when Warren sounded out Moses on making a run for congress. Moses Staats and the Montgomery family had contacts over the years concerning properties that the Montgomery family acquired as sites for manufacturing plants. Staats and Warren's father were approximately the same age.

"Delicate situation," Moses said. "But listen, we've all learned that sunshine and fresh air work. The sooner you get it out, the whole truth, nothing but the truth, the easier it is to control the damage. I don't know why the average citizen has come to respect the truth so much."

"Because we make a practice of bamboozling the average citizen," Warren volunteered.

"What does this do to your future?" Moses asked.

"Well, coincidentally, I decided to call it a day after ten years in Washington and come home. Perhaps try something here."

"Finish your term in Washington?" Moses asked.

"Yes."

"Run for governor?"

"Yes."

"Answer the two questions the press will ask you. Why do you want to be governor and how will you structure your campaign?"

"I want to be governor because I'm ambitious, self-centered, egotistical, and I know that I can do a better job than any other candidate."

"You'll have to clean it up a bit," Moses said.

"As for campaign, I want to run on the issue that Minnesota must start doing the things the federal government fails to do in order to turn the country around."

"Such as?"

"In Washington they don't talk about runaway population, vanishing farmland, immigration that's out of control, a national debt that's starting to choke us, introducing loser pays to bring lawyers under control, and introducing a simple tax code."

"You want Minnesota to take these steps so that Washington gets the picture and follows suit?"

"That's about it," Warren said.

"Suicidal streak?" Moses asked. Then he said, "You know, they'll kill you at the polls with a platform like that."

"I know, but it would be fun," Warren said.

They ordered dessert. Warren had always wondered how Moses stayed trim even though he ate everything on the menu.

"Here's what you do," Moses said. He had summation in his voice. "Write a statement as the spokesman for the family. Just present the facts about Ralph and this new woman. No opinions. Find out from them whether they plan to marry. Pass it by your parents as a matter of courtesy. You'll have to ask Marla if she's filing for divorce. Get glossy prints of you, of Ralph, the woman and Marla. Let me have some biographical data. On the subject of not running again, forget that for ninety days. You don't want to force people to make a connection that may not exist. On the matter of running for governor, forget that for four years. I believe in you, Warren, but we have work to do. Can you pull all that together is a week?"

Warren thought a moment. "I guess so. It might take two weeks."

"When it's ready," Moses said, "we'll have lunch here. I'll invite the publisher and the editor. If we promise them there's no more to the story than we're giving them, they might agree to run it just a couple of days and keep the reporters away. Some reporters are OK, others are attack dogs. And I want to go over your material before our lunch."

"What about television?" Warren asked.

"If Ralph agrees to do an interview, the stations might leave the woman and Marla alone. They love this scandal business."

"I'll put it to Ralph. I'll tell him to wear a suit, no collar. And the woman's name, by the way, is Colleen Murphy. I've grown to like her."

# The Brothers 16

Warren took Moses' advice. His statement had the effects that Moses predicted they would, that truth, the absolute truth, would silence commentary. Warren speculated that some of the following might take place as a result. Men could analyze their feelings for their wives and the conditions of their marriages. Wives in failing marriages might wonder about their husband's longings. Participants in happy marriages would try to figure out the reasons for their good fortune.

Moses ventured that friends of the family would find forgiveness at the ready because over the years society had learned, or taught itself, neither to take sides, nor throw stones, nor feel proud.

Warren's statement acknowledged that his brother and Colleen Murphy had been adulterous. He announced that there was a child on the way and gave the approximate date of birth. He confirmed that Marla had initiated divorce proceedings. He noted Ralph's resignation from his parish. The statement left nothing unsaid.

Ralph installed himself in the guest cottage at the lake. It still belonged to his parents so that he was required to obtain their permission. They were in their late seventies and Ralph found them more accepting than he expected. Ralph's father took the occasion to ask him for the reasons behind the breakup. He made it easy on Ralph by saying, "Many married men who commit adultery are driven to it by an unresponsive wife. Was that your case?" To this Ralph answered, "I could agree with you and make it easy on myself, but I can see now that there was lusting for Colleen on my part, lusting not related entirely to Marla. It appeared easier to do what I did than to clear the air with Marla."

Ralph's father answered, "You'll pardon me the continued metaphor but allow me to observe that clearing the air is followed often by a severe tempest, and after that you might get some fair weather. It's like that for all of us."

The severe tempest arrived in Ralph's life soon enough without any contribution from Marla. He interpreted it as guilt. On his walks around the lake he went over his last night with Marla when she put on her perfumed extravaganza. Why could he not have insisted years earlier and produced the same results? Now he was starting a new life with a woman selected on the basis of her easy availability. In the past, before Colleen appeared, he had gone over the steps he might take to select a second wife and how he would make certain that there would be ample opportunity to be satisfied. Never again would there be long stretches of abstinence. Now that Colleen had started to show he lost some of the enthusiasm for the enterprise. He would be required by Colleen, Warren and Alice to demonstrate happiness and pleasure over his new position, none of which he felt deeply.

Ralph was thankful that a rough schedule had been worked out. He had the children on alternate weekends and Colleen the other times. He would drive down on Friday afternoon to fetch one or the other and return them Sunday evening. No matter who came to the lake over the weekend, he stayed at Colleen's Sunday night.

More than anything, Ralph dreaded the arrival of depression. He knew the symptoms, having had parishioners taken by the disease. It had rendered some incapable of reacting to events and leading what was considered a normal life. He was thankful when Friday came and his loneliness was made to vanish. Alcohol, walking, literature and television were his friends on weekdays.

Marla was not shocked. She reasoned that her husband reacted how so many men had. Thinking back to their courtship she understood that Ralph was ready to find himself in bed with her after the first ten minutes. The men in her life had wanted that. She put her equipment on display and they had reacted as she knew they would. Ralph represented the best catch of the lot. She allowed him to touch so that he was certain of what he was getting. After the children came, something deep inside her took over. The purpose of the equipment was procreation and when that time in life passed, the sex act became vulgar. The kissing, the hands, all that motion, and finally the climax. If she could just have the climax without the rest of it. Marla would examine herself in the mirror as she was drying herself after a shower and she admitted to the beauty of her body. On one occasion Marla put down her towel, placed her hands behind her head and moved her elbows back. That's what the men were after. If she gave one of them unfettered access, she would make him deliriously happy. She saw the equation. She was on the left, giving. There would be an equal sign in the middle. And on the right would be the man, taking. It appeared out of balance. What was there for her to take? The inability to construct a relationship in which the equal sign was not trampled upon was at the center. Marla understood that about herself and was willing to continue through the remainder of her life without sex. She knew that other men would come around and she wondered how she might treat them. Perhaps one would be forceful enough to order her to take off her clothes and get into his bed. She grew disdainful of Ralph's weakness. After all, they were a foot apart in bed. Why couldn't he tear off her pajamas and take what he wanted? Why did she have to be an accomplice when it was not in her heart? She wondered why women differed on this matter, why some women liked it and others shied away. She could not trace back to the origins of her feelings.

Colleen remained Ralph's salvation. She was not saccharine sweet but always pleasant and complying. It was obvious to Ralph that she enjoyed him and the situation she found herself in. He doubted that she understood the little piece in the recess of his mind, to the effect that he had selected her in desperation, before he knew anything about her. There would be no opportunity for him to explore and sample so that he might come across a spectacular woman who had every possible virtue covered. He was surrounded by the impossibility of escape, what with their baby on the way. He did admit that she had solved his problem.

Alice and Warren patched it up. She was pleased that he would be giving up Washington. It seemed to her that it would be an easy matter to plan a stimulating life together. There would be activities they could work on. She did her best to understand her views on sex. It was certain that there would be a great deal more of it in their new life. Alice concluded that the whole business was not important to her, but that having Warren in her life was. She could not imagine being unmarried and without children. Having accepted Warren's need for her, she transformed herself into someone more desirable than she had been in their sixteen years of marriage. It did not surprise her that the decision to give herself to her husband awakened interests and appetites below the surface.

When Colleen stopped working, Alice installed her in the guest bedroom. Colleen thought she had three weeks to go. Alice's question removed any objection. "In Ralph's absence, who will take you to the hospital?" The boys were encouraged to feel the unborn baby's kicks.

Warren delayed announcing his retirement from Congress. When it came, he indicated his satisfaction over contributions to the tax code. He thanked his constituents for according him the privilege of representing them. He noted, as most politicians do at the moment of retirement, that he wished to spend more time with his family and that he would look into opportunities around Minneapolis.

After Colleen's child was delivered, Warren telephoned Ralph with the news. He reported to Alice that while his brother sounded coherent, he didn't indicate a pressing need to see his child and Colleen. Ralph spoke to Colleen, congratulated her, and said he would show up very soon.

"Sounds like he's drinking himself to death," Alice said.

Warren said, "You and I aren't about to get him out of there. Colleen wouldn't have any influence over him. You might not like this, but I could try Muriel and Monty."

"Your Muriel?" Alice asked.

"There must be a more delicate way of phrasing it, but yes, my Muriel."

"And Monty is her man?"

"They were married once ten years ago. Divorced promptly. She's back at the University for a doctorate in history and they're contemplating marriage again."

"You two stay in touch?" Alice asked.

"No. Her call to me in Washington was a goodbye of sorts, an update on how it played out and that she wasn't at loose ends."

"And what makes you think they could do anything with Ralph?"

"They would be new faces. I met Monty once in the apartment's lobby. Nice looking man. Plenty of handshake. Looks tough."

"So they drive to the lake, find Ralph and bring him back. Where does he go?"

"We stick him in Colleen's apartment. I see him regularly. We knock some sense into him. Get him working somehow. Get him interested in Colleen and the child."

"It's worth a try," Alice said.

Over the years, Monty had owned several four-door sedans with large trunks. On occasion he might drive a few coworkers to a restaurant, or take his mother and father to visit relatives, or move a small piece of furniture.

As he and Muriel drove north, he guessed that he would have enough room for Ralph, his books and his belongings. They stopped for a bite and then again at the general store. They asked the clerk for directions to the Montgomery's place. The owner asked, "Looking for Ralph? May take you a while. He moves around the lake a lot. It's not good living alone like that."

They found Ralph sitting on the porch of the guest cottage. He had been in a rocking chair, reading, when they drove up. Although it was

December, the early afternoon sun was strong and the air still and warm. Ralph came off the porch and walked toward the car. They introduced themselves.

Ralph looked at Muriel and realized that she must be the woman in Warren's previous life whose voice he had heard on the phone. He looked at Monty and said, "Warren called and said you'd be up today. Have you had lunch?" Monty said they had stopped on the road. Ralph asked them to come into the cottage. Monty reflected on how clean and orderly it was.

"Did Warren go into why we're here?" Monty asked.

"That I should return with you. I'm to live in Colleen's apartment, I take it."

"Did you agree with Warren's plan?" Muriel asked.

"Not really. I'm still sorting through my troubles, but I suppose I ought to listen to the older brother."

"His point is that if you stay here, you'll freeze to death about January. Ever read any Jack London?"

"A lot of it. I know the story you're referring to. I don't know the title but it's about winter in the Arctic."

"Ralph, I'm going to call you Ralph if you don't mind," Monty said. "You have to confront the world. You're hiding behind a half-bottle of booze each night. I don't care about all the problems you've lined up for examination. I don't want to hear them. You only have one choice left, and that's to come home and commit to Colleen and the child, work at your profession, and restore your good name. Any other choice is a coward's choice. It's that simple. So let's get the stuff packed, close up this place for the winter and get out of here."

"What did Colleen name the baby?" Ralph asked.

"They're waiting for you to come home before they fill out the rest of the birth certificate," Muriel said.

The End